i

# IMPACT!

The Second Novel In The Roll Models Saga

# D. A. CHARLES

# IMPACT!

by D.A. Charles
Published 2023 by Gray Tail Press

### First Edition

All Rights Reserved
ISBN 979-8-218-31868-0

In Memoriam

*Alec Frazier left this world far too soon. He was a relentless advocate and mentor who championed initiatives that enrich the lives of others.*

*Alec had a youthful spirit—snuggling with stuffed animals, entertaining a family of Tribbles, and speaking the language of Pandora. I miss his laugh and long-winded tales. Alec left a huge footprint, and I know he'll never be forgotten.*

*Alec was persistent and rarely deterred when he felt something must be undertaken. The Roll Models Saga was no exception, and I will be forever grateful for his support and enthusiasm.*

*Thank you, friend, for sharing your encouragement and guidance. We will see this through to completion.*

*Wherever you are—because I know you could never simply cease to exist—I hope you're having the grandest of adventures.*

*I miss you!*

*~nise*

# Chapter One

Steven Chandler raised his face upward and screamed.

*I'm so over today!*

The night sky was crystal clear when he'd left Moe's Diner, but now, the heavens were battering New Haven with rain, the accompanying cloud cover obscuring the street. Steven shivered and pulled the sleeve of his jacket down over his hand. He gripped his joystick and hunkered down in his chair before setting off into the cold.

*It's going to be a miserable night.*

The ambitious neurologist had put in a long workday—one that commenced in celebration with his fellow research colleagues and ended as one of the most heartbreaking of his fledgling career. Saying goodbye to a patient was something every doctor faced, but when that patient was a beloved friend and mentor, loss felt a lot like failure. Not one tidbit of knowledge Steven had gleaned from twelve years of college could have prepared him for the feelings of desperation that made him want to pull out all the stops to prevent an outcome that he knew was inevitable.

With his belly full, Steven just wanted to get himself home, crawl into bed, and pull the blankets up over his head.

Steven frowned and cursed his friend for leaving him stranded as he surveyed the landscape ahead. He needed the security of a companion to help navigate the route full of dangerous obstacles and pitfalls. He craved companionship that made him feel less vulnerable.

To Steven's right, the city's streetscape and curb cut project was in full swing and obstructed his access to a safe path of travel through his neighborhood. Orange barrels studded the landscape, long strips of yellow caution tape whipped in the wind, and a folding barricade with a blinking light on top blocked his path to the opposing sidewalk.

To his left, the path was unobstructed. It detoured through an isolated neighborhood known for its criminal element. A fellow med student had gone missing close by and was found murdered just a few weeks before.

Steven had yet to run the gauntlet unaccompanied. He closed his eyes and took a deep breath before rolling off the curb.

*There's a first time for everything.*

Steven was a few blocks from home, entering the street mid-block at the one location he knew held an opposing ramp. When his phone rang, he glanced at the display. Logan. Steven silenced the ringer. Steven loved his father dearly, and he'd expected a phone call from him all day—a conversation that would be filled with hope that new lines of stem cell funding might allow Steven to walk again. As a fellow physician, Steven understood Logan's desire to want the very best for another, but Logan's dream to restore Steven's mobility wasn't a dream Steven shared, and the junior Chandler struggled with the feelings the situation stirred up.

*What about what I want? What about my happiness? Why can't he accept me the way I am?*

The tension Steven felt at the possibility of another heated argument distracted him.

Distracted—as he pulled into traffic from between two parked cars.

Distracted—as he drifted just a bit too far onto the roadway.

Steven never saw the minivan as he propelled his wheelchair onto the pavement.

The driver never saw the young man in the wheelchair.

Hearing a horn beep in the distance, Steven snapped to attention, quickly steering his chair as close to the row of parked cars as possible.

It wasn't close enough.

He wasn't quick enough.

He felt the rush of air the approaching vehicle created.

He heard the hum of the tires on the pavement.

Blinded by the lights, he was certain the driver saw him and would steer out of his path.

❖　❖　❖

Logan Chandler had just poured a coffee when the radio report came in. "Ambulance 22 en route to your facility. Patient is a thirty-three-year-old male who was struck while operating his motorized wheelchair. Crush trauma to the lower extremities. Current vitals are . . ."

Logan's heart stopped, the paper cup slipping from his fingers. Before he could make sense of the words, dispatch had signed off.

*No! No, no, no!*

A dozen anxious faces studied Logan as he paced the ER, waiting for the ambulance that they all somehow knew would be carrying his adopted son. Some of them were present back in '93, the night they'd flown Steven Maxwell in on a chopper from the hospital in Putnam. The Chandler family had already been through so much. It just wasn't fair.

When the gurney carrying Steven Chandler was pushed through the ambulance bay, the department became a flurry of activity. They were the absolute best at what they did, and they'd never worked harder to keep a patient alive.

Logan took a deep breath and steeled himself before heading to the triage room. A Chandler family friend, Spencer Grady, stepped into Logan's path, placing his hands on Logan's shoulders. "You know I can't let you go in there right now. You're too personally involved. You're not doing anyone any favors by rushing in there half-cocked, least of all Steven."

But Logan saw his son lying on that gurney, the blankets a bloody mess. He fisted the front of the paramedic's shirt. "Spence, please, I have to help him."

"Yes, you do, but not like this. Let someone who isn't so emotionally overwrought stabilize him."

Logan's shoulders dropped in defeat. He opened his mouth to speak, but his breath hitched. Spencer embraced him as he sobbed, overwhelmed with the gravity of the situation.

When Logan eventually pulled away, he searched the other man's face. "How bad?"

Spencer raked his hands through his hair and looked at the ceiling before letting out a noisy breath. "It's not good. Not good at all. We almost lost him coming in; it's a miracle he's still alive."

❖   ❖   ❖

As the Director of Family Medicine, Logan had seen all sorts of atrocities during his career, but nothing could have ever prepared him for Spencer Grady's account of his son's accident. The room spun and Grady grabbed his arms, guiding him into a chair just outside the trauma room where the staff continued to work diligently.

"He was trying to cross that construction nightmare down on Davenport. A car hit him at approximately 30 miles per hour."

"Jon was supposed to walk home with him--is he all right?"

"Steven was alone at the scene. Driver says she never saw him."

Logan fought to swallow back the bile that rose in his throat.

As he'd done some sixteen years before, Logan reached deep inside himself to find the resolve necessary to get his family through whatever lay ahead. His responsibility to his nephew, and for over a decade, his son, demanded that he keep his wits and distance himself from the situation. That imminent obligation was the only thing keeping him focused enough to remain objective.

Spencer's voice pierced Logan's reflections. "The trauma to his lower extremities is extensive. Thank God he was in that beast of a wheelchair. If he'd been in the other one, he'd already be gone."

Logan's hands clenched into fists, his anger momentarily overriding the crippling fear of losing his only child. Logan knew that if that driver were in front of him, it would have been impossible to rein himself in. He picked up the chair he'd been sitting in, screamed loudly, and launched it across the room. When security approached, Spencer held up an index finger in their direction before speaking firmly to Logan.

"Come on, buddy. If you're not careful, you'll get us both thrown out. Steven needs you to keep your cool. He needs you, Logan."Spencer took his friend's arm and guided him into a private family room.

Logan ran his fingers through his hair, embarrassed by his unexpected outburst. "I'm sorry. I don't know what that was. I'm so mad right now."

"I am too, but we've got people counting on us to keep it together."

"I have to see him. Tell me what to expect."

"His torso was protected by the wheelchair. He was crossing at an angle mid-block. She hit him head-on before pushing him down the street. The injuries to his face and head appear to be superficial; we'll know more after they get a CT. His legs are a mess. If they don't get the bleeding stopped soon, it's all over."

*How could this happen to someone like Steven?*

"I'm not going to lie to you, Logan. It's really bad."

Logan frantically pulled at his hair.

*He doesn't deserve this!*

"What is his level of consciousness?"

The devastation that flickered across Spencer's face said what he didn't verbalize; they'd both experienced horrific injuries in their careers, and Logan knew his boy had to be suffering immeasurable pain. The seasoned ER doctor prayed that if the end was near, God would let Steven slip away swiftly and peacefully—and he was immediately overcome with guilt. What he prayed for was unthinkable, yet what he had seen personally and heard only moments before told him his boy was barely hanging on. Still, if there were even one shred of hope, Logan would fight with everything he had to save his adopted son.

"What does he know?"

"He's been in and out. He knows his prognosis is pretty grim. He was aware enough to ask me to talk to you, to keep you occupied."

Ethel Boyer, the head trauma nurse, opened the door and poked her head inside. "Dr. Chandler, he's asking for you," she said, wringing her hands. "Hurry, there's not much time. We're ready to roll."

Logan was thankful when Spencer accompanied him into the claustrophobic room; the paramedic's hand reassuringly gripped his elbow. The doctor's stomach lurched as he took in the articles of bloodied clothing that littered the floor—Steven's black leather shoes, mangled and covered in blood, lay on opposite sides of the room.

Logan was overcome with the smell of blood. Normally, he was able to tune out such things. He'd worked at the level one trauma center for more than a decade, and he thought he'd seen the worst of the worst, but nothing could have prepared him for the situation before him.

Steven turned his head slightly as they entered. Logan choked back a sob and attempted to keep his emotions in check, looking down into the eyes of his son.

*My son.*

Steven was barely recognizable—his forehead swollen with a purple hematoma—the rest of his face bloody and bruised. A central line pierced his neck. Nurse Boyer hung a fresh unit of blood as she held up four fingers to indicate it was the fourth unit he'd received. There were tubes and monitors everywhere. Logan flashed back to that night so long ago, but when Steven tried to talk, his bloody hand frantically groping for his uncle's, Logan leaned in close.

"Steven?"

"No heroics."

"There isn't time for this; you've lost too much blood. Let them do what's necessary to save your life."

He frantically shook his head. "Promise me."

*I'll do everything I can to save you.*

"Please."

Logan was still Steven's healthcare proxy; all responsibility lay in his hands. This was probably goodbye. In all his years as a doctor, Logan had never had a patient live through such devastating trauma. Still, if there was any chance···

"I promise to act in your best interest." *I don't know how to let you go.*

Nurse Boyer and Corey Tucker came into the room. "Steven, it's time to get you to the OR." Corey had the gurney in motion almost immediately as Logan jogged alongside, praying to whatever deity would listen. His son's future held so much promise. To see it clipped short— was unconscionable.

Again in the elevator, Steven grasped Logan's hand with surprising strength.

"Remember your promise, Dad." He rasped, in obvious pain. "Please."

Logan nodded. "I remember."

With a resigned expression that rocked Logan to his core, Steven said, "Please tell Aunt Sophie I love her."

"We'll be right here, son. We'll see you soon." Logan emphasized the words as if his pledge would make it so. He prayed Steven couldn't detect the doubt that hung over him like an ominous cloud.

He squeezed his nephew's hand and leaned down, placing a kiss on his forehead.

*"I love you."* Please come back to us.

Steven closed his eyes and a tear slipped down his cheek.

# Chapter Two

Arnie Glover, the head of the operating room, intercepted Logan outside OR reception. "Dr. Mills has begun working. Provided you abide by department protocols, I'll allow you to observe; however, if it's too difficult, I understand."

"I'd like to be present, but I need to go to Sophie." Logan hung his head and turned to walk away. Glover grasped his arm, stopping him.

"Logan, Steven is a promising physician. We all care about him. Everyone is praying for him and the rest of your family as well. I can't imagine how difficult this is for you."

"Losing Grace left a hole in Sophie's heart. I don't know what she'll do if we lose him too."

"We'll do everything in our power to prevent that from happening."

"I know you will. Thank you."

"Go call your wife, and if you'd like to observe, get suited up and scrubbed in."

Logan reached into his pocket and pulled out his phone with every intention of stepping into one of the private waiting rooms to call his wife, but when his colleague stepped away to give him privacy, he couldn't seem to find the words.

He felt dizzy . . . sick to his stomach, the taste of bile an overwhelming presence in his mouth. It was all too much. He didn't know how they'd get through the night; he couldn't envision any sort of favorable outcome. Every scenario he conjured up concluded with them burying the boy they both loved. Logan slid down the wall, dropping his head into his hands.

❖    ❖    ❖

That was how Skyler Jacobs found him. The hospital chaplain had spent her evening in the OR lounge with the parents of a small child who'd needed emergency surgery. She was heading home for the night when she practically tripped over Logan.

Skyler dropped to the floor and placed a comforting hand on Logan's arm, imploring him to explain what was wrong. She automatically assumed something had happened to Sophie; never in her wildest dreams was she prepared for the news Logan shared.

Skyler had grown up with Steven. Both of Steven's parents and his aunt and uncle had been members of her father's charge back home. She knew the family well and found she had trouble swallowing the lump in her throat as Logan told her about the catastrophe that had occurred earlier that night.

Logan's chest heaved as he drew in a breath and shared Steven's parting request. "I have a duty to Steven to do the right thing, but how do I know what the right thing is?"

Skyler smiled gently when she spoke. "Logan, the responsibility you've accepted directs you to act on Steven's behalf and to do as he's directed because he's unable to speak for himself. We both know that when a person accepts this obligation, there is no room for selfishness."

"I know," Logan whispered.

"If something were to happen tonight that would require you to invoke the instructions in Steven's living will, would you abide by his wishes, or would you do what you felt was appropriate?"

Logan gave her a pointed look.

She squeezed his hand and smiled. "Carry out your nephew's wishes, and put the outcome in God's hands."

"What if he dies because of the decision I make?"

"It sounds to me like that's a very real possibility no matter what you instruct the medical team to do."

Logan nodded. "It is."

"I know your family wouldn't want you to be facing this alone. Sophie should be here. It's going to be a very long night. Would you like me to bring her here? You can stay with Steven, and we'll be here waiting for you when you return."

The doctor nodded, and after a short prayer with his pastor, he walked into the OR reception area, feeling like a burden had been lifted from his shoulders. Bess Scott, the receptionist, addressed him immediately. "As soon as you're ready, go right on back, Logan. They're expecting you. Room twelve."

He knew that was where they'd be working. Room twelve was the largest of the operating room suites, reserved for the most critical cases.

❖   ❖   ❖

The tech who had assisted Logan to gown and glove quietly accompanied him to the surgical suite, but it was Dr. Mills who spoke up. "Logan, I know this is difficult for you, but I'd like for you to be as involved as possible."

Logan was shocked at the vast number of his colleagues who were present. Jim Mills was the vascular surgeon on board; Djenii Grey was his assistant. Vance Harrison, an orthopedic surgeon, acknowledged Logan with a curt nod. Three surgical nurses and a number of OR techs were busily assisting. A central supply tech sat near the door on a stool, at the ready to grab whatever supplies might be needed through the night. Logan's colleagues had pulled out all the stops; the night would be a long, drawn-out series of procedures, but a relief team had already been organized to step in when the first team grew fatigued. Logan felt the dedication coming off his work family in waves, and he was overwrought with emotion.

"Thank you. Thank you all for helping us tonight." Logan choked on a sob, and one of the OR techs directed him to a stool they'd prepared for him in a spot that was out of the way but where he could still interact with the team and watch on the monitor if he could stomach it. Logan wasn't sure he could.

*This is it . . .*

While he was speaking with Skyler, anesthesia had put Steven under, his body shielded by drapes. With the draping and equipment obstructing the view, Logan could almost forget that it was his boy they were working on.

Almost.

He shuddered, resisting the urge to rub his arms in an attempt to warm himself. The room itself was unnaturally cool, perfect for keeping the staff alert and on their toes, but for Logan, who would be spending a sedentary evening in the OR, it would be a very long night.

For Jim Mills, the vascular surgeon, attempting to put Steven back together ended up being the most challenging case of his career. The destruction was so vast that Mills began working on the blood vessels closest to Steven's torso, first clamping off the larger vessels that had allowed the greatest amount of blood to be lost.

The conversation quickly turned to the practicality of a double amputation. Logan squeezed his eyes shut and prayed for guidance.

"I think you should try to preserve his legs," Logan said.

Vance Harrison walked over to the x-rays of Steven's legs that were being illuminated on the light box. "These legs look like bags of broken china. Certainly you don't think it's worth it."

Logan looked at his boy, waging the fight of his life, and he made up his mind.

"I do. I'm sure you think I'm just being melodramatic because he's my son, but I know both of you would fight if this were your child."

The orthopedic surgeon, known for his lack of bedside manner, glared at his colleague in shock. "Logan! For God's sake, the boy can't even stand by himself. His legs are nothing more than decorations!"

The hemostat Dr. Mills was holding clattered to the floor as a collective gasp filled the room.

"Vance, I'm going to pretend I didn't hear that!" Arnie Glover made his presence known from where he stood close to Logan. "Mills, what have you got?"

"Djenii?"

Ms. Grey looked up from where she stood at the foot of the table and smiled softly as she replied, "The Doppler sounds indicate the foot is still getting some level of circulation. I've got a weak pulse in the extremity, doctors, but it's there."

"I guarantee you'll be amputating in a matter of hours." Harrison scoffed as he slammed down instruments and stormed out.

Mills continued to work while orthopedic surgeon Robert Wesley scrubbed in. A hush fell over the room as the team worked in perfect synchronization over Steven's motionless body. There was nothing Logan could do but watch and pray for a miracle as the night dragged on.

# Chapter Three

Sitting in an isolated corner of the emergency department all that night, Dottie Myers hoped for a tidbit of news, some scrap of information that could somehow assuage the immense guilt that had felt like a boulder crushing her chest from the moment she'd realized what she'd done.

It had been hours since the mess had been cleared away, and the officers had finished with their questions, but their words played over and over in her mind on a continuous loop.

She'd been a hysterical mess when they'd arrived but had pulled herself together enough to answer basic questions. Supporting her by her elbow, one of the officers had helped her into the back seat of the cruiser.

She'd sat on the edge of the back seat, her feet dangling over the pavement, as the paramedics finally stabilized the injured man enough to transport him. She watched absently as the wrecker arrived, and the accident response team began documenting the accident and clearing away the debris.

"Where were you going?" the officer asked.

"To work," she'd replied, her voice barely above a whisper.

The man glanced at the hospital ID that dangled from around her neck, shifting his gaze toward the hospital that loomed in the distance. "You're a nurse?"

"Third shift, Cardiac Care-ICU."

The officer glanced at his watch.

"Isn't it a little late to be starting your shift?" he asked.

She tried to swallow the lump in her throat.

"Were you distracted?"

*I was.*

Her stomach twisted uncomfortably, and she thought she might be sick. "I never saw him." And she hadn't. Instead, her mind had been on that rat bastard husband of hers and the thought of him driving his girlfriend's new car when her own vehicle was on its last legs.

"That was a mighty large object to miss."

She waved her hand, gesturing to the mess of caution barrels that lay scattered in front of her vehicle. "I thought I hit one of those barrels or maybe a shopping cart."

She hadn't known the truth until she'd exited the car and encountered the macabre scene—the sight of that chair combined with the unmistakable shock of wild blonde curls was what had sent her into hysterics when she'd realized who he was.

She'd personally encountered young Chandler's gentle soul during his cardiac rotation as a resident, watching as he interacted with patients and their families.

*Oh, how he'll be missed.*

It was everything she could do to wrench her eyes away from the sight in front of her. They were saying something about her van.

". . . to impound until the investigation is complete," said the male cop, whose badge identified him as Officer Clouser.

As badly as Dottie needed her car to get to work, she didn't know if she'd ever be able to get behind the wheel of any car again—or if she'd even have a job to go to.

Her eyes studied the accident response team while they walked in front of her van with measuring wheels and chalk, ascertaining the distance he'd been hurled by her van. Her breath hitched, and she stifled a sob with her fist when they began photographing the spot where his body had lain, the macadam stained with his blood and covered in chalk markings.

Dottie jumped when the female officer touched her shoulder. "Were you under the influence of any intoxicating substances?"

"No, never."

She broke down again, too distraught to answer any more questions, too shaken to sufficiently navigate the field sobriety test.

"You need to come with us, ma'am."

"Am I being charged?"

"Not at this time."

She buried her face in her hands and sobbed in the back seat of the cruiser. Even worse than taking her to the precinct was the realization that they were taking her to the hospital lab.

*My hospital.* The one where not only she, but the Doctors Chandler were employed.

It was all she could do to put one foot in front of the other as they shepherded her to the reception desk. She'd had a bird's eye view of paramedics Grady and McEntyre as she sat in the corridor outside the lab between the two officers waiting for the phlebotomist—her light blue uniform sandwiched in between the two crisp navy of New Haven's finest.

Spencer Grady, the paramedic who'd exiled her to the van like an errant child being sent to their room, sat slumped in a chair away from everyone else in the ER, sobbing like a baby—until a big brute of a man stormed through the door and approached him, sinking to a crouch in front of the paramedic. He listened intently as Grady spoke, wiping his eyes on the sleeve of his hoodie and nodding his head. The two men stood, and Dottie watched as the pair walked down the corridor toward the elevator with their heads down, their shoulders slumped.

Dottie choked back a sob. *What have I done? Is he still alive?*

The way the two men walked away, there was no way of knowing.

She'd watched at the scene as they loaded him into the ambulance—the white cotton blanket stained crimson with his blood.

*Blood that I spilled.*

If he'd succumbed to his injuries, surely it would have already spread like wildfire through the rumor mill.

*He has to be all right.*

Late into the night, staff gathered in small groups. They all loved him, from housekeeping to administration. He treated everyone with respect, and during his greatest hour of need, they'd come to repay his kindness, waiting patiently to enter the cubicle designated for blood donations.

Long after her blood was drawn, long after the officers departed, Dottie remained. She was unable to take her eyes off the steady stream of health system employees as they flowed in and out of that tiny room. It was a huge hospital, but the employees treated one another like family, and as the news spread, so did the need to do something, anything, even if all they could do was donate on his behalf.

As the sun began rising over a new day, Dottie heard someone say both Doctors Chandler were still in surgery, one observing and the other still being treated as a team of the hospital's best continued to fight to put the young doctor back together again.

On shaky legs, she made her way to the hospital chapel where she dropped to her knees and begged for a miracle.

❖    ❖    ❖

Unit after unit of blood was poured into young Chandler that night, and miraculously, with the introduction of vessels from a cadaver, the copious loss of blood was staunched. Steven finally had a viable chance at survival.

One by one, intricate surgeries were performed to repair his injuries with an assortment of hardware to hold the shattered remains of Steven's extremities in place. The vertical fracture of Steven's pelvis was repaired with plates and screws. The completed project was packaged in a bright blue body cast. From chest to ankles, Steven was wrapped in fiberglass.

Surprisingly, none of the bones above Steven's waist had been broken, nor had he suffered any traumatic brain injury. After eighteen hours, the young doctor remained critical but stable, his overall prognosis positive; however, the prognosis of his repaired extremities was still shaky at best. Only time would tell if he was out of the woods.

As they wheeled Steven into recovery, Logan realized with a start that he'd never gone to find Sophie. Once in the operating room, his focus was solely on Steven. Now, Logan had an overwhelming urge to go find her, comfort her. Despite knowing the staff was providing regular updates to the OR waiting room, he knew she'd be worried sick.

Exhausted, both physically and mentally, Logan trudged to the waiting area. As soon as he opened the door, Quinn Eastman, a close Chandler family friend and the hospital's infectious disease specialist, shot up from his perch in the corner. He took Logan's arm and in a low voice said, "What do we know?"

Quinn's wife, Maddie, stepped out of the adjoining restroom and hurried to where the men were talking. Logan scanned the room, searching out the other half of his soul. Almost immediately, he spotted Skyler sitting on one of the couches on the far side of the room, but she appeared to be alone.

"Sophie?"

He hastened across the large room, and as he came around the end of the long couch, he saw her. A small pillow lay on Skyler's lap, and Sophie's head rested there as she slept. Skyler ran her fingers through the ends of Sophie's hair as she hummed softly.

Logan knelt next to the face of his beloved, troubled even in sleep, and began waking her. She opened her eyes and gasped. Before he could register what was happening, she'd launched herself at him, and they were both on the floor.

Logan steadied himself and tried to stand. Reaching down, he offered his hand and guided his wife to a small grouping of chairs. Sophie sobbed openly, her eyes pleading for answers that Logan couldn't have given even a short time before. He glanced from face to anxious face, grateful that Steven had such a solid support system.

Sophie looked up, stroking Logan's cheek ever so gently. "Are we going to lose him?" They were the first words she'd spoken since she'd awakened moments before.

"Right now, Steven is stable, but he's suffered extensive injury to his lower extremities."

"What's his mental status?" Quinn asked.

"He was lucid before going into surgery, and we have no reason to believe that he has experienced any sort of brain injury. I believe he understood how grave the situation was."

Logan pulled Sophie to her feet and without further explanation, led her to the recovery room. Looking through the small window in the door, Logan pointed to a bed along the wall. Although Steven lay in the middle of a mass of cords and tubes, he was alive.

Logan pulled his wife into an embrace and uttered a prayer of gratitude.

# Chapter Four

By the second day post-op, Steven's foot had grown progressively worse, and Logan berated himself the moment it was evident Steven's condition was deteriorating. Vance Harrison's words echoed ominously in Logan's mind.

The exposed portion of Steven's foot, ghoulish gray the day before, had quickly turned purple. The discoloration, rimmed with angry red, crept closer and closer to the fiberglass of Steven's body cast as the day progressed. The toes themselves began splitting and seeping due to the volume of fluid the injured doctor retained.

The knowledge that he'd had the power to prevent the current situation, yet had allowed hope to cloud his judgment, caused Logan to sink into despair. In his heart he knew that had Steven undergone the recommended double amputation, they'd already be seeing signs of improvement.

*Why did I have to be so stubborn?*

Steven had lapsed in and out of consciousness since he'd left the recovery room the morning before. He began to stir once again as Logan examined his toes, but the elder Chandler was bereft with guilt over his desperate plea to save Steven's legs at any cost, and he found it impossible to make eye contact with his nephew.

Skyler Jacobs's words twisted and churned inside Logan's head: ". . . to act on Steven's behalf . . . to do as he directed . . . there is no room for selfishness . . . would you abide by his wishes . . . or would you do what you felt was appropriate?"

Did I act on his behalf?

"Dad?" Steven whispered sleepily.

Logan turned his back to Steven, his head hanging in shame. "I made an unforgivable decision during your surgery. I think I should step down as your POA and let Sophie manage everything until you're capable of determining the direction of your care."

Logan's admission jarred Steven awake. "What? No. I trust you."

"You shouldn't."

"I put my care in your hands because I knew you'd do what was in my best interests."

Logan turned finally, beating his chest with clenched fists. "But I wasn't able to do that. I did what I thought was best, and I was wrong!"

Steven sighed. "Tell me."

Logan slumped into the chair closest to Steven's bed and slowly explained the events that followed the accident, but Steven was snoring softly before Logan was able to lighten the burden which weighed so heavily on his soul. He adjusted his nephew's blankets and went in search of his wife who had taken up residence in a secluded corner of the ICU waiting room for the indeterminate future.

In his haste, Logan nearly slammed into Jim Mills as they passed in the corridor; the vascular surgery hospitalist guided Logan back into Steven's room, his facial expression serious. "I hoped I'd find you here."

"What's wrong?"

"I've taken the liberty of scheduling a procedure for two this afternoon, with your consent, of course."

Logan shook his head. "I—I can't, Jim. My wife will be making all the decisions concerning Steven's care from this point forward—"

"That won't be necessary," Steven whispered, turning his head to address his visitor. "Please bring me up to speed, Jim."

Mills nodded. "I need to go back in today and attempt a different approach. My standard protocol in cases of massive extremity trauma that's to the extent and severity as yours was, is amputation, rather than salvage of the limb. At your uncle's direction, we made every attempt to salvage both limbs. There was an adequate pedis pulse yesterday; however, one extremity is no longer getting sufficient circulation. We're at a point where it would be prudent to reconsider amputation of the foot."

"What? And destroy all your hard work? I overheard my nurses say your masterpiece will end up in The Journal. People will be talking about your amazing save years from now." Despite the gravity of the situation, it made Logan smile to hear humor in Steven's response. Perhaps hope was not lost.

"So, it's your wish that we continue efforts to spare the foot?"

Steven's expression grew serious. "Did you have a contingency plan in place if Logan refused to let you amputate?"

Mills paled. "I suppose we'd have attempted to decompress the extremity, debride any necrotic tissue, maybe introduce a shunt, or replace the dorsalis pedis with a vessel from a cadaver."

"You're a talented surgeon, and I'm humbled that your team worked so tirelessly to patch me up. I think your contingency plan sounds reasonable; however, if your efforts should fail to produce an outcome you're comfortable with, I trust you to use whatever course of treatment you deem necessary. Logan will consent."

Mills studied Logan's face. "Will your wife—"

"That's not necessary. I trust Logan to act on my behalf."

"But-but I—,"

"Don't want to burden Aunt Sophie with the responsibility of making a decision she might struggle with any more than I do."

Jim Mills squeezed Steven's shoulder. "Thank you for entrusting me with your care. I'll do what I can to reestablish circulation."

"And if the procedure is unsuccessful, you understand it's my wish that you do whatever is necessary."

Mills nodded and turned to Logan. "The consent form will be at the nurse's station. I'm heading to surgery."

As he did thirty-six hours before, Steven reached for his uncle's hand, his earlier plea now an ardent command.

"No heroics. I mean it."

Logan nodded. "Understood."

"What's done is done, but if Jim has to amputate, you'll let him. If I take a turn for the worse, you'll follow my advance directive—to the letter. I forgive you for letting emotion dictate your decisions. I can't imagine the weight you've had to carry since we lost Mom and Dad, but I need you to understand—this isn't a decision you have to make. I've already made it."

Logan squeezed Steven's hand, a wan smile on his face. "I promise, Steven," he whispered. "I promise to uphold your wishes."

"Thank you. I love you."

"I love you, too, son. Sophie is asleep in the lounge, but she'll want to see you before they take you. We'll be right back."

❖   ❖   ❖

The nurse's station was a hive of activity until Logan approached. Looks of concern greeted him when he reached for the forms.

"We're all pulling for him."

"Please give him our best."

"He'll get through this."

Logan looked from one face to the next. "He will. I'll tell him, thank you," Logan replied before hurrying off to find his beloved. He scanned the cavernous waiting room, remembering the weeks they'd spent there sixteen years earlier. The décor was different, the cool blue tones at some point replaced with warm hues of brown, but the emotional climate hadn't changed. It was as much a place of great sorrow as it was one of great joy.

Sophie stood, as he'd found her so many times in the past, with her palms on the glass, gazing out over the city. Logan grasped his wife's shoulders, turning her gently. Sophie studied his face and frowned. "It's not good, is it?"

"Jim's, uh, Jim's gonna go back in and fix this. If anyone can, he's the one."

Sophie wrapped her arms around Logan's waist and embraced him.

"Is he very upset with you?"

"Not as upset as he should have been, but he's still pretty heavily medicated."

Sophie glanced at the clock. "We should go wish him the best."

Logan entwined their fingers and tugged on her hand. "Come with me."

❖　❖　❖

Logan followed Steven and his entourage to the OR, scrubbing in and gowning up as he had just hours before, but this time, both his mind and his heart were in a better place.

As the vascular team worked, Logan castigated himself for acting so selfishly, for creating a situation which might have been resolved more expediently and with a more favorable outcome had he not intervened. From the moment Steven became paralyzed, Logan struggled between wanting the very best for his son and accepting the reality that Steven's disability was something he did not have the power to change. Through years of praying for a miracle—some medical intervention that would restore Steven's ability to walk—Logan never gave up hope, but the consequences of his last-ditch effort could still cost Steven his life.

*This mindset has to end if I'm going to preserve what's left of our relationship.*

Logan stood and walked to the table where Mills worked on his son. "Steven has directed you to use your best judgment. He trusts you and I do, as well. I'll be in the waiting room with my wife."

❖　❖　❖

As Steven fought for his life, Logan watched his beloved wife struggle to remain strong for their son. Even more painful than losing her sibling, he suspected, was the fear of losing Steven—a fear that kept Sophie shackled to the ICU by invisible tethers.

"What if something happens, and I'm not here?" she'd asked.

Logan wanted nothing more than to insist that Sophie go home and sleep or to take her out, his assurance she was eating. Logan knew his wife needed a respite from her heartache. More importantly, he suspected Steven needed a respite from his aunt's desperate need to remain close even though Logan knew Steven would never push her away.

Logan found himself lingering at the hospital long after each shift in order to remain close to his family. And when he couldn't bear to go home to an empty house or a cold bed, he'd make his way to the little corner where Sophie had staked her claim in the ICU waiting room, snuggling in alongside her on the recliner where she attempted to sleep.

After several such nights, Logan gathered his wife's backpack and the small pillow and blanket she kept rolled in a duffel. Sophie balked. "What are you doing? I'm not going home until he's out of the woods."

"And I wouldn't ask you to, but it's impossible to get a decent night's sleep with all this chaos. How can you be here for him if you're not taking care of yourself? He'd be the first to tell you that it's impossible to get a decent night's sleep in the ICU."

She put her hands on her hips and Logan could feel the heat of her glare. "You never answered my question."

Logan sighed. "I'm hoping to convince you to move into my office. It's private and quiet—secure, so you don't have to worry about leaving your things."

"But the faculty offices are so far from the ICU."

"Only a few floors away." Logan draped a lanyard around Sophie's neck, a shiny new key dangling from the clip. "Please, sweetheart. I'd feel so much better if I knew you were getting adequate rest. Spend your days on the floor; sleep on the couch in my office; shower in the nurses' locker room. I have a small closet you can set up with some clothing and toiletries."

"You're sure it's okay?"

"I cleared it through the proper channels, and security is aware. The only concern was protected health information, and we already keep that under lock and key."

"It really means that much to you?"

"Your well-being means everything to me."

Sophie nodded. "I'll do it for you."

"Do it for all of us."

❖   ❖   ❖

Steven continued to spend many of his hours in a peacefully medicated cocoon, but as the days progressed, he had more and more lucid moments. The recovering paraplegic was already receiving antibiotics when he suddenly spiked a temperature of 105 degrees. Steven begged Maddie for help as fever overtook his body, the bulky fiberglass cast elevating his temperature by trapping Steven's body heat inside.

A team meeting commenced in a conference room with Quinn Eastman and his infectious disease residents at the helm.

"Fever is the body's way of fighting infection," one of the residents said. "A fever with infection shouldn't cause brain damage."

Sophie clutched Logan and began softly sobbing. "We need to consider extenuating circumstances." Logan pressed. "The cast poses a risk."

"He's declined cognitively. He's no longer aware of time or place."

"Well, what are we gonna do? Can't submerge him in water."

"What about an alcohol bath?"

"Not enough skin to make a difference."

"We've started a broad spectrum antibiotic."

"If the cast is the problem, why don't we just remove it?"

"That's the dumbest idea I've ever heard."

"No, Quinn, the kid has a point. If we cut the cast off, we could use more conventional methods to control the fever."

"Oh, I don't think that's a wise idea at all."

"What if he suffers a febrile seizure? Any sort of uncontrolled movement could be detrimental."

"I beseech you to give the antibiotics and Tylenol time to reduce Steven's fever," the on-call orthopedic surgeon said. "Wesley will kick my butt if we cause further injury."

Quinn gave his wife's hand a squeeze. "Keep an eye on him, babe. I want temps on the half hour. Any signs of distress, you call me or Logan immediately. My senior resident has things under control. I'm not leaving the floor."

Quinn squeezed Logan's shoulder. "We both know these things take time. Try not to worry."

Two hours later with little relief, Steven was suspended in a medically induced coma to prevent any movement or subsequent injury to his healing extremities, and the body cast was bi-valved, a procedure where the plaster and padding on either side of the cast was cut, allowing either half of the cast to be removed individually. The procedure allowed medical personnel to cool Steven's skin, and eventually the fever relented.

# Chapter Five

Logan's younger cousin, Sydney, stretched and let out a deep sigh. It had been weeks since she'd slept in her bed, and she had slept like a log. Sure, her bed in the spacious apartment overlooking the Seine had been like sleeping on a cloud, but Sydney missed waking up in her own bed in her own place, and she was happy to be home.

Sydney was perched in front of her computer with a vat of hot coffee, picking at a bagel when she stumbled upon the article in the paper. Placed inconspicuously in an obscure corner of the Lifestyle section, it told the story about up-and-coming stem cell research fellow Steven Chandler and the accident that had nearly claimed his life.

Sydney was confused at first glance, thinking it was some sort of human interest piece on Steven's history; there'd been quite a hub-bub when Steven had completed his residency in neurology. One of the first paraplegics to achieve that honor, his story had been the center of attention throughout the local medical community.

Expecting to learn that the whiz kid had discovered some medical miracle in the research lab where he spent all his free time, Sydney read on.

It had been late the night before when she'd landed at Tweed Airport, and she'd yet to speak with any member of the family. The online copy of *The Register* was the only interaction she'd had with her community since she'd set foot on American soil.

Sydney was horrified as she read the account of Steven's accident and then angered knowing they'd purposely kept the news from her; a frantic call to her beau, Spencer Grady, confirmed it. Based on the circumstances of her trip, Sydney understood, but she was livid when she learned how close they'd come to losing Steven. She ran from her home office without even grabbing a jacket.

❖   ❖   ❖

Sophie barely recognized the disheveled, pajama-clad girl who burst into Steven's hospital room, sobbing inconsolably. She could hardly understand the strangled words that escaped Sydney's lips, holding the girl for what seemed like an eternity until she was able to carry on a coherent conversation.

"Oh Sophie, how did this happen?"

Steven had been sleeping until the outburst occurred, and before Sophie replied, he coughed and answered the question. "I was trying to cross the street. The driver never saw me."

At that, Sydney once again burst into tears, clinging to Sophie until her shuddering stopped, and she had regained some semblance of composure.

Sydney stepped away from Sophie, and her hands went to her hips. She wrinkled her forehead causing her eyelids to form little slits as she gave Sophie her most serious stink eye. "Why didn't you let me know?"

"Because," Steven said from across the room, "you could have never kept this from Brooke, and she needed you more at the time than I did. Now, did you come here to see me or Aunt Soph?" He gestured to the chair next to his bed. "Come, tell me about your trip. How's Brooke?"

❖   ❖   ❖

Sophie sat reading a magazine as the two younger Chandlers spoke quietly, discussing the accident and how everything might affect Steven's future.

"What's the prognosis?" Sydney asked. "Will you be able to manage the workload you've been juggling?"

Steven smiled but shook his head. "I don't know, Syd. I've got months of therapy ahead of me before I'll be able to jump back into the ring."

"Where will you go?"

"Logan's visiting a place out in Hartford next week. It'll depend on who has an opening when I'm ready."

Sydney frowned. "But that's so far away."

"It's a good facility, Syd, and that's what I'm gonna need. I don't know if I'll have a job to go back to. I may have lost my fellowship." Steven blew out a long breath. "I don't want to be working to pay off my debt for the next twenty years."

"We both know you won't let this hold you back."

"I don't plan to, but I've got contractual obligations I won't be able to fulfill until I'm cleared to work again. If Trey was still around, he'd whip me back into shape."

"If you need a hand with that, my dance card is looking pretty bleak."

"I'm sorry about your client. No new assignments?"

"I got in late. I was checking in with my agency when I stumbled across the article about your accident. I'm sure they'll line something up right away."

"How's Brooke?"

"It's been a rough couple of months, but she seems to be in a good place. I suspect she'll be by once she hears about this. I still can't believe you kept this from us!"

"You'll have to take that up with the 'rents. I was unavailable for consultation."

Fearing the discussion would turn to intimate details about Brooke and the loss of her baby, the room suddenly became claustrophobic for Sophie. Too much loss, too much pain and sadness.

Knowing Steven was in safe hands with Sydney by his side, she walked down to the chapel in need of a visit with Skyler Jacobs or one of her colleagues.

When she returned an hour later, Sydney was preparing to go. "I'm sorry for the intrusion, Steven. I just read the article in the paper and ran out of my apartment without thinking." She patted her hair and tried to smooth the wrinkles out of her sleep clothes. "I must look a fright; I really need to get home and shower. I'll stop back soon. If you need anything at all, don't hesitate to call."

"Thanks for stopping by. Think about what we talked about."

"I will. See you soon."

Sydney wrapped her arms around Sophie and squeezed her hard. "Please let me know if you need anything, any of you."

Sophie nodded. "We will. Thank you."

❖ ❖ ❖

When the door thumped closed, Steven cleared his throat. "Aunt Soph, there are some things I need. I was wondering if you'd mind."

"Not at all, hon. What can I get you?"

"You're aware that Sydney has been on a brief sabbatical."

"I am."

"I've offered her a job for the foreseeable future. I won't officially need her until they spring me from this joint, but I'd like her to start coming in a few hours each day to get used to my routine."

His aunt began to argue, but he interrupted her. "You've been living here since I was admitted. I've got so many things I need your help with, things Sydney can't do for me. Please, Aunt Soph. I need you to take care of yourself."

"This will be different from hiring a nurse from an agency, Steven. I wonder if it will be difficult for us to get everything put together for her employment."

"I just need you to reach out to the agency she works for, set up an intake, and manage all the necessary paperwork until I'm able to handle that sort of thing on my own.

"Syd was telling me about a residential rehab that one of her clients received services through." He held out a scrap of paper. "Could you or Logan make a call tomorrow? See if they might be a suitable fit?"

Sophie studied the information. "Absolutely. Is there anything else you need me to take care of?"

Steven nodded. "I'd like you to make a trip down to the gym. There are some folders on rehab services in the cabinet next to Karla's desk, and grab that binder on accessible housing too, please. It's big and heavy; you can't miss it. It's time I take this bull by the horns and show him who's boss!"

Sophie was embarrassed. She hadn't even thought about the support group since the accident. The group she'd helped Steven get off the ground during pre-med offered a myriad of information on assistive technology, social services, and accessible housing—of course he knew what needed to be done.

Sophie smiled at the first true signs of her nephew's steely determination; she couldn't wait to share the news with her husband.

"If you don't need me, I am going to join Logan for lunch. Is it all right for me to make it all in one trip?"

Steven smiled. "Of course. Enjoy your lunch."

Sophie bought herself a coffee and went to their usual spot in the corner, but Logan never arrived. She left a message at his office and read several articles in a magazine that lay on the table, looking up periodically as she waited. The emergency room was full of surprises. *I'll only be a distraction if I go looking for him; he'll immediately think the worst.*

As she stood to leave, she ran into Corey Tucker.

"Hello, Mrs. Chandler."

"Good afternoon, Corey." She greeted the perpetually happy young man with a smile.

"Dr. C asked me to keep an eye out for you. There was an accident, and he's overseeing several critical cases. He asked me to apologize for him and said he'll see you this evening."

"Thank you. I figured he got held up. If you see him, please let him know you found me and I'll see him later."

"Will do, Mrs. Chandler. How is Steven? Has his condition improved?"

Sophie smiled. Whenever someone asked how Steven was doing, she'd felt like she'd been punched in the gut, but it had been a good day so far, and she fought to contain her excitement. Instead of swallowing down her concerns and providing a vague reply, she had a positive feeling about his condition, and it bubbled out before she could contain it.

"He's having a remarkable day; thank you for asking."

"Tell him we're all pulling for him, please."

"I will, Corey. Thank you."

As she made her way up to the fourth floor, the expressions of encouragement and support repeated themselves numerous times. Steven was a popular doctor . . . especially with the nurses. Visiting the rehab gym was even worse than braving the halls. Everyone who worked in the gym knew Steven Chandler. He held his support group meetings there, and it wouldn't be an understatement to say he stalked the gym for potential members. They all adored him, staff and patients alike.

Karla was no exception. She was the first to comment as Sophie exited the elevator. "I saw Steven a few days ago; he seems to be in good spirits."

"He's the reason I'm here. He asked me to come down and get some things for him."

Sophie ticked the items off her mental list as Karla began stacking them into a neat pile. She handed everything across her desk but didn't let go as Sophie reached for them. Her face broke into a wide smile.

"I'm pleased to see he's looking into attendant services. He's such a great advocate for Independent Living Philosophy and the part attendant care plays, as long as it's for someone else."

When she finally let go of the binder, Sophie nearly dropped it, not realizing how heavy it truly was.

"He needs to hear that from someone besides me. They want to start working his arms on Wednesday, so I imagine you'll see him around."

"Oh, that's great. I can't wait."

❖      ❖      ❖

Sophie hugged the heavy binder to her chest and took the elevator up to Steven's floor. When she walked into his room, the curtain was pulled, so she placed the binder on the counter and sat down.

"Sophie, you can come in; we're just changing my dressings."

Sophie walked around the curtain, relieved to find their friend Maddie working with Steven.

When they'd bought their first home in Woodstock, Logan opened a small practice at their home in addition to his work at the hospital in Putnam. Maddie began working for Logan fresh out of nursing school. A few years his senior, Maddie watched Steven when his parents needed a sitter, and as he grew older, they attended concerts and music festivals. They were close like siblings, but Sophie was relieved that Steven was comfortable with Maddie attending to his personal care.

Some of these young nurses—that Johnson girl, especially—spent more time ogling Steven and flaunting themselves in front of the male patients than they did caring for them. Logan would tut-tut his wife and suggest she was making too much out of it, but those girls made her uncomfortable. Maddie adored Steven, and Sophie wished there was a way to get her assigned to work with him every day.

When Maddie pulled the dressing off Steven's ankle, Sophie gagged. It looked like raw meat. The tissue was purulent and smelled rotten. Aghast, Sophie covered her mouth and nose before she could stop herself. Maddie looked over at Sophie with an understanding smile. "Sophie, honey, do you need to step outside? You don't look so hot."

Shaking her head, she closed her eyes and clutched the railing on Steven's bed until the wave of nausea passed. Her husband and son were both doctors. Things like that didn't usually bother her, but because it was Steven, it had.

She took a deep breath and composed herself. "No, I'll be okay. I was just caught off guard, that's all.

Sophie gaped at Steven's ankle as Maddie cleaned it. Steven seemed to be deeply engaged in something on the ceiling, so she followed his gaze. She wasn't surprised to see a mirror hanging at an angle from the trapeze bar. Steven was carefully watching as Maddie worked.

"Did you debride all the dead tissue on that one edge? What about that necrotic tissue where they drained it? Is it still pooled with blood?" Steven asked. Sophie had heard Logan use the term, "debride" when discussing a burn case once. He'd explained it as a painful process where any dead tissue was removed from burns or skin abrasions to allow new tissue growth.

Sophie was thankful for Steven's diminished sensitivity to pain. He didn't appear to be in any discomfort, but instead, busied himself with observing the procedure.

Maddie let out an exasperated sigh. "Yes, Steven. I got it all."

She turned to Sophie and winked. "See what I have to put up with?" There was a twinkle in her eye that told Sophie she wasn't offended. In fact, Maddie seemed delighted that he had enough spunk to pester her. Sophie was relieved at their banter. Steven needed someone who could keep things light.

Maddie picked up a white tub, covered a piece of gauze with its cream and applied it to the angry sore. "Trade me sides, dearie. This one isn't nearly as angry."

They switched sides and Sophie watched as the bedding was pulled back to expose Steven's other foot.

"Look at all that pink granulation tissue," Steven remarked.

"I see. It does look healthy, doesn't it?" Sophie smiled. Progress, no matter how small or how slow, was important.

Maddie adjusted the mirror and Steven again watched intently as she worked. Maddie used more of the gauze squares and sterile saline to clean the still-healing wound. "This one looks great."

She looked at Sophie expectantly. "Hon, could you help me roll Steven? I just need to check his backside for pressure sores."

Sophie took hold of the body cast, one hand resting on her nephew's hip and the other, just under his arm. Maddie took the draw sheet and rolled Steven towards his aunt.

Sophie pushed a pillow between Steven's chest and the railing to keep him from bumping his face against the barricade. As she supported Steven, Maddie worked, washing him and applying lotion to prevent skin breakdown. Sophie thought about the decision to hire Sydney. She would care for Steven like that too.

Sophie snickered as she took in the body cast that covered Steven completely. Someone clearly had a warped sense of humor. After they cut the cast, someone chose to re-cast him with pink camouflage tape.

Everyone had laughed, including Logan. Steven had been so sick that his aunt couldn't bring herself to add insult to injury.

Now that he was improving, her mood had turned lighter.

"So, Steven, how long are you stuck with that cast?"

"I don't know. Less than two weeks, I think. If there are no setbacks,

X-rays are scheduled to be two weeks from the last surgery. If there are, well, who knows?"

"That's a rotten trick to pull on a guy when he's down."

He smiled wryly. "As long as it keeps me all together, who cares about the color? It was all in fun."

Perhaps, Sophie thought, it had been a way to add some levity to such a grave situation. So many of his caregivers knew him personally and had been affected by the accident.

Sophie retrieved the information she'd picked up in the gym, and before the sun began its early descent, she and Steven made the necessary arrangements with Sydney's employer. The need to be at Steven's side since he'd been injured had been all-consuming in a way Sophie couldn't explain, but it finally felt like things might be looking up.

# Chapter Six

Wednesday morning loomed ominously for Steven, who knew exactly what awaited him with the dawn of the new day.

*Torture.*

Finally declared medically stable, he was scheduled to begin hand therapy with his old buddy, physical therapist Owen "Mac" McCrea.

In recent years, their circle of friends spent a lot of downtime working out and shooting hoops behind Mac's gym. If the manner in which Mac gave Steven a run for his money recreationally was any indication of what was to come, Steven knew he was in trouble.

❖　❖　❖

From the time they met, Mac had encouraged Steven to push his physical limitations, enabling him to be as physically fit as possible, so it seemed symbolic, some sixteen years later, that Mac was at the helm of the team tasked with the process of getting Steven's body back on the road to recovery.

A grueling session in the gym with Mac left Steven tired and sore. With the splints removed, he was slowly put through his paces, bending and stretching, forming shapes with his fingers and attempting to grasp objects which frustratingly slipped through his fingertips. The session concluded with another gentle massage and an order for ice therapy several times a day to help reduce swelling.

Maddie was Steven's nurse that day and after positioning him, returned with a basin filled with ice and water. After a few minutes of icing, Steven was asleep. He awoke some time later in his semi-dark room, the blinds and heavy curtains pulled shut. Disoriented by the lack of natural light, Steven tried to discern the time of day. He didn't smell the food carts that one could often set their watch by, but Sophie dozed in the recliner next to the bed, a light afghan covering her.

*Did I sleep through the entire day?*

As his eyes grew accustomed to the light, Steven spied a stress ball on his blanket. He stretched his fingers and smiled.

*Maddie.*

He pulled the ball into his fingers and began to tentatively flex and extend them around it; some degree of manual dexterity was necessary to palpate a patient, to make notations on a chart, to drive his wheelchair.

*Whatever it takes to get my life back!*

Steven studied his aunt, her beautiful features peaceful in repose. As if she could sense his gaze, Sophie stretched and opened her eyes, smiling sheepishly as she yawned. "I didn't know I was so tired. I'm sorry, Steven."

"I was asleep when you came in. You need to take better care of yourself."

Sophie frowned. "I'm trying. I feel like I need to stay on top of everything."

"How can you help me when you're not taking proper care of yourself? Have you any idea how terrible I'd feel if you got sick?" he asked.

"We almost lost you again. I–"

"I want you to get out of here and do something for yourself this afternoon. You need a break."

She sighed. "I do have a few errands I should run, I suppose."

"I don't want to see you back here again today, Sophie. I mean it."

She crossed her arms and scowled. "I'll go when Sydney comes."

"You'll go now. Go home. Soak in the tub. Take a nap in your own bed. Cook a decent meal for yourself and Logan. Please?" Then he went in for the kill. "If you won't do it for yourself, do it for him—do it for me."

❖    ❖    ❖

As soon as Steven pushed his aunt out the door, he called Sydney to alert her that he was being moved to another floor. He then commenced to have his nurse pack his meager belongings in a plastic bag, which had the hospital logo plastered on the front. An hour later, he was settling into an unoccupied two-bedroom.

*Every goal realized is a step closer to regaining my independence.*

❖    ❖    ❖

Steven's thoughts were interrupted by a sharp rap on the door. Logan had pushed him to consider legal action against the driver who had hit him, and it was Brooke Grady, his friend and attorney, who had arrived to begin the preliminaries on his case.

Steven had known the Grady siblings for a number of years; Sydney met Spencer when he provided treatment to one of her homecare patients. The pair began dating, and in no time, Sydney and Brooke became thicker than thieves.

Back when the Gradys had first entered their lives, Sophie, in a misguided attempt to fix her nephew's love life, attempted to unite him and Brooke as a couple. It didn't take long for the two young people to realize that invitations to family functions had been manufactured as a way to bring them together.

No romantic chemistry existed. The two did, however, become close friends and confidants, and over the years, they leaned on one another for support. That was, until Steven started at the stem cell center. Between Brooke's work with the firm of Emmerson and Reese and Steven's lab schedule, the two grew apart, and unwittingly, Steven failed his friend at the time she needed him the most.

Steven smiled at the sight of her. Brooke's attention to detail was impeccable, from her crisp navy pantsuit to her perfectly styled, auburn locks. The attorney carried herself across the room with the grace, poise, and confidence of a runway model. Steven was concerned about her mental state since learning of the premature death of her daughter and the subsequent departure of her long-time partner, but seeing her in person eased his mind.

*Paris has been good for her.*

Brooke squeezed Steven's hand, her tan skin and perfectly manicured nails a sharp contrast to his pallor. Brooke's smile was warm and genuine. "Steven, I'm so sorry. *How are you?* Sydney called me after she came here, but the minute I walked into the office, the firm handed me the full caseload I'd begged them for last fall.I haven't been able to get away."

"I'm glad they made the decision not to tell either of you. Everyone was afraid you'd cut your vacation short. You needed the time away, and you needed someone like Syd in your life."

"Damn right I would have come home."

Steven laughed softly. "That's exactly why you weren't told. You're here now when I need you. Back then, I wouldn't have even known you had come."

It amazed Steven that for someone who was as fierce as she was in the courtroom, Brooke could be the gentle and compassionate creature he knew and loved.

Brooke's gaze traveled the length of his body. "Word has it you're on the mend."

"That's what they tell me. It's all hard work from here on out." His eyes drifted over her abdomen, and he couldn't pull his eyes away. He closed them, praying for the right words before meeting her gaze again.

"How are you doing? I'm so sorry for your loss, Brooke."

Brooke offered Steven a sad smile. "I'm doing much better. I was having a hard time in the beginning. Caine and I had been having problems for a while. We tried to make things work, but losing Emily was the last straw. We decided it would be better if we separated. I think I would have moved on without much heartache if Caine and I had recently split up; I almost expected it to happen, eventually. But losing the baby—that was more devastating than anything I've ever experienced."

Brooke paused before meeting Steven's gaze.

"Paris was exactly what I needed. The partners at the firm demanded that I take a six-month sabbatical. It was non-negotiable."

"Well, it looks like six months of rest and relaxation was just what the doctor ordered, Brooke. You look wonderful."

Brooke pulled a legal pad from her briefcase, and Steven marveled over her smooth segue.

"Can you tell me everything you remember from the night of your accident?"

Steven shuddered as an ice-cold chill ran down his spine; goose bumps prickled his arms; his throat went dry. He'd never talked about it with anyone other than the officers who investigated the accident. Dredging it up again was nauseating.

"What were you wearing that night? Was your clothing dark?"

*Was it?* "I don't remember."

"Did the wheelchair you were operating have lights and a horn? Were they operating properly?"

"Yes." *But were they bright enough?*

"Did you attempt to warn the driver?"

"No." *I didn't have time.*

"Why were you in the middle of a busy street in the dark? Why weren't you at the designated crosswalk?"

The questions had only begun, but Steven was already growing frustrated. "The street was deserted. My roommate was supposed to meet me at the diner, but ran late at his new job as the Bulldogs' Mascot. I had my accident on the night of The Game." Steven referenced the years-long rivalry between his alma mater and Harvard. "Jon never showed, so I went home alone. Does this matter?"

"If we pursue this in court, a good defense attorney will attempt to place the blame on you. We'll work on your responses when the time comes. Now, please finish answering my questions."

"I was walking home from dinner. All the curb cuts on my route were under construction. The accessible path of travel was obstructed, so I had to enter the street where I could."

"Was the area where you crossed well lit?"

"No, but the moon was leaving its full phase."

"When you are well enough, we'll go to the site. An accident expert will recreate the scene with similar conditions to determine stopping distance. He'll use meteorology reports to determine cloud cover and moon brightness similar to that night."

Steven's stomach rolled. "I don't know if I can go there."

"You can and you will when the time comes. We'll start out with the easy stuff: a court stenographer will meet with us here to depose you since you're unable to travel."

Steven groaned. *Easier said than done.*

"When am I going to have to face her?" *Is it someone I know?*

"The other driver and the emergency personnel who were at the scene will provide their depositions at the courthouse."

Steven sighed and he felt his body relax.

"You can do this, Steven."

He watched as Brooke gathered her things from the bedside table and systematically placed each item back into her bag. She leaned in and gave him a one-armed hug. "Merry Christmas, Steven. I'll be in touch soon."

"And to you as well."

Steven registered the squeak of sneakers on linoleum before he heard the *whoosh* and soft *thud* of the door closing. He looked up to see his buddy, Mac, wearing a face-splitting grin.

"Stevie! Was that Grady's sister? I haven't seen her in years! What a beauty! Did you see that tan? She didn't get that in New Haven. She's not looking for a man, is she?"

Steven shot his friend a pointed glare. "You're wasting your time, buddy." With one friend acting as his attorney and the other having an active part in his rehab, their paths were bound to cross, yet Steven refused to share anything that would reveal Brooke's very private pain.

"Mac, please, she's recovering from something devastating. Promise me you won't hit on her every time you see her. Please?"

"Nothing like being cryptic. I'll leave her be . . . for now. But you can't expect me to ignore her forever. I think I'm in love, Stevie."

When Mac fanned himself, Steven snickered. Little did Mac know, Brooke would wipe that goofy grin right off his face.

*Live and learn, buddy.*

Mac sat in the chair Brooke had recently vacated, balancing Steven's rehab folder on his knee. "Despite the pain and inflammation, which is to be expected, your progress has been great. I've assigned an occupational therapist to assist with your fine motor skills, so you and I can begin rebuilding some muscle mass on those arms."

Steven frowned, rubbing over his casted abdomen. "This thing is pretty snug. I'm afraid I'm getting paunchy."

"I'd like to see you regain as much tone as possible before that body cast comes off. You're going to need to rely on those arms when you begin core-strengthening exercises down at the rehab center."

Steven's face broke into a goofy grin. "I can hardly wait."

"Man, you're one of the only patients I have who doesn't complain."

"I don't have anything to complain about."

Mac shook his head, but Steven stopped him.

"By the grace of God, I'm still here. I'll do whatever I have to, to take my life back."

Mac's chest got tight when he thought about that night and the hours and then days that followed—the rollercoaster ride Steven's accident had taken them all on as they waited and wondered if he'd come out of it alive. Mac had shed more tears than he'd ever admit, but his friend was on the mend, and he'd do whatever he could to help him achieve his goals.

Afraid of embarrassing himself, Mac cleared his throat and stood to leave. "You've got your work cut out for you, Steven."

"I've got this."

"I know you do."

# Chapter Seven

True to his word, it was only a few days, and Steven was in the U-gym, lifting light weights with Mac. The melancholy that had come from lying immobile in a body cast began lifting as well.

A smile broke across Steven's face when Sydney bounced into his room three days before Christmas. "Hey!" she exclaimed, plopping down into the vinyl recliner. "How's your day been so far?"

Steven shrugged. "Same old, same old, ya know? Not a lot of change from day to day."

"Mac says you're getting stronger."

Steven pumped his bare arms with a chuckle. "They still look scrawny to me." He knew it would take weeks of hard work to regain the strength necessary to successfully execute transfers in and out of his chair.

❖   ❖   ❖

Sydney loudly patted the huge, ring-bound notebook she carried everywhere. On the first day of their arrangement, she'd entered his room clutching the thing, and in the days that followed, she'd added to it. Sydney had arranged each section relating to a specific aspect of his rehabilitation: lists of procedures and test results; therapy care plans and progress notes; long-term goals for his independence.

"So, I know something we can work on to occupy your mind and get you to stop moping around when I'm not here."

"I'm not moping!"

"You are too."

"Okay, maybe a little. I feel like these walls are closing in on me."

Sydney looked around covertly before leaning in close to his bed and whispering, "I thought maybe we could start working on your home plan."

"Home plan," Steven murmured with a smile. "I've been so busy feeling sorry for myself that I haven't put a whole lot of thought into where I'm going from here."

"Sophie and I have been scouring the papers for accessible housing, and we found a nice building that is being renovated into visitable apartments. I thought perhaps I could go by and check the model apartment out, maybe take a few pictures. You need to start thinking about the next step of your life."

"So you thought you could take my mind off my boring lifestyle by discussing apartments?"

"Well . . . I was *thinking* that we could make a wish list of all the things you want and need in a place, everything you'll need to outfit a new home. Do you have much stuff over at the house you were renting with those guys?"

"No." He snorted. "Nothing but a coffee maker, a microwave, and some personal stuff—maybe a few electronics."

"I hear there are some nice two-bedrooms over at the place I was telling you about. You mentioned wanting me to live in until you got your bearings. Once I leave, the second bedroom might make a nice study for you."

Steven reached for the bed rail and pulled himself towards Sydney. "Could you help me get up on my side so I can see you a little better? I hate talking to the ceiling."

Sydney moved behind Steven and wedged in a bolster behind his torso, using bed pillows to support the legs of his cast and make him more comfortable.

"How's that?"

"Much better, thanks. Now, what I'd rather do is get some information on local real estate. I think it's time for me to put on my big-boy pants and start thinking about something a little more permanent. I'm so tired of dorm life. I mean, it was okay renting a house with the guys during our residencies, but I'd like to have something to show for my hard work."

Sydney squealed and clapped her hands. "Oh, this is so exciting!"

Steven scrubbed his face with the palm of his hand. "I hope Sophie isn't too upset. I almost expect her to ask when I'm moving back in with them."

"You know they'd never turn you away, but she seemed relieved when I offered to live in if you need me till you're back on your feet. I don't think she's planning for her adult child to return home."

"I think Logan is happy to have his wife sleeping in her own bed again."

"I do too, but if you're gonna get out of this place, we need to quit talking and whip you into shape."

Progress became a huge motivator for Steven, and he found himself becoming enthusiastic while conquering the simplest of tasks; Sydney put together a fine motor tool set with various household objects that Steven could independently use to improve his manual dexterity.

Any time she was with him, she was vigilant about working any part of Steven's body that was accessible: hands and arms, fingers and toes. Pulling back the sheet that afternoon to check his toes for circulation, she let out a horrified gasp.

"Oh, Steven! This looks terrible! Does it *hurt?*"

He cocked his eyebrow and shot her a glare. "Seriously, Syd?"

"Sorry. It didn't look like this yesterday."

"It looked pretty angry when April changed the dressing this morning. She reported it to Dr. Wesley. Quinn or someone else from Infectious Disease will take a look at it in the morning."

Sydney pulled on her jacket. "I'll be interested to hear what they have to say." As she walked toward the door, she added, "Hold that thought. I'll be back right back."

*Not like I'm going anywhere.*

❖    ❖    ❖

Steven jumped with a start when the door to his room slammed against the wall, and his small-statured cousin re-entered the room, pushing a cart laden with shopping bags. She struggled to push past his bed, and he laughed when she flopped into the recliner with a huff.

"I got everyone on your list. I hope I did okay, I wasn't sure about a couple of things."

"It'll be fine, Syd."

One by one, Christmas gifts were revealed: travel mugs and coffee shop cards from Blue State for his former roomies; gift cards for local eateries for Spence—the guy couldn't cook to save his life; a custom printed sweatshirt with a caricature of Mac's likeness and the logo for his gym. Sydney decorated the packages with the speed and precision of a shopping mall gift wrapper.

"You sure you don't need me to come by this weekend?" she asked over her shoulder.

Brooke and Spencer's parents were visiting from Houston, and it had been the first time they'd seen their daughter since she'd lost Emily. "I'd never expect you to spend your holiday with me; you need to spend Christmas with your loved ones."

Sydney whipped around, her expression a mixture of anger and sadness. "Steven Chandler, I'm not some random employee. *You* are one of my loved ones."

"You know I didn't mean it like that. I try to remember this is a professional relationship we have. If the lines get blurred, things can become complicated. Please forgive me?" He offered her his most endearing smile, but she glared at him.

"You might be able to charm these nurses, but don't even try that one on me."

Steven knew Spencer desperately wanted to move forward with his girl. They'd spent years spinning their wheels, both career-driven workaholics. It had taken the sight of his best friend laid out on the pavement, clinging to life, for Spencer to realize that he couldn't live any longer without his lady love. Steven hoped the two would make some sort of formal commitment over the holiday.

"I want you to have a nice holiday. I know things have been a little uncertain with Spence. Go have a nice time with him." He waggled his eyebrows suggestively. "See if you can't rekindle something."

❖  ❖  ❖

Maddie frowned as she placed a basin of bathwater on Steven's nightstand. "Syd said you barely touched your dinner. Are you feeling okay?" She brushed a hand over his forehead.

"Yeah, a little tired. I think we overdid the Christmas spirit this evening."

"I thought we'd get an early start. Tomorrow sounds like it'll be a long day."

While Steven was bathed and lotioned, Sydney chattered away from the other side of the curtain, inquiring about Maddie and Quinn's holiday plans. When the curtain was pulled back, Steven was shocked to see a tiny tree surrounded by gifts.

"Sydney Chandler! I thought we agreed on no decorations. I don't have much to celebrate this year." Sydney's face fell as he berated her, and Steven wished he could backpedal. It wasn't that he didn't appreciate her efforts; he simply wasn't in a holiday mood.

Sydney put her hands on her hips, and the words she uttered nearly broke his heart. "You realize this is the only Christmas tree Logan and Sophie will have this year?"

Steven frowned, having assumed things on the outside were back to normal. "Are you trying to tell me she didn't decorate for Christmas?"

Sydney shook her head.

"But she loves to decorate for Christmas," he whispered.

"She loves you more. Do you honestly believe your family would celebrate at home with you here?"

"I didn't think about how things were at home," Steven said softly.

"We're all celebrating the fact that you're still here to share the holiday with us."

"We have every reason to celebrate this year," Maddie added, throwing the soiled linens in the hamper and washing her hands. "I'll stop back for a minute before I leave at eleven. Merry Christmas, Sydney."

"Merry Christmas."

As soon as Maddie had gone, Sydney began to pull items from the bounty of beautiful gifts that surrounded the tree and plopped them on the foot of the bed.

"What did you do, Syd?"

She pulled the chair up next to the bed and lowered the rail. Holding the gift bag by the bottom, she offered it to Steven so he could reach inside. Several articles of clothing dropped out onto the mattress.

"I found this wonderful shop that tailors adaptive clothing. I hope you're not offended. I got your measurements from Sophie. I thought they'd be perfect for rehab."

Steven eyed a pair of pants skeptically. "Uh, Syd, you do realize I'll still be in casts when I go to rehab. Pants will be nearly impossible."

"Velcro," she replied. With a quick jerk of her hands the outer seam tore apart, exposing the soft fabric fastener that ran from waist to ankle.

Steven smiled at her thoughtfulness. "Perfect. I love them."

A flannel-lined poncho, adapted to cover his legs and keep him dry while allowing safe entrance through doorways.

"I don't know what I'd do without you. Thank you so much."

She leaned in and gave him a hug and a sad smile. "You're welcome."

He pointed to the bedside table. "Why don't you lift the mirror on that thing. I think Santa left something for you, as well."

She rummaged inside, withdrawing a small box. She lifted the lid and gasped. "Steven, I can't take this." Her finger drifted over the delicate opal ring that had once belonged to Grace Maxwell, Steven's mother. "It's too much."

"I've been meaning to give it to you for a while, but I wanted to wait till I could do it in person. She'd have wanted you to have it."

She gave him a teary smile as she slipped it on her finger. "You're sure? What about Sophie?"

"Who do you think had it cleaned and gift-wrapped?"

"Thank you. I'll treasure it always."

They chatted until the voice on the PA announced the end of visitation. "I better go before they kick me out. Merry Christmas," she sang as she skipped out the door, leaving Steven alone with his thoughts.

*Goodnight, Syd.*

Steven stared out the window for hours. The moon shone brightly over New Haven, and he watched as the sleeping city was blanketed under a layer of newly fallen snow. As Steven drifted off to sleep, he gave thanks.

# Chapter Eight

Abby Harris lay in her hospital bed, listening to the strains of "Ava Maria" as it was piped softly through the hospital's PA system. Not one to feel sorry for herself, she'd sucked it up and agreed to do what her doctor recommended in order to keep her disease in check, but the irony wasn't lost on her that she'd spent the same holiday on the same floor of the same hospital one year before.

While her abrupt admission was in no way expected, it didn't hold the same level of fear or uncertainty that her first MS hospitalization had. If there was one thing Abby had learned in the twelve months since her diagnosis, it was to expect the unexpected when it came to her MS.

Unlike the flare the year before, where the MS came barreling into her life like a freight train, this one had crept in quietly and with little fanfare—blurriness in her left eye that started as little more than an annoyance a few days before was followed by a dark shadow that settled around her field of vision. Her balance had been a little off, but she'd brushed that aside, chalking it up to another bad day.

Abby had been under a lot of stress at work; her school's ranking after the spring's standardized testing had been lower than anticipated. In order to target areas of weakness, the director of the Bridgehaven Academy had mandated that students undergo assessment tests the week before Christmas break.

While performance testing was not state-mandated for private institutions of learning, with tuition at nearly twelve thousand dollars a year, the school relied on its proficiency rating to boost enrollment and guarantee waiting lists.

If a particular classroom's proficiency was lacking, it would reflect poorly on the entire school. Abby, like most of her colleagues, had spent the first two weeks of December prepping her students for the tests, all the while trying not to appear too blatantly obvious.

Abby hadn't done that much bookwork since studying for her teaching certification, so when the visual disturbance first occurred, she was certain it had simply been a reflection of her recent work habits.

A piercing headache and stabbing pain behind her eyes woke Abby the day before Christmas Eve, but the issue that troubled her most was the absence of vision in her left eye—all that remained in her field of vision was a pinpoint of light centered in a sea of blackness.

Abby took a deep breath and with shaking fingers dialed the number that had become her lifeline when it came to crises related to her disability. When Dr. Jeffries's receptionist answered, Abby nearly sobbed with relief.

"Danni, it's Abby Harris. Thank goodness you're open today. I'm in trouble."

❖     ❖     ❖

Dr. Jeffries stopped at the door and took a moment to center himself. There were days when it was hard to school his emotions from one patient to the next. One minute he might be laughing with a real wisecracker, and the next he'd be walking into a situation that required a modicum of seriousness such as the one that awaited him on the other side of the door.

He was taken aback to find Abby Harris sitting on the exam table, carrying on a light-hearted conversation with another young woman. When she'd called his office a few hours before, her voice was filled with concern.

When she looked up as he was drying his hands, she gave him a tight smile.

"Hey, Doc."

"Abby."

Abby turned toward the girl who sat off to the side in the visitor's chair. "This is my classroom aide and good friend, Brenda Callahan."

He extended his hand to Abby's companion. "Nice to meet you."

"Nice meeting you, too."

Jeffries turned his attention back to his patient. "So, Danni said you're experiencing a visual disturbance?"

Abby stared at her lap as she wrung her hands. "I've noticed a few things the last week or so, a darkening around the edge of my field of vision, and my colors seemed off; things were sort of washed out. But this morning when I woke up, I couldn't see out of my left eye."

"Let's take a look."

Jeff lowered the lights and went through a cursory eye exam with his patient. As he examined the reaction of her pupils, he began asking questions. "Are you experiencing any pain?"

"I find I'm turning my head because it hurts so much to move my eyes."

"Headaches?"

Abby grimaced. "Splitting headaches."

"Look straight ahead for me, Abby."

After peering into her eye with an ophthalmoscope, he backed away making several notations on her chart.

"Your optic disk appears swollen."

"What does that mean?"

"In your case, the inability to distinguish color, the slow response of the pupil to light, the swollen optic disk are all indicators of optic neuritis. It's a condition that is quite common in patients with MS."

"So this is definitely part of the MS?"

"Optic neuritis is often the *first* event that presents itself in many MS cases, and it can most definitely be indicative of an attack. Have you had any other symptoms that would indicate you're experiencing a flare?"

"Nothing I can think of, other than this annoying blackness." Abby kicked Brenda's foot and shot her a stern glare, praying her friend wouldn't open her mouth and throw Abby under the bus.

Jeffries studied the silent conversation going on between the two women. "Let's get an MRI and see what's going on in there. The test will tell us more about the inflammation of your optic nerve, and it will also tell us if there are any new lesions on your brain."

Abby drew in a shaky breath and asked the one question she most feared. "Am I going to lose my sight?"

"Optic neuritis often improves on its own, but your condition will improve drastically and in less time with IV steroids. Most insurance companies consider hospital admission to receive intravenous therapy medically necessary in cases of acute visual loss such as you're experiencing. It would be justifiable to admit you for treatment."

"But it's Christmas! I was here last year over Christmas," Abby whispered.

"Normally I could order the treatments on an outpatient basis, but as you said, Christmas is in two days, and unfortunately, the infusion center will be closed. There are a number of side effects that can occur with the medication. I don't allow first-timers to do the treatments at home. I don't want you to have to wait to be treated. It would be best to admit you for a few days, Abby."

When she expressed her concerns that her insurance might not cover a treatment that could be performed on an outpatient basis, her doctor put his hands on her shoulders and calmly but insistently implored her to follow the course of treatment he felt was best for her.

"And will this therapy help me?"

"While most patients begin to notice changes within a few days, there have been a rare few who have begun to notice an improvement in as little as a matter of hours. Many times, optic neuritis will gradually improve with no treatment at all. But I'm not a firm believer in the wait and watch approach when it comes to early MS. When exacerbations aren't fully resolved, the lingering effects can build up, leading to permanent disability."

He smiled at Abby and added, "Like dealing with a troublesome student, we like to nip it in the bud and deal with it swiftly and aggressively after it manifests. Based on the severity of your exacerbation, we'll do a seven-day course of the medication, and you'll be well on your way to recovery when you go home."

And there it was, the word she'd come to loathe: exacerbation.

Abby answered despairingly. "I understand."

"I'll stop by to see how you're feeling at the end of the day."

❖   ❖   ❖

Dr. Jeffries groaned when he looked down at his watch. Helena had no doubt cleared away their dinner and retired to the family room with a glass of wine. It had been a long day, and he still had several patients to check in on before leaving the hospital.

He hated standing up his wife each evening, something that had rarely happened since he'd taken a partner two years before, but Jeff had been spread thin since young Chandler's accident, and even though they'd rescheduled a number of routine wellness appointments in order to allow him time to care for the most pressing cases, it was nearly impossible to fill the gaping hole Steven's absence had left at the practice.

Jeff had done fine by himself before offering the partnership to the budding neurologist, but the attractive and charismatic young man had managed to accumulate a staggering number of new patients since joining the practice, and Jeffries was feeling the brunt of it tenfold. Despite the corners Jeff cut, he never seemed to have enough time to get everything done.

He needed to find a suitable replacement to cover some of the backlogged cases that had piled up since the accident. No matter how he spun it in his head, a difficult conversation was in order. Who knew when or if Steven would ever be able to return to his position within their practice?

Jeff chastised himself as soon as the thought crossed his mind. Not only had Steven proven himself as a fine physician and a competent businessman, but he had also become Jeffries's close friend, and it felt wrong to even consider replacing him. Eventually, some sort of decision would have to be made, but until then, he would cope.

*I'll find a way.*

Abby had heard horror stories about the massive doses of steroids her doctor wanted to pump into her system. Her MS support group members each had their own interpretation of how the drug performed—from miraculous results to rather disconcerting accounts of "roid rage."

Once Abby had resigned herself to the fact that she was going to spend the majority of her vacation as a hospital guest, she tried to find the silver lining in her bleak situation. She'd been bone tired since she started helping her students cram for the assessment testing. A week in the hospital with nothing more pressing than watching TV while someone else cooked her meals and fluffed her pillow might not be such a terrible thing.

Dr. Jeffries had stopped by to monitor her body's reaction to the first megadose of steroids, and so far, it had been a doozy. First, it had been the unrelenting taste of metal on Abby's tongue. Then it was the itching—the IV drip made Abby's skin crawl, and she had to go through her meditation exercises in order to resist clawing herself raw. The worst part of it all, though, was the overwhelming urge to pace the room like a caged animal. With her diminished vision and unsteady gait, Abby was afraid of tripping and falling in the unfamiliar surroundings.

Waking up to little change the next morning had been disappointing. Abby had hoped that she'd be one of the rare cases who found instantaneous relief from the medication, but by the time she'd received her second dose, she was a little more sure on her feet, and it felt as if the pinpoint she'd been trying to look through had grown, increasing her field of vision if only by a fraction.

Abby had awakened before the sun was peeking through the clouds that morning, and while she was picking at a cup of fresh fruit and eating yogurt with granola, someone tapped on her door. A petite girl with a ponytail and pushing a wheelchair stood in the doorway.

"Dr. Jeffries has requested that we take you down to work with one of the physical therapists while you're here. Have you finished your breakfast?"

Abby surveyed the remains of her tray. "Yeah. I wasn't that hungry.

These treatments have my stomach all jumbled up." She frowned at the chair. "I suppose it was wishful thinking when I stuffed my wheelchair into the closet."

"Not at all. It's simply a precaution. We transport everyone to the gym. Trust me," she added with a grin, "you won't be sitting for long. We're planning to put you through your paces."

Abby groaned, muttering under her breath. *Some vacation.*

It was true that the MS left her stiff and sore, and sitting behind a desk almost eight hours a day did little to keep her body in motion, but by the end of her workday, the last thing she was capable of was more physical activity. Sure, there had been stumbling blocks along the way, but Abby would be the first to admit that after regaining her mobility and returning to work, the exercises fell by the wayside.

"Oh, goodie. Sounds like I'm getting the full tune-up while I'm here, aren't I?"

"Your doctor wants to be sure you haven't lost function as a result of your flare."

"Well, I suppose he's the expert," Abby replied as she dropped into the chair.

❖ ❖ ❖

Abby took in the holiday decorations while her chaperone chattered, expertly snaking the wheelchair through the labyrinth that led to the gym. Abby's thoughts drifted to the daybreak conversation she'd had with her neurologist. It hadn't been the first time he'd implored her to explore disease-modifying drugs, and she was sure it wouldn't be the last.

Over the past year, she'd had three flares, each one a bit more troubling than the last, the most recent one causing her current situation. Each episode left Abby feeling wobbly and unsteady on her feet—tripping, stumbling, and falling were common occurrences. Abby's doctor had beseeched her to try something more long-term than the occasional hookup with the heavy-duty steroids that had been coursing through her veins since her admission.

Abby had to give him credit. While she was certain many doctors were motivated by big name pharmaceutical companies offering incentives to prescribe particular drugs, Dr. Jeffries seemed to take her concerns seriously and had offered to discuss the pros and cons of each of the disease modifying drugs with Abby, so she could make an informed decision.

The bottom line was that those drugs scared the hell out of Abby, and she simply wasn't ready.

*"Ready for what?"* a little voice whispered.

*The onslaught of side effects I've read about in the neurology magazines that come in the mail each month.*

*The constant monitoring and testing to ensure the drug isn't causing further damage to my body.*

*The need to inject myself on a daily basis with something that could make me feel ill.*

*Or perhaps even though I've come to accept it, using those drugs is acceptance that this disease is here to stay . . .*

*No, I'm not ready.*

The wheelchair's abrupt stop pulled Abby out of her thoughts, and she looked up at the girl who'd been pushing her. "Here we are, Abby. I'll park you here till your therapist is ready."

"Thanks."

Thankfully, the pounding pain in her head was gone, and with her one good eye, Abby took in the gym filled with people and bustling with activity—such a far cry from the cheery gathering place where she'd made so many new friends a year before. Sometimes she regretted the decision to join a more convenient support group. Those *New Haven Newbies* were quite the bunch.

Abby smiled when Mac McCrea waved, and she followed his gaze to the gurney that was parked across the gym from where she currently sat.

Despite her compromised vision, Abby would recognize that head of tight blonde ringlets anywhere, and that voice . . . Without a second thought, Abby locked the wheels on her chair and folded up the footplates. Drawn like a moth to a flame, she stood and slowly made her way to the gurney parked along the wall.

She gazed down into the angelic face of Steven Chandler—*Doc-*

*tor Steven Chandler*—who apparently was also a holiday patient. *Doctor Steven Chandler* who lay directly before her.

The attractive, young doctor looked up, and recognition flickered across his face. Tentatively and without thinking, Abby reached out to touch his bare shoulder, both of them gasping at the sensation. As Abby stood over Steven, she took in his appearance with a frown. His bare chest was covered with angry pink scars, evidence of his rumored accident. A bright blue cast ran from his sternum down to his toes. He was a traumatized visage of the confident, self-assured man she'd met only a year before, and still, he took her breath away.

Steven smiled and very softly said, "I know I know you. I'm sorry—I can't recall your name."

"Abigail Harris—I have MS. It was your uncle who admitted me last Christmas."

Steven chuckled. "You are the spitfire who put me in my place."

Abby laughed in response. "I was hardly fair to you. It wasn't your fault."

"Abby." He breathed her name and smiled warmly. "You accompanied me to the support group."

Abby realized with horror that as she was leaning very close in order to hear, she had invaded the man's personal space. Apparently he realized it as well. "You have to excuse me; I can't project my voice very well, confined like this. The cast is quite cumbersome." He turned his head and coughed.

"I see you have a lovely dime-store bracelet like mine. No special plans for the holidays?" He raised his wrist as he spoke, showing off several bracelets of his own.

FALL RISK.

ALLERGY.

BLOOD BANK.

Abby looked down and rubbed her fingers over her blue ID band. "I've had a flare. Dr. J put me on steroids for a week; he thinks it'll help me bounce back."

"There are much more effective drugs out there for someone who is currently ambulatory. We should be *preventing* these flares instead of treating them. Jeff"'s selling you short if he doesn't encourage you to investigate them."

Abby looked away, hoping to temper her mood. She'd lashed out at Steven Chandler during their first encounter, and she refused to let history repeat itself. "The side effects scare me, Dr. Chandler."

"I appreciate that, but if you ever want to talk, I can offer my professional opinion on what's been most helpful for my patients. Even though I'm not your physician, I *am* qualified to give you reliable advice. You can find me in the gym most days around lunch, and Abby, please call me Steven. Dr. Chandler is my uncle." Steven wore an endearing smile, and Abby reckoned it might not be such a bad thing to get to know the good doctor better and hear what he had to say.

As she opened her mouth to respond, an orderly she recognized from her floor stepped up to the gurney. "Sorry to interrupt, Doc, but it's time to go. I have strict orders not to detain you today. We need to go have that ankle looked at." As his gaze swept the length of the gurney, Abby looked, too, gasping when she took in the seeping bandage peeking out of Steven's cast. Before she could utter another word, he was gone.

❖　❖　❖

The therapists in the rehab gym were evil slave drivers who thought Abby was a contortionist with unlimited stores of energy; after her session, she promptly fell asleep.

The sound and smell of dinnertime trays being delivered drew Abby from her slumber. She sat up, rubbing her eyes and glanced at the whiteboard at the foot of her bed. Feeling more than a little sorry for herself, she'd scowled that morning when her nurse had scrawled December 24th across the top of the board, assuming her holiday was going to be bleak.

The knowledge that Steven was currently under the same roof caused Abby to smile. That he'd referred to her as a friend made her insides do all sorts of squishy things.

Suddenly and unexpectedly, Abby's holiday no longer appeared so dismal. The stay in the hospital didn't seem as confining, and the hospital food seemed almost appealing.

Perhaps her Christmas wouldn't be a disappointment after all.

# Chapter Nine

Christmas passed with little fanfare for Steven. The highlight of his holiday had been seeing that girl again.

Abby.

Steven thought back to the previous Christmas when he'd made the diagnosis that had irrevocably changed her life. He'd tried to soften the blow by inviting her to his support group. He knew the friendships she'd cultivate and the resources available to her would help her navigate the path she unexpectedly found herself on as a person with a disability.

Somehow, that brief meeting had left a lasting impression on the young doctor, and he'd caught himself thinking about Abby Harris on more than one occasion.

*Why hadn't she ever come back to The Newbies?*

Steven smiled at the memory of their interaction shortly before his accident—that day at the food trucks when she'd practically fallen into his lap. Abby was nearly half a block away until he'd figured out who she was. Was it that way for her too?

Steven dissected their short encounter in the gym. They'd only had a moment to talk, but Abby had taken the initiative and reached out to him. Literally. And the expression on her face when she'd touched his skin—as if she wasn't quite sure he was real. Steven knew his time in the gym that day was limited, and he'd felt an inexplicable urge to connect with her in some way until they were torn apart again. Steven grasped at straws for a reason, any reason, to get to know the beguiling creature a little better.

It felt like fate was constantly interrupting their encounters. But what if Steven's buddies had been right? It felt wrong to pursue her romantically, and he rarely warred with his conscience, but Abby Harris was not his patient, and like his buddies pointed out, as long as he wasn't treating her . . .

❖   ❖   ❖

Steven had given up the notion of ever having love in his life, but this girl . . . This girl made him hope for something he hadn't realized he was missing, and maybe it was time to play devil's advocate with his conscience.

A short time after seeing Abby in the gym, Steven lay in pre-op, waiting for someone from anesthesia to come in and prep him for yet another surgery.

Minutes later, Steven was on an operating table counting backwards as he waited for sleep to claim him. Each surgery was another bump along the road to recovery. In the end, he knew he'd be leaving the hospital behind to begin his journey through rehab, and for the first time since his nightmare began, it felt like there was a light at the end of the tunnel.

With the infection cleaned out of the wound and a new antibiotic, which had begun to kick in, Steven was feeling well enough to interact with the visitors who happened by on Christmas day.

❖   ❖   ❖

Sophie and Logan came early, so they were there when Mac came barreling through the door, a huge gift bag in his hand.

Steven's face grew hot when his friend relentlessly teased him about distracting the other patients while attending sessions in the gym, half naked.

Logan, who was normally so proper and reserved, laughed deeply and heartily as he read the shirts, helping Steven pull them out of the bag.

The first sported a bright blue parking placard with a caption underneath that read "I'm only in it for the parking."

The second shirt had Steven holding his stomach while he laughed. The screen print had a red and blue triangular traffic sign in the center of it. The image was an inclined path with the universal wheelchair symbol, and at the bottom of the incline sat a hungry crocodile with his mouth wide open. Underneath the sign, it bore the caption: "Please don't feed the animals."

Sophie gasped when she saw it. "Owen McCrea! That's one of the most tasteless things I've ever seen!"

"I love it!" Steven replied. "I can't wait to wear it."

It felt so good for Steven to joke around with his friend. Mac was the person who could pull Steven out of any self-deprecating mood.

"I'll probably have people in the gym throwing hand weights at me. How is it going to look for me, a doctor, who works with people who have disabilities no less, wearing shirts like these?"

"Steven, they were made by people with disabilities, for people with disabilities. If anyone complains, it'll be because you don't have anything on, not because of what you're wearing."

"Thanks, Mac. I'll wear them proudly."

Steven pointed to the bag on the windowsill with Mac's gifts inside.

His friend grabbed the bag, pulled out a shirt, and yanked it over his head. As he looked in the mirror at his caricature and the logo for his gym, he grinned and said, "This is the shit, man. I'll wear it all the time!"

There was no doubt in Steven's mind that he would. Mac teared up when he opened the framed and signed artwork that the shirt had been designed from.

"Man, I don't think anyone has ever given me a more heartfelt gift." He leaned down and put his big arms around Steven, giving him a hearty squeeze before turning away and wiping his eyes.

Mac said his goodbyes to everyone, explaining that Mrs. McCrea was putting on a huge spread for the entire family, and if he arrived late, there would be nothing left.

When it was finally the three of them, Sophie pulled out an insulated bag, revealing three divided, resealable dinner trays. "I couldn't bear to think of you eating hospital food on Christmas day." She fluttered around trying to set up a suitable dining area for her family. Steven wasn't hungry, but he knew it wouldn't do to tell Sophie that.

Logan leaned close and whispered, "I tried to rein her in."

"It's okay. Don't spoil her day, please," Steven replied, Sydney's words about the holiday fresh in his mind.

Dinner was delectable. It was the first home-cooked meal Steven had eaten since his accident, and he ate as much as he could. He cursed the body cast, his stomach uncomfortable. Everything tasted so good! Oh, how he missed the Sunday dinners that occurred at Sophie's table.

"That was delicious, Aunt Soph." He patted his stomach. "I can't eat another bite, but if either of you want cookies, my favorite nurse left goodies for us all. I haven't eaten too many of them."

Logan didn't need any more encouragement, and he reached for the tin on the windowsill. Steven regretted his offer at the sight of Logan, a cookie in each hand, wearing a huge grin on his face.

"Mmm, she never disappoints, does she?" Logan mumbled between bites. Steven squirmed as his uncle repeatedly opened the coveted gift and helped himself, his heart sinking with the realization that, in no time, they'd be all gone.

Sophie saved the day when she took the tin from her husband's hands and broke out gifts even though Steven had specifically asked them not to do anything special for Christmas.

Sophie kissed him before setting a few packages on the bedside table. "Sweetheart, you were here last year as well. You didn't think I could go two years in a row without celebrating Christmas, did you?"

"I'm sorry for being a brat, Aunt Soph. I've been so miserable, I didn't think about how all of this was affecting the two of you. Thank you for everything. You guys are so good to me."

"We love you."

"I know. I love you too."

Sophie engulfed her boy in a warm embrace. "Having you here to spend Christmas with is the best gift I could have received this year. Knowing our family is together is all I need." She kissed his face as she rubbed her hand over the opposite cheek. "I love you so much, Steven. I was so afraid we'd lost you." Before she could stop herself, the waterworks began.

Wanting to divert the conversation from his near demise, Steven said, "You'll never guess who I saw at PT yesterday."

"No idea, son. Enlighten us."

"Do you remember the gal you admitted last Christmas? I consulted on her case and helped diagnose her MS."

"I do. Pleasant girl. Kind of cute too."

Steven glanced around and whispered, "She's here."

"Oh, that's unfortunate, but now Mac's comment makes sense."

"It's actually pretty great. I mean, well, it was great seeing her again. I never saw her after we went to the support group that one time."

Logan cracked a smile. "You've isolated yourself from the fairer sex for so long, it's high time you start living your life."

Steven felt his face growing warm. His aunt looked simply gleeful. "It's not like that. I mean, she's a nice girl, but she's here again. I only wanted to share . . ."

"I hope it's nothing serious."

"She said she was having a flare. I think she's in for a tune-up. We only had a moment before they whisked me away to Infectious Disease. I'm a little miffed as to why she hasn't considered any of the meds on the market. She could manage her symptoms so much better. I offered to sit down and discuss them with her, as friends." Steven emphasized the last word.

"Your patients relate well to you because of your situation. If anyone can convince the young lady to investigate the drug therapies that are on the market, it'll be you."

"She won't be here long. I'm a little worried she'll sneak off without talking to me. Is there any way you could help me find her before she goes?"

"I'd like nothing more than to help you in your quest for happiness, but you know I can't break confidentiality, even for you."

Steven hung his head, feeling every bit like a child who had been chastised. "I know, but what if I don't see her again?"

He hadn't been drawn to a woman in such a long time. There had been no shortage of nurses who'd approached Steven since he'd settled in New Haven, but every time someone approached him, the words of his former girlfriend echoed in his mind. *You'll never be a whole man. No one will ever want you. I need more than you can ever give me.*

Steven had accepted his lot in life when it came to romance. It was so much easier than putting himself out there only to get his heart trampled again. For some reason, he felt differently about Abby. There was something warm and genuine about her that made Steven want to get to know her better.

Steven felt the radiance of a million suns when she was near, and he wanted to bask in that warmth, even if only for a moment.

"What I can do is drop in on her and apologize that you haven't been back to physical therapy because you unexpectedly needed surgery. I assume I have your permission to share your room number with her?"

"Yes, please. And thank you."

Sophie, being the attentive mother, jumped right into the conversation. "So tell me about this Abby, sweetheart. Do you like her? What do you know about her?" She turned to her husband. "Logan, is she a nice girl? I don't want Steven getting involved with another Courtney!"

Steven's hand went to his forehead, and he grimaced. He immediately regretted having acted so impulsively. "Aunt Soph, please. . . I'm sitting right here! She's only a friend, and yes, she's a nice girl. You'd love her, but I'm sure she'd never be interested in someone like me, so you don't have to worry if she's good enough."

Anger brewed in Sophie's eyes, and she lightly slapped the back of Steven's head before he saw it coming. "Don't you ever,"—smack—"say you're not good enough"—smack—"again, Steven Chandler."

Steven put his hands in front of his face in a mock attempt to protect himself. Under his breath, he muttered, "I don't have anything to offer her." Thankfully, his words went unheard, and the droll voice of the hospital operator alerted all guests that visiting hours would be over in fifteen minutes, effectively bringing the conversation to an end—at least momentarily. Steven had no doubt his aunt would gnaw on the subject like a hungry dog with a bone.

She hugged him tightly and confirmed his fears. "This conversation is far from over," she whispered. "I want to hear more about this Abby."

Sophie scurried around the room, cleaning up everything from their celebration. Out of the corner of his eye, Steven saw his uncle lift the lid off the tin of cookies, and he yelled in protest. "Aw, Dad, come on! Don't eat all my cookies!"

Logan laughed heartily, a cookie in each hand yet again. "It's one for the road, Steven. There are more in there. You can't possibly eat them all before they get stale."

*Not much chance of that happening.* Every Tom, Dick, and Harry took a cookie as soon as they spied the can. He'd almost considered having his nurse stash them under the blankets.

As they were heading out the door, Logan leaned back in. "I'll see what I can find out. I'll see you tomorrow. Goodnight, son. Get some rest."

Steven was asleep that night before his nurse came in to turn off the lights.

❖   ❖   ❖

Repeatedly over the next several days, he inquired about Abby to no avail. Logan's schedule never seemed to coincide with her lunchtime slot at the rehab gym, and Mac was away taking care of business.

Steven had resigned himself to the probability that Abby had been discharged. Even if her treatment had been extended to provide her the optimal benefit of the steroids, her stay in the hospital would be drawing to a close.

He'd become so desperate, he'd almost asked his aunt to drop by the gym. Almost. But, left to her own devices, he was afraid Sophie would have him engaged to the girl before he ever had a chance to talk to her again on his own.

If only he had access to the network at his office, he could pull her up on his computer and creep through the appointment calendar, but at the rate he was progressing, it could be years before he set foot in the office again. Steven huffed and punched his pillow.

*Thoughts like that are exactly why we don't date patients!*

After a protein shake for lunch, Steven asked his nurse to turn down the lights and close the blinds so he could take a nap. A few hours of sleep was the only way he could think of to avoid the blues for the afternoon.

❖   ❖   ❖

Abby Harris zippered her small duffel bag. It was the last day of her hospitalization. The next morning she'd be leaving, and she'd yet to reencounter Steven Chandler in the gym. Not more than a few minutes after her last session, the kindly nurse who had cared for her the Christmas before came into her room pushing the med cart. As she hung a new bag of the drug they all jokingly called "Joy Juice," Abby questioned her.

"I was wondering," she asked her caregiver, "are you the nurse who knows the Chandlers?"

Maddie peered over her glasses at her patient. Many knew of her relationship with the family, and since the accident, she'd been inundated with inquiries about Steven's condition. There was something about the girl's sense of urgency that caused Maddie to take pause and allow the conversation to play out, rather than shutting it down abruptly as she normally did in order to protect her friends' privacy.

"I am."

"Do you know what happened to Dr. Chandler? Dr. Steven?"

Maddie smiled, but kept her answer vague. "That I do, Miss Abby."

Abby sighed, clearly frustrated with Maddie's reticence. "Can you please tell me where I can find him?"

The hospital was a breeding ground for gossip, and Maddie didn't like being in the uncomfortable position of deflecting questions about Steven's personal information, but when Abby explained their encounter in the rehab gym, it softened Maddie's heart. "I can't discuss another patient's information. Breaching confidentiality could get me fired. Surely you wouldn't want that to happen."

When it appeared that Maddie would not be more forthcoming, her patient played the one card that had the power to change everything.

"I was so lost when we met, but you were right. Steven showed me a path where I could find a happy and fulfilling life despite how drastically my situation had changed. I wasn't as receptive as I could have been at the time. Things are going well for me, Maddie. I regret that I don't have any way to thank Steven."

"We ran into each other briefly in the gym, and he asked me to seek him out; he offered to discuss more effective therapies for my MS, but as you know, I'm leaving in the morning, and he hasn't been back to the gym."

She had Maddie at the life-changing gratitude, but it was the yearning in the young lady's eyes that caused Maddie to do an about-face and march out the door and down the corridor without another word.

❖　❖　❖

Steven felt like he'd just drifted off when a noise in his room awakened him.

"Good afternoon, Steven. Are you up for some company?" While Steven adored Maddie, he was in an unusually sulky mood and wanted to be left alone so he could wallow in self-pity.

He reached out and took the hand she had resting on the bed rail. "I'm sorry, Maddie. I feel like being alone right now. Can we make it another time? I don't think I'll be very good company." He tried to manage a smile, but it felt like he couldn't even get that right.

"It's okay, sweetie. One of my patients asked about you and said you knew one another. Something about encountering you in the rehab gym, but you never came back. I didn't understand. But I'll tell her you're not up for visitors this afternoon."

As Maddie turned to go, he gripped her hand.

"You've talked with Abby?"

"I have, but I'm sure she'll understand."

*She was looking. For me.*

"Maddie, wait. I need to see her before she leaves. Could you bring her to my room? Can you help her? Please?"

When Maddie stiffened, Steven realized his gaffe. He was dismissing his old friend but welcoming Abby.

Like the imp she'd babysat, Steven turned on the charm and gave her his award-winning smile. "I'm sorry, Maddie. I didn't mean to offend you. I'd like to get a little better acquainted with Abby, if you know what I mean. I'm afraid she'll leave before I get a chance to talk to her. What if I never see her again?"

Steven didn't think his friend understood until she smiled and said, "I'll be right back."

# Chapter Ten

Abby stood at her hospital window, staring at the snow on the rooftop below her. When her door burst open, she turned immediately, losing her balance.

Maddie reached for Abby, struggling to sort everything out—disentangling the IV pole from the phone cord, moving it away from the bed. Abby's heart began to pound when Maddie handed over her shoes and draped a robe over her shoulders.

*This is it.* Realistically, she'd known he was there all along, but the reality that she was going to see him again set her insides aflutter.

"Can you walk, Abby, or would you prefer the wheelchair?"

"I'm fine to walk."

Maddie placed her hand on the small of Abby's back, and began guiding her out of the room. "Come with me, then." They only walked past a few rooms before Maddie tapped on the door.

*So close all this time but so far away.*

"Come in."

Steven's voice was quiet, but Abby's face broke into a smile when she heard it again. Maddie pulled back the room divider. Propped on his side in bed, wearing a neon green cast, lay Steven Chandler, the blankets pulled to his waist, his chest, breathtakingly bare.

Her name left his mouth, breathy and soft. "Abby."

The smile on his face mirrored the one she could feel on her own.

Abby gestured to the chartreuse cast. "You changed."

"Another one of many, I'm sure."

"I came to the gym every day. You weren't there. I'm leaving tomorrow." Abby recalled the disappointment she felt each time at not finding him in their pre-arranged meeting place.

Steven awkwardly dragged his fingers through his hair. "Yeah, about that, I'm sorry. They dragged me off to surgery, and I haven't been able to return to rehab."

The door *whooshed* softly and then closed with a quiet thud.

Abby stood next to the bed, peering down at the man who'd consumed her thoughts on so many occasions. Her hands gripped the rail for support. "You missed the Buddies meeting in Boston. I was hoping to talk with you there, but we didn't find out what had happened to you until we were leaving."

"I believe my accident was the weekend before. It was touch and go for a while."

Abby stared past his shoulder, weighing the words that were at the forefront of her mind.

"Abby? You seem like you're a million miles away. What is it?"

She shook her head, fearing it would seem too forward to come right out and ask what had happened even though her curiosity was killing her.

He stared up at her with a knowing smile. "It's okay. Go ahead and ask. News around this place spreads like wildfire. I'm surprised you haven't already heard all the gory details of my brush with death."

"I haven't. Really." She stood next to him, staring beseechingly, willing him to spill the words. *Please just tell me, so I don't feel guilty for asking.*

His face devoid of any emotion, Steven swallowed loudly and began to explain. "I was traveling home alone from work one night, and the only accessible place to exit the sidewalk was between two parked cars. The driver, she, um . . . she never saw me."

Abby could feel her breakfast trying to come up, and her hand shot to her mouth. She felt for the arm of the guest chair, lowering herself into the seat.

"Oh, Steven."

Steven smiled gently, his voice soft. "I'm okay, Abby."

Abby pressed her hand to her pounding heart.

*How does one even respond to something so horrific?*

She let out a gust of air she hadn't realized she was holding, and her body melted into the cushion of the recliner. The air hung pregnant with silence for what seemed like forever.

"I truly am fortunate."

"Will you be all right?"

"I've got a long recovery ahead of me, but everyone here has been wonderful."

"That's great. I'm glad they're taking good care of you."

"They are, but let's talk about you. Maddie said you wanted to explore other treatment options. I'm still having trouble wrapping my head around the fact that my partner isn't using disease modifying medications to slow the progression of your disease."

Abby could feel herself blushing as the warmth crept up her neck and bloomed on her cheeks. *Caught. Red-handed.*

"Don't be upset with Dr. J. He's tried to convince me. Your invitation to discuss it further was the first thing that came to mind. Your friend was so protective, and I was afraid I'd leave here and risk never seeing you again. I wasn't intentionally trying to deceive anyone."

"So, essentially, you're here for my good looks and charismatic personality?"

Abby's head bobbed. "Essentially. I'm sorry."

"Don't be. I've been trying to coerce my old man into reaching out to you. I don't know where I'll end up from here, but I have a fairly long road ahead of me. I was hoping, maybe, we could keep in touch?"

Abby's entire body warmed, and she smiled a big, goofy grin, but she didn't care. *He wants to see me again.* "I'd like that."

The pair visited uninterrupted nearly the entire afternoon.Abby had already endured the last PT session of her stay, and the bag on the IV pole continued to drip a steady stream of steroids into her system. Thankfully, with the use of ancillary medications such as Benadryl and antacids, they'd managed her side effects to a tolerable level, and she was able to enjoy the afternoon.

Steven was relentless in his quest to convince her that the use of disease modifying drugs would make her symptoms so much more manageable. They discussed the side effects at length, yet Abby still hadn't been convinced that the route of therapy was for her. When Steven finally drifted off, she sat mesmerized, watching him sleep. *Such an attractive man.*

As they got to know one another that afternoon, it had become apparent how truly caring and compassionate Steven Chandler was. Abby was consumed with guilt over her behavior during their first meeting. He had never been anything but considerate toward her situation. It was her own insecurity and fear that had made her lash out at him, and watching as he lay in slumber, she knew she had to set things right.

❖　❖　❖

When the sun began to set over New Haven, Abby stood to return to her room. Steven had dozed off, and she'd be embarrassed to get caught watching him sleep. It was time for the dinner trays to be delivered, and while the food was less than desirable, the steroids had made her ravenous, and she was in need of sustenance. Her tummy had been rumbling loudly, and at one point, she was sure she'd awakened Steven, but he'd resumed snoring softly.

Any chance of a silent escape was foiled when Abby lost her footing and tripped on the IV pole. In an attempt to right herself before falling, she grabbed for the bedside table, but it skidded away as she put her weight on it. Before she realized what was happening, Abby was practically in bed with her new friend. *So much for a quiet departure.*

Steven stirred, rubbing his face with his hand, his voice gravelly from sleep. "Abby?"

"I was leaving. It's time for the dinner trays to come. The food here isn't great, but it's even worse cold."

Steven looked thoughtful for a second. "If you're not opposed to meeting my parents, I could have them grab some takeout. There's a wonderful Mexican place right down the street."

"Oh, no, I can't impose. It wouldn't be right to expect them to make a special trip. It's only one more night. Tomorrow I'll eat real food. I'm not that hungry anyway."

Steven scoffed. "Don't lie, Abby. Even semiconscious, I could hear your belly growling! Humor me and tame that monster. Now that I'm out of intensive care, they bring something in nearly every night. Do you actually think I eat the food here?" he asked with a grin.

Abby got Steven's cell phone from the bedside table and dialed the number he rattled off, but apparently it went to voicemail.

"Hmm," he muttered, "I wonder where they are."

Abby was almost relieved. "It's okay, Steven. I'm leaving in the morning. I haven't died from the food yet." While the conversation with Steven had come easily, and even though his uncle had seemed nice, she didn't know if she was comfortable spending the evening with his entire family.

Steven reached out past the bedrail. "Don't go. It's been so nice spending the afternoon with you. Fresh faces are a rare occurrence when you've been here as long as I have."

Abby glanced at the door. "Let me go grab my purse. I don't expect you to buy my dinner."

"*No, Abby.* I'd actually be imposing on you. It would be my pleasure to buy us dinner."

Abby cocked her head to the side.

"I rely on Aunt Sophie to help me with dinner," he explained, "and it appears she's unavailable. If I ordered something soft and self-contained, would *you* mind helping me? I'm sort of at a disadvantage here." He looked down, the corners of his mouth pulling into a frown.

Abby mulled over her predicament. Certainly she could handle assisting Steven—how difficult could it be to unwrap a burrito or something? While she still wasn't sold on his MS drugs, he had been attentive when she voiced her concerns and assured her those concerns were valid. He even offered her a number of helpful hints on managing her disease process. If one were keeping track, surely it was she who was indebted to him.

Before Abby could protest, Steven flicked the phone open and held a number down. He rattled off a list of food and finished up with two bottles of water.

"You didn't object to Mexican. I hope that's okay."

Abby dragged her eyes up his body, her face flamed when she met his boyish grin. *Busted.*

"Oh, yeah, Mexican is fine as long as it's good."

A nurse entered the room, interrupting their moment. Without prelude, she pulled the curtain, leaving Abby sitting alone next to the door. A few minutes later, a man cleared his throat from the doorway, pulling Abby from her thoughts. "Dr. Chandler's dinner. May I leave it here on the counter?"

Steven called out from behind the curtain before Abby could respond. "Please set it on the counter, Pete, and could you put it on my bill? I'll even up with you next time. Is that all right?"

"Sure thing, Steven. Enjoy your dinner." His gaze returned to Abby, and he dipped his head in her direction. "Miss." Before she replied, he was gone.

When the nurse pulled back the curtain, Steven had his back to the room.

"Abby?"

"I'm still here, Steven. Are you ready to eat?"

As Abby picked up the bag, he replied, his voice filled with humor. "Can you please push that table around to this side? But for God's sake, don't use it to support yourself. You'll fall and break your neck!"

*Oh, Steven, if you only knew how uncoordinated I truly am.*

Abby fashioned a makeshift tablecloth from napkins and laid out their Mexican fiesta. When Steven's tongue peeped out and swiped over his lips in anticipation, a shiver ran down her spine. Sights like that made her hungry for something other than the abundance of food that was spread before them.

Abby's eyes scanned the meal, knowing the two of them would never consume it all. Her abuela's meals were always so filling. As if Steven could read her mind, he said, "We'll eat what we want, and then I can have someone put it in the fridge for tomorrow."

"Where would you like to start?"

"Come here," Steven replied, pointing to an alcohol prep pad on the table. "Open that and hand it to me, please." When she handed him the pad, he grasped her hand and began removing the tape from her wrist. He unhooked the connector from the site on her wrist and cleaned everything with the prep pad when he finished.

"There, that's better. Now you can eat without being encumbered," Steven said as Abby gaped at him.

"What?" he asked, his voice playful. "I'm more than qualified to unhook you. The bag was done a while ago. Loop the tubing up over the hook so you don't trip on it."

"When I asked where you wanted to start, I was talking about food."

Steven laughed, still holding her hand, his casual attitude taking her by surprise. "Hmm. . . a burrito, please?" he asked, releasing her.

When the little bundle was free of its wax paper prison, Abby perused the little cups of goodies that were in the bag. "Condiments, sir?"

He laughed. "Sure, if you want to go to the trouble, it's probably easiest if you open it and spoon some of each inside, or you can dip as we go. Whatever is easiest for you. Normally, I dunk it, but it's not like I can sit up right now and do that. It looks like he only brought one cup of each . . ."

Abby opened the burrito with unsteady hands and ran a strip of each condiment down the center with a plastic spoon and then did the same with her own. *I hope he can't see my hands shaking. Focus, girl! There's no reason to be nervous.*

Filled with condiments, Abby knew it would be a challenge to keep the burrito intact, so she reached for a towel, covering her dinner companion from his chin to his cast, knowing it was the only protection he'd have from what was sure to be an onslaught of messy burrito leavings.

Abby touched the burrito to Steven's lips, and a trail of sauce ran down the corner of his mouth as he took the first bite. He moaned in satisfaction as Abby tried to clean off his face. She gave him another bite and it happened all over again. Between the laughing and chewing, they'd made quite the mess.

Not able to wait a moment longer, Abby set Steven's food on the tray and picked up her own, taking a tiny, ladylike bite. The authenticity of the food was amazing, and as the different flavors burst over her taste buds, she completely forgot about the hungry man beside her.

Abby gasped when he cleared his throat. "Oh my gosh! I'm so sorry, Steven. This is so . . . wow."

"I know." He chuckled. "Take your time."

"It's rare to find a Mexican joint that compares to my *abuela*, my grandma."

Steven nodded and smiled. "Pete has the food truck—"

"Over on Cedar! How could I forget?"

Steven waggled his eyebrows. *I practically had you in my arms that day.*

Abby's stance wobbled, and she looked for a chair, disappointed to find the only one on the opposite side of the bed. "I'm sorry, I'm a little unsteady." As she attempted to lay the burrito down without destroying it, he reached for her arm.

"You were a little unsteady that afternoon too." Steven said, chuckling.

"Hey, now! You practically barreled me over!"

"I wouldn't have let you fall. Sit down on the bed, sweetheart. I don't bite."

Abby drew in a stuttered breath. *Sweetheart.* That word. Coming from his mouth. It made her swoon.

She surveyed the narrow strip of mattress, surprised that he'd want a complete stranger so close.

"But what if I hurt you? I'm not the most graceful."

Steven snickered. "We've already established that, hon, but trust me, you're not gonna hurt me." He knocked on the chest of his body cast. "Perfectly safe. See?"

There was barely enough room for Abby to shimmy in next to her companion, and she was careful not to jostle him as she pulled her knee up and tucked her other foot underneath. Facing the head of the bed, everything was easier to access.

"That's better, isn't it?"

She nodded. It was, until he needed a drink. Abby felt like a bumbling fool as she ended up dumping more of the water down the front of Steven than she got into his mouth. The two burst into peals of laughter. They'd spent as much time wiping up messes as they had consuming their meal.

Abby couldn't remember the last time she'd felt so carefree with a member of the opposite sex. She'd had a steady boyfriend during her sophomore year of college, but his focus had been hanging out in the bar with his buddies while she studied. After showing up at her dorm room intoxicated and abusive, Abby asked campus security to remove him, and she ended the relationship.

Aside from a few guys in her study groups over the years, her only close male friend was Corey Tucker, a Yale-New Haven orderly who hailed from the same hometown as Abby. *But being friends with Corey has never felt like this.*

As Abby attempted to put the last bite of burrito into Steven's mouth, a huge glob of guacamole oozed down her finger. Before she could pull away, Steven grasped her wrist and guided her fingers to his mouth. Mesmerized, she watched his tongue snake out from between his lips and lick from the junction of her fingers to the tip before he sucked the burrito into his mouth with a smirk.

Steven chuckled before schooling his features into a more serious expression. "I'm sorry, Abby. I shouldn't have been so forward. That was inappropriate."

Abby pressed her hand to her chest. "Um, no . . . that was . . . I didn't . . . it's okay," she stammered, not knowing what to say or feel. While his actions were totally unexpected, she wasn't offended. *Is his heart pounding as hard as mine?*

Abby tried to concentrate on the rest of her burrito, but her stomach was so full of butterflies, she couldn't eat another bite. Between bites of burrito, they'd indulged in hand-rolled tortilla chips and a Mexican spoon bread that melted in Abby's mouth.

Steven looked like she felt—uncomfortable.

"Ugh, my eyes were bigger than my stomach. I haven't eaten anywhere near this much since my accident."

"Why don't you eat, Steven? Don't you get hungry?"

He patted the fiberglass cast over his stomach. "Have you ever over-indulged in a pair of tight jeans?"

It took a moment for Abby to follow. "Oh. *Ohhh!*" she exclaimed, slapping her hand over her mouth.

"Not much wiggle room. I try not to eat too much at one time. Most of my meals are protein drinks or smoothies. I usually eat only one meal a day if my family is here to help me maneuver everything." He covered his mouth, failing to stifle a belch. "I ought to be more comfortable in an hour or so after all that settles. Excuse me."

Glancing out the window, Abby realized it had gotten dark; they'd talked for hours. "I should be getting back. They'll think I ran away. Thanks for dinner. It was great."

"It's all good. Maddie knows where you are and that you're safe with me." He reached for her hand. "Abby, I don't know when I've encountered anyone like you. You don't treat me like I'm different. It's refreshing."

Abby studied the floor, a little embarrassed, a little overwhelmed. "You're kinda nice yourself."

Steven squeezed her hand. "I'd hate to lose touch. Will you come back and visit me, please?" His pout tugged at Abby's heartstrings.

*Do I want to get involved with someone right now? He seems like a nice enough guy. Isn't it wrong to be involved with a doctor who has seen me professionally? Could he get in trouble because of me?*

Abby needed to think. "I was lucky this happened over Christmas break. I've used so much leave since my first exacerbation. I don't know how much time I'll have."

Internally, she was struggling. *So many excuses . . . Is that all they are? Excuses?*

"I didn't expect you to take time off work, but don't you get a lunch break?" Abby wavered at the desperation in his voice. "What about after school? I'd seriously like to get to know you better."

Abby didn't want to put him off, but there were so many things to consider. Since her diagnosis, even simple tasks were more time-consuming. She volunteered after work nearly every day, and transportation was an issue. "I get an hour, but I'd have to get a cab. I wouldn't have a lot of time."

"I understand. It's okay."

The disappointment in his voice made Abby relent. Perhaps they could get to know one another better during his hospital stay. But *will he forget all about me when he goes back to his busy life as a doctor?*

"I'll be here."

"Thank you," he whispered.

The following morning, Abby left the hospital, her heart heavy with the knowledge that her new friend would be there for an indeterminate length of time but hopeful that her presence could make his stay a little brighter.

# Chapter Eleven

Abby had reservations about getting involved with the handsome neurologist. *Is he just looking for a friend? Does he want more?*

There were days when Abby barely had enough energy to get herself through the day, let alone worry about bolstering someone else's spirits, but who was she kidding? Steven Chandler was quite the dish, and Abby understood how lonely and boring a solitary hospital room could be.

Abby's school was close enough to the hospital that she could visit for lunch and be able to make it back to work in time. Conveniently, their schedules coincided, Abby entering Steven's room as the transport from PT was leaving with an empty gurney.

Lunches were fun, the pair talking about whatever they could fit in between bites of their lunchtime fare. Some days it was takeout that Steven ordered before Abby arrived, and others, it was something delicious the enigmatic Sophie Chandler had thoughtfully delivered for their enjoyment.

One day, Steven promised, the ladies would meet. He said it matter-of-factly, but the notion filled Abby with trepidation. Was it no big deal to him because it was no more than a casual friendship? Or had Steven already grown so comfortable with Abby that in his mind, meeting his aunt was the assumed next step.

*Am I reading too much into this? Is he reading too much into it? Are we only friends? Or is this headed somewhere else?*

❖    ❖    ❖

The lunchtime visits came to an abrupt halt after the new semester began. Abby awoke one Saturday morning too sick and too feverish to get out of bed. She burrowed into the covers and let sleep pull her under. The fever broke time and again, but she didn't have the energy to bother with a thermometer. Every inch of Abby's body ached, and her head pounded. Half her kids had been out with the flu—it was only a matter of time till it hit Abby too.

Abby wallowed in her sweat-soaked nest, attempts to get to the toilet or quench her thirst, an insurmountable struggle. She moaned and clutched her head in her hands when someone began relentlessly pounding on the door.

"Go away," Abby moaned, her voice raspy, her throat on fire. When the pounding ended, Abby pulled the blankets over her head and drifted back to sleep.

Abby jerked awake when her classroom aide began speaking from a spot by her bed. "You scared me half to death when you didn't show up for work this morning," Brenda yelled. "I wanted to come over here first thing, but everyone is out sick. Even the subs are sick. I've been trying to call your phone all day. The super let me in."

"I think my phone's dead. I haven't been out of bed since Friday night."

"After I get you something to eat, we're going to the ER."

"No, we're going back to sleep. Well, I am. You're going home; I'll be fine."

"They admitted Principal Gibs this morning. Her illness turned into pneumonia. You can't afford to get worse."

❖    ❖    ❖

After Abby coughed her way through triage, and they confirmed her temperature of 102 degrees, she was sent off to a quiet corner, a surgical mask covering her face and a warmed blanket wrapped around her shoulders.

Abby was thankful that her well-meaning friend and assistant had gone home after delivering her safely to the ER intake desk. Brenda was a godsend, and Abby was eternally grateful that she was part of Abby's life, but Brenda was a social butterfly, and the last thing Abby wanted at the moment was someone who felt the need to fill the silence Abby desired with inane chatter.

After what seemed like hours, Abby's name was called, and she attempted to follow the nurse through the labyrinths of the Emergency Department, but another nurse scooped Abby into a wheelchair, and she was delivered to a room where she dozed until a cool hand touched her cheek. Abby opened her eyes to meet the gaze of the senior Dr. Chandler.

"Abigail. I hear you're under the weather."

"I wish the truck that hit me would come back and finish the job," Abby replied.

The doctor frowned, and Abby heard him mutter something about her joke not being funny as he put his stethoscope to her back. Logan instructed Abby to take a deep breath; she wheezed on the intake and coughed a great, rattling cough on the exhalation.

Chandler squatted in front of Abby and began discussing complications and treatments, but Abby struggled to follow the conversation.

"You're not productively coughing up the secretions in your lungs. I'm concerned that you've not only contracted the flu but bacterial pneumonia as well. I'd prefer to err on the side of caution and admit you before this gets out of hand. We can have a bed for you soon." He squeezed Abby's shoulder. "I'll put a rush on it."

"No! I just got out of the hospital. Isn't there another way?" Abby tried to argue, but her voice was barely louder than a whisper.

"All the more reason to be proactive. Your recent admission makes you more susceptible. Let's get some X-rays, and then we'll make an informed decision."

Abby groaned, too exhausted to argue any more. Helped into a gown by an orderly, she settled onto the gurney, drifting in and out as she was transported to and from radiology. She slept soundly until Dr. Chandler returned some time later.

"Miss Harris, I appreciate your concerns about missing work, but hospitalized or not, you cannot work in this condition. I know you don't want to risk exposing your students to your illness."

Abby opened her mouth, but words escaped her. "I—"

Dr. Chandler's expression of consternation scared Abby, and she quietly listened while he discussed her options. "It's against my better judgment to allow you to go home. You've admitted yourself that there is no one there to help you. While most people are able to recover from pneumonia without incident, with your compromised immune system, you should stay here. I understand your reticence, but the most expedient and effective way to treat this is with IV antibiotics in the hospital."

"I can't afford to miss any more work. I was hoping if I came here today, I could leave with something strong enough to get me back to work and let me finish the week."

"Please tell me you haven't been working in this condition, Abby."

Abby shook her head, "No, I took ill over the weekend; my friend got concerned when she couldn't contact me. She dragged me out of bed this afternoon and made me come here. Can't you write me a script for an antibiotic, and send me on my way? Brenda said she'd drive me home when I'm ready."

"It's already after midnight, Abby. Certainly you don't want to drag your friend out in the cold at this hour. Let me set you up with a room tonight, get some meds into your system, and if you're truly feeling better tomorrow, we'll discuss outpatient options."

Hopefully, Principal Gibney would understand since she was waging her own battle against the scourge of New Haven.

When Abby agreed hesitantly, Dr. Chandler smiled. "Thank you, Abby. I'll feel better knowing you're in good hands. I promise to get you out of here as expediently as possible."

When Abby awoke Tuesday morning, feeling marginally better, a typical New England blizzard was brewing outside her hospital window. She burrowed under the covers and went back to sleep, relieved in the knowledge that no one would be attending school for the next few days, nor would she have to go out and battle the bitter weather—at least not for a little while.

True to his word, Dr. Chandler had Abby back on her feet and feeling more like herself in time for the weekend. He poked his head into her room as her nurse was going over discharge instructions.

"Good morning, Abby! You look like you're feeling much better this morning."

"I am, thank you," she replied.

"I'm glad. Take care of yourself." As he was leaving, he handed her a card. "I want to see you in my office the day after tomorrow for a follow-up. Drink plenty of fluids, and take it easy this weekend. I'll see you Monday afternoon."

❖　❖　❖

After resting all weekend, Abby returned to work and made her way to Dr. Chandler's office in the family medicine department Monday afternoon. She walked into his office unassisted, and her cough had greatly improved. The fever had not returned.

Dr. Chandler put Abby through her paces, appearing pleased with her vital signs and her lung sounds.

"I'd like to see you again early next week. Please make an appointment with Camryn before you leave. Steven asked me to tell you he misses you, and he hopes you feel better soon. He's still vulnerable, so please wait to visit him until after you come back to see me. We don't want him becoming ill."

He smiled sadly as he said it, but Abby understood. The last thing she wanted was for Steven to catch the bug she'd recently done battle with.

❖　❖　❖

The elder Chandler was visibly distressed the following week when Abby returned for her appointment.

"Is something wrong, Dr. Chandler?"

"Steven is very ill." Logan's hand shook when he ran his fingers through his hair. "I was certain he was out of the woods."

Abby was at a loss, unaccustomed to the emotions that swirled around her. She'd come to enjoy Steven's company, but her feelings for him were growing into so much more.

*What if something bad happens to him?*

*It already has.*

"Can he have visitors?"

"I'm afraid not. He's in isolation."

Abby felt her eyes begin to water. She turned toward the window and wrapped her arms around herself. "I understand. I'm so sad for him. If he's up to it, can you have him call me on the phone? I'd like to talk to him at least."

Logan put a hand on Abby's shoulder and squeezed reassuringly. "I think that's an excellent idea. Camryn will have a script ready for that cough. No need to follow up unless your symptoms return."

❖   ❖   ❖

More than two weeks passed before Logan reached out to Abby, granting her request to visit Steven again, but instead of being greeted by the cheerful, charismatic guy Abby had grown fond of, she was met by a gaunt, distant shell of the man.

During three solitary lunch hour visits, Abby chattered away about anything and everything that would have previously interested her companion. When Steven didn't partake in the conversation, she changed her tack and peppered him with questions, certain that he'd feel compelled to reply. Abby knew Steven was listening. His gaze followed her as she paced the room, but not once did he utter a sound, his arms crossed stoically over his chest.

When Abby arrived on Friday afternoon, he was lying in wait. "Abby, will you please go home? This situation"—Steven gestured back and forth —"just isn't working."

"What are you talking about?" Abby's tears fell freely.

"I can't do this, Abby. I thought we could be friends, but I've had a lot of time to think about things. It's for the best this way. Please go, and don't come back."

"If this is about the ethics of seeing a patient in your partner's office, I'll find another neurologist. Please don't do this to us."

"There is no 'us,' Abby."

Before she could argue, Steven squeezed the call bell, and a nurse appeared almost immediately.

"Miss Harris is leaving, and I'd like to get some rest. Would you please restrict my visitors to immediate family until further notice?"

Steven was curt but never rude, and Abby fully believed that her visits might have been taxing after everything Steven had been through, but she didn't understand the abrupt change in his demeanor. She felt cut to the core.

Abby's cheeks burned as if she'd been slapped. She wiped her eyes as she stumbled out the door, slamming face first into Logan Chandler's chest in her haste to flee. When Logan grasped Abby's upper arms, the girl pushed him away and bolted down the corridor. She made it inside the ladies room before her meltdown began. The crying turned to sobbing, which in turn led to fits of coughing and dry heaves. After Abby's breakfast came up, the anguished woman slid down the wall and sank to the floor of the tiny stall. She pulled her knees to her chest, dropping her cheek to her knees.

Abby froze when the restroom door opened and closed, hoping the intruder would do their business and be on their way. Soft footsteps drew closer, a pair of black pumps stopping right outside the stall. A quiet tap on the door broke the silence in the room.

No.

Abby shrank as much as she possibly could, leaning in close to the disgusting toilet and squeezing her eyes tight.

"Abby?"

Abby pressed the heels of her hands into her eyes, trying in vain to rub away the tears. Examining the situation, she realized there was nothing to grab but the toilet and she refused to use it to steady herself. Like a newborn foal, it took forever for Abby to get up on her wobbly legs to open the door.

Abby straightened her clothes and patted her hair, coming face to face with a woman who could only be Sophie Chandler. Between Abby's illness and Steven's setbacks, the two women had never met, but Abby realized she would have known the woman anywhere, her hair and sad eyes so reminiscent of her nephew's. Sophie held a pair of leather gloves in her hands, wringing them nervously.

"I'm sorry. I didn't mean to intrude, but Logan asked me to follow you to make sure you were okay. You seemed so upset when you left

Steven. I'm sorry if I've upset you further. I'm Sophie Chandler. Are you okay, Abigail?" She held her hand out.

That was the thing. Abby wasn't okay, and she didn't know if she ever would be. She hadn't realized how hard she'd fallen for Steven until he'd pushed her out of his life. Abby had yet to utter a word, and she could only imagine what Sophie Chandler must think. Abby hesitantly took the stranger's hand and said, "I'm not sure what I am right now."

Instead of shaking the hand she held, Sophie drew Abby into a gentle hug.

"Oh, sweetheart, I'm so sorry. Let's get you cleaned up, and we'll go get some lunch."

*Lunch! Oh no!*

"I have to get back to work! I'm in so much trouble!" Abby was horrified when she turned to the mirror. Her makeup was smeared, her eyes red and puffy. Abby's long hair was matted, and there was something from the floor all over her pant leg. She could never return to her classroom looking the way she did.

Sophie quietly took charge. "Let's get you sorted out, then we'll go by Logan's office to call your employer and explain you're here at the hospital and feeling under the weather." She looked down at her watch. "You haven't been in here all that long."

While Abby washed her hands, Sophie grabbed paper towels and wet them, handing them to the younger woman. Abby cleaned her face and fixed her makeup, ran her fingers through her hair, and drew it up into a messy bun. Sophie nodded and grasped Abby's elbow, gently leading her out of the restroom and through the corridors until they stopped outside Logan Chandler's office.

Steven's uncle sat behind a desk, his head in his hands. He looked up, frowning when his gaze settled on his guests.

"I'm so sorry, Abby. I know it's no excuse, but Steven isn't himself right now."

Abby sagged into the chair across from Logan's desk; Sophie perched herself on the arm of the one next to it. "Logan, can we please call Abby's school and explain that she's under the weather?" Logan turned the desk phone and pushed it within Abby's reach. Abby feared Principal Gibney would be upset, yet within a matter of minutes, her schedule had been freed for the day.

Logan stood and placed his cool hand to Abby's forehead and then her cheeks. "Are you all right, Abby? You were pretty worked up."

"I think so."

*Geez, did they both follow me to the toilet?*

Sophie walked behind the desk and gave her husband a quick peck on the lips. "I'll see you this evening, dear. Abby and I are going to have a bite to eat and get to know each other."

She smiled at Abby and offered her arm, and within a few minutes, Abby found herself standing next to a tan SUV. Sophie drove them through the outskirts of town to a less populated suburb of the city. A long winding drive led them to a beautiful, sprawling ranch house. Sophie pulled into the garage and parked.

"I'd have loved to take you somewhere nice so we can get to know each other, but we can't have you getting caught playing hooky out on the town. You don't want to end up in the principal's office."

They hung their coats on hooks in the kitchen, and Abby followed Sophie to a huge center island. "Make yourself at home while I find us some lunch."

"How can I help?"

"You've had quite the afternoon. Let me take care of you, Abby."

Abby perched on a stool, and her eyes wandered the beautiful kitchen. In contrast to the exterior's modern design, the huge kitchen with old wooden cabinets was a step back in time. The granite countertops, white with swirls of gray and copper, added country charm and supported a huge porcelain sink. Cast iron cookware hung over the island, and it didn't escape Abby's notice that the underside of the sink was fully open nor that a section of the counter was the perfect height to roll a wheelchair under.

Abby smiled at the old stainless steel breadbox and the vintage appliances. Mismatched pieces of china were showcased in an open oak cabinet.

"They were my mother's, although my guilty pleasure is exploring flea markets and antique malls up the coast. You never know what kind of treasure you might find."

"They're lovely. You and Dr. Chandler have a beautiful home." Abby's gaze returned to the lowered sink. As she glanced again, she noticed other nuances: the table with only three chairs and one space left open; the hooks where they'd placed their coats, all within easy reach for someone who no longer stood. "I know Steven came to live with you when he was young. Did you build this with his needs in mind?"

"Oh, goodness no. Not that we wouldn't move heaven and earth for that boy, but the house was on the market when we moved here for Steven's recovery. It was the perfect fit. The previous owner was an architect who lived his adult life with polio. He created a handful of accessible homes throughout New England before being visitable was en vogue.

"This kitchen is Steven's favorite room. I've tried in vain to teach him how to cook, but everything he's tried to make has bordered on being toxic. He loves to eat and experience different cuisines, though, and he spends as much time here as his schedule permits." A sad expression softened Sophie's features. "I mean, he used to come home often. Obviously, he hasn't been home all winter." She wiped her cheeks and sniffed. "Enough of that. He'll be home again soon."

Sophie placed a board of food on the island and settled into a stool across from Abby. Handing a bottle of water to her guest, Sophie began the conversation at hand.

"Okay, what's my boy gotten himself into this time?"

Abby studied the food, picking up several pieces of fruit and cheese from the charcuterie board. She wasn't hungry, having left her appetite in Steven's room along with a bag of burritos she'd ordered from Pete's in hopes of raising Steven's spirits. Hopefully, someone would find them and make sure that he ate.

"We met in the hospital a year ago. When I was a patient this Christmas, we ran into one another again in the gym. We began having lunch each day. I thought we were becoming close friends until I got sick three weeks ago, and it turned into pneumonia."

"And then Steven had the bout with sepsis," Sophie added.

"Yes. When I was finally able to visit again, he pushed me away. He even asked his nurse to restrict his visitors."

Abby played with the cheese on her plate, refusing to meet Sophie's eyes lest she fall apart again.

"Do you want to continue to visit him?"

"I want to visit the guy I spent time with a few weeks ago, not the one who ignored me for three days and then kicked me out."

"Abby, if I know my nephew, he's berating himself right now for his poor behavior. Please don't give up on him. He's been solitary for years, and the last few weeks, he's been a different person. He talks about you constantly. I'm not certain what's going on in that head of his, but I intend to find out."

Abby sighed. While she knew Steven's absence would create a hole in her life, she couldn't ride an emotional rollercoaster and remain healthy.

"How are you feeling, Abby? Logan said you were very sick." Abby smiled at the concern in the older woman's voice. She appeared to be as compassionate as her husband.

"I've been feeling much better physically, although today's outburst has taken a toll on me. I'm sorry. I should call a cab and get going. I'm exhausted."

When Abby stood to clear her plate, she was surprised to see it empty. "Thank you for lunch, Mrs. Chandler. I appreciate your concern. I was a real mess when you found me."

Sophie put the plates in the sink and held Abby's coat at the shoulders. "Nonsense, my dear. You're absolutely delightful. And you're not calling a cab; I'll drive you."

Abby sank into the buttery leather seat of Sophie's car and remembered reciting her address. It came as a surprise when Sophie gently shook her shoulder.

"Abby? We're here. Wake up, dear." Abby blinked and took in her surroundings. Sure enough, they were parked in front of her brownstone.

"I'm so sorry I fell asleep. I've been so tired, and today was a little more than I'm used to." She got out and leaned in to bid Sophie goodbye, but the driver's seat was empty, Sophie already on the passenger side of the car. "Thank you so much for everything, Mrs. Chandler."

Sophie pulled Abby into a motherly embrace. "Abby, dear, I'm sorry we didn't meet under happier circumstances. Please, don't give up on him. He hasn't been himself since the accident. Feel better soon, Abby." She pressed a card into Abby's hand. "Here's my phone number. If you need anything, don't hesitate to call me."

Abby took the number and tried to smile, unsure what to make of the woman who had cared for her. She trudged into the building, unlocking her door. She took a few steps to her bed and collapsed.

When Abby awoke, it was pitch dark. Next to her pillow was a crumpled piece of paper, the business card that contained Sophie Chandler's home and cell numbers as well as Logan's office number. Scribbled at the very bottom, as if it were an afterthought, was Steven's name and a cell number. Abby threw it into the trashcan next to her bed.

# Chapter Twelve

"Steven Chandler! What in the world has gotten into you?"

Sophie stopped in her tracks when she burst through the door. She had no idea what to make of the situation in front of her. Steven was lying on his side in his bed, his back to the door. Everything from his bedside table covered the floor. The receiver to his hospital phone hung from his bedrail, the cord tangled. The base to the phone lay on the floor, covered in food. Ruined papers, booklets, and Steven's glasses were there, too, amongst the disaster. His cell phone lay in the center of the room. Hospital dishes lay in pieces, chaotically mixed into the mess.

Sophie approached the bed and Steven pulled her to him, sobbing the most heart-wrenching sounds into her chest. Steven hiccupped and gulped air as Sophie attempted to calm him. She frowned as she pulled tissues from the nightstand and wiped Steven's face.

"Why, Steven?"

"I want her to have all the experiences I can't share with her, all the ones I can never have. That's not possible if we get any closer."

"Do you have any idea how unfair it is for you to make that decision for Abby?"

Steven sniffled and wiped his nose on his sleeve but didn't even raise his eyes to meet his aunt's.

"I didn't come here to belittle you, Steven. Son, look at me. Please."

Steven looked up, and Sophie's heart broke for him. "Do you like her?"

His lips turned up into a tiny smile. "I think I love her."

"And you sent her away because . . .?"

He shrugged. "I don't know. I don't want to hurt her. I don't want her to stick around out of pity or some misguided sense of obligation."

"Is this about sex?"

"That's something I can't ever share with her. If she's with me, she'll never have children. That would be tragic. She's an elementary school teacher. I know she loves kids."

"But how do you even know if she wants children of her own? And what if she does? If you can't produce a biological family, you could adopt."

"That's not good enough."

"Not good enough for whom? It was good enough for me. You are my world, Steven. You are my son, as surely as if I'd carried you for nine months."

"And you've always made me feel that way. I've never felt unloved by either of you. I love the two of you so much."

Steven's heartfelt words made Sophie's heart squeeze. Although Steven had alluded to it before, hearing him say the words helped erase the fear Sophie had always had that they weren't enough . . . not enough to fill the gaping hole that losing his parents had left behind.

"As for the sex . . . if Logan could no longer give me intercourse, it would be okay because we are intimate in so many other ways. That is such a small part of sexual intimacy. We constantly share little touches. He rubs my neck; I touch his hand. We kiss, we nuzzle. We have hushed conversations in our own little world. I would miss those intimate gestures so much more than the act itself.

"Do you think I could turn my back on your uncle or stop loving him if he could no longer get an erection, if we could no longer share intercourse?"

Steven rolled his eyes. "Of course not. Everyone knows you love him."

"And I love sex but only with Logan. Do you think I'd be unfaithful if he could no longer give that to me?"

"No, I never implied anything of the sort."

"But you doubt Abby. You say you care about her. You want to protect her from things you have no control over. If you care about her the way you say you do, you need to allow her to decide if this is what she wants. You can't make unilateral decisions."

"I haven't been fair to her at all . . . have I?"

"Do you have any idea how I've spent the last two hours?"

Steven studied the floor and shook his head.

"I've been consoling Abby. She sobbed until she made herself sick. So sick, in fact, that she couldn't even return to work." Steven jerked his head in his aunt's direction.

"So you see, son, you may think that you are protecting her from getting hurt, but you've already hurt her deeply. You keep saying you are concerned about Abby, and you want to protect her, but I'm more concerned that you've pushed her away out of fear of rejection. If you ever hope to reconcile this with Abby, I think you need to sort out your own feelings first."

Sophie watched Steven's quivering lip and heard his breath hitch. Then finally, he spoke. "I'm so confused. Abby is the first woman who has given me hope that there might be someone out there for me. Everyone I know is in a committed relationship, but I'm afraid to put myself out there only to be rejected again. When I wanted to get closer to her, I panicked and pushed her away. Do you think she'll ever be able to forgive me, Sophie?"

"I don't know, son. Only Abby can answer that question, and right now, I doubt even she knows."

Steven held his head in his hands. "I've ruined everything."

Sophie leaned down and kissed his forehead. "You'll have to find a way to fix it."

He frowned. "I have no idea where to begin."

Sophie patted Steven's shoulder. "You're an intelligent man. I know you'll figure it out."

"Thanks, Mom," he replied, softly.

"I love you, son. Good night."

# Chapter Thirteen

*I've broken her spirit through my actions.*

The realization hit him like a wrecking ball, the knowledge that he'd harmed Abby. Harming another, especially someone he cared about, went against every grain of his being.

Steven hadn't been prepared for the emotions that assaulted him as a result of spending time with her or later at the thought of being separated from her. Despite the fact that they had each been seriously ill, he'd allowed his old insecurities to come back to taunt him in her absence.

*She doesn't want to spend time with you.*

*You're not enough.*

*Why would she want you when she could have anyone?*

It had been a little more than a decade since Steven's previous relationship went sour, and the girl, Courtney, had paid for her actions with the loss of her freedom. The situation cost Steven, too, with setbacks to his physical health as well as his ability to trust—not only in the opposite sex but in himself as well. The situation squashed Steven's desire to foster a healthy relationship with a woman who would value him for the man he was, not for the man she wanted him to be.

There had been so many opportunities with women over the years, but it had been easier for Steven to fall back on that old excuse than to invest the time and messy emotions in a relationship that was destined to fail anyway—until Abby Harris tumbled into Steven's life, and he'd been powerless to get out of the way.

*If only I'd talked to her.*

❖    ❖    ❖

Abby Harris had never been one to simply give up without a fight. After lunch with Sophie Chandler, a hot shower and a long nap had given her fortitude. With a clearer head, Abby was ready to go into battle.

Despite being pissed at the way Steven had treated her, she understood that his entire existence had been turned upside down. Hopefully, he'd come to his senses because damn, that man was worth the investment of her time even if he didn't get that.

Abby pulled the crumpled scrap of paper from the trash and squared her shoulders.

*It's time to show him I'm not going anywhere. You might be a stubborn man, Steven Chandler, but you're about to meet your match.*

Abby punched Steven's number into her phone with purpose, but her balloon deflated when it went straight to voice mail.

"Hi, Steven, this is, um, Abby. I get that it's been a rough couple of weeks. It's been hard for me too. I'm hoping today was simply a bad day. I wanted to let you know I'm here if you ever want to talk. Um, okay, catch you later."

❖    ❖    ❖

The following afternoon, as Abby was falling into her after-work routine of correcting homework and grading tests, her phone rang. She hadn't entered Steven's number into her phone, but she had already committed it to memory. Abby wrapped her hand around the phone and closed her eyes, grounding herself before she leapt.

"Hello?"

"Abby."

"Hey." The beat of Abby's heart kicked up a notch, and she put her hand over it. Steven's telephone voice was silkier and smoother than she remembered. *Was it only yesterday??*

"I wanted to return your call. I can't talk for long. I have to get down to rehab soon."

"Yeah, I'm working on my lesson plan and grading homework."

"So . . ."

"I wasn't sure if you'd return my call. I wanted to see how you were doing."

"Abby, I have to apologize for my behavior. I truly am sorry for the way I treated you. In time I hope you can forgive me."

Abby sighed. "I've already forgiven you, Steven, but you have to understand that I don't deal with stress well. I become physically ill when I get overwhelmed. This was your free pass. I refuse to allow you to put me in a position like that again."

"I understand, and I can't begin to tell you how sorry I am. I'd like to go back to how things were in the beginning. Can we do that?"

Abby suppressed a growl. "Going back to how we were doesn't address whatever it was that brought us to this point in the first place. I like you, Steven, but instead of rushing to define this, let's start over with a clean slate and get to know one another as long as you're willing to talk to me instead of pushing me away if something is bothering you."

"I promise. I'd like that." And so softly and reverently that it sounded like a prayer, Abby heard Steven whisper, "Thank you."

❖     ❖     ❖

Steven struggled with self-doubt, but he desperately wanted to foster a lasting relationship with Abby. She had extended an olive branch and he intended to hang on with everything he had.

*She's not taking your crap, Chandler. Don't screw this up. The pity party is over.*

Steven knew from experience that the best place to get out of a funk was in the gym.

As Steven worked with his therapists, his hands and fingers became more flexible, his manual dexterity improving. Steven's arms grew stronger by the day. He was determined to get his shoulders toned enough to be able to propel himself in the manual chair when the body cast came off.

*Stop moping and take back your life!*

The workouts were brutal, leaving Steven too exhausted to mope or brood over his misgivings. Three weeks into the new routine, Mac attached a trapeze to the bar above the gurney and encouraged Steven to lift his torso off the mattress as far as he was able. Steven's newfound strength was empowering, and he'd worked out vigorously until the day the body cast made a loud "snap!" and split down the side.

Steven's regular hospital orthopedist, Dr. Wesley, had taken a family leave to help his wife get settled in with their newborn. An orthopedics resident assessed the damage to Steven's cast, but due to the nature of Steven's injuries, Wesley had been consulted by phone, and as the cast was being cut away from Steven's body, he came rushing through the door.

"I want an x-ray of his pelvis as well as the ball and socket joint of his left hip." Ever so gently, Steven was removed from the body cast and returned to the gurney. A portable X-ray machine was wheeled into the room, and the necessary films were exposed. Steven had started to drift off to sleep when Wesley returned with the films in his hands.

"I'm sorry it took so long, Steven. I wanted a second opinion on these films. How would you feel about something different?"

"What do you mean, 'something different'? What do you have in mind?"

"I thought you'd like to shed the body cast for something a little less constricting. Look at this!"

Wesley pushed the gurney over to a light box on the wall. He flipped the switch, and it came to life, illuminating Steven's pelvis, full of plates and pins. The break that had been there so obviously a few weeks before had knit back together.

"It's healed." Steven said it more to himself than anyone else, but his doctor clapped him on the shoulder.

"Amazing, isn't it? I'm sorry, but you'll still have long leg casts. As you know, the damage was much worse in your tibia and fibula, but they are improving." And then, almost excitedly, he asked, "Have you seen the films?"

Steven shook his head slightly.

"Would you like to? I have the ones from the night of your accident."

*Do I really want to go there?*

Morbid curiosity won out, and Steven nodded. As Wesley removed the film of Steven's pelvis and began pulling out the films from the accident, Steven could feel his heart begin to race.

When he looked up, there it was—the ghost-like outline of his leg. Encased in the shadow were fragments of solid matter.

*Bones. My bones.*

Like a giant jigsaw puzzle that had been dumped from a box, the pieces lay waiting for some expert to merge them together into some semblance of their former selves. Wesley had been that expert.

Before Steven could stop himself, he retched, and breakfast covered him.

Wesley reached over and flipped the switch on the light box, effectively obscuring the proof of Steven's worst nightmare. He motioned with his hands, and a nurse entered with a trashcan and a box of wipes. The blanket covering Steven was rolled up and discarded, replaced immediately with another. His face, hands, and chest were wiped clean. The girl was efficient and had come and gone before Steven even had a chance to thank her.

"Are you all right, man? I was going to show you the after shots, but I don't know if you can handle any more excitement."

"It was a shock. I know Vance Harrison felt it was unrealistic to attempt saving my legs, but I never saw the films."

"You're a miracle, Steven. The fact that you didn't bleed out before you even got here is a miracle in itself. I came into the reconstruction a little late. I was on the B team waiting to relieve Vance when he got tired. When he stormed out, I was brought in. Wells had already transplanted the cadaver arteries. You're lucky to be alive. As people learned about the accident, they came in to donate blood. Nothing was spared to save your life. I hope you know how much you mean to all of us."

Steven's throat was so dry, he couldn't swallow, let alone speak. The hospital staff treated one another like family, and that was how they had cared for Steven in his time of need. He attempted a weak smile, letting Wesley know he was all right.

"Would you like to see how they look now?"

"Please."

When the light box came to life again, Steven was amazed. Most noticeable was the long rod that ran from knee to ankle on each leg. Around each rod, the bone fragments had been pieced together to perfection. He could see screws scattered across the negative, each bone fragment tied into the rod.

"You did an incredible job, doc. I didn't give you much to work with, did I?"

"You gave me just enough, Steven, and thank you, but it was my pleasure. Your case has been the highlight of my career as an orthopedic surgeon. After putting you back together, I know I can do anything."

Steven chuckled, suddenly thinking to himself that he'd be one noisy SOB going through airport security in the future. "I feel like Humpty Dumpty."

Wesley laughed, pausing as if in thought. "So I was thinking long leg casts would be appropriate today. How does that sound?"

*Like freedom.* Free of constriction, free from the bed that had been like a prison for four months. But he was apprehensive.

"Are you sure? Am I ready?"

"You won't fall apart. You'll be a little ouchy for a few days. You'll want to take it easy. Work those hips carefully. Don't let anyone force it. Other than that, you'll be fine. You'll be stiff for a while, but I imagine it'll feel great to move around more. You've got some osteoporosis but much less than I expected for someone who's been non-ambulatory for so long. Do you do a lot of weight-bearing with your work?"

Steven smiled. His electric wheelchair was his pride and joy for so many reasons, but now he had one more to add to the list. "I had an electric stander. I spend much of my day over at the stem cell center, so I'm on my feet a lot. I did standing pivots before the accident as well. I'm not sure if my level of function will change."

Wesley scratched his head before he smiled. "There shouldn't be many changes once you've healed. You'll have to work to regain muscle tone, but I have faith in you. That and I know a lot of people who will kick your ass if you start slacking. When you needed them, they didn't hesitate to give your case one hundred percent."

"I understand. I won't disappoint you, any of you. I promise."

"I know you won't, bud.

"Tell Mac to quit experimenting. Not so adventurous with these casts, okay? I want you to start doing adductors and abductors. Gently. Slow and steady . . . hips pulled out to the side and pushed back to the center. That's all. In a few days, when you feel up to it, begin core training. Sit-ups are your friend, Steven. You're top heavy, and your core is weak. You'llneed to use a chest support for the time being. You may begin using the wheelchair as soon as you feel up to propelling it. I'll send a memo to the rehab department for Mac."

"Thank you. I'm excited to be moving forward. I was afraid I wasn't ready yet."

"You're ready. Pace yourself. I've got to get going. I'll let the residents put your casts on, and I'll see you in six weeks."

"Congratulations on your new daughter."

"Thank you, Steven. I'll bring pictures next time."

"I look forward to seeing them. Please congratulate your wife as well. I'm sure you're proud of both of them."

Wesley's smile was huge as he made his way through the door. "I am. Take care, Steven. See you soon."

# Chapter Fourteen

During a number of evening phone calls, Abby and Steven had begun building their friendship in a healthier manner. While Steven's meltdown had hurt them both, it instigated necessary conversation.

"I'm not marriage material."

Abby chuckled. "I'm not looking for a husband."

"I can't have kids."

"We haven't gotten anywhere near first base, and you've fast-tracked all the way to the house with a picket fence and the two point five children you're afraid you can't father. How about we start this thing off as friends and go from there?"

"I'm sorry, Abby. I've gone about this all wrong."

"Hey, don't be so hard on yourself. It's true, I love kids. That's why I'm a teacher, but in my physical condition, kids are the last thing on my mind. There are days I can't put on my own coat or make my fingers work to tie my own shoes. Finding out I have a permanent disability has rocked my self-esteem. I need to learn to love myself before I'm ready to love somebody else."

"I do too."

Abby smiled when her phone started playing "Sexy Back." *It's him.*

"Hey."

"I was wondering if we could talk."

"We are talking. We talk every day."

"Not like this, in person. Tomorrow."

"I can come by for a little while. Then I have a math project to work on."

"They moved me down the hall, right across from the elevator. See you tomorrow."

Without giving Abby a chance to say goodbye, he hung up.

Abby stared at her phone. That was odd. *Is he having second thoughts?*

When Abby stepped into the elevator the next morning, a shiver went down her spine. *What if we aren't ready?*

She took a deep breath. She was fumbling with her gloves, trying to get them into her purse, when the elevator lurched upward, and Abby lost her balance. She reached for the railing to steady herself when someone gently grasped her elbow. Abby looked up into the friendly face of Logan Chandler.

"Abby, what a pleasant surprise! Are you here to see Steven?"

"Yes. We've been enjoying one another's company for a little while now."

"I hope he's working on being someone worthy of your friendship."

"He's always been worthy of my friendship. The problem is that *he* doesn't seem to realize that. You know, there are so many reasons why Steven could trudge through life with a chip on his shoulder, yet he's always seemed so content. He showed me a different view of life when I wasn't well. Maybe he needs me to do the same for him now."

Logan gave Abby's elbow a squeeze. "Enjoy your visit, dear. This is my floor. Perhaps you'd join Sophie and me for dinner one evening. We'd love to see you again."

"Thank you, I'd like that. I'm sure we'll talk sometime soon. Have a nice afternoon, Logan."

"So long, Abby. Enjoy your visit."

The door closed on the third floor, and the elevator car lurched again as it headed to Abby's destination.

Abby smiled when she got off the elevator. Even though it was weeks since she'd had pneumonia, Abby still tired easily. It was a relief to know she wouldn't have to navigate a long maze of hallways to get to his room.

The door was partially closed, so Abby tapped and waited, not wanting to intrude on something private.

"Come in."

*He sounds so much louder, so much stronger.*

Abby pushed on the door to find Steven sitting in an electric wheelchair at the window, looking out over the city of New Haven.

*Sitting in a wheelchair. He's sitting!* Abby gasped and dropped her purse. "Steven! The cast is gone!" She looked down before meeting his gaze sheepishly. Embarrassed that her hands acted as if they had a mind of their own, Abby couldn't seem to make them refrain from patting Steven down like a common criminal.

"Well, hello to you, too, Abby."

"I'm sorry; I don't know what came over me. I didn't mean to be so handsy."

"It's okay. It's caught most of the regulars off guard, too, although no one else has been quite as enthusiastic about it as you." Steven continued to chuckle as he reached out and took Abby's hand while she gawked.

Steven wore a T-shirt that had some snarky comment about accessible parking on it and a pair of long Bermuda shorts. Long, sky blue casts now covered his legs, which were sticking straight out in front of him.

"I'm so happy for you. How? When? Why didn't you tell me?"

"I wanted to surprise you."

"You did! I bet you feel so much better, sitting, driving."

He chuckled. "You have no idea how liberating this is. I was beginning to wonder if I'd ever see my toes again. Bending, it's surreal. I'll never take anything for granted again."

Losing the heavy cast seemed to liberate Steven in more ways than one.

Abby pulled a chair next to Steven's and slumped into it, sighing when she was finally off her feet.

"How are you feeling, Abby? Are you bouncing back from having pneumonia?" Steven asked, his features etched with concern.

"Uh, yeah . . . I'm okay. I still tire easily. I don't know that I can say I've bounced back, but I'm improving."

"Have you spoken with Dr. Jeffries about some of the other drug therapies we discussed?" He playfully nudged her shoulder with his elbow as he chuckled.

Abby didn't think they'd get to that conversation so quickly. Suddenly her lighthearted mood disappeared. "No, Steven," she snapped. "I haven't. I'm not ready for that yet."

He seemed taken aback by the defensive reply, his eyes filled with regret when they finally met hers. Barely above a whisper, he asked, "Why aren't you ready? What are you waiting for? Are you going to wait till it gets so bad that you are no longer independent?"

Abby shrugged. She had no answer other than fear of the unknown.

"You realize it'll be too late for disease modifying medications then."

Abby's voice caught in her throat. Steven's comment wasn't a question. He was stating what he knew to be true.

"I'm scared," she whispered. "There's so much to consider. It's a big decision."

He smiled softly. "It's not that big a decision, Abby. It's a matter of doing what you have to do. Sometimes our choices are taken away from us. We have to pick the lesser evil. You have advantages with these therapies that patients didn't have twenty years ago. You're at liberty to choose."

"If I decide I want to explore it, I'll talk to you about it then, okay? Please understand."

*How can I make you understand that I'm not taking my disease lightly?*

"Abby, please, don't wait too long. You can walk, write, dress yourself, feed yourself. Don't take those things for granted. Not everyone gets to decide."

Abby thought about Steven's situation and how precious the liberties she took for granted were. "I understand."

Apparently trying to lighten the mood, Steven switched gears. "Speaking of walking, come on."

Abby frowned. She was certain her explanation that even a short walk would be exhausting would circle right back around to Steven's recommendation of disease modifying meds.

"Um, we don't have to. We can hang out here. I know you're trying to make me feel better. It's okay."

"Abby, I want to show you something. Hop on my wheelie bars and hold on to the back of my chair. Come on, grab your coat!" A hoodie had seemingly materialized out of nowhere and lay across his lap.

Abby glanced down at Steven's legs. "Do you need a blanket or something?"

"Nah, come on. The casts keep me warm." His feet had purple non-skid slipper socks stretched over them. Gingerly, Abby took hold of the handgrips and stepped up onto the wheelie bars.

"Hang on, Abby! Here we go." Steven switched on the electric wheelchair and turned toward the open doorway.

They whizzed down the hallway so quickly, Abby's head began to spin. She smiled, remembering the adventurous side of Steven, which had accompanied her to the self-help group, and the considerate side that said, "Maybe you should get off here and let me back into the elevator. I don't want to hurt you." After Steven was situated, he reached out and pushed the button for the seventh floor, bringing the car to life.

"What's on the seventh floor?"

He simply shook his head and chuckled. "You'll see."

When they exited the elevator, Steven said, "Put on your jacket. I'll need you to open that door."

Abby held the door for Steven, the sun showering them with light. When Steven pulled through, he reached for her hand, leading Abby into a rooftop garden. It lay dormant in a deep winter's sleep, but Abby could visualize its beauty come spring.

"Wow. Has this always been here?"

"I think it was installed shortly before I finished med school. When I first came home for my residency, this was my favorite place." Steven took a deep breath and smiled. "I love the fresh air. I'm still not at liberty to leave the hospital, but my hospitalist has agreed that it would be beneficial for me to come up here for short periods of time with supervision."

"Is this here for the staff?" Abby asked.

"It's here for everyone to enjoy, but see those windows off to your left?" He turned his chair and pointed.

"Stop pointing!" Abby whispered loudly as she tried to push his arm down. Suddenly, she felt self-conscious. There were people inside in chairs, facing their direction. "Someone will see you!"

Steven ignored Abby, his gaze still on the window. "That room is where the chemo patients receive their treatments. This whole area was designed with them in mind; no matter which window you look out of, you have a view of this garden."

Gazing at the large fountain in the middle of the garden, Abby could imagine the sounds of it babbling like a brook during warmer weather. A huge metal chime hung next to a pergola, the individual chimes emitting rich tones as the gentle breeze moved them about.

The plants bore delicate buds waiting to burst. Abby could picture tulips, daffodils, and azaleas in bloom. She closed her eyes and listened to the beautiful song the birds were creating as they, too, anticipated the arrival of spring. The breeze picked up, and Abby shivered. "Can we come up here again when it's warmer?"

"Yes, on a day when we're better prepared. For now, we should go back inside."

Abby stopped, her gaze settling on the windows once more. "Let's stay out a little longer."

"You promise to tell me if you get too cold?"

Abby nodded as she followed the winding path through the garden, marveling at its beauty. "I think this might be the most incredible thing I've seen since I came to the city."

"Some of the patients clock hour after hour in that room. This is a pleasant distraction compared to the monotony of staring at the walls all day."

Steven turned his chair and followed Abby along the garden pathway. "You can see everything from here," he said as he pointed. "New Haven Harbor, City Point, the marina."

"This is simply breathtaking. Thanks for sharing this with me, Steven." Abby's praise earned her a face-splitting smile from the most gorgeous of men.

"It's my pleasure, Abby." He shivered as he said it, each word creating a small, misty cloud as his breath hit the air.

Abby sighed, wishing she could enjoy the garden's beauty a few moments longer. "Come on, let's go back inside. We've both been sick; we don't want to tempt fate too much."

"I suppose you're right. I hate to go back. Coming up here like this with you, well, this is the first time I've been outside since the night of the accident."

Abby's hand went to her chest. *Another way I've taken my liberties for granted.*

❖   ❖   ❖

Back in the room, Abby helped Steven get free of his sweatshirt. It was exciting for Abby to see him more self-sufficient, imagining the boost to his self-esteem.

Abby studied the wheelchair. "I thought your chair was destroyed in the accident."

Steven frowned. "Beyond repair. Mac arranged a loaner for me until mine actually arrives, but I've got no clue how long that might be."

He motioned to a chair that sat close to his window. "Here, take a load off. Thanks for humoring me. I haven't been to the garden in so long. I didn't realize how much I'd missed it. I'd gotten so busy with everything before the accident that I forgot to enjoy the simple things around me. Even barren as it is, the garden is beautiful."

"I can't wait until it's warmer." Abby's mind went to the beautiful marble fountain, one of several focal points of the healing garden. "That fountain is amazing. I can't imagine it brimming with water.

The sounds must be soothing."

"There's a lot of history surrounding its existence."

Abby quirked an eyebrow. "Oh?"

"Back when State Hospital opened in 1833, that fountain sat in the hub of the surgical department. It was actually the scrub sink used to prepare for every surgery. The water that flowed was warm. Countless hands were washed and scrubbed in the large basin on the bottom, and then the clean water continuously flowed from the top for rinsing. Clean hands never touched anything dirty. Now, we simply have a foot switch."

"I had no idea it had been a fixture here for so long."

"It was in storage someplace, but someone had the foresight to hold onto it while the hospital evolved into the facility that it is today."

"Speaking of sinks, I've been to dinner with Logan and Sophie several times," Abby said. "Sophie's kitchen is to die for." Abby secretly hoped she'd have the opportunity to cook in that kitchen one day; the place was a chef's wet dream.

"Oh yeah, she remodeled the kitchen with me in mind. Unfortunately, my cooking skills did not improve."

"I thought she was exaggerating when she said eating something you'd cooked could send me to the ER."

Steven laughed. "Could, but Logan would treat your food poisoning at the house even though he doesn't like to talk shop at home."

"Your aunt said they moved here when you had the accident. They seem to be very dedicated to your needs."

"Logan and Sophie have always put my needs above everything else. When I lost my parents, they stepped up to the plate without being asked. While they've never tried to replace what I've lost, I don't know that I'd be where I am today if they hadn't been present in my life. It's a shame that they never had their own children. Sophie was born to be someone's mother. I feel fortunate that she's mine. I owe her and Logan everything."

Abby's heart swelled at the devotion behind Steven's words. How fortunate to not only have experienced one incredible set of parents but to also have surrogates who loved him so deeply as well.

"They've been through so much because of me."

"I'm sure they'd do it all over again."

The corner of Steven's mouth turned up. "Well, they say the third time's the charm, but I don't think I'm ready to tempt fate again anytime soon."

Abby playfully slapped his arm. "That wasn't what I meant!"

"I know you didn't, Abby."

Abby's gaze settled on Steven's legs. She was quiet a long time before she looked up.

"When I met you, you seemed so matter-of-fact about your situation; you've had to face so many challenges since this accident. There are still days when I want to pull the covers up over my head and go back to sleep. Where do I get some of that attitude?"

"We are forced to make the best of our situations. Look at you. I know you get up early every day and nurture young minds. I know there are days when your disease process steals every ounce of your energy. I know you come home and spend countless hours of your own time preparing for the next day for your students. Do you call in sick? Do you actually pull the covers over your head and ignore the world? No, you don't, because you have a purpose in life. Those kids are depending on you to be there the same way my patients depend on me. You don't need my attitude. You've got your own."

"Your recovery will be a lot different this time, won't it?"

"In some ways. I did a lot of rehab in '93, but after my spinal injury was healed, a lot of my rehab was relearning—learning how to navigate the world as a pusher, learning how to care for my body so I don't get sick or injure myself. This time I already have that knowledge, but the damage to my legs was extensive."

Steven ran his hands through his hair and looked away. "When the car hit me, I felt more pain than I've felt since I first became paralyzed. They say sometimes sudden trauma can cause something like that to happen. I felt like my body was on fire."

He turned back and met Abby's gaze. "I'm happy that sensation has since gone away. My spinal cord injury is incomplete, so I still have some sensation. I can transfer independently, or at least I could in October. I can drive, although I prefer public transportation. I have an incredible amount of work ahead of me if I want to be as independent as I was before I got hit."

"What kind of long-lasting effect will the injuries from the car have on your body? When will you know how much function you've lost?"

He smiled wistfully. "Spoken like someone who is all too familiar with the ways and means of the disability population. When I was out of the body cast, my team did several stimulation tests, much like we do with your MS: the tuning fork, the Babinski test on the sole of the foot. I was responsive to stimuli. I still have some sensation, but very little movement; my legs have been immobilized in the same position for months. I could easily require physical therapy for a year or more. I want my life back, Abby. I'll do anything I have to in order to regain everything I possibly can."

"Do you have much physical therapy now? I mean, I saw you in the gym." Abby knew he was there for something, but she wasn't sure exactly what he would have accomplished in a full body cast.

"When you saw me in the gym, Owen McCrea—Mac—was working on loosening up my hands and wrists. When muscles stay at rest in the same position for a long time, they get contractures. I've worked with Mac and an occupational therapist to regain the use of my hands and fingers. I lift weights. Mac has a special machine he designed for people on stretchers or wheelchairs. Now that my torso is free, I do core exercises so I can support my trunk independently. I put in several hours a day in the gym now." Steven rubbed his hands over a chest harness Abby hadn't even noticed until he drew attention to it.

"How about you, Abby? When we first met, you were going home in a wheelchair. You're walking now. What do you do to keep yourself moving?"

Abby frowned; she loathed PT. "Well, I live in an apartment with a few steps, so it was hard at first with the wheelchair. My place is small. We had to move my bed into the living room because I couldn't get down the hallway to the bedroom. I went to PT daily on the bus with an attendant. By the time I went back to work, I was walking—not well, mind you, but I walk every day, now. I don't drive right now; my dad has my vehicle in his garage until I feel safe driving. As for exercise, I walk and do stretching and range of motion. I hope the wheelchair stays in the closet."

"So you still live in the place with steps? Have you considered something more accessible? I mean, MS has its ups and downs."

"I signed a one-year lease right before I had my first episode. It rolled into a month-to-month commitment this past November. I think once it gets warmer and travel is easier, I'll look for another apartment. It's much more comfortable riding the bus in nice weather."

"I know you only went to my support group a few times . . ."

Abby frowned; of course he knew.

"We support the philosophy of Concrete Change: housing with at least one no-step entrance, apartments that are accessible. The local chapter of the organization has been working with a developer in New Haven. They've recently renovated a church into accessible apartments. It's called The Sanctuary or something like that. You should check it out. I hear it's quite classy and not terribly expensive."

"I've had some interaction with that organization through my involvement with the Center for Independent Living, but I don't know . . ."

While Abby appreciated his concern, she'd feel funny living in a place that was segregated. "I don't know if I'd be comfortable in a disability community. People look at me like I'm a criminal if I use my parking placard when I'm out with someone because they can't see anything wrong with me."

"No, Abby, you misunderstand. It's not segregated. It's a housing complex that is accessible for everyone. Mothers with strollers and old women with shopping carts benefit from no step entrances as much as you and I. I'm sure if you wanted to ride over there, Sophie would love to drive you. I could ask her . . ."

Abby interrupted Steven's enthusiasm. "I'll think about it, but I want to wait until it's a little warmer to look for a place. Thank you." She quickly turned the conversation around.

"How about you? Where will you go when you leave here? Your Aunt Sophie said you had to give up your share of the apartment you lived in off-campus. Do you have a plan?"

"I have no idea what's in store for me. I won't be going home for a while.I'll most likely end up staying with Logan and Sophie temporarily even though that's the last thing I want. I may enlist the help of my attendant to locate something suitable before I leave rehab." He looked at the floor as he said it. Abby was sad Steven's life was currently so uncertain. She reached over and squeezed his hand.

"Hey, it won't be that long, eh? You're on the mend." She was going for the positive, not being patronizing.

They were interrupted by a tap on the door. A young girl Abby remembered from her last stay stepped into the room, carrying a tray that exuded an aroma one could recognize only as hospital fare. It didn't seem to ever matter what it was; it all smelled the same. The girl set it on the bedside table and lifted the lid with a flourish. Abby half expected the dietary aide to say, "Ta-da!"

Steven groaned. "Lisa, please cover that. I cannot stomach another bite of hospital macaroni and cheese."

Abby laughed at his outburst even though she understood his complaint. "On that note, I need to go. Try to enjoy your dinner."

"Are you sure you won't indulge in some takeout with me? I can call the Mexican place." Abby shook her head. "Hoagies?" She shook her head again. "Pizza?" Steven sounded desperate.

"Sorry, Steven. I have a few other things to do today. I'll come back soon."

"I would like that very much, thank you, but at least let me walk you to the elevator, Abby."

Abby smiled a little inside each time her name passed his lips. She hung her head to hide the blush.

"No, eat. I'll be fine. I really do have to go. We'll talk soon, okay?" Abby gathered her coat and purse as she headed toward the door.

"Can I call you later?"

"I'll be home this evening. Talk to you soon." Abby rushed through the door and onto

the elevator before Steven followed her home.

The ride to the grocery store took forever, but when Abby exited the bus, the sun was shining, and birds were singing. She took a deep breath, feeling revived, exhilarated even. She couldn't help but wonder if the rush she was feeling had more to do with where she'd come from than it did with the emergence of spring.

# Chapter Fifteen

Abby trudged into Steven's room carrying two cups of Blue State Coffee. Steven sat tall in his chair.

*He looks healthier every time I visit.*

They weren't back to the daily visits they shared after the holidays, but Abby visited regularly and tried to spend part of each weekend with him. They were growing closer, and Abby enjoyed spending time with him. She almost dreaded the day he left the confines of the hospital.

*Everything will change! He's a busy doctor. He'll go back to his old life with his real friends.*

*Will he even need me anymore? I'll miss spending time with him.*

Abby was still rambling to herself when she handed Steven the large coffee. She'd come to expect a wide smile and his happy sigh after he took a big swallow, not the serious expression that clouded his features, the same expression he wore every time "Brahms' Lullaby" played over the hospital's PA system.

"Why does this piece seem to upset you so?"

Steven's voice was filled with melancholy when he replied. "It shouldn't bother me, truly. It's a blessing."

"What's a blessing?"

"They play "Brahms' Lullaby" to announce the arrival of a new little someone here at the hospital."

"Oh, wow. I never realized. That's such a cool thing to do."

"It is, but . . ." So softly Abby nearly missed it, he muttered, ". . . it's not like it'll ever play for me."

"Why? I'm sure they'd be happy to play it for you too." Abby teased as she nudged him with her shoulder.

Steven gripped the armrest of his chair until his knuckles were white, his gaze focused on the floor. "I'm almost certain I'll never have that. *Look at me.*"

*Well damn . . .*

Abby had heard the female staff talk about her friend, and she'd heard fellow patients drop comments in the waiting room of Dr. Jeffries's office. Fact was, Steven Chandler was a hottie, and plenty of women knew it.

"I am looking at you, and if you want to have children, I'm certain there are plenty of women who would be happy to oblige."

"I'm not destined for that kind of a future, Abby."

"Not to pry, but since you brought it up, what could possibly make you come to such a conclusion?"

Steven turned away from Abby, and when he spoke, his voice was quiet. "I can't exactly, you know, make love with a woman."

Abby understood the mechanics of paralysis, but sexuality had been the subject of conversation around the water cooler at The Center, and she knew guys who had higher cord injuries than Steven who happily indulged.

"Why? Since the accident? Have you tried?" Abby slapped her hands over her face. She could feel the flames burning behind her fingers.

"Not since the first one."

*The first one. What? The first accident? Is he trying to tell me he hasn't since . . . No way.*

Abby put her hands on her hips. "But that was a long time ago. Certainly you've . . ."

He shook his head.

"Never?"

A blush crept up Steven's neck, and he looked as heated as Abby felt. "I haven't dated since right after I left the hospital in 1993."

"But *why?*"

He paused before answering, looking at her skeptically. *"Seriously,* Abby? You have to ask? Why would anyone want *me?*"

Suddenly Abby found herself pacing, her hands balled into fists. She turned and marched into Steven's personal space. "Wait, wait . . . *wait!* Let's back up here. In January this was what you alluded to, wasn't it? Do you care to explain?"

He sighed. Abby was crushed by the expression on his face: devastation, sadness, heartache . . . longing for the one thing that was missing in his life.

*A man so handsome should never look so desolate.*

"I had a steady girl before the accident. We'd been together for a couple of years. She stuck around after the accident, all through rehab. She didn't run screaming when I pulled out the books on sexuality for the disabled."

His head was in his hands, his fingers gripping his hair.

"After I got home, she became involved in my routine and made a half-hearted effort to learn to assist me. The winter of '94 was horrendous. Aunt Sophie and I had the worst case of cabin fever. We constantly snapped at each other. Logan was stuck for days on end at the ER. We all needed a break from one another, so Sophie and Logan decided to check into a nearby hotel. None of us dreamed a weekend getaway would end in disaster or change all of our lives. They trusted Courtney and knew if I had any trouble, we'd call."

When Steven turned to Abby, his face was streaked with tears.

"I'd been seeing a specialist for a long time. He provided me with the proper tools, and I was confident that with some creativity, we could enjoy ourselves if we chose.

"When she realized my 'issues' hadn't been resolved, she said the words I'd expected her to utter since the day I woke up from the coma: 'I love you, but I'm eighteen, Steven. I need a whole man. I want kids someday. I can't do this.'

"She left me in a situation where I couldn't even go after her. Instead of chasing her down, I ended up falling and knocking myself out. I couldn't access a telephone, and I lay in my own filth until my family came home and found me.

"That is why I'll never put myself in a position where I'm dependent on another human being, why I don't engage in sexual encounters, and it's how I know a hospital will never play Brahms to welcome my child into the world."

At some point, Abby had moved closer to Steven. She stood next to him, rubbing circles on his back as he choked out the broken words between sobs. She wiped her own tears on the sleeve of her shirt.

*Damn the girl who did this! To lose his parents, his independence—even his home—and then to lose the person he thought would be there for him, no matter what.*

"I'm *glad* she's not with you because you deserve so much better. You'll have that someday. You'll find your happiness. I hope she's miserable."

"No, Abby. I've made my peace. And Courtney? She's made a life with some rich plastic surgeon. She got her happily ever after."

Abby could see Steven mentally slathering bricks with mortar and erecting another wall like the one he'd surrounded himself with after Christmas, and she wasn't about to let him pull that move again.

"Stop it! I know what you're doing, and I won't lose you again!" Abby grabbed their coffees and shoved one toward Steven. He needed some sort of fortitude, and it was all she had to offer.

"I don't date either. But I have to believe that someday the right person will come along."

Steven took a long draw from the coffee and swallowed. "And if he doesn't, Abby? You're setting yourself up for a fall . . ."

"No, Steven. If they don't . . . I'm still a good person. I have a full life. I don'tneed another person to define who I am. Being alone doesn't mean I'm lonely. You know, I went to your support group, and through that, I ended up getting involved with another organization that provides services to people with disabilities. I've met some great people. There are lots of men with cord injuries who have healthy sex lives. They have kids, too. God, you're a doctor. You must say things like this to your patients all the time."

He gave Abby a mischievous smirk. "Don't tell anyone, but we doctors don't always practice what we preach."

"So are you saying you lie to your patients? How can you give them advice if you don't believe it yourself?"

"I believe it for *them*, but not for *myself*. The bottom line is I don't handle rejection well. Like you seem to be, I was content before I got hit. When I'm working, I have little to no free time. I work at the office, I'm active at the hospital, and several times a week I work in the lab. Most days, I eat dinner when other people are heading to bed, but all this free time has made me wonder what my life could have been if so many things hadn't happened."

"You shouldn't let what's happened in your past determine your future. You're far too pretty to remove yourself from the dating pool." Abby winked at him, hoping to lighten the suddenly oppressive mood in the room.

"*Pretty?* You're not helping my fractured ego here. Thanks."

Abby nudged his shoulder. "Broken ego? Are you kidding? Do you not see how all the nurses here salivate over you?"

He laughed. "Oh sure, I see how they *look* at me, but I'm certain that if any of them found out what they were getting into, they'd run away screaming. I seem to have that effect on women."

"I haven't run. In fact, I think you're quite a catch."

"Don't blow smoke up my hospital gown, Abby. I know what I am. I look in the mirror every day."

"Then I think your self-image is a little warped. You're an attractive man, Steven, but it's not only a physical thing. The first time we met, I was so mad at you, but that attitude of yours, *that* was what made a lasting impression on me. Your self-confidence—it's empowering."

"Perhaps I'm good at putting on a show."

"I don't believe it!"

Steven tilted his head, a thoughtful expression on his face. "Abby, would you like to go on a non-date?"

"Trying to test my theory, Chandler?"

He chuckled lightly. "You don't have to go if you don't want to."

"You want to see if I'll put my money where my mouth is?"

"I can understand why you wouldn't want to."

Abby smacked him dramatically. "I can't say no, can I?"

"I was probably wrong to presume . . ."

"Stop it! Of course, I'll go on a non-date with you. What *aren't* we going to do?" Abby giggled.

"Let me worry about that. Do you think you could come to me? I don't think I'll have any trouble getting a temporary leave for a few hours."

"I'll be here."

The rest of the afternoon sped by, and it was soon time for Abby to go. She was nervous about their impending outing. It didn't matter what you called it . . . a date was a date.

*But, are we ready to go there?*

Abby liked Steven, but she didn't want to be in a position where their friendship would end if it didn't work out.

While Courtney's rejection had undeniably affected Steven, his rejection of Abby had broken something inside of her, and she was still a little skittish about getting close to him again.

As she walked through the hospital to leave, she passed Logan's office. The door was ajar, and she could hear voices. Abby tapped softly on the door and waited. The voices grew quiet, and the door opened. When Logan saw her, he smiled handsomely. "Abby! Please, come in."

"I heard you talking to someone. I wondered if we could talk when you are done."

"Oh, no. I was merely dictating a few notes for my secretary to type up. I'm done now. How can I help?" He seemed genuinely interested, and immediately Abby felt at ease.

"I was wondering if we could talk about Steven."

Logan moved a stack of folders off the adjacent chair and patted it for his guest. He slipped behind the desk and sat down.

"Did you have a nice visit? He seems to be in good spirits, doesn't he?"

"Mm-hmm, he does. And yes, we had a very pleasant visit."

"But? What did you want to talk about, dear? Is everything all right?"

"We talked about Courtney. My heart hurts for him. I don't want him to think I pity him, because I don't. I can't comprehend how someone could be so cold-hearted, so cruel."

"It's not my story to tell, but if he already shared, what has he told you?"

"He told me she stuck with him through his recovery, but when they tried to be intimate, and he couldn't perform, she deserted him."

"That girl abandoned him. She neglected him with no regard for his safety or comfort."

"He said she left him in a position where he couldn't call for help."

"If I ever see Courtney Green again, I swear . . ." Logan's hands curled into tight fists. "It's been nearly twenty years, and I'm still furious over what we found. I had my reservations about her dedication to Steven. I thought maybe she had some sort of Florence Nightingale complex. But in her defense, she spent a lot of time learning how to assist Steven with his routine, and when she waxed poetic about her desire to learn how to make a relationship with him work, well, we were hopeful for them both. I wanted him to experience everything life has to offer. He'd lost so much.

"They were both adults and had been in a physical relationship for some time. Sophie and I went away for a weekend, a local getaway. She begged me to let her call and check in, but I didn't want to upset Steven. The kids promised they'd call if there were any problems. When they didn't, well, we thought everything was all right."

Logan ran his fingers through his salt and pepper hair. "When we went home on Sunday evening, Courtney's car was gone. We didn't think much of it because her sister Elaina had a fiancé here in the city, and the girls shared a car. When we got inside, the house was dark, the silence deafening. Immediately, Sophie went to Steven's room. I heard her suitcase hit the hardwood floor before she began to scream. The stench hit me before I got anywhere near the bedroom. All sorts of scenarios ran through my mind. We found Steven on the floor of the guest room, broken pieces of furniture all around him."

Logan wiped his eyes. "In that moment, I thought we'd lost him. The concussion he endured from falling out of bed was the least of our worries. Between the dehydration and the bedsores that had already begun to develop, losing Steven was a very real possibility."

"You must have been beside yourselves."

"Walking into that situation was almost as bad as . . . well, I've never seen a worse case of neglect."

"Steven's reluctance to get close to anyone makes more sense to me now. I like him, and I think he likes me too. I would like to enjoy his friendship and see what comes of it. Even if we were to become more than friends, there's so much more to a relationship than sex. There are lots of ways to share intimacy with someone you care about."

"Thank you, Abby. I hope you're able to share your thoughts on that with him one day."

"Yeah, I hope so too. No matter who he ends up with, I think he needs to look at the big picture. As a doctor, he should understand better than anyone."

Logan held his side as he laughed. "Oh, Abby. We doctors are the worst patients!"

Abby shared Logan's laughter until she saw the darkening sky and realized how late it was getting. "I need to go before it gets dark. Thanks for taking the time to talk with me. I appreciate it."

"Safe travels, Abby. Have a pleasant evening."

"To you as well. Please tell Sophie hello for me."

"I will. Goodnight, dear."

❖　　❖　　❖

Abby crawled into bed that night, mentally exhausted. *This non-date business is no different than all the afternoons we've spent together at the hospital, right?*

As Abby was drifting off, her phone chirped.

Are you busy tomorrow?

Tomorrow? Abby gulped. Isn't that your family day?

Not this week. Plans changed. Would you like to go bowling?

LIKE BOWLING, BOWLING?

THAT'S WHAT I SAID.

YOU BOWL?

SURE. :-)

SERIOUSLY?

YES. I THINK BOWLING DEFINITELY QUALIFIES AS A 'NON-DATE.'

IS IT FAR? HOW WILL WE GET THERE?

I HAVE THE ELECTRIC WHEELCHAIR. I'LL DRIVE US. :-)

CAN YOU DO THAT?

MY DOC APPROVED IT. CAN YOU BE HERE AT NOON?

I'LL CYA THEN, STEVEN.

GOODNIGHT, ABBY. SWEET DREAMS.

YOU TOO. 'NITE.

Abby tucked her phone under her pillow and went to sleep with a smile.

*I'm going bowling. On a non-date. With Steven Chandler.*

# Chapter Sixteen

*She said she'd go! She'd go out. On a non-date. With me!*

Steven giggled. *I am* such *a dork! Do I dare to hope that one day it could be something more?*

❖     ❖     ❖

Maddie came in at eleven o'clock to assist Steven onto his side. "What has you so happy tonight?"

"Nothing." Steven couldn't help feeling smug and hoped it didn't show.

"You can't hide anything from me, mister."

Steven sighed. "Promise you won't tell anyone?"

"Cross my heart, hon."

Steven grabbed the bed rail and pulled himself in Maddie's direction. "You can't tell Sophie . . . or Logan."

"I won't." *Yeah right.*

"I may or may not be going out tomorrow."

"Oh, that's nice, dear." Maddie picked up a pillow and gently put it between Steven's knees.

"With a girl."

"Anyone I know?"

"Mm-hmm."

Maddie dropped into the bedside chair. "Do tell."

"Do you remember Abby Harris?"

"She's such a sweet girl! I thought someone said she'd been visiting again. Oh honey, she's perfect for you!"

*We need to nip that in the bud right away.* "It's *only* a little bowling. Nothing romantic. You know I don't date."

Steven's friend stood and tried to look busy, but the smile on her face was undeniable.

"I'm happy you've made a new friend. She's a nice girl. I don't care what you want to call it. Don't mess this up! I think you really hurt her before."

She covered Steven with the blanket and pulled the string on the fluorescent light above his head.

Jeez, does everyone know? Steven closed his eyes in shame. "I won't."

"I know you won't. It's been nice to see a smile on your face. I've missed that. Ring the buzzer if you need me."

Sleep was evasive. Steven was restless, but there was nothing he could do about it.

*I refuse to whine to Maddie. No amount of positioning will make these butterflies go away.*

At two o'clock, Steven was rolled onto his back, propped and positioned with the appropriate pillows. Maddie handed him a urinal and a straight catheter so he could empty his bladder.

When Steven was done, he rang the call bell, and Maddie cleared everything away.

By three o'clock, Steven had counted all the holes in the ceiling tiles above his head and found himself perking up each time he heard footsteps in the corridor. Never in his life had a girl made him feel so unhinged. Each tick of the clock reverberated off the walls.

At four, he pushed the call bell, realizing that his battle with insomnia was not something he could conquer on his own.

Maddie came quickly, a worried expression clouding her typically cheerful face. "What's wrong?"

"I can't sleep. I can't get comfortable."

"How can I help, Steven? Where does it hurt?"

"No, it's not physical . . . it's the date . . . but it's not supposed to be a date . . . and I don't know how I'm supposed to act or feel. While we both agreed we *don't* date . . . it's a *date* . . . and I'm just . . . so . . . tired. Please help me. I need something—a hot toddy or a pill—anything that'll knock me out."

Maddie smiled. "You can act like it's nothing, Steven Chandler, but I've never seen you so worked up over a girl that you're sleepless and slaphappy. Why didn't you say something sooner? I'd have brought you a sleeping pill. It's a little late for that now. You'll sleep right through your"—she cleared her throat—"what did you call it?"

"I have tried everything to distract myself. I've counted sheep and the holes in the ceiling tiles. I've even come up with the outline for a sensitivity training the nursing staff should attend."

Maddie laughed. "You'll have to tell me about that one sometime." She clicked the mouse as she looked through Steven's chart. "There's an order here for something to help with anxiety. All these doctors would rather leave an order for anti-anxiety meds and sleeping pills in every chart rather than be awakened in the middle of the night for a restless patient. I swear they teach you that in medical school."

"They do." Steven chuckled. "I can give you an order if there's not one in my chart. I have privileges at this hospital, you know."

"And you know that's not permissible. If there's no order, I have a couple of doctors on speed dial."

Maddie soon returned with a pill cup and a drink. "Here, this should let you calm down and make you a little drowsy without making you all hung over in the morning."

Steven swallowed the tiny pill and took a deep breath. Maddie leaned him forward, fluffing his pillow and tidying his blankets. Then she put her hands on her hips, surveying him.

"I don't want to disrupt you in an hour. While you're waiting for that pill to kick in, let's get you rolled onto your side. I wish I'd thought of it before I got you comfortable. Would you like the urinal again?"

"No, I'll be okay till they come in with morning meds."

Maddie helped Steven roll to his side. Then she said quietly, "Sweet dreams, my friend. Have a wonderful day. Don't overthink it; have fun. Tell Miss Abby I said hello."

"Thanks. I will, Maddie. Have a wonderful day off."

Maddie snorted in response. "I'm going to go home and sleep, and then I have to be back at seven tomorrow night." Without another word, she was out the door.

Steven began a deep breathing exercise and closed his eyes, walking his mind through the relaxation techniques a massage therapist had taught him years before. Steven imagined each of his limbs growing heavy with sleep. By the time he got to his hands, he was adrift in some faraway land.

❖　❖　❖

Refreshed by a bath and hot cup of coffee, Steven was contentedly lost in hisreverie when a hand touched his shoulder, but he knew who it was without opening his eyes.Abby was so close, he could feel her breath on his face. "Steven?" she whispered.

"Abby?"

"Are you ready to go?"

Steven yawned loudly and stretched as much as he possibly could. "Sure, hop on. You've got door detail. I'm sorry you have to get on and off the back so many times, but I'll try to make the ride a smooth one."

When she went to the back of Steven's chair, Abby laughed. "What's this?"

"It's a skateboard that some of my friends invented. They call it the 'Care-E-On.' Hop on and let's give it a whirl!"

Abby climbed on, and Steven looked over his shoulder to check on her.

"You holding on tight?"

Abby gripped the push handles and giggled. "Take it away!"

"Hold on, Abby!"

Steven spun in a wide circle, ever mindful of the precious cargo under his care. His passenger let out a squeal, but a playful smack on the shoulder reminded Steven to be attentive.

❖   ❖   ❖

When the doors burst open, and they headed toward Davenport Avenue, Steven's chest grew tight, and he began to sweat. He let go of the joystick, the abrupt halt causing Abby's body to slam into the back of his chair.

*I can't do this.*

Not once as he'd devised his grand plans did Steven consider the fact that he would have to drive unprotected in traffic —with a passenger, no less —if they were to go through with their outing.

*Why did I think this was a good idea?*

# Chapter Seventeen

Abby sensed Steven's hesitation and stepped directly in front of him. "What's wrong? Steven?"

Steven swallowed, staring at the busy street before making eye contact with Abby. He opened and closed his mouth, but nothing came out.

"Steven?"

"I'm sorry. I don't think I can do this."

"Nonsense, Chandler. Do you intend to be a hermit the rest of your life?"

"Apparently I didn't think this through."

"Is there a sidewalk the entire way?"

Steven looked off into the distance. "Yes, I'm pretty sure there is now. They were paving and installing curb cuts when I had my accident."

"So we won't be playing in traffic as long as we use the crosswalks. We'll be all right; I risk my life like this every day."

"Please don't make light of it. Do you have any idea how dangerous a busy street is for a person with a disability?"

Abby rubbed Steven's shoulder. "I'm sorry. The best way to squash our demons is to face them head-on, but you don't have to do this alone."

"I trust you, Abby."

"Here's how my kids and I confront overwhelming projects—taking it step by step. Let's not worry about the entire street. We'll take one curb at a time." Abby held out her right hand, and Steven grabbed it tightly. He looked once, then twice after the light changed and the audible and visual signals prompted them to cross. He took a deep breath and held on as he inched out into the street.

❖　　❖　　❖

Steven's heart beat against his ribs; his head throbbed in tandem.

When they were safely on the opposite sidewalk, Steven gasped for air. He let go of the joystick and slapped his palm to his chest.

Abby swiped her fingers across her damp cheeks. "You okay?"

Steven swallowed the lump that had formed in his throat. "I think I will be."

"I'm right here with you."

"I know," Steven replied. "Thank you."

Abby stepped back up on the little platform Steven's friends had installed on the back of his chair. She gave his shoulder a squeeze, and Steven began moving down Davenport, enjoying the newly poured sidewalks. As he drove, Steven remembered that it hadn't always been so nice. Out of necessity, he often rode in the street.

*I don't know if I can do that again!*

When they approached Vernon Street, Abby tapped Steven's shoulder. When they slowed to a stop, she hopped from her perch and took his hand once again. Steven gave her a squeeze and looked both ways before venturing into the intersection. Time stood still as they inched their way across. Steven's mind screamed for him to go as fast as he could, to rush her out of harm's way, but Abby grounded him, and they crossed at her pace.

Coming upon Ward Street, Abby tapped him again, but Steven shook his head and continued on his way without stopping. Steven didn't want Abby expending all her energy to quell his fears when they had a fun afternoon planned.

The next time Steven stopped for a light, Abby grabbed his shoulders and gave them a squeeze. She leaned down and spoke firmly in his ear. "I'm proud of you, Steven." Steven's face split into a smile as he pulled into the crosswalk. *I'm kinda proud of myself, too.*

When they rounded the corner, the brightly colored façade of the bowling alley came into view. As they drew closer, bass from the sound system pounded and pulsed. Steven's heart sped up. So much had happened since he'd done anything for pleasure.

Steven looked over his shoulder. "This is us. Can you open the door?"

Abby hopped down, but instead of reaching for the handle, she hit a silver button, and the double doors opened wide.

"Well, that's a pleasant surprise!" Steven exclaimed.

The staff had always been welcoming. They were the first place in town to offer ramps and bumpers for people in wheelchairs, and they had put in a lowered section at the bar so a patron could roll right up to it to get their order. While the place wasn't fully accessible, the bathrooms passed muster, and the staff went out of their way to be kind, so Steven never complained.

While Steven paid for their games and Abby's shoes, his guest excused herself to the restroom. Her breath tickled his ear when she leaned in close and whispered, "I've got a tape measure in my purse. You want me to see if it complies with ADA regs?"

Steven barked out a laugh. "Sure, let me know what you find!"

Abby returned with a wide grin on her face. "I *love* this place. You should *see* the restroom. It's incredible. The grab bars are at a good height, the sink is accessible, and the baby change station doesn't sit directly on the grab bar."

*My Abby has become an undercover accessibility inspector! That shit is so cool.*

Single fathers were the norm in a way they'd never been before, and as such, the changing table was a dilemma Steven faced in the men's accessible stall as well. "I'll have to check out the men's room, too."

Steven led Abby to the lane where an attendant was placing the ramp. She turned to Steven and Abby with a smile. "Dr. Chandler! So nice to see you again. Will you be using the bumpers today?"

Abby cocked her head, her eyes big. "Will we? I've been bowling once in my life, and even then, we used bumpers."

"Really?"

"Really."

Steven smiled at the attendant. "We'll start with the bumpers."

❖   ❖   ❖

Steven looked down at his outstretched legs and frowned. "We need to set up our lane to get started. Can you type our names into the computer? I don't think I can get close enough."

Steven glanced up at the screen and couldn't contain his smile. When Steven had paid, the attendant had entered CHANDLER into the computer to indicate the lane, but seeing Steven and Abby Chandler emblazoned across the huge screen filled Steven with a warmth he'd never experienced in his thirty-three years.

That warm, fuzzy feeling turned into a chill at the frown on Abby's face. *Had she seen it too?*

"Is everything okay?"

She looked down at the floor, her cheeks nearly as red as the hideous shoes on her feet.

"What's wrong, Abby?"

"I tried to pick a ball, but I don't remember them being so heavy."

Steven sighed in relief. *That's something I can help you with.*

"Come on, we'll pick together. I might need your help too." Steven led the way to the back, examining the balls for something that was heavy enough to gain momentum coming off the ramp but light enough for him or Abby to lift. He sighed audibly as he studied the choices. The balls had been stored with no sense of order.

"Why don't you get one for me first? I think I know what I want. I just need you to find it and set it on my lap."

"Gotcha. What size do you want?"

"First, open my backpack. There's a small pillow in there. Can you hand that to me?" Steven placed it mid-thigh so the ball would rest securely and not escape. "Now, I think I can handle about fifteen pounds. So just look for the number fifteen. When you find one, I'll get close so you don't have to carry it too far."

Abby turned the ball carousel. She smiled and reached down to the bottom shelf. She made a grunting noise when she lifted the ball, and Steven's grunt echoed hers when she dropped the black Brunswick onto his lap and silently thanked God for pillows and fiberglass casts. *The girl's aim is perfect . . . if she intends to incapacitate me.*

She blushed and giggled softly. "Sorry, Steven."

"Come on, let's find one for you. We'll start with an eight pounder. You have small hands, so we'll need to look for one with smaller openings for your fingers. You want it snug, but not so tight that your fingers get stuck in the holes."

"Got it."

Abby walked from one rack to the next, eventually choosing a Columbia with a dark purple swirl. "Is this okay? The holes are a little big, but it's the only eight I could find."

"You should be okay. Do you want to go first?" Steven asked her.

Abby's eyes grew wide, and she shook her head. "I'd rather wait."

Steven approached the ramp and lined up his shot. He was used to bowling from a standing position, so the difference would be to Abby's advantage.

Happy with his adjustments, Steven gave the ball a firm push. He returned to where Abby sat, offering his hand, but she batted it away, her eyes on the lane as the ball hit the pins—six, with the remaining four pins split. He had no chance of a spare, but Steven wasn't there to show off.

Steven's next roll netted him two more pins.

Abby had gotten up and was now bouncing from foot to foot.

"Are you cold?"

"Nervous. I don't want to make a fool of myself."

"Don't stress. It's only a game."

"I know, but I'm afraid I'm going to fall on my ass."

"The shoes are supposed to be slippery; you want to be able to slide in them. Would you like a little refresher?"

Abby nodded.

As she cradled the ball to her chest, Steven led her to the approach. "Visualize the pins. Hold the ball in front of your chest with both hands. When you're ready, bring the ball down to your right side, and take four steps to the line. Step one—lead off with the back foot on the ball side. Push the ball straight in front of you until your arms are extended and level with the floor. Your opposite hand should be helping to support the ball in front of you."

"Okay, anything else?"

"Yes, step two, swing the ball straight back. Step three, swing the ball forward. Your last step is your ball release. You want your feet to slide forward, and your left foot will be behind you.

"Think you're ready now?" Steven asked.

"Can't I just push it down your ramp? It feels like I have to do a lot more work."

"I have the utmost faith in you, Abby. Just take your time. You don't need to hurry. Use the arrows on the lane to line up your shot. You don't even have to look at the pins; in fact, maybe it would be easier if you don't."

Abby grabbed her ball and followed Steven's instructions to a T, except on the backswing, she must have loosened her grip. Steven sat dumbstruck as the purple ball flew in his direction instead of rolling down the lane. He jerked out of the way as it narrowly missed him.

Abby turned, her face crimson. "I think the holes are too big." She walked over to retrieve her ball and apologized again before she tried to take another swing. Her second release was done like a pro, and Abby turned and began walking toward Steven.

Steven watched, his mouth agape, as the ball made its way right down the middle, zeroing closer and closer to the center pin.

"Abby, turn around!" She swiveled just in time to see her ball meet the center pin. The remaining nine pins fell in its wake.

"*Strike!*" The word flashed on the screen along with an instant replay of her ball hitting the pins. Abby jumped up and down, clapping her hands. When she got close to Steven, their palms collided in a high five.

"That was an awesome throw for a beginner! Now let's see what I can do."

Steven returned to the ramp and proceeded to roll nothing. Abby had to hide her good-humored grin.

Round after round, they played and they laughed. Steven couldn't remember having such unabashed fun, and if the perpetual smile on Abby's face was any indication, she couldn't either.

Steven frowned when he looked down at his watch. Abby had the last throw of the second game, and they'd soon have to go. He watched with a smile as she picked up the ball, lifted it to her chest, and walked to the lane. She swung and followed through, but in her enthusiasm, she lost her footing, sliding to her behind with an *"Oof!"*

"You okay, Abby? Are you hurt?" Steven cursed his inability to pull her off the floor to make sure she hadn't injured herself.

Abby shook her head. "Only my pride." She got up gingerly and looked around to be sure no one had seen her fall. Abby blushed as she walked over to the ball return, finishing her game.

"I won both games! Can we do this again?"

Steven held his stomach as he laughed. "So you did, and yes, I think I enjoy this non-dating stuff with you. Are you hungry? We could get something here or go grab something on the way back."

"I'm okay with it if you want to eat here. Did you want anything in particular?"

"Let's go see what they have." Steven studied the many choices on the menu board.

The food was hot and greasy and covered in breading—such a far cry from the hospital fare that Steven consumed much more than he'd intended. The hand-cut fries were to die for, drowning in salt and dark, malt vinegar.

Steven patted his stomach. "It's been so long since I had something that good. How are the chicken fingers?"

Abby smiled with a mouthful and held one out in offering.

"I don't want to eat your dinner. I'm quite satisfied. I seem to have a voracious appetite out here in the wild."

"Because the food tastes so good!"

As Abby finished her meal, they watched other patrons bowl. It had been Steven's first carefree day since the accident, and he dreaded going back.

He was so lost in his thoughts that he hadn't realized Abby was finished until she began clearing their spots. She took the baskets to the counter and returned with two colas.

"Here, yours was gone. I thought you could use a refill."

Steven took a deep draw on the straw. He never enjoyed fountain soda much, but maybe, Steven thought, it was the company that made everything taste so much better. He took a few more swallows as he watched his companion. She was so cute in a bashful, awkward sort of way. She was also humble and reserved and extremely polite.

Longing tugged at his heart. *Mom would have loved her.* Sophie adored her, and his

uncle. . .? Well, his uncle had had a soft spot in his heart for Abby from the day they'd met.

Steven wanted to spend lots of time with Abby Harris, and he prayed that the lovely young teacher wanted that too.

*Do I dare to hope?*

Steven could feel Abby's eyes on him, and he lifted his gaze.

"Penny for your thoughts?"

Steven felt the corners of his mouth lift into a smile. "I was thinking, Miss Harris, that I'd love to do something like this with you again if you'd be interested. I can't remember when I've had this much fun."

"It hasn't been that long since you've been laid up, but I'm glad I amuse you."

"No, it hasn't been that long since the accident, but coming here with a bunch of guys from the ER or the stem cell center isn't nearly as entertaining as coming here with you. I've never done anything like this with a girl."

"Really?" She sounded shocked.

"Life was full before my accident. I worked four days a week with Jeff—your Dr. Jeffries. I have to do at least one ER rotation a week, and normally I do several so Jeff can be home with his wife. At least twenty hours a week, I'm required to work in the lab, playing with DNA. I squeeze more lab time in where I can between patients at our office. It helps get my student loans paid off."

Her eyes got huge. "When do you sleep?"

"It's not all that bad. All my office time is during the day. I alternate Saturday mornings with Jeff. I don't actually have to be present in the ER for my rotations as long as I remain on the premises. Normally I'm holed up in my office catching up on notes, reading new information in journals, or catching a snooze. There is someone present around the clock at the lab, so I can sneak in whenever there's a decent break in my schedule. Most scientists have non-existent social lives."

"It doesn't seem like you're in the lab a lot. Isn't that your career goal? I remember your saying something about your desire to work in stem cell research. I'd think you'd devote more of your time there."

"I do have to put in a specific number of hours to retain my loan repayment contract, but they've been extremely generous and allow me to log my hours whenever I can. Perhaps it helps that my last name is Chandler. At least, that was one of the reasons Logan used to convince me to change my name. Personally, I think he's holding out hope that I'll one day pass on the family name. Who knows what the future will hold?"

Abby's gaze was pensive.

"What is it, Abby?"

"Who were you before your accident?"

"I was Steven Maxwell."

"Well, hello, Steven Maxwell. So nice to make your acquaintance." Abby giggled and thrust her hand across the table.

Steven didn't often dwell on his circumstances, but his heart warmed hearing his birth name cross her lips, and suddenly he wanted her to know him—really know him.

"My parents were Oliver and Grace Maxwell. Mom and Sophie were sisters and Dad was an only child. I'm the end of the bloodline for both families."

"Yeah, me too. I mean, there's my stepbrother and stepsister. They aren't Harrises, but we've been close for so long, I don't think of them as anything other than family. God help us all if Penny procreates again. You haven't had the pleasure of meeting her." Abby laughed nervously, and Steven remembered hearing Logan's first impression of Abby's mother. No, Steven didn't think he'd enjoy meeting the woman at all.

"I met your dad that one time. He seemed nice, and it's obvious he thinks the world of you."

"Yeah, we're close in our own way. He's not overly affectionate, but I know he loves me."

"That's good." Steven was relieved she had someone to go to for support. He knew the past year couldn't have been easy for her.

Abby stood up and smoothed her hands down her pant legs. "So, should we blow this popsicle stand? Do you have a curfew, Dr. Chandler?"

"No, but I said I'd only be gone a few hours. Technically, you're completely responsible for me, you know." Abby blushed and burst into a fit of giggles, and Steven couldn't help but notice how pretty she was.

"Nothing like putting pressure on a girl. If I'd known that, we would have found an accessible bus rather than play chicken in traffic."

Steven grew serious. "We should probably go. Thank you so much for humoring me."

"Thanks for asking. I had a blast! Let me go visit the ladies' room again, and I'll be ready."

While Abby visited the restroom, Steven sought out the manager and thanked him for the changes he had recently made in regard to accessible accommodations. Even though it was required by law to have an accessible establishment, it was important to Steven to let the manager know how much he appreciated the work. Steven left a card from The Newbies as well, explaining that the group was compiling a database of disability-friendly establishments in the Greater New Haven area and assured the manager he would have them added to the directory.

As Abby came out of the restroom, the owner waved them over to the counter. "Steven, please take these for the members of your support group. We'd love to have you come back." Steven smiled as he studied the booklets the man had put in his hand. Free games and shoe rentals for each guest.

*There must be fifty of these!*

"Wow! Thanks, Otis. I'll be sure to spread the word. We love to support businesses that make an effort like you have to make us feel welcome."

"Any time, Steven. Have a safe trip back to the hospital. Come see us again. If you'd like to use those for a large group outing, give me a call. We could accommodate your group for an evening of private bowling. I'll even throw in pizza and sodas."

"We will. Thanks again."

"Bye now. Take care."

"See ya later, Otis."

Abby looked confused. "What was that about? Did I miss something?"

"Well, yeah, sort of. The guy who owns the place gave us a huge stack of coupons. He essentially invited the entire support group to come over and bowl—on the house."

"That was nice."

"Yeah, it was. I wanted to acknowledge the splendid job they did renovating. I've always liked this place, but this makes it even more inviting. I didn't tell him my friend was wielding a tape measure in the ladies' restroom. That might have freaked him out."

They both laughed as Abby climbed onto the back of Steven's wheelchair. With a lurch, they were off. Steven's heart sped up at every intersection, but he refused to let his fears dampen what had turned out to be one of the best days of his life.

As they rode, it began to rain, and by the time they arrived at the hospital, they were soaked but laughing like teenagers as they shook the rain off their jackets in the ER entrance. They passed the senior Doctor Chandler in the corridor, and Steven mirrored the grin his uncle wore.

*Yeah, the cat is definitely out of the bag now.*

"I had a nice time, Steven. Thanks for inviting me."

"You're welcome, Abby. I enjoyed myself too. If you'd like, maybe we could do it again."

"I'd like that."

Steven smiled to himself. He considered himself an old-fashioned guy, and it felt a little weird to reverse their roles. After all, Abby had picked him up and had returned him safely to his doorstep. A few of the nurses gawked from their station in the center of the corridor, and Steven beamed with pride. Some of those girls wanted to get a little too close to him, and Steven hoped seeing him with someone—a very pretty someone—would serve as a deterrent. He couldn't help but think Abby had the same idea when she leaned in and pecked him on the cheek.

"Thanks for dinner, Doc."

Steven's hand seemed to rise of its own accord, and he couldn't seem to pull it away from the place that was still flushed from her kiss.

"Thanks for going out on my first adventure."

"Goodnight, Steven." With that, Abby turned and walked back to the elevator, leaving him outside his room with his hand on his cheek and a goofy grin on his face.

# Chapter Eighteen

Abby met the elusive Sydney Chandler on Friday when she breezed into Steven's room as Abby was putting on her coat. "Hi, Abby! I'm Sydney. Steven's told me so much about you!"

Steven's forehead wrinkled as he witnessed the interaction. "Don't overwhelm her, Sydney. I'll kick your butt if you scare her away." The serious tone of his voice made Abby feel all squishy inside. To hear him make a comment that implied he desired her continued presence in his life was rather nice.

"I'll see you tomorrow, and maybe I'll bring a surprise. Sydney, could you walk with me to the elevator?"

Steven perked up and whipped his chair around. "I'll walk you to the elevator, Abby!"

"Sorry, Steven, girl stuff. Have a nice Easter, I'm headed home to spend the weekend with my dad. I'll see you on Monday." Abby grinned and walked out the door, hoping Sydney would follow. She didn't get far before Sydney fell into step.

"What's up? How can I help?" The girl radiated kindness, and while Abby could only make assumptions based on what she'd learned from Steven and his family, she thought it could be easy to be Sydney Chandler's friend.

Still, uncertainty had Abby rambling. "I saw these things called Cast Tats. I'd like to buy some for Steven, but I didn't know if that was something he'd take offense to. I mean, people sign casts all the time, but Steven's are a clean slate. Maybe he's not into that sort of thing."

"Ooh! I think I've seen those online. They're like a decal you adhere to the cast?" Sydney asked.

"Would he be upset if I got him something like that? We've never discussed gifting."

"I believe he'd be flattered. He's quite taken with you, Abby." Sydney winked, and Abby felt her face flame.

*I'm quite taken with him too.*

"He'll love the tats. I've only ever seen them in medical magazines. Where did you find them?"

"I was shopping for a cane when I saw them."

"I hope you found something to meet your needs." Whether Sydney knew or was simply being polite, Abby was relieved that she didn't appear to be the prying type.

"I did."

Sydney smiled. "At least they're not so utilitarian anymore."

"Yeah, it's girlie but not obscenely so, if you know what I mean." The elevator dinged, signaling Abby's escape route.

"That's me. Have a nice Easter, Sydney. Nice meeting you."

"It was nice meeting you too."

❖   ❖   ❖

Abby stopped for the tats on her way home. As she waited in line, she studied different medical equipment displays and pondered Steven's daily life.

*How does he get into the shower? Does he have a shower chair? Does he use a transfer board, or does he do standing pivots? He's so tall, and Sydney's so tiny. Can she pivot him?*

*Does Steven sleep in a special bed at home?* Abby realized she had no idea what home life was like for him . . . or how it would change since his accident.

"Miss? Can I help you?" the cashier asked.

"I'm sorry, my mind was wandering. I'd like to buy these."

The woman rang up the purchase and put it in a small paper bag. "Now be sure to follow the directions carefully, and they'll go on real easy."

"Thanks."

❖   ❖   ❖

Spending Easter at home with her dad was enjoyable, but the house was difficult to navigate, and the long ride was draining. When she got back to her apartment, Abby went straight to bed, snuggling under the covers. When she opened her eyes, the sun was coming up.

Abby stretched and smiled, wiggling her fingers and toes. She felt rested for a change. After showering and dressing, Abby pulled out all the ingredients for blueberry muffins onto the counter.

As soon as they were cool, Abby put them into individual zipper bags. She lined a basket with a clean tea towel and arranged the muffins inside.

Realizing the challenge of juggling the basket, her backpack, and coffee, Abby didn't stop at the coffee shop down the street but opted for two cups from the hospital snack shop instead. She ran into Maddie, who gave her a hurried hug.

"What do you have in your basket, dear? You look like Little Red Riding Hood." Abby looked down and laughed. She had thrown on a red hoodie before she left and was carrying a basket of goodies. Abby supposed she did look like the fairytale character.

Abby held out the basket. "Blueberry muffins. I made them a few hours ago."

"Are you sure? I don't want to deprive my favorite patient. I know how he loves the breakfasts here." Maddie rolled her eyes as she laughed.

"I made plenty. I can't think of anyone he'd rather I share with. We all know he adores you."

Maddie blushed as she reached into the basket. "I adore him, too, but I can't wait for the day he's discharged."

"I hear that day is coming in the not too distant future."

Abby noticed that Maddie was checking the time. "I'm sorry. I didn't mean to hold you up. Enjoy the muffin."

Maddie gave her a quick squeeze. "I'm sure I will, honey. Have a nice day."

"You too, Maddie."

Abby had dismissed an available elevator as they had visited, so she found herself waiting for the next one.

Abby backed into the elevator and felt someone gently take her elbow. "Abby, good morning."

She turned and said, "Dr. Chandler, how are you?"

"Couldn't be better. The sun is shining, it's a lovely spring day, and my beautiful wife is meeting me for breakfast on the rooftop."

Abby noticed he was holding a cup holder with two coffees as well. She was surprised she didn't run into him at the snack shop. "Is that all you're having? It doesn't seem like a very filling breakfast."

"I wanted to get some sort of pastry, but they were all gone. I figured a hot coffee was better than nothing."

She extended her arm. "Go ahead."

"Pardon?"

"Go ahead. Breakfast. Take one for each of you."

"Are you sure?"

"I insist."

"Is this my nephew's breakfast?"

"It's fine. I have four."

"What did you *do*, Abby? Are these—"

"Blueberry muffins, fresh this morning . . . with a crumb topping and cream cheese filling."

"Oh my! Steven doesn't need an entire basket of these."

"As long as we each have one for breakfast . . ."

The elevator dinged for the fourth floor. It was becoming evident that none of the staff ate before coming to work. "Enjoy the muffins, and please give Sophie my best."

"I will! Thanks, Abby."

Abby got off the elevator, and a maintenance man passed her, smiling down at her basket.

*Don't even think about it, buddy!*

Abby scurried into Steven's room and backed against the door, slamming it shut behind her.

"Good morning, Abby! What's got you so frazzled?"

"Argh! Don't any of you eat before you come to work? I swear getting here was like being chased by a pack of hungry wolves.

"I brought us breakfast. In fact, I made enough muffins to last you several days. I narrowly escaped with one for each of us. Someone almost snagged my coffee too. The maintenance man was looking at me like I was some sort of oasis in the middle of a desert. I made a run for it."

"So you came to save me from a hospital breakfast?"

Abby nodded.

"Coffee too?"

"It's hospital coffee." He looked at her basket and raised an eyebrow.

"No, these are homemade. I baked them a few hours ago."

"A few hours ago? Like . . . *this morning?*"

Abby nodded.

"When did you get up?"

"Early."

He seemed excited. "So . . . you brought me something?"

Oh yeah . . . muffins. She rolled her eyes. "Here, take your pick."

He pulled them both out, opening one of the baggies and inhaling deeply. "I think I love you, Abby. This is heaven."

Abby swallowed hard at his admission even if it was an off-the-cuff comment. She wasn't anywhere near ready to share the *L* word with anyone. It had crossed Abby's mind, but she wasn't *there* yet. She wanted someone to share her days and nights with . . . someday.

Abby listened as he moaned and sighed his way through breakfast.

When he finally stopped, she began to regale him with the tale of her adventure through the hospital with homemade food. Next time, it's going inside the backpack.

Abby had only eaten half her muffin. Steven kept looking at it with those puppy dog eyes. She pushed it across the little table to him. "Go ahead. You know you want it. It's all right. They're almost too big for me."

"I don't want to steal your breakfast, babe."

Their relationship had been slowly shifting and, Abby felt special when Steven used little terms of endearment.

"You're not stealing it. I offered."

"These are dewishus," he mumbled with a full mouth. "Quit your job and become my personal chef? I'll pay you well."

"How do you know I can even cook? Maybe I can only bake muffins. My cooking could be toxic." Abby laughed. "Regardless, I love my job, thank you very much."

Steven pouted. "I'm a terrible cook. I'll waste away when I go home."

"Liar! Sophie would never allow that!" They both laughed, and she remembered the gift in her backpack when he told her again how much he loved his surprise.

"Ooh, Steven, I have another surprise."

Abby felt guilty when his face lit up, and he asked, "Did you bake something else?"

"Sorry, nothing else to eat, but it's still cool. Do you trust me?"

His excited tone turned quiet, and he swallowed. "Completely, Abby."

"Good! Close your eyes, and don't move."

When Abby asked Steven to close his eyes, his heart began to pound. Steven had no idea what she had in store for him, but he wouldn't blink an eye until she said it was okay. He was a little apprehensive . . . and a lot excited. Abby was more relaxed around him, and Steven liked the direction things were headed.

He trusted her implicitly. There was nothing she would do to harm him.

Steven heard rustling and the sound of paper crinkling. *What in the world is she doing?* He almost hoped for a smooch, but it was evident he wasn't getting that.

*Don't let your disappointment show, Chandler. Man up!*

"Don't peek."

Steven shook his head. *I won't.* He swallowed.

It sounded like she was . . . *cutting something?* She was so close, he felt the warmth of her breath, and occasionally her hair would brush over his arm. When she put pressure on his leg, he could feel the movement all the way up to his hip.

He raised one eyebrow. "Abby?"

"Shh, I'm almost done. Don't move." She put her hand on his arm for a moment. "This is it. No turning back. Are you sure you trust me?"

"Unequivocally."

"Okay, here goes. I'm not going to be able to talk to you till I'm done. You're sure?"

Steven nodded.

She gave his hand a squeeze. "No matter what, don't move."

He held his breath in anticipation. He heard Abby fumble with something, and suddenly there was a loud noise and a rush of heat blowing up under his shorts.

*What in the world?*

*Trust, Chandler.*

Steven relaxed into his seat and enjoyed the sensation of the warm air blowing all around him. He inhaled deeply, and the scent of Abby, enhanced by the heat, swirled and settled in his soul. Then, as suddenly as it began, it stopped.

His eyes snapped open, and he looked at her in dismay. "Why did you stop? That felt incredible!"

"Don't fret, Chandler. I'm all done now."

"I'm not fretting. I liked it. I've been cold for so long." Abby picked up a blanket from the foot of the bed.

"Why is this on the bed if you're cold?"

"The cold . . . it's one of those annoyances you get used to, I suppose. My circulation has been poor for years. I didn't realize *how much* I enjoyed the heat until you started blow drying me." He reached for the towel. He wanted to know what was under it. "May I?"

"Not yet. Let me explain."

Steven cocked his head. *Why is she nervous?*

"I noticed there was nothing on your casts, no graffiti or anything, and. . . I don't know. You're so outgoing and positive, it felt like you needed something fun."

"Okay, you've piqued my curiosity."

"I hope I didn't overstep my bounds. These are permanent until the casts come off." She was blushing and nervously toeing the floor with her foot.

He took her hand and pulled slightly. "Hey, I'm sure it's fine. You couldn't overstep your bounds. Can I see?"

She hesitantly pulled the towel back to reveal a number of comic book superheroes stuck to his casts. "Superheroes, Abby?" Steven was in awe.

"Are you angry? I, um, I didn't know. They had other things. There were Chinese symbols, but I saw these, and I thought of you."

"You thought about me when you saw these guys?" He had to hear this explanation.

"Well, I think about how they all go from being these mild-mannered characters to heroes who can take on the world. I think of you—how compassionate you were when you met me, all serious Mr. Doctor, and then you have this accident, and it seems like you've taken on the world, like you could conquer anything. When you sit and talk to me about my health problems, it's as if you're trying to save me—at least that's how it feels."

"The artwork on these is seriously cool. Where did you *get* these?"

"Oh, I saw them at a medical supply store, and I couldn't help myself."

"Do you often shop in medical supply stores?" He couldn't resist teasing her.

"No, silly, I was buying a cane. I saw them while I was at the register paying. They're called Cast Tats. I thought they were pretty cool."

Steven considered asking about the cane but decided that if she was having trouble, and she wanted him to know, she'd tell him.

"They are *very* cool. They remind me of happy times with my dad. We loved indulging in vintage comics. I imagine Sophie has my comic books stashed away somewhere with the stuff from my mom and dad's house. Collecting comics was something I loved doing with my dad. Those are good memories that I haven't revisited in so long. I can't thank you enough for giving me that." Steven thought about what she said about the bare casts. It wasn't like he was a party pooper or anything. "Nobody has ever asked if they could write on my casts. It's not like I would have minded."

Grinning, she pulled out a Sharpie and sat next to where his legs rested. Leaning over his leg, she began doodling. "There. I added my name."

She had angled it so he could read it any time he glanced down. "You can be my superhero!"

*Be still my heart!*

"Thanks for being a good sport."

"Thank *you* . . . for everything."

"Hey, I'm sorry it's been a short visit, but I can't stay very long. I have stuff to do for school tomorrow."

"It's okay. I understand. Thanks for breakfast. It was incredible."

"The next time I have goodies, I won't advertise with a basket."

"Next time? I can't wait, but perhaps a knapsack would be less conspicuous."

"Of course there will be a next time. I enjoy surprising you."

"I enjoy your surprises."

"I'm glad. See you tomorrow."

"So long, Abby."

Steven laid the blanket on the foot of his bed. There was *no way* he was covering up those tats.

# Chapter Nineteen

Abby heard the yelling before she turned the corner to Steven's room.

"Brooke, that's ridiculous. *No,*we're *not* going to drop this!"

"If you go through with this, he's going to be found completely at fault."

"But she nearly *killed* him—she didn't even attempt to stop."

"Do I even have any say in this? I don't think . . ."

At the same time, two voices yelled, "Shut up, Steven!"

*Good lord, what am I walking into? This conversation is not meant for my ears.*

Abby headed down the corridor to the fourth floor solarium. There was only one other person in the room, and she appeared to be as lost as Abby felt.

Sophie Chandler had her back to the door, but Abby recognized her immediately. The younger woman thought back to the day Sophie rescued her. *It's time for me to return the favor.*

"You look like you could use a friend, Sophie. May I sit with you?"

"Abby," she said, relief evident in her voice. She gestured to the chair by her side. "Please."

"Is everything okay? I was coming to see Steven, but his room sounds like the last place I belong right now."

"They're discussing the accident case with Steven's attorney. Some new information has come to light since the re-enactment of the accident, and Logan is distraught. I don't know if I've ever seen him so angry. It's very intimidating."

Abby didn't know how to respond. She hadn't known Logan for very long, so she had no idea if he had a temper, but Sophie had known him most of her life. If she was intimidated, Abby was concerned.

"You don't have to tell me any details, but is it going to be okay? Steven's case, I mean?"

"I don't *know* all the details, but no, I don't think so. I'm sure when Steven's had time to digest this, he'll explain it to us."

Abby thought of the non-date and the anxiety Steven exhibited the first time he attempted to cross traffic. Her stomach was in knots, knowing he had been made to go back to the crash site.

When Steven returned to the hospital after the re-enactment, Abby received a curt text saying he was too tired to talk.

The following night when Abby called, it went directly to voicemail.

*Please don't shut me out again.*

"I haven't been able to talk with Steven all week."

"This has been very difficult for Steven. The news this morning has made everything worse."

Abby stood to go. "This isn't my place. I should go."

"Please stay. He needs you."

Sophie cleared her throat before she spoke again. "Steven says you've been spending a lot of time together. I see such a huge difference in him, Abby. He's so *alive* now. More than he's been in a very long time."

Abby shook her head defiantly. "He was energetic and full of life the very first time we met."

"That's the persona he *wants* patients to see. He *wants* them to be hopeful even if he doesn't believe in that for himself."

"Surely you don't think I'm the responsible party. I haven't . . ."

"You've changed *everything*, my dear."

"It's easy to be around him. He's warm and funny, and he likes to tease and joke around. We have a lot of fun together."

"Do you see this blossoming into something more? I'm sorry, I shouldn't pry."

Abby smiled, her face growing warm. "I like your nephew. He says he doesn't date—heck, I told him I don't either, but all these little outings certainly *feel* like we are."

"You've been good for him." Sophie leaned over and pulled Abby into a one-armed hug.

"Come on, the yelling has died down. Let's go see if there's anything left of the room. There was a huge crash shortly before you came in here. I've been afraid to look."

Sophie stood and offered Abby her hand. They locked arms as they made their way through the solarium. Abby leaned into Sophie's warmth and smiled. She hadn't been mothered in a long time.

❖　❖　❖

Steven's door was closed, the room quiet. Sophie knocked softly, and a pretty brunette opened the door.

The woman was tall and sophisticated, her crisp black suit pinstriped, her nails, salon perfect. She was stunning.

Abby frowned when she spied her own reflection in the large mirror over the sink, her hair tumbling out of a messy bun, a comfortable hoodie covering her Bridgehaven Bandits T-shirt. She glanced down at her Chucks and nearly laughed at the contrast between her own shoes and the model's Louboutins.

*This is the kind of woman Steven is destined to spend his life with; she's hot, and I'm a hot mess!*

The brunette hugged Sophie, then took Steven's hand. When she leaned down and hugged him, he kissed her cheek. A feeling Abby wasn't accustomed to squeezed her chest. *Is this what jealousy feels like?*

"I was just leaving, Sophie. We've got some things to work out, but it'll be okay. Steven, I'll see you next Monday. Don't worry about Logan. He'll come around."

As if she could sense Abby's unease, Sophie squeezed her hand. "Brooke, this is Abby Harris. She's a friend of Steven's . . . and mine too. Abby, this is Brooke Grady. She's not only Steven's attorney but also a family friend."

"So nice to meet you, Abby. Sophie, I'll be in touch."

The designer shoes clacked across the floor, and Brooke Grady was gone.

❖   ❖   ❖

Steven seemed sad but appeared calm and collected.

"Ladies, please, sit down." He gestured to the chairs on either side of where he sat.

Steven gazed at his aunt. "Sophie, I'm sure Logan will fill you in. When he does, please understand I love him and respect him. He thinks he knows what's best for me, and usually he does, but in this, I can't agree with him. He may have power of attorney, but I'm not incapacitated, and I won't allow him to make this decision based on some warped idea of what's in my best interest. I'll rescind the POA if he pushes this."

"I should go to him."

Steven nodded. "That might be wise. I believe he went to his office to cool off. Did you know they sent security to tone us down?"

Sophie hung her head. "This is so embarrassing."

Steven laughed. "*You're* embarrassed? We both know how people talk. The rumors spread like wildfire. I wish I was going home with you."

Sophie stood and hugged Steven. "I wish you were coming home with me too. I can't wait until this is behind us. I love you, son. I'll see you tomorrow."

"Thanks, Mom," Steven replied softly. "I love you too."

Sophie turned to Abby and took her hand. "Thanks for being here today, Abby. Maybe we could get together some afternoon? Have a coffee or something?"

"I'd like that, thanks. I'll call you."

Sophie gave her hand a squeeze. "Until then, dear."

❖   ❖   ❖

Abby and Steven spoke at the same time.

"Busy place—"

"You missed the show—"

"You first," Abby said.

"It got pretty rowdy here this morning. Brooke came to discuss a turn of events in my case. While I was surprised, I agree with her. My uncle does not. I fear I've done irreparable damage to our relationship. In anger and in front of him, I actually askedBrooke if I could revoke his POA."

Abby squeezed his hand. "I heard the yelling, so I went to the waiting room. Sophie was already there. She was concerned, so I sat with her, but she didn't tell me anything private."

"She doesn't know much—she stepped out when Logan got belligerent. I want to forget about it for now. Can we talk about something else?"

Abby spied an iPod on the nightstand. "May I?"

Steven nodded.

Abby scrolled through Steven's playlists until she found a jazz collection. *We can chill with this one.*

Abby looped one headphone over Steven's left ear and the other over her right ear. Then she snuggled in next to him in her chair. Abby draped her sweatshirt across her chest like a blanket and closed her eyes.

A song or two played, and Steven reached under Abby's makeshift blanket, grasping her fingers and warming them. Soon they were woven between hers as if they were made to fit together. Abby smiled and snuggled in a little closer.

Since Abby had gotten to know Steven, she'd decided that exploring a relationship with him might be rewarding.

They listened in silence for more than an hour. Their hands were still clasped, and Abby wondered if Steven had fallen asleep. She peeked out of one eye; he was watching her, a sheepish smile on his face. "Hey."

He let go of her hand, looking down to where they'd been joined.

"I'm sorry. I didn't mean to . . ."

She stretched and yawned before slipping her fingers back into his. Abby hadn't slept, but she was so relaxed. She hoped he'd been able to relax as well. She was pretty certain he needed it.

"It's okay. You're warm and toasty. It was nice."

Steven smiled down at her. "I was afraid you'd get upset at me for being too forward."

"It wasn't like you groped me. We held hands, Steven. It's fine."

"So if I were to do it again?"

"It would be fine."

"And if I did *accidentally* grope you?"

"We'd *both* know it wasn't *accidental*, and I'd have to kick your butt, injured or not. *Comprende?*"

He laughed, deep and hearty. *What a pleasant sound.* He held his hands up in surrender. "Just establishing boundaries."

"Hopefully I've made them clear?"

"Crystal."

"Good. I'm going down to the drink machine. Can I get you anything?" Abby stood up and smoothed her clothes. She'd heard about the rumor mill and didn't want to give the gossiping staff any ammunition.

"I'll go along if you don't mind getting the doors."

"Let's go!" She held the door as he made his way through. They entered the solarium, and Steven rolled over to the window.

Abby bought a root beer for herself. "Steven? Do you want something? Root beer. . . cola?"

"Nothing unleaded."

Abby laughed. "So Coke? Or do you want a Mountain Dew?"

"Mmm, Dew sounds great."

She carried their bottles to where he was sitting. Abby opened hers and took a sip. She held Steven's out to him, but he stared at her. "What?"

"Would you like to go up to our roof for a while? The flowers should be in bloom."

Steven and Abby hadn't been there in a few weeks, and while she liked their weekend outings, Abby had wanted to see their roof bursting with color. *Our roof.*

"Sure."

Steven took the sodas and stuffed them into the sides of his chair. "After you," he said with a flourishing gesture of his hands.

Abby led the way through the doors and followed the maze of the hospital passageways. She remembered, not all that long ago, when she had no idea how to find her way, but now she was an expert at navigating the corridors.

When Abby opened the door, she gasped in surprise. Immediately, her senses were bombarded with the scents, the sounds, the warmth. So she said the one thing any teacher with an undergrad degree in English would say. "Wow."

"Pretty awesome, isn't it?"

"Breathtaking." As she walked the paths, she stopped to dip her head and smell flowers along the way. Roses and beautiful vines covered trellises which were bursting with morning glories. It was simply amazing. The soothing flow of the fountain could be heard from one end of the garden to the other. Like a child in some magical garden, Abby twirled in circles with her eyes closed and her arms outstretched.

Abby heard Steven roll up behind her. She opened her eyes, and he held out his hand. "Come with me?"

Abby walked along, her fingers entwined with Steven's; Steven's pace matched her gait.

They stopped at a raised bed of flowers. Like the rest of the garden, the bed was beautifully manicured. "We've gotten so much enjoyment out of this place. I wanted to give something back."

Abby didn't understand until her gaze landed on a brass plaque that had been mounted on a small granite rock. "In loving memory of Steve and Grace Maxwell."

"You did this? It's lovely."

Steven's cheeks flushed. "Yeah, the hospital auxiliary accepts donations to help defray the cost of caring for the garden."

"That's so cool. I didn't know they did that."

He looked across the rooftop to a wooden bench that sat next to a blue hydrangea bush. "That bench over there recently got a plaque as well. The couple was friends of my aunt, much older friends, who owned a pharmacy close to Logan and Sophie's home. The wife had cancer. Sophie and I saw them not long ago, but . . ."

"I'm sorry."

"Me too. It happens to the best of us though. We're all terminal . . . from the day we take our first breath."

*So true.*

Abby walked over and ran her fingers over the name on the bench. She didn't recognize it, but it had belonged to someone's soul mate. Abby never thought she'd have that, but she had begun to hope.

Life was short, and it would be much more fulfilling having someone to share it with.

Abby lowered herself to the bench and closed her eyes, allowing the warm sunshine to bathe her. Steven pulled up next to her, and they basked in the silence.

*Is that someone sitting next to me right now?*

Abby could feel herself getting drowsy when Steven began to talk.

"Brooke wants me to drop my case."

*"What? Why?"*

"Technically, I'm at fault. My insurance company would be within their legal rights to come after me for damages—make me compensate the driver for the value of the car."

"Didn't *she* hit you?"

"Yes, but—"

"But what? What could you have possibly done wrong?"

"When the collision occurred, I was mid-block."

"That shouldn't matter. Don't pedestrians always have the right of way?"

"Unfortunately, no. Because I was not crossing the roadway at an intersection, I was required to yield."

"But didn't you say you were unable to access the intersection because of construction work?"

"That's true, but the city can't be considered negligent when there's proof they were in the process of working to become ADA compliant."

"They have to find someone at fault! This isn't fair!"

Steven chuckled sardonically. "Now you sound like my uncle."

"And this is why he was so upset this morning."

"I've never seen him as mad as he was when I told Brooke I won't be pursuing the case. It'll be up to the insurance companies to hammer out the details and decide what my liability is in the whole mess.

"Logan wants everyone held accountable: the city for not having adequate curb cuts but also for having the streets torn up because they were installing them and the woman driving the car for reckless endangerment because the legal team determined she should have seen me with enough time to stop. He wants to place the blame anywhere except where it belongs."

"They call these things an accident for a reason . . ."

"I look at it this way. . . . I'm recovering. Even if I pursued this, and the driver was found negligent in some way, she's a single parent. What could I take from her that I don't already have?"

"Maybe Logan will accept your decision once he has time to cool off?"

"I don't know, Abby. I've never seen him so angry. He threatened to have me declared incompetent so he could abuse the POA and file a suit on my behalf. That's when I threatened to rescind the power of attorney. He was very upset when he left here."

"Wow."

"I think Sophie will be able to unruffle his feathers, but the next few days are going to be uncomfortable for all of us."

"I wish there was something I could do to make this easier for you."

"Don't you see, Abby? You already have." He reached up toward her face, and Abby stayed perfectly still. His palm touched her cheek, and she leaned into the warmth of it. She placed her hands on the armrests of his chair so she could support herself. He pulled her closer so they were at eye level. "May I kiss you, Abby?"

Abby's throat went dry, and she couldn't find words. She swallowed and nodded.

Her eyes fluttered closed, and she let Steven guide her. She felt the warmth of his breath on her face, and she licked her lips. He smelled delicious. His soft lips brushed over hers, ever so lightly.

Abby opened her eyes, and his beautiful face—the face of an angel—was right in front of her. She'd never seen him look so at peace. Leaning in again, he brushed her lips with his before releasing her, breaking the spell.

Abby took a deep breath, and a chill made her shiver. She'd been kissed before, but it was never anything like that. Steven chuckled. "That was nice."

"I think I'd like to try that again, Dr. Chandler."

"That could be arranged, Miss Harris."

He reached out and took her hand. "Come on, let's go inside."

"But . . ."

"Someone is bound to come looking for me soon." He glanced up at the long row of windows.

"They all witnessed our first kiss. Let's not give them too much to gossip about."

Abby drew in a breath and sighed. "Okay."

She led Steven back to his room where they found Sydney sitting in the corner, reading a magazine. She smiled when they came in but went back to her reading.

"I wanted to share the garden with you one last time, Abby."

"What do you mean? You're getting released?"

He nodded, grinning.

"You're getting released! Oh my gosh! That's incredible. When?"

"There's someone being discharged from rehab this week. As soon as the bed opens up, I'm outta here."

Abby held her hand over her pounding heart. "Do your parents know?"

Steven's voice was quiet when he said, "I never got the chance."

"So what does this mean for you? How much longer till you can go home?"

"They say six to eight weeks. It'll depend on my progress. I wish I'd be able to lose the long casts before I get transferred, but that's doubtful. Once they come off, I imagine about six weeks of therapy. My goal is to be home by my birthday."

"When's your birthday?"

Sydney piped up. "June fifth. He'll be thirty-four. Please plan on coming to his party."

"No parties, Sydney."

Steven's cousin laughed evilly.

"I mean it."

Sydney crossed her fingers behind her back and winked at Abby. "Promise."

"I'm serious, Syd."

"Understood."

"So where's rehab?"

Abby was surprised to learn that it was a local facility near her own neighborhood.

"Wow! I was afraid I wouldn't be able to see you when you moved. You'll be closer to my house and my work!"

"It's a great facility. I can come and go whenever I want to. However, the food probably isn't any better."

"Speaking of which, I should go. I have to take the bus to the grocery store. If I don't leave soon, I'll be riding home in the dark."

Steven sighed. "I understand. May I walk you to the elevator?"

"I'd like that."

When Abby stood to go, Sydney excused herself and went into Steven's bathroom.

When the faucet came on, Steven took Abby's hand and said, "I'm going to kiss you again, Miss Harris. Is that all right?"

Abby giggled and nodded. Steven took her face in his hands, pulling her close. The kiss was sweet and chaste, but it made Abby's heart pound and her head spin.

When the water stopped, Steven drew in a loud breath. "Okay, we were walking you to the elevator if I remember correctly."

He flipped on his chair, and Abby followed him into the corridor, walking side by side to the elevator. Steven reached for her hand. "Thank you for today. It had the potential for disaster, but it didn't turn out that way."

Abby licked her lips. "I had a nice day too. Thank you." The elevator dinged and Abby stepped inside. Steven was still sitting there wearing a big smile when the door closed.

When Abby was safely inside the empty elevator, she squealed. If smooching him on the lips left her feeling like this, Abby didn't know if she could handle anything more. For someone who claimed to be sexually repressed, Steven was an amazing kisser.

As she sat waiting under the bus shelter, Abby's phone chirped.

Abby laughed out loud when she read the message.

SEE YOU TOMORROW?

OKAY.

# Chapter Twenty

Abby quickly fell into a restless sleep, but in slumber she found herself wandering a dark, deserted street. In the distance, Abby saw something traveling toward her on the sidewalk. As the object grew closer, Abby recognized the wheelchair and its operator—Steven Chandler, in all his glory—decked out in slacks, a crisp, white shirt, and a leather jacket. He sat tall in his chair, legs bent without casts. She could hear him humming to himself, and he smiled and dipped his head but continued on as if the action was nothing more than a simple pleasantry.

Abby called out as he rolled off a curb mid-block with no opposing ramp. Dream Steven rode in the street. In the distance, a car traveling far too fast careened toward Steven as he rolled along. Abby frantically tried to get his attention, but she stood helplessly as Steven barreled directly into the path of disaster.

Abby watched in horror as Steven swerved to the far left, pushing as close to the parked cars as he could. *He looks so small! It's only a dream, Abby. The car will stop! It has to!*

Abby let out a bloodcurdling scream as the two collided. She watched Steven's body wrap around the bumper of the vehicle before he was thrown past her like a rag doll. Steven's anguished cries filled Abby's head as the vehicle continued on as if nothing had occurred.

*He needs an ambulance!*

Fumbling with the zipper, Abby reached into her coat pocket for her cell phone and found nothing but a gaping hole. She frantically searched the other pocket but found it the same.

Steven lay crumpled on the ground, the metal frame of his wheelchair ensnaring his body. Abby knelt in a rapidly growing puddle as Steven's lifeblood slipped away. Taking his face in her hands, Abby looked into his eyes and begged him to hold on.

The street was deathly quiet except for their screams. *We need help! I can't leave him!* Abby's hands and clothing were covered with blood. With no other way to save Steven's life, Abby screamed and screamed until she was jolted out of her tortured sleep.

❖　❖　❖

Leaning over the side of her bed, Abby grabbed her trash can and vomited. Gasping for air, she lay back and tried to calm her racing heart.

*It was only a dream. Get a grip, Abby! Only a dream . . .*

Abby rubbed her face with clammy hands. Her clothing was sweat-soaked, the sheets wrapped around her legs. She looked at the clock. *Three a.m. No way I'm going back to sleep. It's too late to call anyone to check on him.*

With shaking hands, Abby pulled out her phone and typed a quick text, sending it off to a hospital room a few miles away, praying somehow he would answer.

Psst! You awake?

No, I'm sleeping, silly girl. Are you awake?

I need to hear your voice. Call me?

The phone rang immediately. "Abby? What's wrong?"

Breathlessly, Abby tried to explain. "Dreams. No, not dreams. Nightmares." She shuddered as the bloody scene flashed before her eyes.

"Are you all right?"

Abby realized the images her mind had conjured up were probably closer to real life than she'd ever want to come. *Am I? It doesn't feel like it.*

"I needed to hear your voice." There was no way she would ever tell him what she'd seen. The images had been so real . . . and the blood. Abby's fingers felt sticky from it, and almost compulsively, she wanted to wash her hands even though she knew they were clean.

When Steven yawned, Abby apologized. "I'm sorry I bothered you."

"You could never be a bother. I'm glad you texted me. I hope it helped ease your mind."

"You have no idea."

"I hope you can get back to sleep."

"I think I'll get up."

"Put your headphones in, and listen to something classical."

"Can't sleep with headphones. I'll strangle myself."

"How about I sing to you? Are you in bed?"

"Yes."

"Lay back and put the phone to your ear."

As Abby put the phone under her head, she could hear him already humming a tune. Listening, Abby found it hauntingly familiar. As she drifted off, she recognized it as the piece he'd been humming as he passed her on the street in the dream.

The nightmare shook Abby to her core. Seeing him so vulnerable, so seriously injured was something she'd never get out of her head even if it was only a nightmare. The thought of losing Steven was incomprehensible.

*I'm falling so hard.*

❖    ❖    ❖

Abby tumbled out of bed, feeling like she hadn't slept a wink. It was nearly noon before she arrived at the hospital, feeling hung over from the worst night's sleep she'd endured in years.

Abby's rational side knew everything would be fine, but she crept through the doorway to Steven's hospital room half afraid she'd find a complete stranger in his bed. Relief washed over her to find Steven sitting up in his chair, appearing happy and healthy.

Being around him was a rush she could feel washing over her every time she entered the hospital and made her way to the fourth floor. Being away from him left her painfully craving more.

*I want the kind of relationship that makes me feel the way I feel when we're together.*

They had both been hurt and had endured painful breakups, but it was time to leave the past where it belonged and move into the future. *I'm ready to take the initiative today if I need to!*

It appeared Steven had something on his mind as well. "Come in, Abby. Good *afternoon.*" It was a relief to see him happy even if it was at her expense. Perhaps the decision to drop the case was cathartic for Steven. The change in his demeanor was palpable.

A shiny new laptop and a stack of file folders were on Steven's over-bed table.

"What's all this? Back to work already?"

"Please, sit down. I've wanted to share something with you for a while, but I wasn't sure if you'd be receptive to what I'd like to discuss, but time is of the essence."

"You aren't hoping to convince me to investigate those drug therapies you're intent on me trying?"

Steven laughed. "I'll leave that one be for now."

"Okay, I'm game. What's up?"

"How's the apartment hunt going? Are you still hoping to move?"

Abby dropped into a chair next to him. "It's not going well at all. Either I find something nice, but I can't afford it, or I can afford it, and it's a real dive. I'm losing hope."

"That might be a good thing . . . I think."

"I find it extremely frustrating."

"I'd like to ask you something, but I need you to hear me out before you say anything, okay?"

"Sure."

"I'm building a house. It's completely accessible.

"I was wondering . . . would you be interested in moving in with me?"

Abby gasped. What? "I, uh, I couldn't impose like that."

He put his finger to her lips. "Abby . . . please . . . let me finish."

"Okay."

"Sydney has offered to provide live-in assistance until I regain my independence, but once she leaves, I think my family would be more at ease if I wasn't entirely on my own. Syd has started seeing Spencer again, and I don't want her to feel obligated to stay longer than she'd like."

"Why does that name sound familiar? Does he work here?"

"Yes. He's a paramedic."

"That's it! He brought me in when I was paralyzed. Man—he's cute."

Steven's jaw clenched, and his brow furrowed.

*Is he jealous?* "Sorry, I didn't mean to interrupt."

"Where was I?"

"You were right at the part where you suggested it would be a huge favor on my part if I moved in so you can convince me to accept your extremely generous but impossible offer."

"Right." Steven chuckled and ran his hands through his hair. "Was I really that transparent?"

"Uh, yeah."

Steven hung his head, but when he finally met Abby's gaze, he was smiling again.

"Look, I have a brand new house that's more than large enough for two people. You'd have your own room. I'd never try to pressure you into anything you're not comfortable with. You said yourself that you've been looking for something more accessible. This is in a safe neighborhood in a gated community. You could bring your own stuff, anything you wanted. It would be cheaper in the long run than renting. Would you please *consider* it?"

Abby stood and paced the perimeter of Steven's room. *It would be wonderful not to have to worry about housing, especially if I have another flare. It would be fun to live with Steven, but what would happen if something goes sour? Is it an ethics violation if someone from the hospital finds out? What if he wants to bring a random girl home? Can I handle that? What if I want to bring a date home? We are, after all, still only friends.*

"I don't know. It's a huge step, and there's a lot to consider."

"Like what? I'd think it would solve so many problems for you." Steven spoke as if it was such a simple solution. Then he grew quiet, allowing Abby to voice her concerns, and when she was finished, Steven let out the breath he'd been holding.

"I'mnot your doctor, and I agree the situation *would* be unethical *if I were.* If you had a bad spell, I'd offer you advice but only if you asked for it. I promise not to stick my nose in your business. As far as whether your housing situation would be stable if we had a disagreement, we could sign a lease for a predetermined length of time. I won't throw you out if we argue, and you don't have to worry about random girls. That's never occurred before, and it's not going to start now. I told you, *I don't date.* If I were to make an exception, it would be with you—no one else. Please consider the offer. The house is nearing completion and should be ready by the time I'm released. While you're considering this, would you at least like to see where I'll be living?"

"Sure, I'd love to."

Steven pulled out brochures from the developer, explaining the homes they were building in the development.

Abby smiled. "I heard about this development. The land was donated for residences that adopt Universal Design."

Steven spread out a map. "This one is mine. It's a T-shaped ranch with an open floor plan. I can't wait till you see it." Steven swiped his finger across the mousepad, and his laptop came to life. He clicked the mouse, and a video began. Sophie was asking questions, and a gentleman responded as they drove along in a vehicle. The homes were nice, the neighborhood well kept. Abby noticed that the road signs took them out near Long Island Sound in East Haven.

The screen went blank for a minute, but the audio continued, and suddenly the camera panned across the front of a gorgeous home. The bottom half of the exterior wall was mountain stone, and the upper half was a lighter gray siding. Redwood trim added to the rustic charm. It was easy to picture Steven living there.

The sidewalk rolled right up to the front door with a no-step entrance. When the door opened, the interior was spacious. Abby immediately thought *art gallery*, even though the walls were still white drywall, and the floors were plywood.

As they viewed each room, Steven would tell her what they were. He didn't hesitate to say "your room" as they looked at one of the bedrooms. Abby wasn't prepared to move into his home, but her heart sped up when she realized he had already set aside space for her.

Abby gasped when she saw the kitchen. The linoleum was installed and she could envision where each cabinet would go.

"What an amazing kitchen! I'll at least agree to come over and cook so you don't starve."

"Thanks."

Steven started the video again, and it took them out onto a concrete patio and panned the back yard before it ended.

"I don't know, Steven. Your home is beautiful, but there's a lot to consider. Please give me time and I promise I'll think about it."

"I'll try not to harass you. Although I can't make any promises."

"Assuming I did agree to this, how would expenses work?"

"Simple. You wouldn't have any."

"Wrong, Chandler! That's a deal-breaker. You've gotta do better than that. I'm not a kept woman. I've been self-sufficient for nearly ten years. I'd have to pay my own way if I were to accept your offer."

"How about I pay the mortgage, and we split the other expenses?"

"We split the mortgage in half."

"No way, Abby. It's my house, and I refuse to allow you to invest in my mortgage."

"Well, I refuse to stay with you for free."

"What if I paid the mortgage, and we split the utilities equally?

"I can't let you pay the entire mortgage, and don't forget groceries. Do we each get our own food and keep it separate, or do we split it and take turns cooking?"

He snorted. "Not if you value your life! You don't want me to cook. How about I pay the mortgage, and you buy our food and cook it? As we agreed, utilities would be split equally. Deal?"

"Deal!"

*Wait!*

*No!*

*What have I done?*

Steven's smile lit the room.

"Hey! *No fair!* You tricked me! I didn't agree to anything!"

He chuckled evilly. "Oh, but you *did*, Abby, or should I call you roomie?"

"You can't hold me to it. I need time to think it over. This is a big step for me."

He held his stomach as deep belly laughs rang through the room. "I wouldn't try to pressure you into something you're not comfortable with, but I think it would be a blast. I'd love to have companionship. You're fun to be around, and I can't think of anyone I'd rather share my home with. And what I said earlier? I don't expect you to be my nursemaid."

"I wouldn't mind helping you if you needed a hand."

"I don't need much. You might have to help me put on a pair of socks or pick up the TV remote from time to time. I don't want to bother Sydney for something trivial. She's agreed to stay a few weeks till I get my bearings. We'll probably taper off services as I regain my independence. I won't have you do personal care for me. I have a nurse for that reason. In the same sense, if you ever needed anything, she'd already be there. I know she'd never hesitate to help you."

"I'll think about it. I promise I will." Abby knew she would be having another sleepless night. So many things ran through her mind. The house was gorgeous. Having a roommate wouldn't be terrible.

Abby loved to cook, and apparently he could not, so that beautiful kitchen would be her territory. Cohabitating with Steven would get Abby into a safer neighborhood and out of a place with steps. No matter what condition she was in due to her MS, Abby would be able to navigate the house easily.

And the downside of this was . . .

*I can't think of one.*

But that kiss. They crossed a line yesterday, and while they hadn't had any other physical contact today, if Abby had anything to do with it, they would kiss again before she left. That was the thing that would make it messy. There was no way Abby was ready to jump into living together *as a couple*.

It was as if he could read her mind.

"Look, I can understand if yesterday has made you uncomfortable or if you think I decided this because of it. I wanted to ask you this last week, but I didn't have all the information. Sophie dropped off this stuff and my new laptop this morning. I'm not trying to coerce you into a physical relationship or lure you into a bad situation. I'm trying to offer you something that I see only as a win-win situation. Please consider it. I don't need your answer right away."

"Would you be willing to give me a week to decide? I can let you know by next Saturday."

"That's fine. I promise not to pressure you while you're deciding."

Abby stood up. "I've got homework to grade and lesson plans to write for this week. I should go."

Steven grabbed her hand and pulled her down to his level. He looked up and winked. Abby leaned in and they kissed. Their lips smacked once, twice, but the third time, they lingered a little longer, and when he hesitated, she licked his lower lip with her tongue. His flesh was plump and soft, and soon his tongue was caressing hers as they melted into one another. Abby snaked her hand into his hair and his was on her waist, his thumb caressing the sliver of skin above her jeans.

"I can't wait till we're living together."

"No pressure, Steven! You promised."

Abby went home and tried to concentrate on her schoolwork to no avail. She decided to make it an early night and look over the lesson plans the next day while she ate breakfast.

As she was futilely trying to count sheep, her phone buzzed.

HAVE YOU DECIDED YET? I HAVEN'T BUGGED YOU FOR HOURS!

YOU AGREED TO A WEEK.

I KNOW, BUT I COULD DIE OF ANTICIPATION.

YOU COULD . . . BUT YOU WON'T.

I wish you'd decide already.

Okay.

Okay? Okay what?

Okay. I'll do it.

Really?

Yes, really. Can I please go to sleep now?

Absolutely! :-)

Goodnight, Steven.

Goodnight, roomie!

*What have I gotten myself into?*

*But the kiss! That kiss was incredible!*

# Chapter Twenty-one

Spring 2010

Like a triathlete winning a marathon, Steven rolled out of the gym and raised his arms over his head in triumph.

*Today's the day! I'm breaking out of this joint!*

Steven was not ungrateful in any way. When he'd had his emergency, his hospital was the place he needed to be in order to remain alive, but week after week, lying in a bed brought on bouts of depression and self-deprecation. By the time Fate thrust Abigail Harris into his path the second time around, Steven was ready to move forward with his life.

In the beginning, Steven had trouble accepting whatever Abby and he had become, but Abby was different from the others who attempted to enter his orbit. She was snarky and sweet, and she never used her womanly wiles to attract his attention. She was a contradiction to everything Steven thought he knew about the female population, and he truly cherished the moments she shared with him.

His only hope was that she found similar qualities in him, and that one day, she would let him be her knight in shining armor—even if that suit of armor came with wheels and a joystick.

Steven would willingly go into battle for her, leading her, or if she chose, alongside her.

Abby had quickly become his everything.

Abby seemed hesitant to put a label on what they shared, and that was okay. For her, he'd wait forever, the same way she'd waited for him when he let self-doubt creep in—with patience and anticipation. *Because Abigail Harris is someone worthy of being cherished and loved.*

❖   ❖   ❖

Steven's old Econoline van was long gone, replaced by a newer version that was purchased when Steven first came back East. Getting behind the wheel had been overwhelming, and the van sat, for the most part, unused in the Chandler garage. But today, pulling out of the hospital parking garage, it represented the freedom Steven was ready to celebrate.

*I've got a lot of work to do.*

Steven was determined to realize the goals he'd outlined while lying in that hospital bed. He sat tall in his chair, patted the breast pocket of his track jacket, and smiled at the familiar crinkle of paper. He didn't need a list; he knew each line by heart.

*Independence: regain enough function to be self-sufficient at home and in the community.*

*Transportation: purchase a vehicle modified for my individual needs, and learn to become confident in my driving abilities so I can provide safe, reliable transportation for Abby and myself.*

*Assertiveness: take the reins guiding the insurance company who holds the purse strings regarding my medical needs.*

Mr. Reese, the attorney who'd represented Steven against the logging company in 1993, had recently retired, but he'd worked tirelessly for the arrangement which left the medical portion of Steven's settlement open. This meant the logging company was required to cover any and all future medical expenses Steven would ever incur. When they'd learned his two-year-old wheelchair had been destroyed beyond repair in an accident where liability could possibly be placed elsewhere, they attempted to reject Steven's claim for a new chair. Brooke had declared she would straighten them out, but Steven was ready to begin speaking for himself.

*Reconsideration: accept the money in my trust fund as the blessing it is.*

Even though the trust was fully funded, Steven balked at touching one cent of it, but his parents would want him to be happy, safe, and cared for. *I have so much to be thankful for.*

# Chapter Twenty-two

Intake at the rehab facility took nearly an hour, and Steven was exhausted by the time they were done. He was looking forward to finding a bed and taking a nap.

Sydney unpacked Steven's things while Sophie and Logan accompanied Steven and an orderly on a short tour of the facility. When they entered the gym, one of the physical therapists stood with her hands on her hips, watching from across the room. Steven cocked his head. *Is it? Really? Oh my gosh!*

As the woman got closer, Steven began laughing. She was older, and her hair wasn't styled the same way, but Steven would have recognized his old rehab therapist anywhere.

With a huge smile, Jillian Moss came over and bent to give him a hug. "Steven Maxwell! What in the world brings you *here?*" The name struck him like lightning. It had been years since anyone called him by his birth name, and hearing it was a shock to his system.

"I tangled with a car."

"While you were driving?"

"My wheelchair."

His old friend Jillian had the same reaction most people had after learning the details of the accident—first, the surprised gasp and then the "Oh my gosh, are you okay?" followed by "I'm so sorry!"

"I've improved greatly. I was very fortunate. Hell, I'm lucky to be alive."

"I knew we were getting a new patient who had been in a wheelchair versus vehicle collision. I read in the case notes that the patient was a doctor and a research scientist . . . I never dreamed . . . Wait! You're the doctor! You're really a doctor?"

Steven felt his face begin to flame. "I am."

"I'm so glad you followed your dreams! What's with the name? I think that's what threw me off. Did you marry some girl and take her last name?" She was laughing. Steven was sure she knew it was Logan's last name although it made sense she didn't know—their paths hadn't crossed.

"I'm a neurologist with an interest in Pediatric MS, and several days a week I work in the Stem Cell Center."

"I'm feeling a little insignificant now." she smirked. "I guess you didn't waste my time after all."

Sophie piped in then. "He also created a support group at Yale for patients who are newly disabled."

"That's *you*? I've sent patients to your group. I usually talk to some girl named Karla or a guy named Mac."

Steven took his aunt's hand in his own and smiled up at her. She'd given him so much. "Aunt Sophie helped me form the group when I started my residency. Support for people with newly acquired disabilities was inadequate with no place to go for information or referrals to agencies that could help them access the equipment and services they needed. I went through it myself and understood what it was like. Some of those families have no clue where to start."

"Wow! I'm impressed. You've done good, kid." She patted his shoulder. "Would you like a tour of my gym?"

"Sure. How long have you been here?" As they began walking around, Steven took in the various contraptions and tables he'd be using daily so that he could once again be independent.

"I left Guilford around 2000, I think."

"I was at the University of San Francisco, working toward my MD in 2000."

"I saw driver's training on your intake paperwork. Didn't we address driver's ed years ago?"

"We did, but it's been a long time since I've been behind the wheel. When I went off to California, I left the van at home. It was easier to buzz across campus in my wheelchair. Somehow, between classes and rotations, I overlooked the notices from the DMV to renew my license, and eventually it lapsed." He leaned over close to Jill. "To be honest, driving in traffic was a little overwhelming. I think I need a refresher course, but I'd feel more confident having someone from your facility help me prepare for the test."

"We'll get you back on the road."

"This is a nice facility, Jill. You referred to it as your gym earlier. Are you the person in charge?"

"I got my doctorate in physical therapy years ago and opened the business with two of my friends, so technically, it's *our* gym, but I'm the only one with a degree in physical therapy, so I like to call it mine." She winked at Steven with a smile. "That doesn't mean I'm too good to get down and dirty in the gym though. I work the same as everyone else. This just means you have to answer to me."

"I can't wait to get my new electric. I guess they are delivering it here?"

"Oh! Didn't they *tell* you? It's *already* here. I didn't know if you wanted to be fit for it now, or wait till the casts come off. It's a stander, right?"

"Yeah. I know I can't stand yet, but I'd love to be using it. Recline and tilt-in-space, it'll be a relief to do my own pressure releases."

"I'm on the late shift tonight. Once everyone has had their dinner break, I'll get two of the guys to help transfer you, and I'll do your fitting. Once you're bending, we can make adjustments as needed."

"I can't wait. Once these casts come off, I'll be able to do so much more."

"I read that Dr. Wesley was your orthopedic surgeon. He has a clinic here on Monday afternoons. He'll probably X-ray you and change you into short leg casts then. We have the equipment to do everything in-house."

Steven's heart pounded. It had been so long since he'd experienced the freedom short casts would provide him. He nearly choked on his reply. "No way! I could be free of these in a few days?"

"I don't want to give you false hope, but based on the X-rays that came with you, I can almost guarantee they'll come off then."

Steven sucked in a shaky breath. *I'm finally putting this behind me.*

"Look, Steven, I've got a few things to take care of before dinner. It's great seeing all of you again even though I'm sorry it's under these circumstances. I'll come find you when we're ready to get you situated in your new chair, okay? Please make yourselves at home. This isn't a hospital. Feel free to go outside, or go to the rec room. You're free to do whatever you want, within reason." She winked at him.

"If you're leaving the premises, you need to let the receptionist know, and sign the book. Other than that, if you're scheduled for PT or driving, it's your responsibility to get yourself there on time. The rest of your day is free. I encourage you to socialize and take advantage of the occupational therapy sessions in the cafeteria although it's not mandatory. Enjoy dinner. I'll come get you in a few hours."

Jill left them in the gym. Logan had been preoccupied with the equipment, and his fingers ghosted over one of the machines. "Come on, old man. Let's go check out my room. Sydney's been up there unsupervised for an awfully long time."

They made their way back to his room to find all his things unpacked and a colorful comforter on his bed. Sydney sat in a chair next to the window, painting her nails.

"I was wondering when you were coming back! I got you a new set of bedding. I washed it at home so it's nice and soft." Steven cocked an eyebrow at her; he refused to have the staff think he was "special."

"Don't worry. I called last week and asked for a list of suggested items. A lot of people bring their own bedding." She alternated between blowing on her nails and waving her hands through the air. She touched a nail and smiled. Her perfectly manicured index finger touched a leaflet that lay on his bed. "This pamphlet says dinner will be served in a half hour. I should get going. Is there anything else you need before I leave?"

"Nope. See you tomorrow?"

"I'll be here. Have a good night."

"You too, Sydney. Tell Spence he needs to come inside next time."

"He will. He wanted to give you a chance to take care of whatever you needed without interruption." Sydney turned to Sophie and Logan. "Goodnight, guys. See you soon."

"Goodnight, Sydney," they replied in unison.

Logan rested his hand on Steven's shoulder. "Well, son, we should be heading out too. Is there anything else you need?"

"No, I'm good. I'll see you later. Thanks for everything today."

"You're welcome."

Sophie stood off to the side, waiting. She gave Steven a tight hug when Logan stepped aside.

"I love you. I can't tell you how happy it makes me to see you here today."

"Me too, Mom, and by the way, I shared pictures of the house with Abby. It's beautiful. I know 'thank you' doesn't begin to cover it. I'm still speechless. You're amazing. Thank you."

"It was my pleasure. I can't wait till the guys are done so I can get in there and put it all together." That was where Sophie truly shined, and Steven could almost feel her anticipation in the air.

"Thanks for working my mom and dad's things into your plans. I can't wait to see everything put together." It was weird referring to two women as "mom" in a few breaths, but Steven didn't have to explain to her. She knew exactly what he meant.

"It'll be gorgeous."

"Thank you. Love you."

She kissed his head and was gone.

❖   ❖   ❖

Steven considered calling dietary to ask for his tray to be delivered to his room. The intake nurse explained that the facility allowed individuals to make that request but only three times per week. The desire for solitude was understood, but socialization was part of the rehabilitation process, and the administration tried to foster an environment where people would automatically come together. Steven decided to make his way to the dining room to meet the others.

Some of the patients who sat at Steven's table were intriguing, and he enjoyed a comfortable conversation with them. There were people from all walks of life who shared one common goal at the residential facility—achieving the freedom of independence.

Dinner was served restaurant style. The dietary staff came to the table, took orders, and served delicious food. Steven relished every wonderful morsel.

True to her word, Jill sent someone to fetch him directly from the dining room. After a short time in the gym, everything had been adjusted, and Steven was sitting in his new wheelchair.

"Wesley's goal in your case notes is to have you standing and weight-bearing soon."

"I can't wait to shed these casts and get vertical again. It's going to be amazing."

Jill laughed at his enthusiasm. "I can't believe you're the same guy. I was so concerned about your outcome when I first worked with you."

"I'm so sorry, Jill. I didn't get it back then."

"I know you didn't, but I did. You were just a kid trying to muddle through a devastating situation, but I was so afraid you were going to fall through the cracks."

"Thank you for not giving up on me."

"Thank you for not giving up on you. I'm proud of you."

"I owe you so much. I try to pay it forward, helping others adapt to their circumstances."

Jill looked at her watch. "I've got a few things to wrap up before I go. I want to hear all about Dr. Chandler and what makes him tick. Can we make it a date in the morning?"

"I can't wait."

Jill laughed as she walked into her office. "I'll bring the coffee."

❖   ❖   ❖

An orderly helped Steven change before using a lift to move him into bed.

A nurse came in with Steven's meds and changed his fentanyl patch. He'd been introduced to the patch when the hospital discontinued his morphine. It was a synthetic opiate for pain, which was placed on his shoulder every three days. Steven was relieved. His dose had been lowered from one hundred to seventy-five micrograms per hour over his last few weeks in the hospital. Steven's biggest concern was getting hooked on the opiate even if it was synthetic.

Steven pulled his cell phone off the bedside table and dialed Abby's number. She picked up on the first ring.

"Steven."

"Hey, Abby."

"How are you?"

"I'm good. I made a few new friends and ran into an old one."

"Oh, that's cool. I hope the old friend isn't recuperating from an injury as well."

"No, Jill was the physical therapist who worked with me when I first became paralyzed. She kept me focused when so many things were going wrong in my life. She's a doctor here now—a co-owner of the facility."

"Is that why you chose it?"

"No, I haven't seen her in almost twenty years. We had a nice visit. She had a little surprise for me after dinner."

"What kind of surprise?"

"It's black and chrome and goes about five miles per hour. Unlike the one I've been borrowing, this one stands up. Well, it will once I can stand up, that is."

"You got your new chair? Is it more comfortable?"

"I could have slept in it tonight; I've done that in the old one. But they made me get out of it until tomorrow. I can't wait to put it through its paces."

"I'm happy for you. It sounds like it was an amazing day."

"It truly was."

"How was the house?"

"It's incredible! Sydney is free both tomorrow and Sunday if you'd like to go see it."

"Sure, I'd love to."

"I hope you love it as much as I do. I want you to be happy there. I think you'll love the kitchen. It's nearly twice as big as Sophie's."

"Seriously? No *way!*"

"For real, babe. It's *huge.* I can't wait till you see it firsthand."

Steven expected a reprimand for the term of endearment he'd blurted out, but it happened organically, and he felt warm and fuzzy inside when she didn't call him out on it. He made a mental note to be more careful even though he secretly hoped that their friendship would take a more romantic turn once they were settled in the new house.

"Let's plan for tomorrow, so if something falls through, we still have Sunday," Abby said.

"That sounds wonderful. I can't wait to go back."

Abby chuckled. "Anything else happen? Was the rest of your day all right? Did you get settled in?

"Sydney more or less unpacked me while Logan and Sophie toured the facility with me. Oh! I almost forgot to tell you!"

"What?"

"It sounds like you'll have to get me a new tat."

"You're losing the casts?"

"They're hoping to have me in short leg casts next week. I may be able to begin standing, and I can't wait. It's been months!"

"Oh, that's incredible!"

"Isn't it?" Steven yawned loudly. "I'm sorry, but I'm whooped, I guess I should go. Do you know when you're coming tomorrow?"

"What's good for you?"

"I have physical therapy from eight to ten a.m., and then I have a meeting from one to two p.m., so somewhere between the two?"

"I like the idea of ten a.m., if that's okay. I can bring coffee."

"All right. If you need a ride, call and I'll have Sydney collect you. Don't worry about coffee for me. Jill has me covered."

"Thank you, Steven. Pleasant dreams."

"Sweet dreams to you, Abby. See you tomorrow."

# Chapter Twenty-Three

Steven's heart skipped a beat when he found Abby and Sydney waiting in his room. Abby immediately wrapped her arms around him. "I love the new chair. It's kinda . . . sexy."

Steven felt the heat creeping up his neck. He brought his fist to his mouth and coughed. "I think that's the first time I've heard that one."

"No, that's wrong. It's the way you look in the chair—tall, confident, *empowered*."

Steven didn't often receive such heartfelt compliments from members of the female persuasion, and he wasn't sure how to react. He drew in a deep breath and puffed up his chest.

*No, babe, it's you that empowers me.*

He spun in a tight circle, deflecting. "This chair is easy to operate. If I appear confident or empowered, it's because this particular chair, or some incarnation of it, has been an extension of my body for more than a decade. My body has craved this chair since the day I lost it."

"I still say it's sexy." Abby's quip was bolstered with a wink. "*You're* sexy."

Sydney sat quietly and watched them interact. Her smile told Steven that she was pleased with the progression of their friendship. Steven was too. It felt . . . organic. *Does Abby feel it too?*

"So," Abby said, interrupting Steven's thoughts, "I talked with Sophie last night. She said perhaps you had some news. Is there something you want to tell me?"

Steven sighed. "I wanted to surprise you, but I guess the cat is out of the bag . . . or the leg is out of the cast, so to speak."

"Tomorrow? Have I mentioned that the kids are off for parent/teacher conferences?"

"What exactly does that mean? Isn't the teacher an integral part of a parent/teacher conference?" While Steven understood the concept, it almost seemed like Abby was suggesting she had free time.

"Well, the parents come in and meet with me. We're doing them all this week—school in the morning, conferences in the afternoon and evenings—but the students have the entire day off tomorrow, and I don't have any conferences scheduled until after dinner. I think the first one is at five p.m."

"Oh."

"Would you like me to be here with you tomorrow morning?"

"I'd like that. I have to be at X-ray at nine."

"When would you like me to arrive?"

"You can arrive whenever you like."

Sydney looked up from the book she was reading. "I can pick you up, Abby. I have to run some errands for Steven. Would that make your day easier? It's supposed to be rainy."

"Thanks, I'd appreciate that."

"Hey, Syd," Steven asked, "could you grab me some personal products as well? I don't have my own shampoo or soap. The antibacterial soap here makes my skin dry and itchy. I'd like to smell like me again. I can give you a list, if you don't mind."

"Not at all. Whatever you need."

"Thanks. Maybe you could grab some kind of snacks too—energy bars, granola, protein snacks—and a few bottles of sports drinks would be nice."

"Sure, that's no problem."

"While I love visiting with you ladies, it's going to take a while to get me loaded into the van, and I need to be back by one."

❖　❖　❖

"Up ahead on the right is the development." Steven hit the button on the remote, and the gate opened before them, allowing Sydney to pull through.

"Wow, this is an impressive neighborhood! All of these houses are visitable?"

Steven waved his hand toward the other homes. "Yep, I could enter any house in the development and access all the vital parts of the guest areas. It's a nice mixture of visitable and completely accessible."

"Which one is yours?"

They turned a corner, and Steven said, "This one is *ours*. It's your home too, Abby. I might own the house, but it's your home. That's how I want you to think of it."

Abby took off her seat belt and turned.Her face bore a serious expression.

"But it's not . . . It's yours."

"Please don't argue with me about it. I don't ever want you to feel like an outsider. I want you to be comfortable. You can do anything you want here. I want you to be yourself."

"It might take me a while to grasp that concept, but I'll try. It's gorgeous."

"It is. I was blown away yesterday."

Sydney piped up. "Yeah, and there were tears. Don't let him tell you otherwise."

"It was a very overwhelming experience for me." Steven took Abby's hand and led her up the sidewalk. He pulled up alongside the front door and punched in a code. Abby gasped when the door swung open.

*Yeah, babe, I know . . .*

Steven followed quietly as Abby took it all in. Standing in the kitchen, she turned with tears in her eyes.

"Oh, Steven . . ." she cried, "this is too much. This is—it's *way* out of my league. *You're* way out of my league." For a moment, Steven feared she was going to back out.

*Au contraire, my dear. It is you who are out of my league, but I digress. I'm too enamored with you to let you go.*

"Abby, please. You *do* belong here. I can't *wait* till you're here. It *is* an incredible house, but you need to understand. Logan has convinced me to pay for the house out of the wrongful death compensation I received from the logging company that was found at fault for my parents' deaths. The thought of touching that money has always turned my stomach, but my mom and dad would *want* this for me, to be able to move about comfortably in my own home, to realize my full potential and live independently. I have to believe that they would be happy about this. I've been frugal my entire life, but nearly dying a second time has shown me that I need to begin embracing life and enjoying what it has to offer rather than simply going through the motions. I'm not going to feel guilty about using that money to build a house that will be functional for the rest of my life."

"Ollie and Grace would be ecstatic." Sydney rubbed Steven's arm but turned to Abby as she spoke. "They wouldn't want Steven to live here all alone. They would have loved you, Abby. Grace would be plotting away with Sophie to try to get the two of you together." When Steven looked at Abby, she was blushing.

"Come on, let's look around." The rooms were big and nondescript. Steven could tell Abby was trying to picture the finished project. He couldn't wait to see it either. Their home, full of furniture, looking lived in . . .

"I love all the dark woodwork. And this fireplace? The stone is gorgeous. I don't know if I'll ever leave this room."

*Oh, just wait until you see what we have planned.*

They strolled along the wide hallway where Steven pointed out the study and their bedrooms. They entered the study first. "This was the third bedroom. I'm going to make it a home office. There's no reason we can't share."

A few steps down the hallway, Steven stopped outside a door.

"Go ahead, Abby. Check it out."

Abby stepped inside, and the first thing she did was walk over to sit on the window seat. It was surrounded on either side by beautiful built-in bookshelves. "These windows are great. The yard is going to be beautiful! And the bookshelves—I love this window seat; I could get lost here for hours." She sighed. "Oh, Steven, you have an *incredible* room."

Sydney laughed and Steven pulled up next to Abby and leaned in close. "No, Abby, you have an incredible room. I know you love to read, so I thought you'd like this little area to relax and have a sanctuary of your own. I won't ever come in here uninvited."

Abby rubbed her face and sniffled. When she opened her mouth, a squeak came out. "Mine?"

"Yes, yours. Now who's sniffling? Shame on you for laughing at *me*."

Abby put her fists on her hips and stuck out her tongue.

Steven threw back his head and laughed. *Living with you is going to be so much fun.*

"Come on, let me show you your bathroom. I want your opinion."

"My *what?*" Her fists were still on her hips, but now she looked angry.

Steven held his hands up in surrender. "I didn't do it; it was on the floor plan when Sophie brought the builder over. You'll grow to love it."

There was *no way* he'd tell her that it had only been a half bath before Sophie reworked the plans with Aaron to make sure Abby had a full-sized, fully accessible bathroom identical to his own.

Steven showed her the markings on the floor where the fixtures would be.

"This is . . . wow, Steven. I don't know what to say."

"Are there any changes you want made? Is everything all right with the layout? I tried to take our situations into consideration and what our needs might be a few years down the road. I'd rather be practical and make these decisions now than face a major remodel in a few years."

"That makes sense, but I'm perfectly happy the way it is. You don't have to make any changes for me."

They wandered back into the hallway. Steven pointed across to his room. "That one is mine— same sized room, same layout in the bath, but my window faces the street."

"You gave me the nicer view? But why?"

*Because I sense you're going to act more like a visitor in the beginning, and you deserve to have a retreat to call your own.*

He shrugged. "I work crazy hours, and I wouldn't get as much enjoyment out of it as you will."

He thought he heard her growl low in her throat. Before she became argumentative, Steven rushed to move things along. "Come on, you didn't get to explore the kitchen yet."

❖  ❖  ❖

Abby strolled through the kitchen, letting her fingers trail over big boxes and random cabinets as she walked. "And I'm the cook, right?"

Steven nodded.

"Is this like . . . my area? I'm in charge of the kitchen? *This* kitchen?" He could hear the excitement in her voice, and Steven felt his body relax. *You're adorable.*

"It's the only one we have, Abby." Steven laughed. "Yes, you have free rein over the kitchen. Anything you need for this kitchen, let my aunt know. I'd like you to look at appliances."

"I don't feel comfortable choosing your appliances."

"You're talking to a man who thinks Hot Pockets cooked in a microwave are gourmet. I'm counting on you to save me from myself. We could go shopping together, but I know nothing about appliances. I'll buy anything that makes your eyes light up, so either way . . ."

Abby conceded. "Okay, you win, but I have my own gadgets, and I refuse to let you or Sophie buy anything personal for my room. I've got my own things—furniture, towels, bedding, you know . . ."

"I respect that, but for the rest of the house, we need things like curtains and throw rugs, towels, bedding . . . Please understand, Abby, I lived in either a dorm or a shared apartment for almost fifteen years. I have nothing personal to contribute. You'll have the advantage of knowing where your things will look good before you move in. I'm counting on you ladies to make the place comfortable. I know I'll be happy with it."

Steven took her hand. "Come on. Check out the deck and patio." Abby followed him to the fire pit and sat on one of the benches.

"This is so inviting," she said. "I can imagine spending evenings around a fire, roasting marshmallows. Oh, Steven, we can make s'mores!" Steven pulled between the benches and extended his hand. Abby squeezed it and smiled.

*She's delightful. I wish I were brave enough to tell her what she means 2to me, but I rushed things once and almost threw this all away. I won't do that again.*

Neither of them was ready for fast and furious. A nice, steady, slow burn that would eventually catch flame was exactly what they both desired. The little touches, the chaste pecks of a week or so ago were growing into something far more exciting. Their friendship was happily moving forward. *It feels good.*

Steven knew real life would be different. When they were together, he enjoyed indulging in Abby's undivided attention, but he also knew she was a self-professed workaholic who brought materials home, working long into the night throughout the week.

Steven hoped to return to work soon. His life had always revolved around his career, and he wasn't sure he knew how to work a nine-to-five shift and simply come home. In the past when he was done working, he *deliberately* found more things to do because he had nothing and *no one* to come home to.

*I can't even keep a goldfish alive. What if I'm a terrible boyfriend?*

*But Abby seems happy. We'll be okay. We'll be more than okay . . . I can't wait to come home.*

# Chapter Twenty-four

When Abby arrived the next morning, Steven was sitting in his chair, freshly bathed and shaved. When he wasn't fidgeting with his iPod, he was fiddling with his chair controls, tilting the seat, moving back and forth in front of the window. When their eyes met, he stopped in place, and Abby gave him a fierce hug.

*Don't be nervous. It'll be okay.* She inhaled deeply. *You smell incredible. Focus, Abby!*

"Hey, you okay?" she asked.

"I will be. I'm a little nervous."

"Why are ya nervous? You've done this before."

"I have, but I dunno. This is a big step. Losing the long casts will open up so many rehab opportunities. It's not that I'm afraid of the work. The busier I am here, the sooner I'll be able to go home."

"So what is it? Is there some way I can help?"

"Nah. It's—I've got myself so hyped up. What if Wesley comes in this morning and takes a look at the X-rays and decides I'm not ready?"

"If you're not ready, you're not ready. He transferred you to a rehab facility because you're ready. Can you lean forward for me?"

Steven tilted the chair back showing her where to find the connectors. "I'm a little top heavy right now until I recondition my core."

"This thing is kind of difficult to unhook. I think I'll . . . Never mind. It was a silly idea."

"No, it's all right. What were you going to do?"

"I thought a backrub would distract you. I don't want to do something dangerous though. I knew the harness was to help support you, but it never occurred to me that it was more for safety than to ensure your positioning."

"A backrub would be incredible. Leave the harness off. I have a seat belt and a safety bar. I'm not going anywhere. The harness is coming off soon anyway. I can't get myself out of the chair with it on."

Abby walked around to the side of his chair and began rubbing his neck, working her way down as low as she could go. She massaged back up to his shoulders and down each arm.

When Abby went back to Steven's neck, she massaged up into his hairline, and it sounded like he was purring. She used her thumbs around his ears until she had made it all the way to his forehead.

When Abby stopped, he groaned. "That felt incredible." Sitting in a chair facing Steven, Abby took Steven's hand in her own, working the knuckles and fingers with lotion the way she'd seen Sydney do. Steven sighed deeply and closed his eyes. When the lotion was worked in, Abby took the other hand and repeated her actions. "You're incredibly talented, Miss Harris. Thank you."

As Abby was about to acknowledge his comment, her stomach growled loudly. "Oh, excuse me."

He began laughing. "Still neglecting that thing, I see." He pulled the bedside table over and lifted several lids on his tray to reveal a virtually untouched breakfast. "Is there anything here you'd enjoy?"

"You didn't eat? *Why*, Steven? You've still got plenty of time."

"The last time I saw my X-rays, I tossed my cookies. Thanks, but no thanks. Please, take anything you like from my tray. I promise, we'll get lunch together afterward." He pushed a small plate with a huge muffin toward Abby and continued to talk.

"It was the day I finally came out of the body cast. Oh, Abby, I've never seen anything like it. I don't have a weak stomach, but seeing those X-rays from the accident . . . I don't understand how I'm still alive."

"I'm so sorry I wasn't there for you. You're fortunate to have had such wonderful doctors."

"Everyone at the hospital did everything possible to help me. I wouldn't be here if it wasn't for the team who worked on me. I am *very* fortunate."

Abby walked over to the sink, washed her hands, and picked up the muffin to cut it in two. She nibbled on one piece while she raised the other half to Steven's mouth. He took a tentative bite and chewed. As she fed him, he continued to nibble. When it was gone, Abby began pulling a small bunch of grapes apart. One by one he let her feed him.

"Thanks for sharing your breakfast with me."

"Thanks for being here." He reached up with both hands, and she let him pull her in for a kiss. He tasted sweet and fruity, and Abby caught herself licking her lips when he pulled away. Someone coughed behind them, and she turned to see an orderly standing in the doorway. "Steven, they're ready for you."

Steven waved his hand toward the door with a flourish. "After you, Miss Harris."

Abby stepped through the door and stayed to the left side of the corridor. When Steven came out of the room, he took her right hand, and they strolled along, their hands swinging like carefree school kids.

When they made it to the treatment room, Steven motioned for Abby to go first. "Oh, no. Let them get you situated. I'll wait right over here."

The room was spacious, but with the cast table, a huge portable x-ray machine, and Steven's chair, there wasn't room to accommodate spectators.

Reclined, Steven's chair was as flat as a table. The orderly and two nurses gathered around him. They counted and lifted, and as smooth as a hot knife through butter, they slid Steven onto the cast table.

Abby jumped when one of the nurses touched her arm. "I put a chair in the room for you. I'm sorry it's so crowded. When they do the

X-rays, you'll have to step outside."

"Thanks."

Abby walked to the only chair in the room.

Steven turned his head. "Abby?"

"Yeah?"

"It feels like you're in Siberia. You wanna hang out with me till he gets here?" Abby hurried across the room.

"Relax, it'll be okay." Abby ran her fingers through Steven's hair. His eyes were closed, and he was humming. She heard footsteps and looked up to see an attractive man in his mid-forties. He held his hand out. "I'm Doc Wesley. You must be Abby." He winked at her and gestured toward his patient. "He sleeping?"

Steven opened his eyes. "Nah, feigning sleep to see what you were gonna say behind my back." They both laughed. Steven's nervousness seemed to dissipate with the entrance of his physician.

"So are we gonna do this, buddy? I know you're ready to get rid of these casts so you can get down to business."

"I thought I'd have them another two weeks. This was a surprise."

Wesley turned to Abby. "I understand you're the support system today. I apologize there's no room for you to sit closer to Steven . . ."

"I don't want to get in your way." She leaned down, giving Steven a kiss on the forehead, then whispered into his ear, "I'm only a few steps away. Good luck." She gave his hand a quick squeeze.

Steven and Wesley conversed about rehab and the happy coincidence that Steven's first rehab therapist was again working with him. Abby could tell that his doctor genuinely cared about Steven as both a patient and a friend.

Suddenly, the room became a flurry of activity. The nurse who had made a place for Abby came in and stood across the table from the doctor. She picked up several items, handing one to the doctor and placing one on Steven's face. When she turned, Abby could see that she, too, was wearing safety glasses.

*Oh! Of course.*

The nurse moved to the foot of the table and stabilized Steven's right leg. The orthopedic surgeon worked his way down one side and then moved to the other. Back and forth he moved and sawed. After nearly ten minutes, he stopped sawing and picked up a weird-looking pair of pliers. He inserted it into the crevice he made, and Abby watched in amazement as he worked from Steven's groin, then down his leg toward his foot. *Pop, pop, pop . . .*

Soon, the doctor traded sides with the nurse and did the same thing working from the opposite side of the table. Several more pops were followed by a loud hurrah.

Steven raised himself up with his elbows as Wesley stood over him, snipping and cutting. He lifted the long top half of the cast away and deposited it into the trash can. The lower half of the cast followed.

Abby watched from her perch as Steven's leg was washed and gently patted dry. The garbage can and the instrument table were rolled away, and a girl wearing a lead apron entered the room. Abby stepped into the hallway until she saw the girl leave. When Abby stepped back inside the room, Steven was covered from his toes to his chin.

"Hey, you cold?"

"Not too bad."

"Why are you all bundled up, then?"

"I'm not ready for you to see."

"Hey," she said quietly, "I'm here for you, willing to be whatever you need. If you don't want me to see, I won't look."

They chatted until Wesley returned. Without prelude, he flipped the switch on a light box and clipped a series of X-rays up on the screen. Abby could see every piece of hardware from Steven's thigh to his toes.

"All right, Steven. Short leg cast on this one for a few more weeks. I'll reassess it in three, and we'll decide then. What color we goin' with?" Wesley asked.

Steven looked at Abby and smiled. "Can we get more superheroes?"

"They're in my bag; I've got the blow dryer too."

Steven looked at the rolls of tape and smiled. "Bright blue, please."

Abby went back to her perch in the corner and watched as they removed the other cast.

Steven appeared far more relaxed than he had been the first time.

When Wesley put the second set of films up on the wall, he said, "This one looks good, but we'll err on the side of caution and put a short cast on here too. We'll recheck in three weeks."

Steven groaned. "All right."

Wesley went through the process of replacing the left cast while he discussed the next few weeks of rehab with Steven.

". . . you could suffer another fracture."

*What was that?* Abby felt sick to her stomach.

❖　❖　❖

The nurse who'd greeted Abby when she'd first arrived motioned to a chair she'd placed next to the cast table where Steven still lay.

"What was he saying about *another fracture?* I'm sorry, I was trying to be polite and not eavesdrop on your conversation."

"Wes doesn't want anyone but Jill working my knees, which means my rehab schedule will be at the mercy of her work schedule. He's afraid that because of my paralysis, I may not realize I'm being hurt."

Abby shuddered and looked at the floor. She could barely force the words out, but she had to know. "In other words, someone could break your leg simply by *bending* it? What about the rods and plates? Won't they protect you?" Abby rubbed her arms. It felt as if the temperature in the room had dropped ten degrees.

From where he lay on the table, Steven reached over and touched her arm. "Hey, it *could* happen, but it won't, and yes, the hardware will protect the long bones, but the problem would be a fracture closer to the joint where there is nothing to protect it."

Wesley poked his head back into the room. "It was nice meeting you, Abby. Please try to keep him out of trouble."

"It was a pleasure meeting you too. Thanks for everything."

Steven chimed in. "Bye, Doc!"

Turning toward Abby, Steven said, "He's got ten more to see today *before* he heads to his office."

"Wow, I can't imagine living like that. He probably has very little personal time."

"He has a wife and a brand new baby too. This is what it's like, Abby. I don't know how much we'll see each other. It'll be even worse in the beginning because I've been away for so long."

"You mentioned that, but I try not to think about it."

"I work with Jeff, but I'm required to pull a certain number of hours in the lab each week to fulfill my LRP commitment."

Abby cocked her head. "LRP?"

"Loan Repayment Program. It's a federal program that helps doctors repay their college loans through sweat equity."

"Nice."

"It is, but it'll eat up time I'd rather be spending with you."

"We'll learn to adapt, I'm sure. Your aunt and uncle did it."

Steven was beaming, and Abby realized she had admitted that she was in it for the long haul.

Abby looked up to see the three people in the doorway who had lifted Steven onto the table. She stepped into the corridor so they could help Steven back into his chair.

"I get a roomie tonight. I hear he's pretty young. Motorcycle accident, T seven eight. I'm kind of glad he's going to be in my room."

"I hope you become fast friends."

❖　❖　❖

Hours later, as Abby was walking into school, her phone chimed with a text message.

WHAT TIME ARE YOU DONE WITH YOUR CONFERENCES?

*MY LAST ONE IS AT 8:30 P.M. I SHOULD BE DONE BY NINE. WHY?*

MY PARENTS ARE GOING OUT. DO YOU NEED A RIDE?

*NO, BUT THANKS. ONE OF THE OTHER TEACHERS IS DROPPING ME OFF. SHE LIVES CLOSE BY.*

YOU WOULDN'T TELL ME THAT TO KEEP ME FROM WORRYING, WOULD YOU?

*I REALLY DO HAVE A RIDE.*

REALLY?

*HONEST.*

Okay. I'm sorry.

*Don't be sorry. Your chivalry is endearing. I'll call you when I get home.*

Thanks!

*You're welcome. Talk later. And thanks!*

# Chapter Twenty-five

Steven expected his new roommate to arrive around seven. He envisioned an opportunity to mentor a young person facing a recovery similar to the one that had turned into a contented and fulfilling journey for Steven.

In Steven's experience, a guy named Ross had nudged and nudged until Steven accepted his situation and chose to embrace life again.

In time, Steven accepted the baton, choosing to pay it forward any way he could.

Steven rushed through dinner, wanting to have time to tidy up his side of the room they would share. He smoothed his hands over his bedspread and grabbed a hoodie from his closet, smiling at a whiff of Abby's lingering scent from the last time they snuggled.

Like a proper host, Steven intended to be present for introductions, but then he planned to step outside so the kid and his family could get settled in.

Voices in the corridor caught Steven's attention. He backed into his corner of the room to give them plenty of space.

Two guys dressed in the familiar blue and white transport team polos pushed in a gurney. Jill raised the bed to make a level transition, and Steven's roommate was delivered into his new world.

The orderlies from transport left, and Jill put her hand up, mouthing *"Wait,"* halting Steven's departure.

Of course he planned to be social and meet the kid's family, but . . . *where are they?*

*He's . . . alone.*

Jill walked around the bed. She raised it into a sitting position and extended her hand. "Welcome, Alec, my name is Jill. I'll be your rehab doc for the next couple of weeks."

Alec responded halfheartedly. "Hey, Jill," he mumbled, avoiding eye contact.

*Oh, brother, she'll be working to bring you out of your shell.*

Steven silently appraised his neighbor. He was a little guy with dark hair that was worn long; he had a baby face, and his left arm was in a sling but didn't appear to be casted. Alec seemed to be introverted, and Steven couldn't tell if it came naturally, or as a result of recent events.

*Where is his family? Is he more like me than I imagined?*

Steven heard his name, and it brought him back from that dark place where he'd existed another lifetime ago.

". . . your roommate for a while."

"Sorry, I wasn't paying attention. I didn't want you to think I was eavesdropping."

Jill smiled. "I was telling Alec that you've got some time under your belt, and he's fortunate to be rooming with you."

Steven blushed and said, "Well, I don't know about that, Alec, but you are fortunate to be getting your rehab here. Jill's team is top-notch."

Family or not, Steven didn't want to interfere with the kid's intake. "I was headed out to shoot some hoops. You play? Maybe we can play some one-on-one when you get a chair."

When Steven was at this point in the game, he was recovering in a Circ-O-Lectric bed so his position could be changed frequently without causing further injury to his spine.

*Oh, how times have changed.*

"I'm not getting a chair. That's not why I'm here. I might not be back on my feet yet, but I'm here to get better."

Jill spoke matter-of-factly but not at all condescendingly. "We're doing a fitting tomorrow, Alec. You'll be ripping and tearing with Steven soon enough."

"I know you have intake business to take care of, so I'm not going to sit here being nosy. See ya later, Alec. Nice to meet you. See you tomorrow, Jill."

"Bright and early, Chandler. Don't be late!" Steven waved as he made his way out the door. *I'll be there with bells on. I can't wait to go home.*

Steven pulled the door shut behind him. Alec deserved to interact with Jill privately, free from prying eyes and ears that might cause him to hold back.

*This could very well be the most important day of his life.*

Steven grabbed a ball from a bin, and punched the automatic door opener. *"Boom!"* A clap of thunder followed a flash of light, and the sky gave way to a downpour. So much for basketball.

When Steven strolled to the lounge, there was nothing on TV. He saw a teenage girl sitting in a corner by herself. She wore a rigid back brace with both her arms immobilized and perfectly straight. They hadn't met yet, but she looked as bored as he felt. *Perhaps she can use a friend.*

He buzzed over to where she sat. "Hi, I'm Steven."

Her face broke into a big smile. "Hey, Steven, I'm Debbie. Nice to meet you."

"What are you doing over here all by yourself?"

She shrugged her shoulders. "My laptop is charging, there's nothing on TV, and the family is on vacation. Seemed like the logical choice."

Several boxes of pizza sat on one of the tables with a stack of paper plates and napkins. Steven had recently eaten, but the aroma made his stomach growl.

"Want a slice of pizza?"

"Nah, I'm okay, but you won't offend me if you have some."

Impeccable manners dictated that Steven forgo the snack despite his rumbling tummy.

His gaze landed on a deck of cards in the center of the table where they sat.

"Do you play cards?"

She shrugged again. "Sometimes."

"You wanna play a few hands of rummy or something?"

"As long as you don't want to play War or Slapjack. You'd have me at a disadvantage with those." She had a wry sense of humor, and Steven liked her instantly.

Steven had seen some of the others playing cards, and he looked around until he spied them—a dozen blocks of wood with slots cut into the tops.

He grabbed one and took it to the table. "Here, let's use one of these!"

She studied it, frowning. "I don't have a clue what it is!"

Steven dealt seven cards to each of them. He placed one of the jokers into a slot in the holder.

"Oh! I get it!" Debbie squealed. She slowly stuck each card into the holder.

Debbie won the first hand but frowned at the pile of cards on the table. "I can't shuffle or deal."

"Uh-uh, Debbie. I'll shuffle, but you can deal one at a time."

She grinned at him. "I'll probably be slower than molasses in January."

"We've got all night. You can do it."

Debbie carefully dealt out fourteen cards and they began another hand. As they played, they talked a little bit about their situations.

Steven got the impression that Debbie's parents were no longer together. She lived with Mom, and Dad was always traveling for his work.

Before they had a chance to dredge up details about Steven's tragic past, Debbie yawned. Steven glanced at the clock; he was surprised to see it had been nearly two hours since he'd left his room.

Steven stretched. "I think I'm going to call it a night."

"Yeah, me too. Thanks for introducing yourself, Steven. I had fun."

"Me too. Nice meeting you!"

Debbie turned and opened the refrigerator, grabbing two bottles of water.

When she got a few feet away from Steven, she hollered, "Think fast!" and threw one underhand in his direction.

Steven snatched it midair. "Hey, thanks!" He grabbed a tray and some napkins, tucking the water next to his body and went in search of food.

Alec had just come from the hospital, so Steven knew what kind of food he'd been eating.He grabbed a few slices of pizza and a can of cola too. If Alec wanted the water, he could have that. With everything strategically placed on his tray, Steven went to greet his new neighbor.

The room was dark, and Alec was lying with his face to the wall. Steven could hear sniffling and hiccups coming from his roommate's bed.

Steven flipped on a small lamp and unloaded the food onto a table near the window. When he turned and glimpsed Alec's bare back, his breath hitched. The kid's shoulders were bloodied and bruised, but it was the angry, zipper-like scar that began above the brace and no doubt spanned the length of the boy's back that made Steven's insides twist and turn.

Though it had faded with time, it was the same scar Steven wore on his own body, and seeing it,knowing Alec was embarking on the same journey he had spent his adult life navigating, hurtled Steven backward nearly twenty years.

*Get a grip, Chandler. Jill gave you the tools to help this kid begin his journey on the right foot, and she put you together for a reason . . .*

"Alec, I brought pizza."

"Whatever."

"Are you hungry?"

"No."

*Aren't all teenage guys hungry?*

"It's . . . I was in the hospital recently too. I know the food is pretty terrible."

"Whatever, dude."

Steven understood the kid was hurting, knew the past few weeks were probably the scariest time of his life, but that attitude.

*Is this how I treated everyone who tried to help me?*

"If you're interested, there are always activities going on down in the lounge. There are other teens, too . . ."

The kid pulled the blankets up around his shoulder and covered his face.

*So this is how it's going to be. Tomorrow's another day, I guess.*

Steven turned his TV on and popped open the cola. He had some time until bedtime and refused to let Alec's foul mood sully his own, settling on some new rookie cop TV series. From time to time, he heard Alec sniffle, and he knew the kid was going to have a rough first night.

*It's going to be an overwhelming couple of days until he gets into a groove. Hopefully it won't be too long before he figures it out.*

The last few weeks had no doubt been devastating. Steven would never forget what it was like to be thrust into the unknown, but Sophie and Logan were right by his side, supporting him . . . encouraging him.

*Why is this kid all alone?*

Steven was working on his first slice of pizza when his phone rang.

"Sydney."

*"Hey! How's the roomie?"* She screamed at such a high pitch, Steven knew his new neighbor—and probably everyone else in the building—could hear her.

"'It's all good, Syd," he replied curtly.

"Rough evening?"she asked, a little more softly.

"Yeah, you could say that."

"I saw Logan and Sophie out and about, I wondered if you asked Abby if she needed a ride tonight? They said something about offering to give her one."

"No, she's getting a ride from a co-worker."

"Oh good. I'll let you get back to your roommate, and I'll see you in the morning, okay?"

"Mmkay. See you then."

Steven finished his pizza and went to the window, staring out at the city.

Sure, the wheelchair was an inconvenience, and there were times that he thought his world had ended, but Steven was grateful for the life he'd been gifted.

*My life is good.*

*I hope I can be a positive role model for Alec. He needs to be proactive if he's going to prepare his body and his mind for the years that lie ahead. Heck, there are still days I have to psyche myself up for what lies ahead.*

The next morning would be the most strenuous since he himself had arrived at rehab—an early morning where he was expected to dress himself without assistance with legs that were still unbending.

Steven's stay would be intense, and rightfully so, but he refused to sit back and let a single moment slip through his fingers.

*I might have cheated myself the first time I worked with Jill but not this time!*

Last time, exercises to remain flexible and free of contractures had come easily once he learned how to manage the severe muscle spasms that taunted him each time he moved the wrong way. Once he understood how to avoid setting them off or how to use them to his advantage—stiff legs aided transfers in and out of the chair . . . or created a fall risk just as easily. His joints hadn't been injured when he'd become paralyzed, and exercise had come easily once he understood the new mechanics of his body.

*I'm facing a whole new learning curve!*

Steven decided there was no good time to address the elephant in the room, so he went to the far side of Alec's bed, facing him. The kid stiffened as Steven grew closer, his eyes squeezed tightly shut in mock sleep.

"Look, Alec, I don't know what the circumstances were which brought you here, but I've been where you are right now. I know it's scary, and you feel alone, and no one in your old life at home could possibly *begin* to understand what you're going through, but I *do*. If you need anything, if you have questions . . . if I can help you in any way .

. . please ask."

Without opening his eyes, Alec dismissed him. "Yeah, okay, what-ever."

"This is the best rehab facility in Connecticut. If you take the weeks you have here seriously and learn, you will get the best possible out-come for your disability. Once you get your own chair, and you get ac-customed to it, things will become much easier. I know how devastat-ing this must be for you, but I guarantee it's *not* the end of the world."

"You don't know *anything*." And again, almost desperately this time, Alec added, "I'm *not* here to learn how to use a chair. I'm here to *get better*. Now, *please* stop bugging me."

❖   ❖   ❖

Steven's nurse, Leslie, was entering as Steven returned to his own side of the room.

Leslie glanced at the slices of pizza on Alec's tray and back at Ste-ven. "If you're finished with your pizza, I can help you get your shower."

*Huh? I must have heard her wrong. Don't do it, Chandler! Don't you dare get all excited when you know she just misspoke!*

"Bed bath."

Leslie laughed. "No, I said shower. We'll have to strip you in bed and then get into the shower chair, and we'll have to wrap your legs in plastic to keep the casts dry, but I thought you might really enjoy it."

Steven drew in a sharp breath. "Like a real, honest to God, hot wa-ter spraying all over my naked body . . . shower?"

Leslie laughed even harder, holding her stomach. "That would be the one."

"Oh God, yes, please? I haven't heard the word shower in reference to my own body in so long."

"I'll be right back."

Leslie returned with an orderly pushing a shower chair and car-rying several long, plastic cast covers. In no time at all, Steven was stripped, transferred into the shower chair, and his casts were protect-ed. Steven glanced at his plastic wrapped legs and started to laugh. *I look like a leftover.*

❖    ❖    ❖

The shower was euphoric. The only thing that topped it was kissing Abby. Leslie let him revel in it, and he enjoyed every moment. When it was over, he was dried and a robe was thrown over him. Steven quickly brushed his teeth and pulled a comb through his hair. He left the bathroom feeling like a new man. He was warm and felt clean . . . clean like he hadn't felt in months. *I'm going to sleep like the dead!*

Alec lay quietly in the darkness, and Steven prayed that the kid would let someone in. Steven didn't know how, but he vowed to find a way to reach him.

It was still early, and normally Steven would lie awake late into the night, but it had been a long day, and the shower had made his body feel like Jello. Abby wouldn't be home yet, so he left her a quick text.

HEY, BABE. SINCE I KNOW YOU HAVE A RIDE HOME, I'M HITTING THE HAY EARLY. IF ANYTHING CHANGES, PLEASE CALL SYD. SHE CAN BE THERE IN JUST A FEW MINUTES. TALK TO YOU SOON!

# Chapter Twenty-six

Steven quickly fell into the nightmare which had haunted him since the night of the accident. He awoke to the screams that had jerked him out of sleep so many nights only to realize they were coming from someone else.

A nurse brought something to help Alec sleep, and Steven silently thanked her as he watched the kid swallow the pills. Slowly, Steven drifted into a comfortable slumber.

Roused by a brilliant sunrise and the sound of hushed voices, Steven watched as Alec balanced on the edge of his bed, his head resting on a therapist's shoulder. Steven chuckled inside when someone asked Alec if he still felt like he was going to pass out.

*I swooned like a teenage girl at a boy band concert the first few times they sat me up!*

Steven watched as they lowered his roommate back to the bed and explained what was happening. A nurse gave Alec a pill, and one of the therapists wrapped Alec's legs with ace bandages while another prepared a belly binder. They rolled him around until he was trussed up like a Thanksgiving turkey and then let him wait until his body adjusted.

❖    ❖    ❖

Steven used the help of an orderly to get into his chair and then followed his nose to the delicious breakfast being served in the dining room.

As he rounded the corner to the rehab gym, he met Daisy.

"Jill wants you on the machines."

"Sounds good to me! I won't be independent until I can transfer again."

"Start on the Game Cycle. Gotta get that upper body strength back."

The equipment was a hand cycle, which used the upper body to pedal rather than the legs. The pedaling action powered a car chase video game. Entertainment aside, it certainly gave Steven a good work-out. His shoulders were aching after ten minutes.

Next, Steven moved to the total gym, where his body was secured with gait belts so he wouldn't fall off. He did a number of routines that involved lifting weights and working specific muscle groups.

When Steven yawned and said he was tempted to skip lunch and take a power nap, Daisy said, "One more thing on Jill's list, and then you're free to go."

She stepped away and returned with a manual wheelchair.

Steven glanced at the manual, then back to where his power chair had been parked. "Um . . . that's not mine." *How could she confuse that tiny thing with my electric? There's no similarity whatsoever.*

"Jill would like you to use this chair until you return this afternoon. You can have yours back then."

Steven rarely used a manual chair. At work, he needed to stand frequently, and he was on the move far too much to push all day without sustaining injury. Years of pushing had damaged Steven's shoulders, so he only used his manual for leisure or if he rode in someone's car although he'd never pass up the occasional game of one-on-one if invited to shoot some hoops.

Jill smiled when Steven rolled into the gym. "Looking good, Chandler! Good posture, good follow through with your strokes. How do you feel?"

"I'd like to spend more time in this chair."

"That can be arranged, but I don't want you to overdo it."

"I know."

"You ready?" When Steven nodded, Jill locked the brakes, swung the footrests out of the way, and slid him forward until his feet touched the floor. She popped her head under his arm, slid both of her hands under his butt, rocked a few times, and on the count of three, she stood Steven and pivoted him onto the mat table.

Jill scrambled behind Steven and pulled until his legs dangled in mid-air. She put a wedge behind his shoulders and hopped off the table.

A goniometer appeared out of thin air. Jill held the hinged instrument along the side of Steven's knee to establish a baseline range of motion measurement. Every future session would be an effort to increase those numbers. "Fifteen degrees on this side, Steven." With those six words, a goal had been initiated.

Jill rolled her stool to the other knee and repeated the process. "Eighteen here."

Steven smiled. *Could be worse.*

Jill grabbed a pair of weights and fastened them to Steven's ankles. "I'm using the anti-inflammatory gel with the ultrasound on your knees today, Steven. The pulsations will assist with the whole healing process as we try to break up the scar tissue and get you moving again."

Jill sat with Steven's calf resting across her lap and used a gentle downward pressure with her left arm as she worked the wand on his knee. "For a few days, we're going to let gravity do the work."

"I can't wait to begin bending again."

"So I hear you were tired this morning. Are you feeling a little better?"

*Does the woman miss anything?*

"Didn't get much sleep . . . I didn't realize how much I was enjoying the private room until last night."

"You know, Steven, I could have placed him with an older patient, but I thought you'd be good for one another. He's young and impressionable. Right now he's feeling very alone, and if anyone can show him how incredible his life can be, it's you."

"He can't stand me. I brought him food, and he was sullen and rude. I ended up throwing it in the trash. He's a spoiled brat."

"No . . . he's a kid who's scared and alone. His parents blame him for the accident."

"I blamed myself for my parent's accident."

"It was your accident too. A tragic, tragic accident."

"I know you're right, but there are still times when I wonder if things would have been different if we hadn't been celebrating my birthday or if he hadn't been distracted or if she'd been wearing her seat belt. Those things were my fault."

"Do you have any idea how much I wish things had been different?"

"I can only imagine."

"I used to feel my paralysis was punishment for the accident. I wonder if he feels that way too, like he deserves this. I heard him crying after you were done with his intake. I tried to make small talk, but he wasn't interested. We both know he's not going to make any progress until he accepts his disability."

Jill smiled and squeezed Steven's knee. "I remember my first job. One of my earliest patients was a young man who was mad at the world. I'm proud of the man you've become, so very proud, but it took weeks for you to be receptive to the help I was offering."

"The way insurance companies want to rush things, Alec doesn't have weeks to come to terms with this. I'm sorry I got frustrated with him. I'll try to be more understanding. He's a T-seven or T-eight, right? Complete?"

"We both know that discussing another patient is a blatant disregard of HIPAA, and I could get myself into a world of trouble, but as two health professionals consulting on a case that would benefit from peer mentoring, I trust you to keep this conversation between us."

"Understood."

"He's a stable T-eight, and he's healing well. You'd be a great asset to him, Steven. If you can get past the attitude, he's a nice kid."

"Where is he academically? Is he still in high school?"

"He graduates in a few weeks. Apparently, he's met all his graduation requirements, and they'll allow him to take modified finals."

"Does he have a career goal? I mean, did he? Before . . ."

"His family owns Leonard Atlantic Construction. Sounds like he kinda blew the old man's plans out of the water with his accident. You'd think he'd be more compassionate toward his only child, but he's still refusing contact with him several weeks later."

"So . . . Alec was going into heavy construction. Has he considered an alternative? Drafting? Business management?"

"Apparently, the old man built the family business with sweat and hard work, but there's no reason Alec can't still participate by working intellectually rather than manually."

"I think a meeting with the parents is in order. They need to understand that this isn't some temporary setback. They should be making these decisions with him. Someone here needs to be realistic. Someone needs to nudge him in the right direction about his disability. Someone needs to let that kid know he's loved and supported."

"Mrs. Leonard says she understands the gravity of the situation and is adamant that her husband will come around."

"When? He's had several weeks."

"I don't know what he's waiting for."

Steven snorted. "A miracle."

With Steven's knee still resting on her lap, Jill held the goniometer against his thigh and centered the hinge over his knee.

"Twenty-three degrees. I'd prefer you wear the weights whenever possible. Gentle stretching is the outcome we're looking for here."

Jill smiled when she measured the opposite knee. "Twenty-four!"

Steven pumped his fist. "Yes!"

❖   ❖   ❖

Steven went to the dining room after rehab with Abby on his mind. Would the long hours of the conference schedule aggravate her MS?

They frequently talked late into the night. *Am I depriving her of much needed sleep? Is she taking care of herself?*

As Steven got a tray and pulled into the á la carte line, he glanced around the cafeteria, and his breath caught when he spied an attractive brunette sitting alone at a table. She looked lovely in a sleeveless mint green dress that emphasized her sun-kissed skin and accentuated her gorgeous curves in all the right ways.

*Oh, sweetheart, you are a sight for sore eyes.*

Steven rolled back into line and grabbed a second sandwich and drink. He hurried to the table where his girl sat. Afraid his imagination was playing tricks on him, Steven grabbed her face and kissed her thoroughly before she could protest.

"Well, hello to you too." Abby giggled as they separated. A bottle of water toppled to the floor, but Steven didn't care. *Definitely not a mirage.*

"Ahh, Abby. I've been thinking about you all day, missing you. I had a rough night, and then today was so . . . I feel like I've finally made some progress . . . and—"

It seemed like it had been a week since he'd seen her instead of only one day.

"Whoa! Slow down. Why did you have a rough night? Were you in pain?"

"No. Nightmares. And Alec couldn't sleep."

"Alec is the new roomie?"

Steven looked up from unwrapping his sandwich. "Yeah. He had nightmares and woke up screaming. Apparently, I was in the midst of my own nightmare, and I thought it was me screaming. It was terrible."

"How do you like him? What's he like? What's his family like? It must be nice to have someone to talk to." Abby rambled between bites.

Steven groaned. Leaning in, he tried to share his thoughts discreetly. "Quite the contrary. He's got a chip on his shoulder the size of Texas and no family support. They think the accident was his fault. He doesn't talk. He whines. He complains. He's obnoxious."

Abby took a swallow of her drink and wiped her mouth. "Do you think he'll come around?"

"I hope so because he's only hurting himself by being stubborn although I did see him playing catch and using the total gym this morning. There might be hope for him yet."

Abby reached over and took Steven's hand, her thumb rubbing his knuckles in a soothing pattern.

"How was *your* day?"

"I'm tired and stiff. I worked hard. I'm used to the upper body and core exercises, but Jill worked my legs this afternoon."

"How did that go?"

Steven gestured toward his ankles. "I've gained a few degrees using the ultrasound and a few pounds wearing these weights."

"That's wonderful."

Steven looked up to see an orderly pushing Alec into the cafeteria. The kid's posture was good, and he looked comfortable. For once he didn't have a scowl on his face.

"Psst—that's *him*."

"That's *who*?"

"Alec—my roommate."

"Well, invite him over if you'd like."

The kid was heading to an empty table.

"Nah, leave him to his own devices. He'll come around. I don't want to push him."

Abby gave Steven a stern look. "The Steven Chandler I know and love would be over there pestering him until he relented."

Steven felt his eyes grow wide. "Wh-what?"

Abby's eyes twinkled as she continued. "He might not want to sit with us, but he needs companionship. You had no trouble getting in my face and telling me it wasn't the end of the world. Where'd that guy go?"

Steven groaned. *So much for Abby time.* He went over to where Alec sat.

"Hey, Alec, why don't you come over and sit with us? There's no reason to eat alone when there are so many people here."

The kid shrugged. "Yeah, whatever."

*Is that the only phrase you know?*

"I can carry your tray. We've got plenty of room."

Alec pushed the tray towards the edge of the table so Steven could take it. When Steven looked up, Abby was next to him, extending her hand. "Hi, Alec. I'm Abby. It's nice to meet you."

Alec smiled, holding Abby's hand much longer than Steven was comfortable with. "Nice to meet *you*, too."

*What the hell?*

"I noticed the sling. Is it okay if I push you over to where we're sitting?"

Alec nodded. "Thanks."

Steven didn't appreciate the way his roommate gazed at his girl, but he remembered what Abby said and took a cleansing breath. *We've got this.*

"So, first day, huh?" Abby asked.

"Yeah."

"Where are you from?"

"Here in New Haven."

"That's cool."

Alec leaned in toward Steven's girl and smiled— again. "Where are *you* from, Abby?"

"Tiny little town called Woodstock. Have you ever heard of it?"

"Mmm . . . nope."

"I haven't lived there since I enrolled in college. I'm an elementary school teacher . . . here in New Haven."

"Oh, cool. Do you like it? Molding little minds and whatnot?"

"It's rewarding to mentor someone and know that you're contributing to the outcome of their future." She winked at Steven.

Alec stared at his lap, no longer making eye contact with either of them. Abby pulled him back into the conversation. "So, Alec, are you still a student?"

"I graduate high school in a few weeks."

"Are you going to college? What are your plans after graduation?"

Alec sighed and ran his hands through his hair. "My dad wants me to work for him. I've been one of his grunts since I was old enough to push a wheelbarrow."

"What will you be doing?" Abby asked.

"My parents own Leonard Atlantic Construction. We run most of the bridge and highway construction projects in the area. Obviously, that's a pipe dream now."

Alec was playing with the hem of his shorts, and it seemed to Steven that maybe Alec was beginning to accept that his path had taken a detour.

"Have you considered something like engineering? There are lots of ways you can contribute to your family's business."

For the first time, Alec made eye contact with Steven. "You don't know my dad. He has a one-track mind, and if I can't do things his way, it's the highway. I made my bed when I got on that stupid bike and went joyriding. He hates me."

In an encouraging tone, Steven said, "He doesn't *hate* you. He probably needs time to accept all this."

"You don't know what you're talking about." Alec pushed away so forcefully, the table moved. He turned to Abby. "It was a pleasure, Abby. I hope to see *you* around." He winked at her and turned around, singlehandedly wheeling himself away from the couple.

*Seriously? Did he just hit on my girl?*

Steven stared after Alec with his mouth agape. Abby began to snicker. "Well, *he's* sorta cute."

*What the heck?*

"He's a kid."

Abby took Steven's hand, squeezing to get his attention. "Don't tell me you're jealous."

Steven's gaze dropped to the floor.

"Steven Chandler!"

"He was hitting on you, and you flirted back."

"No, I made conversation because it's clear that he's hurting."

"Jerk hasn't said ten words to me in twenty-four hours. You come in here, and suddenly he's a different guy."

"Hey, don't be like that. I'm old enough to be his, well, to be his *older* sister."

"Still . . ."

"Hey, I didn't come here to argue about your roomie. I came here to see *you*."

"I'm sorry. I missed you, Abby. So much. I can't wait till *you're* my roomie."

"I'll be tied up all week during the day, but is this okay instead? I'll stop on my way to conferences."

"Mm-hmm . . ." Steven ran the tip of his finger over her knee and along her thigh at the edge of her skirt. "I like this dress. It's very pretty. Did you wear it to school today, Miss Harris?"

Her breath hitched, and she blushed. "No, I wore a pantsuit to work. I wore *this* for you."

He continued to make tiny circles on the outside of her knee. "Thank you. I like it very much."

"Sydney helped me pick it out at one of those vintage stores."

*Oh, Abby, you're a vision . . .*

"I'll have to thank her." Steven leaned in toward Abby, and she took his face gently between her hands. Her eyes were like melted chocolate before they fluttered closed, and she kissed him softly. "I have to go to work, Steven. Thanks for dinner."

Abby stood and tugged on Steven's hand.

"Walk me out?"

❖　❖　❖

Steven returned to his room and found Alec with headphones blaring. Steven dug through his dresser for a magazine.

When he spun around to leave, Alec was sitting there, wearing a smirk, headphones in his lap.

"She's cute."

"Who?"

"Your Abby."

*Darn right she's my Abby.* "Yeah, she is."

"You two serious?" Alec cocked his head as if he were considering whether that was even possible.

"We're building a house together."

Alec's face fell. "Oh. Is she coming back tomorrow?"

Steven suppressed a growl. "Maybe. *Why?*"

"No reason." He shrugged.

"You'll find a girl, or are you already seeing someone?"

"Who, me? *Like this?* What kind of girl would want someone like me?"

"I thought like that for a long time too. It didn't get me anywhere. You need to have more confidence."

Steven watched the kid's face flame before he exploded. "You don't know anything about me."

"I think I do. I've driven hundreds of miles in your wheelchair. You can sit around sulking, or you can *do* something about it. Either way, life is going to keep going on around you. It would be a shame if you turned into a jaded shell of a person because of your disability."

"Whatever, dude!"

Alec reached to put the headphones on, and Steven put out a hand to stop him. "Look, I'd like to help you if you'll let me. You have to let *someone* in, Alec."

"How could you *possibly* understand? I heard that your family is here all the time. You must have a decent job—you're building a new house, and you have a pretty girlfriend. You've got the *world* in the palm of your hand. I'm paralyzed, and you have the *nerve* to say you understand? You haven't got a clue, dude." Before Steven could respond, the headphones were on, the walls back up.

Steven sighed. *Why is it so hard trying to reach you? I've been nothing but sincere. Why does life have to be so frustrating?*

*Abby will be on my ass till I make nice with you because "that's what the Steven she knows and loves" would do.*

Then, Steven chuckled . . .

*That's right. She loves me.*

*Take that, Alec.*

# Chapter Twenty-seven

Professional Steven struggled with his roommate's demeanor. Mentor, advocate, ally Steven let it go. He had his own life to get in order. He wanted to become as strong and independent as he could possibly be—for himself and for his girl. They might not have officially declared themselves, but it wouldn't be long.

It was both physically and mentally stimulating for Steven to push his abilities. For one hour of his day, Steven was on the floor at various stations. He started out doing a wall routine where he simply sat on top of an air-filled disk, legs spread out in front of him while he balanced. If Steven moved the wrong way, he fell over and had to start again.

It didn't take him long to figure out when and how to shift his weight to avoid toppling. Once he gained a little confidence, Jill switched it up, throwing Steven a Nerf ball, giving him hand weights, or having him do cherry pickers with his arms extended, actions intended to throw off Steven's balance.

*I'm on to ya, Jill.*

Sydney was present every day, participating in every routine. *It won't be long until I can work out at Mac's. I wonder if Abby would tag along.*

❖   ❖   ❖

Despite Alec's apparent disdain for Steven, he seemed to be moving forward.

Another young guy, Zach, transferred to the facility from St. Ralph's. He and Alec hit it off right away. Steven was relieved to see someone challenging Alec in the gym.

Debbie had caught his attention too; a wheelie, no doubt meant to impress, found Alec on the floor. Two orderlies righted his chair, and he was ushered off to X-ray. Debbie blushed and giggled as she hurried away.

It was promising to see the kid socializing and with a smile on his face, too.

*Go, Alec!*

❖    ❖    ❖

Unfortunately, the physical activity Alec was engaging in daily did little to deter the demons the kid still battled at night, and it was Steven who was paying the price.

Alec awoke screaming in terror on Friday night, and the staff gave him something to help him sleep. Steven pulled a pillow over his head to drown out the raucous snoring coming from his roommate's side of the room and awoke to someone giggling. He opened his eyes, surprised to find big, chocolate orbs studying him.

Steven smiled and stretched. "You're here. What time is it?"

"A little after seven. We're going to breakfast. We cleared it with Jill yesterday."

Steven looked at his roommate's bed; Sleeping Beauty was still lightly snoring.

*Figures!*

"You look exhausted. Maybe this is a bad morning?"

"The kid had nightmares, and then they gave him something to sleep. He has been snoring *for hours*."

"Would you like us to come back in an hour? You could catch a little more rest."

"No. Someone is going to come in and start getting him around, and I'll be awake anyway. Breakfast with you sounds amazing."

"I'm going to go find a seat in the reception area until Sydney is done with you. I don't want to make Alec uncomfortable."

Alec was out cold.

*Thanks for understanding I'm still trying to get comfortable with my body image.*

❖   ❖   ❖

Sydney helped Steven dress swiftly. As soon as he was put together, he rang the buzzer. Leslie walked in and smiled. "Wow, you look great, Steven. What do you need?"

"My meds, please. I'm going out."

"Yes, sir! I'll be right back."

Sydney rummaged through the closet. "You don't have much clothing here. Where's all your stuff? You *did* have clothing before the accident."

"Yes."

"What happened to it after the accident? Do we need to get you new stuff?"

"I think maybe Skyler Jacobs stopped by the apartment and picked everything up. It should be at Sophie's."

"I'll have to check. It'll all need to be washed. Maybe Abby and I can take everything to the cleaners next week. What about furniture, appliances . . . electronics?"

"Nah, the furniture we had was crap, the appliances, too. Nothing I want."

Steven heard Alec stirring, and the kid grumbled. "Do you guys have to be so loud? I'mtrying to get some sleep here."

When Steven growled, Sydney giggled. "He's so *cute*, Steven."

Alec's attention turned to Sydney. "Hey, you're not Abby."

Alec shot Steven a sly grin. "You steppin' out on the little lady already, Chandler? I'm sure I could make her happy. I've got a soft spot for older women." He winked at Sydney.

As Steven was considering giving the kid a piece of his mind, Leslie cleared her throat.

"Here's your muscle relaxer, Steven." She opened a little packet and dropped the pill into his hand. Steven popped it in his mouth and chased it with some water.

Leslie winked and said, "Abby said to tell you and Sydney to get a move on. She's hungry."

"Thanks, Leslie." Steven smirked in Alec's direction. *Take that, kid.*

❖   ❖   ❖

Steven and Sydney chatted as they crossed the parking lot, but Steven came to a dead stop when he spied Abby with her arms crossed, leaning against a sweet little ride.

*Where's the van?*

Perhaps it was the lack of sleep. It took a few moments to sink in, but when it did . . . Steven wheeled over to the car and put both his hands on the fender. He rolled around it and looked and touched . . .

*It's done? It's done!*

The little PT Cruiser was gunmetal silver with metallic flecks that sparkled when the sun hit it. Sydney handed Steven the keys. He went to the rear of the vehicle and held the fob to the tail light. Silently the driver's side gull-wing door rose up out of the way. Because the vehicle was small and sporty, and Steven had chosen to keep the rear seat intact, he would have to enter and alight from the driver's side of the car when he drove.

A ramp opened, and Sydney rolled the bucket seat she'd sat on off the ramp paving the way for Steven to roll into the front passenger position of the car.

While Abby climbed in and got comfortable, Steven caressed the dashboard and inspected the glove box. *I wonder if Sydney will let me sit in the driver's position when we get to the house.*

Abby had been quiet the entire trip. When they stopped in the driveway, she hopped out of the back and walked around to the driver's side of the car.

As surely as if Sydney had read Steven's mind, she disengaged the bucket seat and rolled it down the ramp and onto the driveway so Steven could exit the car. "Go ahead. You know you want to."

Steven pulled up into the position that would soon be his. His hands ghosted over the steering wheel, along the hand controls, and across the dashboard. He turned the key in the ignition, and she purred to life. He used the hand control to accelerate, revving the engine a few times.

*Oh, how I love that sound.*

Steven cranked up the stereo and smiled at the thumping bass, the pounding percussion. He beeped the horn, revved the engine again, and flipped the lights on and off. He was totally engrossed and didn't realize there was an audience until his father laughed.

"He's been like this since we got here, Logan. Do you think you can get him out of there so we can go inside?"

"Come on, son. Your mother is setting up breakfast in the kitchen, and the girls have some things to discuss with you."

Steven hadn't been in the new house since he'd first shown it to Abby, and he was amazed at how much progress had been made in such a short time. He went into his room first, and the walls had been painted a beautiful shade of tan, but his bathroom was inaccessible. Tools and materials littered the floor, so he made his way across the hallway to Abby's room.

Steven was surprised to see it completely done. He was impressed. He looked appreciatively at the bookshelves surrounding Abby's window seat. They were finished in a beautiful maple and attractively complemented the rest of the room. The walls had been painted a light blue, and Steven was awash in calmness as he went inside. The cushion and pillows for the window seat were in place. Everything followed the color scheme of light blues, turquoises, and pale greens. It reminded Steven of the ocean. The curtains, which spanned above the window seat, matched the cushions, and they had been hung, as well.

Steven looked up to see his father smiling warmly. "I like your Abby. She's something special."

"Yeah, she is pretty special. I'd like to think we were destined to find one another, but I'll be forever grateful to you for bringing her into my life."

"I'm happy for you, son. Sophie and I had resigned ourselves to the notion that you would remain a confirmed bachelor."

"I never imagined myself with anyone, but now—I don't want to imagine a life without her." Then Steven shook his head. "She's changed my outlook completely."

"She's *the* one?"

"She's the only one for me. She's smart and fun and so compassionate. She always takes my needs into consideration, and I can definitely see this blooming into our once in a lifetime. We're still skirting around what we're calling it, but there's no rush. Neither of us is looking elsewhere."

"I'm happy for you, son. I'm sure you'll both love it here. You have so many wonderful memories to make."

"Come on. Let's find the girls," Steven replied. As he went back through Abby's room, he smiled. There was bedding somewhere that coordinated with the window treatments. Abby would probably be furious, but Steven had turned his aunt loose, and it was no secret she loved Abby too.

Logan stepped out of the room, and Steven spun around one more time. As he was turning into the hallway, Abby practically fell into his lap. Steven reached out and grabbed her waist to steady her.

"Hey, take it easy there. You okay?" He briefly studied Abby, making sure she wasn't hurt by their collision.

"Yeah, I'm good."

"Come here, Abby." Steven reached out his hand, and she took it. "Turn around." He murmured softly. When she turned her back to him, he put his hands on her hips.

"Gently. . . back up to me. Careful. That's it." He guided her slowly onto his lap.

"Now sit. You won't hurt me."

Abby gasped and turned, looking at him like he had lost my mind. "But . . ."

"No buts. It's all right. Please be careful."

Gingerly, Abby lowered herself onto his lap and he positioned her so her legs hung off to the side.

"That's better. You were too far away." Abby sighed and Steven could feel her body relax into him. He dipped his head, and she took the lead, putting her hand on his cheek and leaning in until their lips met. Softly she explored his mouth, deepening the kiss as he shifted her hips so she was nearly facing him, her legs slung over the low armrest of his wheelchair.

He pulled back and looked at her. "Are you comfortable, babe?"

She bit her lip and nodded. "Mm-hmm."

Steven's hands ghosted upward until they came to the soft skin above her jeans. Her breath hitched when his thumbs touched her, moving in circles over her baby soft skin.

Abby leaned in and hugged him, nuzzling his neck. She inhaled deeply, and Steven snickered when it tickled the hairs on his neck. He felt her tongue moving up under his earlobe, and he shuddered. "Baby, that tickles."

Steven pushed Abby back far enough to see her face. Steven leaned in closer to her mouth, wanting to kiss her again. Her eyes drifted shut, and she brought her mouth back to his. She trailed her fingers over the spot where she had tickled his neck, and he couldn't help himself.

*Turnabout is fair play, Abby.*

He ever so gently began to tease and tickle the bare skin where his hands rested.

Abby stopped kissing him and began to giggle.

"It's nearly time to head back. Are you two lovebirds ready?"

*Steven rested his forehead against Abby's and groaned. Cockblocked by Sydney.*

Abby blushed as she tried to scramble off his lap. "Careful, baby. Don't fall. Everything's okay. Don't let *Sydney* embarrass you."

Abby began shifting her weight to get her feet under her, so Steven lifted, helping her to right herself. "Your mom has a breakfast casserole in a slow cooker. Let's go eat."

They found Sophie leaning against a large box, looking through her project notebook.

Steven rolled over to his aunt with outstretched arms. "Breakfast smells amazing. Thank you."

Sophie gestured to a table set with plates of food. "Let's enjoy it while it's hot. We can talk while we eat. I know you're on a schedule."

They discussed various details of the construction project, and when Logan began clearing the table, Steven looked at his watch, sad that the morning had passed so quickly.

"Hey, Ma, we're gonna go. I have to go see my counselor in a half hour. Is there anything else you need from us?"

"Nope. Go be counseled. Put forth the effort. It'll do you good."

"Yeah, yeah . . . I will. I'mso ready to come home. This is beautiful, thank you."

Sophie gave Steven a hug. "It's my pleasure. I love you."

"Mmm, I love you too." He breathed into her shoulder as they said their goodbyes. Her scent reminded him of his mom, his Grace. The emotions it evoked were bittersweet.

"Abby," Sophie said, pulling her into a fierce embrace, "I'll see you soon. Let me know when we can get together to look at furniture."

"I'll check my schedule. We have a science fair coming up, but otherwise, I should be free."

Steven followed Abby outside. He heard noise and poked his head in the garage.

"Bye, Dad. Thanks for everything. I never would have been able to do this without you."

"I'm glad we could help, son. I can't wait until you're home."

"Me either. Love you!"

# Chapter Twenty-eight

The girls parted ways with Steven in the parking lot. He continued to talk as he backed away from them. "When will I see you again?"

"I'm not leaving yet. Sydney and I are going to hang out during your appointment . . . if that's okay?" Abby asked hesitantly.

"Even better. I'll be back in an hour. "

Abby giggled and smacked his shoulder. "Go. You're gonna be late."

Sydney sensed something was troubling Abby. Once they were alone, she said, "It's beautiful outside. Let's hang out at the gazebo."

Silently, the girls walked side by side to the garden. Abby stopped at a bench, then sat and turned sideways with her back against the arm-rest, her knees pulled to her chest. She wrapped her arms around her knees, and she rested her head. Sydney sat at the other end, mirroring her movements.

"Penny for your thoughts. Is something wrong?"

"Wrong?" She lifted her head. "No . . . not *wrong*. I'm curious, and I don't know how to talk to Steven. I don't know . . ."

"What are you curious about? Can I help?" Abby blushed crimson, and lay her head down, facing away from Sydney.

"I'm sorry for walking in on you guys. I didn't know . . ."

"It's fine, Sydney. I'm not sure what is okay to do with him. I was so afraid of hurting him, you know, sitting on his legs like that."

"You have to know he wouldn't do anything to jeopardize his health when he's so close to coming home. He wouldn't encourage anything that would hurt *either* one of you."

"It's not that. I'm not sure how to touch him. I don't know what feels good to him or if he can even feel certain things. I'm at a loss here, Sydney. Tell me what to do."

"It looked like you were doing fine on your own, but I'll see if I can put you at ease. Let's see . . . he's a T-twelve."

"That's the level of his injury. It refers to his twelfth thoracic vertebrae, right?"

"Exactly. Have you talked about what he feels?"

"No. I wanted to, but I don't want to be intrusive."

"You'd never offend Steven by being curious." Sydney put her hands on her own hips at the top of her thighs. "He can feel to about here, and there are areas on his legs that have some sensation and movement as well."

"So sitting on his lap, I wasn't *hurting* him?" Sydney shook her head. "And he couldn't feel me sitting on . . ."

"To quote Steven, *'Fred's dead.'*"

"Yeah, he said something to that effect." Abby's blush grew a furious shade of crimson.

"Don't be embarrassed. I'm a nurse. Maybe it would be easier to think of me that way; it's more clinical."

Abby nodded, her head still lying on her knees. "I don't have much experience with guys. I was with one guy, but he was all wham, bam, thank you, ma'am, and he was out the door. Steven's all soft touches and caresses—affectionate. I'm not used to . . . I've never experienced this."

"Oh, Abby. Never?"

"Not like this, Sydney. It's very overwhelming and, um, stimulating." Abby's voice cracked as she forced the words out. "Is this what it's like when you're with Spencer? I'm tingly all over, and he feels so good in my arms. I don't want to let him go."

Abby looked directly at Sydney. "So Steven really can't, um, you know."

*Would the girl ever stop blushing?*

"What? Get it up?"

"Uh, yeah . . ."

"I've helped him get washed up, and there are erections that happen when a penis is touched. It's not something he can control. It's not like he sees a pretty girl, and he pitches a tent. That type of reaction is gone. But a reflex erection isn't something that would last long enough to satisfy either of you. They don't get very hard either."

"Oh." She laid her head back down. "Are there other things we can do? I mean I know there's like . . . oral stimulation and stuff. Can he even feel something like that?"

"Well, even if he can't feel it, he can watch. The visual is enough to turn him on. You don't have to ejaculate to have an orgasm. It's hard to explain, but people with injuries like Steven's can experience the same type of euphoria that accompanies an orgasm."

"Can we still . . .Um, this is so embarrassing, Sydney. Can we have intercourse? How's that even possible?"

"There are ways. If you want to learn more, there are books we could get. Or we can talk to Logan. Or . . . you *could* talk to Steven about it."

"Oh God, Sydney. I'd die before I asked Logan, and I'd be mortified to ask Steven! What if he doesn't want, you know, something like that . . . with me?"

"Oh honey, that should be the least of your worries. He's smitten with you."

"It's one thing to snuggle and smooch, but you and I are talking about things that spell commitment to me. How can I be sure we're both on the same page? This isn't something to take lightly. I'm not *that girl*. I never have been."

"Abby honey, be honest with him. He adores you, and I know you feel something, or we wouldn't be having this discussion."

"I'm in too deep now. He's sorta stolen my heart. He's *such* a special guy. I truly believe he'd never intentionally hurt me. I feel safe with him."

Sydney got up and wrapped her arms around Abby. "Steven is a special guy. Please, don't ever hurt him."

"No, I won't. I promise."

"Promise *what*, Harris?"

Abby gasped and Sydney whipped around. "Talk about the devil himself! Don't sneak up on a girl like that, Steven. You darn near gave me heart failure."

"I wanna know what Abby was promising you." The corner of Steven's mouth was turned up in a smirk.

Abby blushed and shook her head.

"Come on, Harris, tell me. I know you're ticklish. I have ways of getting it out of you." Steven wiggled his outstretched fingers, and he laughed.

Abby giggled and turned to run. She tripped on the curb, and in slow motion, Sydney watched her go down, putting her hands out in front of her to break her fall.

Sydney grabbed for Abby as she tumbled, but she wasn't strong enough or quick enough. They both landed in the gravel.

Sydney touched Abby's shoulder gently. "Abby? Are you okay?"

Steven, red-faced, began yelling for help. "Get her up! Help her!"

"I'm okay. Please give me a hand." Abby's jeans were torn at her knees, and the heels of her hands were scraped. She wiped her eyes with the back of her hand. "I wasn't looking, didn't see the curb." Her hands trembled.

Steven was practically on top of them.

"Calm down, Steven. She's okay. Only some brush burns."

"Sweetheart, can you sit on my lap again?"

Abby shook her head stubbornly. "I don't want to hurt you, I'm too heavy. I can walk."

"Let me be your knight in shining armor. Please?"

Abby nodded and limped to Steven. She took Sydney's hand as she gently sat, hissing when she bent her knees.

"Let's get you inside and take a look." Steven was in full-on doctor mode.

"It's nothing. I can go home and change. I'll get a few Band-Aids and take care of it."

Steven started wheeling towards the entrance.

When they got to the room, Alec was watching TV. He perked up as the trio entered. Abby's face was red and smudged with tears; her head lay on Steven's shoulder.

"What did ya do to her?" He looked pointedly at Abby. "I'd show you a good time without hurting you, sweetheart." He waggled his eyebrow, and Abby looked sick.

*Really sick.*

Sydney brushed the side of Abby's face. "Hey, are you okay? You don't look so hot."

"I'm a little squeamish." Steven wrapped his arm around her, pulling her tight against his body.

"Sydney, would you go see if there is a first aid kit or some gauze and maybe a bottle of peroxide?"

He looked at Alec. "And you! Go find someone else to bother."

Alec gawped at Steven.

"Now!" Steven bellowed.

❖   ❖   ❖

"Hon, can you sit on the bed for me? I'll make it feel better. I promise."

Abby stiffened. "I'm okay. Let Sydney take me home. Please?"

"I can't let you go until I'm sure you're okay."

Reluctantly she nodded, and Steven breathed a sigh of relief. He needed to see for himself that she wasn't seriously injured. He held her hand as she slid off his lap and sat on the edge of the bed, her knees dangling in front of him.

*I had to fool around and play games, and she got hurt. I'm such a jerk!*

Abby stared at something over Steven's head.

*Maybe I can distract her.*

"Abby? What did you and Sydney do while I was with Melanie?"

"We talked."

"About what?"

"Stuff."

"What kind of *stuff*?"

"Um, you know . . . just stuff."

"I got a first aid kit!" Sydney said, bouncing into the room. She laid the kit on the bed next to Abby. In her other hand, she carried a basin with a bottle of peroxide in it.

Steven surveyed the contents of the first aid kit, pulling out scissors, bandages, triple antibiotic ointment, gauze, and tape. He placed the implements on his bedside table. Sydney moved the table to his right side so he could work.

"Abby, honey, the jeans are ruined. May I cut them off?"

When she nodded, Sydney cut up the front of each pant leg allowing the material to fall away from Abby's injuries. Steven put his hands behind Abby's right calf, gently pulling it up onto his lap. "Is this all right? Does it hurt in this position?"

Abby stared at something on the wall. "It's fine. Do what you need to do, please."

Steven opened a piece of gauze, saturating it with peroxide over the basin. He gently dabbed at the blood on each knee until he could see the injuries. The scrapes were superficial, but he worried more about trauma to the joint itself. He put antibiotic ointment on a clean piece of gauze, taped it over each injury, and gently set it down.

"Abby, I'm going to move your knees and feel, to make sure you didn't tear your ACL or your meniscus."

"My men-*who*?"

Sydney snorted, and Steven smiled. "Your meniscus. Your *cartilage*. I want to make sure you don't have any signs of a torn cartilage."

"Oh, okay." She turned away from him, her face crimson.

"Hey, I'm sorry we laughed. It was cute. I want to be sure you didn't damage anything orthopedically."

"Okay." Abby limped slightly but assured Steven it was from the abrasion itself.

Sydney held up the scissors. "Hey Abby, let's go into the bathroom and turn those jeans into a proper pair of cut-offs."

Steven cleaned up and rinsed the basin in the sink the nurses use to wash their hands. He felt terrible that Abby had gotten hurt, but it felt good to take care of her.

When the girls came out of the bathroom, Abby's jeans were cuffed. Steven was relieved they had managed to salvage Abby's favorite pair of jeans in some form.

Steven looked up to see Jill standing in the doorway. "Everything okay, Chandler?"

"Yeah, a few abrasions, but it's my fault she got hurt."

"I saw it from my office. Clearly you guys were breaking the fun barrier, but it was an accident. You act like you intentionally hurt her."

Abby came over and ran her hands through the hair at the nape of his neck. "It was an accident, so quit trying to take the blame. Don't you have some exercises to do or something?"

Steven sighed. "Come on, Jill. Might as well get this over with."

Abby leaned down and pecked him on the lips. "Thanks for taking care of me. Call me later?"

"Okay." He reached up and pulled her in for another kiss. "I had a nice day."

She seemed to be more and more comfortable around him each time they were together, and it felt nice.

"I had a nice day too."

Sydney gave Steven's shoulders a squeeze on the way out. "See ya later. Have fun with Jill."

Steven heard Jill laughing from the doorway. *Oh brother, I'm in trouble.*

Alec was finishing up with his therapist when Steven and Jill entered the gym. He steered close to Steven as they passed. "What did you do to doll face? She was fine sitting out there on the bench with your little friend all that time. You go out there for five minutes, and she comes back inside in tears. *I'd* treat her like a goddess. Whadja do? Push her down so you had a reason to kiss it and make it all better?"

Steven saw red, and for an instant, he *almost* considered giving Alec a kiss with his fist until he felt a firm grip on his shoulder.

"Alec, why don't you go find something to do? Your session is over, right?"

"Yes, Jill." But he remained, taunting Steven.

Steven growled when his roommate finally left. Jill shoved his shoulder and started talking. "Why do you let him goad you like that? He's doing it because it makes him feel good about himself. He's picking on someone bigger, older, and much more comfortable in their skin. You're *everything* he's not and fears he never will be. Don't buy into it."

"For him to suggest that I would deliberately hurt her . . . I'd rather die before I did anything like that."

"I know you would, and so does he. That's one of the reasons he's the way he is. You've got it all, and he can't possibly imagine what this life holds for him. One day soon, he'll need you for something, and the tables will turn. The day he has to rely on you, trust you, you'll gain his respect. He's merely acting out."

"It doesn't make me feel any better."

"Nope, it doesn't. Now, how was your time in the manual wheelchair? It's a sports edition, so it's incredibly light and fast. Are you getting a manual wheelchair as well?"

"Uh, mine is a little dilapidated. I don't know if I'm eligible for a new one yet. I'll have to call my insurance company. I like that manual chair." *I really like the fact that this chair has no armrests, and Abby can sit in my lap. We could dance in it . . . The possibilities are endless. Yes, I want a chair like this.*

"I'll see what we can do to justify the acquisition with your insurance company. We can ask the insurance to reconsider eligibility because your physical abilities have changed. Were you in better condition five years ago?"

Steven snorted. "Yes."

"Let me see what I can do. Now come on, let's get busy. I have something for you."

Jill walked across the room and came back with a new transfer board.

Steven groaned. *That's something I lost in the accident, my transfer board.*

"Come on, get on my mat. We're wasting time."

Steven placed the board carefully across the gap between his chair and the mat table. Tucking it under his butt, he inched his way across.

"That was good, Steven."

Jill ran him through his mat routine, range of motion, and core exercises before she used the Hoyer to lower him to the floor. "Can you help me relearn getting to the floor without a lift?"

"Do you want to be able to get on the floor?"

"I'd like to at least have the option. I need to be able to get back into my chair if I fall."

"Hopefully, you don't do a lot of that."

"I don't ever want to get myself into a situation I can't get out of."

Steven's mind drifted back to the weekend in hell when Courtney left him. *No, never again!* No matter the circumstances, he'd never be stranded again if he could help it.

❖   ❖   ❖

When Steven rolled into his room, Sydney was sitting on the bed. "What are *you* doing here? I thought you went home."

"Yeah, I did, but I thought I'd help you shower. You know, get the hang of it."

"We'll need help to get in the shower chair. I have been stripping on the bed, and then the orderlies put me in the chair."

"All right. You lead me and tell me what to do; we'll get it. Leslie said she'd be in to help."

"Okay, cool. She'll get some muscle in here for the lifting when we're ready.

"So, um, Abby wanted some advice. I, uh, I took her to a bookstore."

"What kind of advice, Syd? What kind of books?"

"Oh, here." She thrust a brown paper bag into Steven's hands, and he cocked his eyebrow.

"Sydney?"

Pulling the contents from the bag, Steven came face to face with the books that had mocked him in his youth. *Loving Relationships . . . for People with Disabilities. Sex and Disability. Fred's Not Dead.*

"Sydney? This is what you were talking about before she fell?"

"I don't want her to feel I betrayed her trust. I thought this was something important to share with you."

"Wow, thanks. It's nice to know that I'm reading the signs right."

"She didn't ask me not to tell, and I suspect she is secretly hoping I'll mention it to you so she doesn't have to initiate the conversation."

"Thanks, Syd. I'll find a way to broach the subject. Thank you for caring enough about us, both of us, to answer her questions and direct her to information that's appropriate for our situation."

"Sure thing."

Leslie came into the room and pulled the curtain around Steven's bed. "Okay, Steven. Jill says you can use this to get into bed. She also said you forgot it in the gym and that you need to have it with you at all times.

"Let's see what you can do."

Steven put the board across the gap, and the women watched him work his way across. "Jill said you aren't to do this alone yet, so please tell her you got the memo, 'kay?"

"Got it."

Steven scooted onto the bed and slowly lifted himself backward. Leslie swung his legs up onto the bed and removed his pants. She covered him with a towel and rang the buzzer.

The two guys who had lifted Steven before put him into the shower chair, and Sydney threw a robe over him before wheeling him into the bathroom. Sydney rolled up her pants and turned on the water, filling the room with steam.

Steven felt refreshed and renewed when they were done.

He didn't remember Sydney leaving or telling him goodnight. He never heard the staff put the kid to bed, and he never heard him crying out in his sleep. Steven had a long day, and for once, sheer exhaustion was enough to let him reap the benefits of a full night's sleep.

# Chapter Twenty-nine

Steven had never been one to sit idly by if he could be working toward an objective. The average length of stay for injuries such as the ones Steven sustained had been reduced drastically since his first accident occurred. Steven was fully prepared to pay out of pocket for his stay in Jill's facility until he met his goals.

*Every day I'm getting a little closer . . .*

Steven parked his chair next to the mat table and laid his transfer board on the mat. Unhooking his seat belt, he turned his torso and lifted the armrest. He laid his board across the gap between his chair and the mat table. He'd been doing transfers so long, the process had become muscle memory, and then out of nowhere—smack!

"Don't even *think* about it! The last time you attempted a stunt like that, it took two of my guys to fish you out of the space between your chair and my table!"

He smiled sheepishly at his therapist. "Just getting ready for you, Jill."

"Always in such a hurry. One would think you don't want to be here."

"Well . . . you know I love you, but seriously, I can think of a million other things I'd rather be doing."

"Okay, hotstuff, how 'bout you show me what you're made of."

Steven had the utmost respect for his therapist and mentor. Her perseverance and dedication had ultimately changed his life. Still, he found himself growing frustrated with the rules when he was approaching an act he had mastered and performed thousands of times independently.

"I can't begin to imagine the things that go on in that head of yours, but don't let your haste cause a setback in your recovery. Your safety while you're at this facility is paramount. A few more weeks, and you'll be fit to run this place—but not quite yet."

On the mat table, Jill supported Steven's legs and allowed him to get situated. An orthopedic wedge behind Steven's shoulders allowed him to sit without support. Steven clasped his hands behind his knee and pulled toward his chest, holding while Jill counted.

"How about the other one?"

Steven repeated the exercise.

"Great! Let's do some range of motion, then we'll measure."

Jill supported Steven's knee with one hand and pushed his calf with the other. On the count of ten she let go, and his leg slid back down the mat. After fifteen reps, she switched legs.

Next came lifts. Jill bent Steven's straightened leg with no trouble at all, but she was huffing and puffing as she wrapped things up.

"Didn't you say your girl has MS?"

"Well, she's not *my girl* yet, but yeah, she does."

"Please, I thought I was going to have to step between you and Alec."

Steven blushed.

"Why do you ask? You know about her disability?"

Jill reached under Steven's legs and swung them over the side of the mat table; her other arm supported his torso. Steven grabbed the table to steady himself.

He set his board in place and began the journey across the expanse between mat and chair.

"I was going to suggest you leave tasks like these exercises for your aide to conserve your girl's energy for other activities."

"I have no intention of letting Abby do anything like this for me. I don't ever want her to feel like I offered her a home with the motive of snagging a free caregiver. I refuse to be a burden."

"Understood, but I've watched the two of you interact. If you don't allow her to take an active role in your life, and having your needs met is part of that, she'll feel insignificant when you allow others to care for you, but you shut her out."

"I refuse to put her in a situation where she hurts herself."

"Remember to choose your battles wisely. *Let* her do the things you know she can do safely."

"Yeah, yeah. Let's let her get moved into the house first, okay?"

"I want to see this house once you get moved in. I hear there's an entire community of accessible homes. That's progress."

Once he was seated, Steven situated his legs and flipped the toggle to tilt his chair. He pushed up with his arms and slid into place. Seatbelt buckled, he inclined his chair and straightened his shirt.

"I'm pretty stoked about moving in. Abby was a hard sell at first, but I . . . I love doing things with her. She's so easy to get along with. She gets me."

"How long have you been together?"

"That's what I was saying. We'renot together . . . not yet, but I think we're on the same page. We've been friends for a few months. We're doing 'couple things.' I can't wait to get home and start living again."

"Speaking of which, how would you like to bust out of this joint for a while?"

"Seriously? Am I ready?" Steven's heart began pounding so hard he was afraid she'd hear it. He didn't know if he was overwhelmed with fear or excitement.

"See how it goes. You'll need your aide or a member of your family to stay with you overnight."

"I can't go to my house yet, but I can go to my parents'. You're not joking. I can actually get out of here?"

"Do you have everything you need at home?"

"I can have Sydney get any supplies I need."

"After your last session Friday afternoon, sign out, but be back by seven Saturday night so you can get a session in before bedtime."

"Aren't the therapists all out of here early on the weekend?"

"They are, but I'm covering second shift. While I think it's important that you start getting acclimated with the outside world again, it's also important that you don't miss a lot of therapy."

"Yeah, I understand. I'm determined to recover everything I lost."

"I know you are, but I also know it's easy to get lax about your recovery when real life hits. You'll have other things to think about: that new house, work, your girl. You won't want to think like a patient anymore and that's good, to an extent."

"I know. I'll be okay."

"You will."

"Karen will do your range of motion this afternoon. I've got a new admission arriving."

"Thanks, Jill."

❖    ❖    ❖

Steven buzzed back to his room as swiftly as his chair would carry him. *If I don't tell someone, I'll explode!*

Steven punched in Abby's number. It rang—once, twice. *Don't go to voicemail.* Three times. *It's gonna go to voicemail . . .*

"Steven." His name sounded like a song coming from her lips.

"Hey, am I interrupting?"

"No, it's okay. I'm on my break. It's beautiful outside. What's wrong? Do you have to change our lunch plans?"

"No. It's nothing like that. I'm sorry . . ." *Please don't stay away. Our lunches mean everything to me!*

He heard her laughing with someone, her words muffled.

"I'm sorry, Steven. My aide had a question."

Steven's enthusiasm turned to self-doubt, and he found himself stammering through the invitation that he clearly had not thought through.

"I, um, I have some good news, but . . . it can wait."

"If it was too good to wait until lunch, you better spill now, buddy."

*Will she think I'm being too forward if I ask her to join me at my parents? What if we're not compatible? What if? What if? What if!*

*What if she says yes?*

"I have a get-out-of-jail pass—Friday afternoon until Saturday night at seven."

"You're getting out? Oh, Steven! That's wonderful!"

"It's only overnight."

Abby's voice grew quiet. "I wish it was longer. I'd love to hang out with you, but I'm sure Sophie and Logan will be ecstatic."

"Actually, I was wondering . . . Would you join me at Logan and Sophie's? You don't have to if you don't want to. They have room, but I don't want you to be uncomfortable."

"You don't think they'd mind?"

"Mind? Never! They love you!" *And I think I do, too.*

"I have reports to grade, but I can do that Sunday. I'll need directions so I can get the right bus. Sophie has always driven me."

"We'll stop and get you when I leave here."

A buzzer sounded in the background. "Hey, Steven, I'm sorry—gotta go. Talk to you soon?"

"Sure."

❖   ❖   ❖

Standing endurance was the morning objective with Steven's OT, made possible by the standing feature on the Permobile. He felt secure with all the built-in safety features of his chair but it felt amazing to shift position independently. He raised and lowered his chair until the timer chimed, and he was released. Most days he'd find Abby observing from the doorway.

Steven's stomach rolled when she was nowhere to be found, and the message on his phone simply stated, "Something came up. I'm sorry. I'll see you later in the week?"

The days dragged for Steven. Everyone was busy, leaving Steven to toil through his sessions and spend his evenings wearing his headphones to avoid interacting with his roommate.

Sophie was no doubt cleaning like a fool. Steven could picture her airing out rooms, changing linens, and planning elaborate menus despite knowing it was only a twenty-four hour visit.

Syd was busy getting the supplies they'd need for the weekend and to get started at home. There were creams and lotions, catheter supplies, prescriptions . . .

Abby's excuse was doubling down on lesson plans to have more time on the weekend, sessions with her peer mentees, accessible parking, and employment committees.

Steven was a nervous wreck by the time Sydney picked him up Friday afternoon. He groaned when he saw the big bag of supplies. "She's going to see this and decide it's too much! What if she changes her mind?"

The car rolled to a stop, and Sydney turned in her seat.

"You're acting like a virgin on prom night. *Will you please relax?* She won't change her mind. We're going to have a blast. This is a night to have fun and get to know each other. Calm down."

When the car behind them beeped, Sydney hit the gas, and the car lurched. "Oops, sorry!"

Steven was overwhelmed by everything his family had planned—Sydney's movies, Sophie's classic board games. *Has Logan got an agenda too? It's all becoming so complicated!*

Abby sat, sunning herself on a bench in front of the school. Her head was thrown back, her eyes closed. Steven thought she was sleeping, but she hopped up the moment his car pulled into the loop in front of the school.

Sydney opened the door for Abby and stowed her bags in the trunk while she got in.

Abby giggled. "This is going to be so much *fun!*"

❖　❖　❖

Logan and Sophie were on the porch when they arrived, and by the time the engine was turned off, they were standing next to the car door waiting for Steven to exit. The air was filled with excited chatter as everything was unloaded, and their bags were carried into the house.

Steven inhaled the familiar aromas of home. It had been nearly a year since he'd been there, and he was filled with longing for the creature comforts he had taken for granted.

Steven found himself teary-eyed over things like the cinnamon potpourri Sophie loved and the chiming of the grandfather clock in the hallway.

Abby wrapped him in a comforting embrace. "Hey, you just got here. You should save this for tomorrow when you have to leave."

Abby took his hand. "Come on, show me around. I'm only familiar with the kitchen and dining room . . . well, and the restroom."

Steven guided her through the house, depositing Abby's things in the room next to his. He opened the door to his room last. He hadn't slept in his old room in forever, yet it remained exactly as he had left it.

He was drawn to the dresser, and his hand involuntarily touched the photo album and framed family photo. His dad's heavy, cherry jewelry box sat on one corner of the dresser; his mother's sat on the other. He was in no shape to open them. Not today.

From the corner of his eye, he saw Abby pick up the family portrait. When he stiffened, she stopped. "I'm sorry."

"It's okay."

Abby's finger brushed over their faces. "She looks a lot like Sophie."

Steven bit his lip, not knowing if he could answer if he tried. It had been so long since he'd seen a picture of them.

Returning the picture to its place, Abby squeezed Steven's hand.

"Hey, is this okay?" she whispered. "I don't want to overstep my boundaries."

Steven saw nothing but sincerity on her face. He nodded, words still eluding him.

She ran her fingertips from his temple down across his cheek and stopped when her hand rested on the side of his neck. Leaning in, she gave him a soft peck on the lips. "Thank you for letting me into your world."

Her other hand touched the opposite cheek as her thumbs rubbed across under his eyes, softly wiping away tears he didn't realize he'd shed. Steven grasped both of her wrists, keeping her hands there. "Thank *you*, Abby, for not giving up on me."

"Never." She leaned in and snagged another kiss before letting go.

"You're like a perfect blend of your parents. Your dad was a handsome man. I see so much of him in your features, but your hair and eyes . . . those are your mother's. Your mom looks gentle, nurturing. You have that too. You're such an attractive man, Steven."

Abby tugged his hand. "Come on, lead the way."

She started walking, but Steven grasped her hand and jerked her to a stop.

She turned around. "What?"

"You think I'm attractive?"

She sighed and rolled her eyes. "Yes, Steven, you're a very handsome man. I've told you that before."

"*No*, you've said I was *pretty*, not handsome—or attractive."

"I guess you're right, but you are, you know, handsome, that is . . . as well as attractive and sort of pretty, too, in a manly sort of way." The corner of her lip went up, and she winked when she said it.

"Don't patronize me, Miss Harris."

She cocked one eyebrow. "Would I lie to you to get in your pants?"

Steven started coughing. He had just taken a swig of cola from a bottle that he'd had stuffed in the corner of his seat. It burned when it came out his nose.

Steven was searching for a comeback when there was a quiet knock on his door.

"Son, I don't mean to intrude, but is it okay if I bring your things in?"

"Sure, set them on the bed, please. We'll be out in a minute."

Logan did as instructed, winking at Steven as he left. "I think I'll see what Sophie's up to. Abby, please make yourself at home."

Steven pulled clothing from his bag, laying everything on a chair for the morning.

The brand new and very comfortable-looking recliner which sat on the opposite side of the bed caught Steven's eye. *Is that for Sydney? Did they get it for Abby?*

"Where do the other bags go?"

"Bathroom stuff. I can take care of it later."

"If we put this stuff away now, we can forget about it and enjoy our visit. Is it okay if I help you?"

Steven's eyes squeezed shut, and he took a deep breath.

"It's okay."

❖    ❖    ❖

Abby quietly pulled his supplies out of the bags and set them on the counter: a box of catheters, a urinal, disposable gloves, Betadine, baby wipes . . .

An internal battle raged in Steven's head. *Perhaps this isn't such a great idea. But what do I have to hide? This is the real me.*

Steven blanched when she pulled out a pack of adult diapers, K-Y jelly, a box of suppositories, lotion for his butt . . .

*Well, she won't be trying to get in your pants now, will she?*

"Okay, tell me where everything goes, and we'll get it taken care of."

*Stop underestimating her, Chandler.*

"It all goes in the closet. The catheters, Betadine swabs, and blue pads have to be on the bottom shelf where I can reach them. The other stuff can go on the next shelf up. The, um, urinal can go on the back of the toilet. Can you pull the top off the catheter box for me?"

Steven's face warmed, but Abby got right down to business. "Do you need any of these left out?" She held a handful of catheters.

Steven swallowed and took a deep breath.

"No." His voice sounded unusually high-pitched. "I'll get one out of the closet when I need it."

Steven was talking to the floor when Abby's voice grew softer, gently coaxing him for information, things she'd never asked before, personal things.

*I want her to know me. Jill said to pick my battles. I can do this.*

"Does it hurt?"

He jerked his head up. "What?"

"The catheter. Does it hurt, you know, to use one?"

"Oh, no, not exactly. I can feel it deep inside sometimes, but I can't really feel much, you know, down there."

Her head was cocked to the side as if she were deep in thought. "Not at all?"

"Come here, Abby."

Steven flipped the toggle switch that would let him stand. He had only done this with supervision, and if he hurt himself, Jill would have his ass.

Carefully, he raised himself to a standing position. Abby gasped as he ascended. When he was standing as fully as he could, Steven looked into her eyes. They were nearly the same height—*for now.*

With one hand gripping the safety bar, Steven placed Abby's left hand below his ribs. She put her right one on the opposite side. "I have full feeling there."

She moved her hands down a few inches. "Here?"

Steven swallowed and nodded. "Keep going."

Her hands gripped his waist. "Here?"

"Mm-hmm."

Steven giggled when her hands glanced over the flesh that covered the curve of his pelvis. "That's a sensitive spot."

"Good to know." Abby smirked before she continued her exploration of his body.

When her thumbs rested over the ball and socket of his hips, he put his hands over hers. "That's it."

Abby frowned. "Nothing more?"

"There are a few spots that have sensation—mostly on the front of my legs."

She moved her hands up a fraction of an inch and tweaked the top of his butt.

Abby blushed. "Can you feel that?"

"Yep, I felt that."

Abby giggled. "I think I like this chair."

"I think there are a lot of things you *might* like about the chair."

"Are you propositioning me, Chandler?"

Steven frowned. "Nah, just wishful thinking."

"So you really can't"—she glanced at his lap—"you know . . ."

Steven laughed at her hesitancy to ask. "Raise the dead?"

She nodded.

"I haven't figured that one out yet. I'll let you know if there are any developments."

"Okay."

Steven silently thanked Sydney for taking the time to introduce Abby to information that was educational and factual. He wasn't sure that he was ready to have that conversation yet. He needed to explore his options. *Apparently, a discussion with Logan is in order.*

Advances in reproductive medicine had continued to evolve, a subject that had been a source of contention between Steven and his overly helpful uncle for years.

Logan would be all too willing to share whatever knowledge he had gleaned since Steven last considered exploring his sexuality.

It had been easier to ignore his non-existent sex life, his non-existent love life. Eventually, the notion of sharing life with a partner was a dull ache that tugged at Steven when he saw someone he knew in a healthy relationship, knowing that would never exist for him.

*But Abby . . .* Abby gave Steven something he hadn't experienced in a long time.

*Hope.*

Steven smiled. "What I can do is this."

When he put his hands on Abby's hips, her breath hitched, but she allowed him to lead. Abby blinked, and when her tongue slid over her lips, Steven put his hand behind her neck and gently ran his fingers through her hair. It was so soft, and she smelled so good.

He nipped her bottom lip with his teeth before running his tongue over it. Her tongue caressed his, and they deepened the kiss. They both laughed when their teeth bumped together. It was sweet and awkward and perfect all at once. Abby's eyes closed, and she let out another contented sigh.

Steven kissed the length of Abby's neck and nuzzled under her ear. One of her hands gripped his hair while the other dug into his hip. She held on as if he were her lifeline. Suddenly, she raised her mouth to his and they kissed a second time before she broke the kiss and rested her forehead against his.

*Mmm . . .*

Abby stepped away from Steven and swayed slightly. *I know exactly how you feel, Abby.* He reached out to steady her, and their fingers tangled together. Abby stepped to the side of the chair and watched as Steven gingerly lowered it to the seated position, unbuckled his belt, and tilted back. Using his arms, Steven shimmied himself back as far as he could and got situated in the correct spot.

Abby had seen Steven put the chair through its paces a handful of times, yet when he caught her watching, she blushed, and he wondered what she was thinking. He hoped one day he could give her further reasons to blush as they explored other adventures.

*In this chair.*

# Chapter Thirty

"We better go see what's cooking. It won't be long before someone else comes back to check on us. I feel like a teenager again."

Abby laughed as she took his hand. Once through the doorway, they were able to walk hand in hand down the hallway.

"I love the wide hallways and open spaces. This is a beautiful home."

"The architect had a disability. This was his personal residence for a number of years. The open floor plan and the wide doorways are all original. He was designing accessible homes before organizations like Concrete Change existed."

Steven could smell food, and the aroma of it owned him. Food wasn't bad at rehab, but this was home-cooked, Sophie Chandler food. He knew she'd made some of his favorite things, and he couldn't wait to indulge.

"Oh honey, I was about to come looking for you. Everything is ready to eat. Come sit down, and I'll make you a plate. What are you hungry for?"

Steven inhaled deeply. It all smelled so good. "A little of everything, please?"

Sophie had laid out an Italian feast fit for a king. She set a plate down in front of Steven, and he inhaled, clutching his chest. Incredible. The aroma alone had him drooling like Pavlov's dog.

Abby went and got a plate full of food but not nearly as full as Steven's. "It's been a long time since I've consumed so much, Aunt Soph. I hope your eyes aren't bigger than my stomach!"

For the longest time, the only sound in the room was the clinking of silverware against plates.

Sydney elbowed him. "Hey, I'll go take care of your medical supplies after we eat, and if you want, I can get you all ready for bed, so all you have to do later is transfer. We can have an easy evening then."

"You're going to have an easy evening. I showered and dressed in clean sweats before you picked me up. I fully intend to sleep in these. We'll change in the morning."

"Okay, well I'll run in and get your supplies put away, then."

"Wrong. You can relax; we're *all* going to have a stress-free evening. Abby and I put everything away a little bit ago. It's all situated the way I want it."

"Oh."

"Don't worry, there will be plenty of organizing when we move into the house."

From time to time during dinner, Steven caught himself watching Abby. She was adorable. He was delighted she agreed to spend the weekend with them. Steven knew she had things to do. The reports she needed to grade were rather detailed. Abby had explained that they were the written descriptions of her students' upcoming science fair projects. It would take her a while to go through them, and he understood the sacrifice she was making for him by putting them off until Sunday. As Steven swallowed the last bite of his garlic bread, a light bulb came on.

"Hey, Abby, I don't want to intrude, but could I help you at all with your homework on Sunday? I know I can't *grade* the papers, but you said it was science. I was AP science all through high school, and my bachelor's degree is in science."

Her expression went from one that was deep in thought to beaming. "Well, they don'tneed to be graded. I'm reading over them for composition, so I can decide whether the project is something they could actually do at a science fair.

"Some of the ideas are amazing, but some of the students don't put forth any effort, and some are downright dangerous. I'd love your input. I could bring them over on Sunday. Thank you."

Steven noticed everyone else was done, and they were all sitting around the table talking. The coffee maker had clicked on and was brewing. No one even noticed when he went to that familiar cupboard and took out his dishpan. He loved the fact that Sophie was so predictable, and all the things he needed were right where they belonged. Steven rolled up next to Abby first. "Are you all done, Abby?"

Her eyes got big when she realized what Steven was doing. "Oh, yes, it was very good. Thanks." She handed him her plate and silverware, and he lowered everything into the dishpan.

Sophie shot up. "Oh, honey, let me get that. You're visiting."

Logan put a hand on her arm, and Sophie sat back down and nodded. Steven buzzed over to his spot and grabbed his dishes, then continued to make his way around the table. After he gathered everyone's dirty dishes, he made his way to the sink. It had been so long, yet it felt good to contribute.

"Mom, your coffee is done. Could you pour a cup for me so it starts to cool?" Steven hated decaf even if hers was some of the best you could buy, but with her distracted, he could start on the dishes. He knew Logan would run interference for him. Sophie gave everyone a cup, and he could hear the clinking of spoons against ceramic as they added cream and sugar to flavor their drinks.

When Steven heard the scraping of chairs, he turned and looked over his shoulder to see his family quietly making their way out of the kitchen with their coffee. "Abby, could you throw a shot of milk into my coffee? Thanks."

"My pleasure, kind sir."

Steven turned on the hot water and rinsed each plate and utensil, putting them neatly in the dishwasher for his aunt. Abby snuck up behind him and leaned over his shoulder. From time to time, she'd point out a spot he missed. After several comments about his dish-rinsing skills, Steven turned the sprayer over his shoulder and gave it a squirt.

Abby let out a squeal.

She backed away but continued to tease him about his dishwashing abilities. "Hey now, be nice. I might be a horrible cook, but I'll be in the kitchen washing dishes every night that I'm home." He stuck a detergent tablet into the machine but didn't turn it on yet because there would be dessert.

Backing up, he maneuvered his chair under the sink and began washing the pots and pans. It was the least he could do after the spectacular dinner Sophie made. He knew she was up early for his benefit. There was no way he was letting her clean up.

Steven heard footsteps to his left, and as he was preparing to tell his mom to go sit down, Abby cleared her throat and smiled the most endearing smile. "I know you want to do this on your own, but if you'd like some company, I can rinse and dry as you wash?" Steven couldn't take his eyes off Abby's shirt. The thin cotton stretched over her breasts, and after it had gotten wet, he could see . . . everything.

Steven coughed, trying to pull himself together and look anywhere but at her chest. *She must think I'm a cad!*

Steven hesitated. He didn't want her to have to do anything while she was here, but it might be nice to do something domestic together.

"That would be nice, Abby. Thanks."

Steven picked up a lasagna pan, but just as he lifted it into the sink, he felt a tickle on that spot above his hip, and Steven jerked, dropping the pan and causing soapy water to splash everywhere. The front of his shirt was soaked. Steven looked up, and Abby stood with her hand over her mouth. She gasped a fake gasp before she began to giggle.

Steven growled. "Abby!"

Steven had never seen her let loose like this before. It made him love being with her even more. For a while they worked in companionable silence. When Abby went to rinse the big pasta pot with the sprayer, a shot of water hit his chest.

"Oops!"

It was the last of the dishes, and apparently Abby anticipated a reaction.

As soon as she finished rinsing, she turned to make a hasty getaway but slipped on the wet floor. Steven watched her lose her balance and reached out to steady her before she fell. "Careful there, Abby. Wet tile is slippery. It's all fun and games till someone gets hurt."

Abby got serious all of a sudden. She backed up so that her hips were resting on the edge of the table. Her gaze was cast downward.

*Is she embarrassed?*

"What is it, Abby?"

"I'm sorry if I was too pushy, you know, earlier. I've been wondering what home life is like for you. I realized the day I bought the cast tats that I had no idea how things are for you outside of a hospital setting."

Steven took her hand and squeezed it. "Hey, it's okay. I know you're curious. We're about to embark on an adventure together where it will be necessary for you to know this stuff anyway. I'm not offended. This is my life."

Steven went to a small closet that housed cleaning supplies. He pulled the mop off its hook, buzzed over to the puddle on the floor, and wiped it up. It wasn't enough to even warrant wringing out the mop, but he didn't want anyone to fall and get hurt.

"Come on. Let's go see what kind of movies Sydney is going to torture us with."

Abby looked down at her shirt. "I need to find something dry. Would anyone be offended if changed into my pajamas, quick?"

"Not at all. I need to grab a dry shirt too. Come on." They headed back to their rooms, and before he knew it, Abby was standing in his doorway.

"I'm done." She was fresh faced, and her hair was pulled back into a ponytail.

When they got to the living room, everyone was sitting around talking quietly, their coffee cups abandoned on the cocktail table. Sydney stood up, gathered the three cups, and headed to the kitchen.

"Sydney, where are you going?"

"We have to have popcorn and something to drink. I won't be long. Go get comfy."

Steven parked perpendicular to the couch. After he undid his seatbelt and the safety bar, he looked at Logan. "Would you mind spotting for me?"

"Not at all, son. I'd be delighted."

Inch by inch, Steven worked his way across his board. Patting the space beside him, he silently asked Abby to join him when she returned. She curled up under his arm, pulling her feet up. Steven gave her a gentle squeeze.

Sydney carried in a tray of goodies and sat it on the coffee table. She opened a folding table and slid it against the arm of the couch so Steven could reach it.

Grabbing a few things from the tray, Sydney filled the table with two paper cups of popcorn and an assortment of theater boxes of candy. Last but not least, she set two small bottles of root beer on the tray. Steven groaned. *Sophie and her root beer.*

Sydney held up *Revenge of the Nerds, The Breakfast Club,* the very first *Nightmare on Elm Street*, and *Grease.* She raised one eyebrow. "Steven?"

"I'd like Abby to choose. I know I'm only good for one or two movies."

Abby looked up at Steven and blushed. *"Grease?"*

"Sure, that's fine. Do you want to pick the other one?"

"Nah, I'm good. What do you want to watch, Steven?"

He looked at Sydney, her smile triumphant. "Abby already picked my favorite. It's up to you."

*"Elm Street."*

Abby's eyes got big. Steven gave her shoulder a squeeze. "I'll protect you, Abby."

He felt her shudder, and he mentally pumped his fist.

They watched *Grease* first. Abby and Sydney sang along. Sydney recited most of the words too. Occasionally, Abby would put a piece of popcorn or candy against his lips, and Steven would take it from her. His arm had slipped from her shoulder and rested along her side, and when no one was looking, he'd rub little circles with his thumb on the side of her breast. He wondered if it was too much, but she snuggled in closer and took a deep, contented breath.

*She's okay with this.*

When it was time to swap movies, Abby hopped up to use the bathroom. Steven realized he hadn't done that since he left rehab hours before. He tried not to slack when it came to bowel and bladder care. It was difficult sometimes when he was working to stay on a rigid schedule, but there was no excuse to neglect his bladder while he was relaxing at home.

"Sydney, could you grab my urinal and a catheter? It's been a while since I've taken care of business."

Sydney and Abby came back down the hallway together. Abby made an excuse and went to the kitchen to see Sophie, giving Steven privacy. He finished quickly, calling Abby as he removed his gloves and handed the urinal to Sydney.

Everyone got settled, and Sydney turned off the lights. Whenever something scary happened, Abby got impossibly closer. Steven was sure Abby had drifted off, but when Johnny Depp got sucked into the mattress, Sydney shrieked, and Abby jerked up off the couch.

"Come here, honey. It's okay," Steven whispered. Abby smiled and settled under his arm again. They both drifted off, and Steven awoke to Logan shaking him gently.

"Son, wake up. The movie is over."

Steven yawned and stretched. Abby's head rested on his lap, and someone had covered her with a blanket.

"We missed the movie."

Logan chuckled. "Yeah, most of it. You fell asleep right after you got Abby back to sleep."

Steven reached out and shook her. "Abby . . . hey, Abby . . . wake up. It's time for bed."

Abby rolled over and pulled her arms into her chest. When she opened her eyes, she gasped and sat up so quickly that she nearly fell off the sofa. Steven grabbed her arm to catch her.

"Oh God! I am *so* sorry!"

"Hey, it's okay. Come on, it's time for bed."

Abby looked around. "You're waiting on me. I'm sorry." She fumbled with the blanket and righted herself.

"Please stop apologizing. It's fine. I woke up a minute or two before you did."

Abby stood and folded the blanket, watching as Logan helped to get everything lined up so Steven could move back to his chair. He'd gotten stiff on the couch, and it was difficult to transfer, but he wouldn't have traded his night for the world.

Sydney waited in Steven's room where she had the blankets turned back, and a few extra pillows for positioning filled the recliner. Sydney laid two self-contained catheter bags on Steven's nightstand. They not only had a pre-lubed cath tube, but a sealed bag was attached. The unit was fully self-contained, and Steven could use them independently.

In the bathroom, Steven's pills were laid out on the counter. Taking them before brushing his teeth, he cathed one more time and washed his hands.

Sydney was patiently waiting in his room, flipping through his photo album. "Do you think about them much anymore?"

"Every day, Sydney. Every day." Sydney nodded a few times and closed the book.

Steven backed up to the head of the bed and readied his board. After everything was set, he inched his way into bed. Sydney reached down to swing his legs around for him. "No, let me. Please spot me."

"Okay."

Steven made fists and locked his elbows, lifting his behind off the mattress. He moved his butt backward as far as he could before hooking his hands behind his right knee. In one fluid movement, he leaned back and swung his leg up on the bed. Once Steven braced his heel on the bed, he hooked his hands behind his left knee and swung it up onto the bed as well. He moved them around until he got them where he needed them, then he rolled onto his right side, facing the recliner. It was the first time he had been able to keep himself balanced enough to do it independently.

Sydney flitted around, putting pillows between his knees and ankles. Once she was satisfied, she covered him.

"Should I leave your bathroom light on and leave the door ajar?"

"I have no intention of getting out of bed by myself."

"I better leave it on. That way, I won't need the overhead light when I help you turn."

As Steven was drifting off, he heard the shuffling of feet. It was far too early for Sydney. His door creaked open, and a soft voice called his name. "Steven? I can't sleep."

"Can you sleep in the recliner? I don't know how comfortable it is."

"Yeah, that would be great."

"Well then, come on."

Abby shuffled across his room with a blanket and climbed onto the recliner. When she leaned the chair back, she was mere inches from his face. Reaching out, she took his hand.

"G'night, Steven."

"'Night, hon. Get some sleep."

Steven had barely uttered the words, and Abby was snoring softly. Giving her hand a squeeze, he snuggled down into his pillow. He didn't know how long he watched her before he drifted off himself.

Steven was awake early, so the house was silent.

If he were at rehab, they'd be dragging him out of bed soon, and if he were back to work, it would be time to get up, but this was some lazy daisy, Saturday morning, and it was the first time he'd slept at home in forever.

He heard Abby yawn, her bedding rustling, and Steven pictured her as she stretched, eyes squeezed shut, reaching for the sky as her little T-shirt crept up her belly. He smiled at the thought.

"Be right back," she muttered, and he heard her slippers shuffle across the floor. When Abby returned, she plopped down on the edge of his bed and yawned again, rubbing her eyes. Her hair stuck up everywhere, and her Hello Kitty pajamas were rumpled. She looked endearingly like a little girl.

"What are we doing today? Do we have plans?"

"Dunno. Is there something you'd like to do? I'm not the social butterfly I used to be. Have you ever walked the campus at Yale? We could do one of the self-guided tours downtown."

"Is there something we could do on the waterfront?"

"Sure. Would you feel up to walking the promenade along the Sound? We could stop and get pizza at Zuppardi's."

Her face was split with a huge grin. "Oh, I love their pies! I haven't had one in forever."

"Maybe Logan could drive over and meet us at the house around five."

"We could go pick up some things for the house while we're out, if you'd like. It sounds like it's going to be a gorgeous day. Not too warm. I'm sure Sydney would love going with us as long as you don't let her tire you out."

"I've shopped with her before. I'll be all right. She's always mindful of my needs."

"Should we go get some breakfast, then?"

# Chapter Thirty-one

Apparently the entire populace of New Haven had the same idea. They were all there—on the green, at the fountain, in the park.

Navigating the crowds was difficult. Steven felt invisible. People were inconsiderate. They stepped in front of him, pushed into him, and one woman even leaned against his chair while she talked on her phone.

While the trio shopped, Steven handed over his credit card and allowed the girls to load him up like a pack mule. He didn't think they needed everything they bought, but planning for a future with Abby was exhilarating.

Steven was exhausted when they returned to the car, and he dreaded the deal he'd made with Jill to put in his PT time that evening.

Later, meeting with the contractor and Logan, Steven signed off on the house. With the closing on Monday, Logan would pick Steven up to meet Brooke at the bank and finalize the paperwork. Steven looked forward to the upcoming support group and Concrete Change meetings to praise the work of Aaron's team and to encourage others to meet with him.

❖   ❖   ❖

Steven signed back in to rehab more than twenty minutes early, so he hung out in the garden with Abby until Jill's shift started.

Steven was so tired that Jill had to harp on him about staying on task. He was cranky, but she was persistent. They finally agreed to call it a night, and Steven went to his room to get ready for bed.

A new nurse, Chelsea, worked with Steven that night. She convinced him a hot shower would wash all his troubles down the drain. Steven was thankful when he snuggled into bed. He was warm and sleepy, and his muscles no longer ached. He settled in for a long night of sleep, and Chelsea bid him goodnight.

Steven's slumber was interrupted by Alec sniffling and snuffling and blowing his nose. Steven yawned and looked at his clock. *After ten! I haven't gotten a decent night's sleep since this guy moved in!*

Steven smiled when his roommate started snoring softly. He pulled the blankets up to his neck, and sleep quickly claimed him.

In dreamland, Alec called out, begging Steven to wake up. Steven couldn't imagine why. During every encounter they'd shared, Alec acted like a spoiled brat. Steven tried to reposition and realized the kid really was calling his name, begging for help.

*What in the world?*

"Alec? What's the problem?"

"My head hurts."

"You sound like shit. Do you have a cold?"

"I don't think so."

"How long have you been congested?"

"I don't know. Since right after bedtime? I feel like my head is going to explode. I can hear the blood rushing through my head. Please, get help. It hurts so bad."

*Something is seriously wrong!*

Steven reached for his call bell, but it wasn't clipped to his blanket. *Of all nights to be without it!*

*Damn new nurse.*

Steven didn't want to start screaming and create hysteria when he was capable of helping his neighbor.

*I can do this!*

Steven burned precious time fumbling with the release on the bed rail. It was fortunate that the nurse neglected to engage the one on the lower half of the bed.

Steven reached for his chair and grumbled when he realized Chelsea had left the tiny manual chair next to his bed after the shower. *I'd rather have the electric for my first solo transfer, but there's no time to be picky. The kid is in trouble!*

Steven slid one leg at a time off the bed and thanked his lucky stars that the transfer board was on the seat of the chair where he'd left it. Making sure that the brakes were locked, he laid the board across the span between bed and chair while Leslie's words rang loud and clear in his head: "Jill said you aren't to do this *alone* yet."

*Alone.*

*What am I doing?*

*The kid has treated me like garbage since he arrived, yet here I am risking life, limb, and quite possibly a severe thrashing because of him. Jill will probably kick me out.*

Steven couldn't shake the feeling that something was terribly wrong. Alec would never ask him for help. *Not if I was the last person on earth. Not unless it was a true emergency.*

Steven knew he could get to Alec and check on him in less time than it would take to conjure up a nurse so late. He wheeled the loaner chair to Alec's bed.

Steven yanked the cord for the light over Alec's head, and the kid moaned painfully. "God, that light is stabbing through my head. Can't you *please* turn it off?"

Steven would have, but one look at Alec told Steven the kid was in a life-threatening situation. He pulled the blankets back to assess him.

"Sorry, buddy, close your eyes, and let me take a look."

Alec's face was covered in red blotches, and his T-shirt was soaked with sweat. Reaching out, Steven took Alec's wrist in his hand and counted. His pulse was so slow . . . *way too slow.*

"Alec, look at me. Can you tell me what's wrong?"

Immediately, the kid's hands went to his hair.

"My head! Oh God, my head . . . it feels like it's going to explode."

"Is your stomach upset?"

"Yeah, I feel like I could hurl."

As he asked questions, Steven was visually inspecting the kid, searching for the offending object he knew to be the culprit.

*Think, Chandler! It could be anything in any place. There's no time to waste!*

"I'm gonna sit you up, buddy. Let me know if it helps. I have to figure out what's making you sick. It'll be okay." Glancing down, Steven noticed the overnight collection bag for Alec's catheter. Empty. Something would have accumulated since bedtime.

BINGO! Now to solve the problem.

Steven followed the tubing up to the edge of Alec's shorts, and nothing was kinked. Steven reached into Alec's boxers and found the tube. It was folded in half and bunched under his thigh. *Someone is going to be in a heap of trouble!*

Steven straightened out the tubing, and a rush of urine flowed through the tube.

"What the hell, man? Leave my junk alone!" Steven sat back and watched the clock. Suddenly, Alec's distress was replaced by utter disbelief. "The pain. It's gone. *What did you do to me?*"

"I took care of the problem. How's the headache?"

Alec scratched his head. "Almost gone?"

Steven had to stretch to pull the blood pressure cuff from the wall and put it on Alec's arm. He reached for his stethoscope and sighed when he realized it wasn't there. He wasn't a doctor in the hospital, just some good Samaritan trying to help.

"You're feeling better, then?"

Alec nodded and answered quietly. "Yeah."

"Good. Let's get someone in here to check you out."

Alec clutched the blankets to his chest. "I'm telling them you were all up in my junk. That shit's not right, man."

Steven shrugged. "Whatever, dude."

Steven's call bell lay on the floor next to his bed. He pulled his reacher from the clip on the side of his power chair and retrieved the bell, breathing a sigh of relief when the light over the door came on.

Steven went back to monitor Alec until he could hand him off to a member of the staff for a professional assessment. Alec was still clammy, but a quick check of his pulse confirmed that his heart rate had returned to normal. Alec tried to jerk his wrist away but relented when Steven refused to let go. The ruddy blotches had faded, and before a single staff member burst through the door, the kid was snoring.

Leslie was the first to enter the room, appearing startled to find the lights on and Steven out of bed. "What the . . .?

"Steven? How did you get out of bed? You didn't . . .?" Steven followed her gaze as she looked to the floor. His blankets were half off the bed. His transfer board was several feet away.

Steven looked down; he was wearing boxers and nothing else.

"Uh, yeah. He was in distress. I think he'll be okay, but someone should look him over." Leslie began assessing Alec as she talked.

Shaking Alec to rouse him she asked, "How do you feel?"

"Better now," he answered groggily. "But my roommate is a perv."

Leslie laughed and looked at Steven, silently mouthing the words. *"What in the world?"*

"He had his hand in my pants. That shit's *not* cool."

Leslie cocked her eyebrow as she took out her stethoscope and began taking Alec's blood pressure. "It's slightly elevated but nothing serious. What gives?"

"The catheter tube was kinked and pinched off under his thigh." Steven's retort left him feeling a bit smug. *Careful, Chandler. Jill's gonna hand you your ass!*

"You realize that any other patient would have used the call button. Only *you* would drag yourself out of bed." Steven pulled a T-shirt from his dresser. *Please don't feed the crocodiles . . .* He rolled back to Alec's side of the room.

"I didn't have the call bell, and neither did he. He woke me, complaining of a severe headache. He was congested and sweating profusely; his face and chest were covered in red blotches . . ."

Leslie studied Steven's face. "Autonomic dysreflexia?"

"Imagine what could have happened if I didn't wake up." Steven took stock of what he had done. Without putting conscious thought into it, he had gotten himself out of bed and answered the call. He'd assessed Alec's condition and solved the problem.

*Dr. Chandler is on his game!*

Leslie stuck a thermometer in Alec's mouth. When it beeped she flicked the plastic sheath into the trash. "Who put you to bed?"

Steven rubbed his eyes. "Some new girl."

"Chelsea?"

"Yeah, she was professional, seemed attentive . . ."

"She's not too attentive if she missed something like providing a call bell or a patient lying on a kinked catheter tube."

"We both know this conversation isn't appropriate in front of a patient. I'd like to talk to Jill about how this will be handled."

"I'll say something to her."

She took Alec's wrist, checking his heart rate again. "How are you feeling, Alec?"

He shivered. "All right, I think. My head still hurts a little, but not like it did."

"Let's get you into a dry shirt; the one you're in is drenched." Steven moved so Leslie could do what she needed to.

Someone cleared their throat from the doorway, and Steven cringed.

"Chandler?"

"Jill."

"Do you mind telling me why I have the distinct feeling you've been up to no good?"

"Um, can I plead the fifth and say that I was working toward my occupational goals?"

"I was leaving and saw the lights on in here. What's up?" she asked, motioning to Alec.

"Autonomic dysreflexia. He had an episode. The catheter was kinked, and I couldn't get to my call button, so I did the next best thing. Look, I'm sorry if you think I acted rashly, but there was no way it could wait."

Jill picked up Steven's blankets and sat at the foot of his bed. Sighing, she ran her hands through her hair. "Look, I understand, and you did do the right thing, given the circumstances. It's surreal having a patient here with your background." She chuckled. "I think this is a first in my career. But I have to ask you to refrain from treating the patients. You know . . . insurance liability and whatnot."

Then she grinned at him. "Does it feel good to be getting your feet wet?"

Steven puffed out his chest. "I didn't even realize that I was acting on instinct until I reached for my stethoscope and didn't have one."

"I heard him say something about your getting friendly with him? He's not going to sue us or anything, is he? What did you *do*?"

"I, um, I sorta reached into his boxers and took care of business. The problem was inside his pants. I didn't mean to freak him out."

"From now on, stay in bed, Steven. I'm not ready for you to fall and break something. Not in my facility. You got it?"

"Mm-hmm. I hear ya."

"I mean it."

"I understand, Jill. Scout's honor?" He held up his fingers, trying to remember if it was supposed to be two or three.

"Were you even a scout, Chandler?"

*Busted.* Steven hung his head. "Uh . . . no?"

"I suppose I should call Alec's family."

"Can I talk to you about Chelsea?"

"She's gone for the evening. We'll talk tomorrow. In my office."

"I don't want you to be too hard on her."

"I'll listen to what you have to say, but this . . . it's not only up to me."

Jill quietly left the room. Steven prayed Alec's family would begin to be receptive to his needs.

After she left, Alec turned toward Steven. "I suppose I should be thanking you. Leslie told me I could have died if you hadn't helped."

"You could have. It's a fairly common occurrence in people with spinal cord injuries. It's more common in the first six months or so."

His eyes grew wide. "Will it happen again?"

"It's possible. Some people have frequent episodes, others hardly ever. It happens most commonly in individuals with injuries above T-six, but it can happen with lower injuries."

"But why? What happened?"

"Because some part of your body below your injury encounters an irritant, a stimulus, if you will. Because your nerves can't send the impulse to your brain, your whole body sort of goes into overload. Your blood vessels constrict, and your blood pressure rises. That's why you had the headache."

"What kind of things set it off? What kind of irritant?"

"Hmm, let's see. A backed up catheter is probably the most common. Being constipated or having a bladder infection can cause it; pressure sores, something as simple as a bruise, a stone in your shoe, or even an ingrown toenail. For a woman, it could be menstrual cramps or going into labor. If it happens a few times, you'll learn to recognize the symptoms early enough to call for help. Sometimes you can find the trigger and fix it yourself, like the catheter tube tonight, although you should always get checked out. Monitor your blood pressure. If your blood pressure is too high for too long, you could have a stroke."

"How do you know all this? Has it happened to you before?"

"No. My injury is at T-twelve. It's not entirely impossible, but it would be rare for me to have an episode like yours. I'm actually surprised that you had an episode at T-seven-eight."

"What do you mean yours is at T-twelve? You've got casts on your legs. Actually, I didn't think you . . ."

"You never asked. I've been in a chair for a while. I did tell you I understood; you weren't listening."

Alec cast his gaze to the floor, and his face and neck reddened for an entirely different reason. "Man, I'm so sorry. I . . . I don't know how people can say they understand when they have no idea. My entire life has changed."

"Yeah, mine too. More than you'll ever know, kid."

A petite brunette rushed into the room, wearing sweats and looking slightly disheveled.

Steven knew her.

"Alec? Oh baby, I'm so sorry." She touched Steven's roommate everywhere—his face, his arms—as if he were a mirage that would disappear before her eyes. "I've missed you so much."

The pair sobbed, and Steven felt out of place. He turned to the window and took in the New Haven skyline.

"Mom? What are you doing here? How . . ." Alec asked, but the woman interrupted him.

"They said you suffered some kind of episode, that you could have died. I didn't even wake your father. I had to see for myself that you were okay."

"Yeah, I think I'm all right. You can thank my roommate, Steven. He helped me out tonight."

Not wanting to appear rude, Steven turned to greet Alec's mother. A warm smile graced her features, and Steven made the connection: Kristle Leonard. She was a patient at the practice.

"Dr. Chandler, I heard you were under the weather. How nice to see you again."

Steven extended his hand. "Mrs. Leonard. It's nice to see you too. Alec and I have been roomies since he was admitted here. I'm sorry I never made the connection." He knew her husband was in construction. Coming face to face with her now made him feel embarrassed.

Alec had buried his face in his hands; his ears burned red. *Is he okay?*

"Alec? What's wrong? Is it happening again?"

Alec groaned and lowered his hands. "This just gets better and better. You're a *doctor* too?"

"Yeah, I *was* . . .before my accident. Right now, I'm only your roommate."

Kristle beamed like a proud mother. "Dr. Chandler is a neurologist. He's a scientist too. He works in stem cell research. He's living proof that you can be anything you want to be, kiddo." She fussed with Alec's hair and kissed the top of his head.

"He, um, he tried to take me under his wing. I haven't been very receptive." Alec leaned forward to look around his mother. "I owe you a huge apology, man. I don't know how to channel this anger and you're so . . . perfect."

"Perfect? Hah! You've got to be kidding. I'm far from it."

"But I've acted like such a jerk."

"Look, I understand where you're coming from. I understand your anger. Jill reminded me none too subtly that I was very much like you at eighteen."

"Eighteen?" He nearly choked on the word. "But I thought . . . I guess it's true what they say about assuming things."

"Yeah, well . . . look, we can talk about it some other time. I'm going to see if I can find someone to get me back into bed. I know you want to visit with your mom for a while."

Steven headed into the corridor and encountered Leslie. She carried an irrigation kit under one arm, a bottle of saline and a bottle of drinking water under the other, *plus* she had a pill cup in her hand.

"What can I do for you, Steven?"

"I was wondering if I could get back into bed after I use the restroom."

"Sure, let me get Alec's cath irrigated and taken care of real quick, and I'll spot you."

"Thanks."

As Steven was dumping the urinal, Alec began to yell. Steven washed up and opened the door to a confrontation.

"*Seriously*, Mom. Please? She's taking care of my *catheter*. She'll be done *soon*." Once again, Alec's face was flushed. *Oh* . . .

"Kristle, would you mind coming down to the solarium with me since Leslie is helping Alec? I don't know if I can open the door, but I could use a cold drink."

He winked at Alec as Kristle exited ahead of him.

"Thanks, man."

Steven nodded.

They walked quietly to the small room off the foyer, and Kristle opened the door for Steven.

The fluorescents flickered and hummed while the room came to life. Steven motioned to a couch.

"Why don't you sit down? It's late; you look exhausted, and please, call me Steven."

"The last few weeks have been tough. I haven't had a good night's sleep since his accident."

*Me either.*

Kristle had suffered debilitating migraines which brought her to Steven's office after a referral from the emergency department. "You need to take care of yourself, Kristle. The migraines will come back."

She hung her head. "I know."

"You can't help your son if you don't take care of yourself. I've been trying to spend time with Alec, but until tonight, he's pushed me away. I'm hoping in the light of day, he'll still be receptive to interacting with me. He doesn't realize how much potential he has."

Her puzzled eyes bore into his. "What do you mean he *pushed you away?*"

"He's angry, has quite the chip on his shoulder. But rehab is going pretty well for him from what I've seen."

Kristle wrung her hands in frustration. "He's his father's son. He has Patrick's temper, and it doesn't help that he's terribly spoiled. My husband rules with an iron fist and only seems to know how to show affection through grand gestures. Do you know what I mean?"

"Yeah, I think I do."

"Patrick and Alec went everywhere together. Long trips over school breaks, white water rafting, skydiving, hang-gliding, Canadian adventures to hunt big game. They've been skiing in Vail and sailing in British Columbia. He'd never admit it, but since Alec became a teenager, they have been nearly inseparable."

Kristle's shoulders shook as she choked out her account of the night of Alec's emergency. "My husband came to the hospital as soon as they brought Alec in. I was in Oregon taking care of my mother. When he found out what happened, he told our son that he wanted nothing to do with him—that he was a disappointment, that he'd ruined our dreams with his carelessness. Our boy went into surgery thinking we hated him. Oh God, Steven, what if he had died in surgery?"

Kristle wrapped her arms around her torso as she crumbled. Steven got as close as he could and reached out to her. She fell to her knees and sobbed into his chest as he held her.

Steven rubbed her back, and eventually her sobbing was reduced to hiccups and sniffles.

"It would do him a world of good to have the support of his family. You know, I was eighteen when I became paralyzed. It was the love and support of my family that helped me to get through it. I thought my world had come to an end too."

"I've never seen my husband so lost. He hasn't been able to control his anger, but deep down, I can see how broken he is. He almost acts as if"—she shuddered before continuing—"as if he's grieving Alec's death."

Steven remembered that first night when, like a mantra, his conscience kept chanting . . . *Where is his family?*

"Your husband can't be completely unfeeling. It sounds as if they were close. Doesn't he . . . How could he not be pacing the floor with worry? If he were my son . . . Some people aren't as fortunate as you are—to have a child and nearly lose him . . . But you *haven't* lost him. You're shutting him out. It's hurting Alec's progress. If he cares at all, he'll make the effort."

"Patrick was away overseeing a huge project, so we hadn't seen him for weeks. Alec had been driving for some time, and he'd talked with us about getting his motorcycle endorsement, so I wasn't all that surprised when he asked if he could sign up for a course. Alec's very mature for his age, and I trusted that he would be a safe operator."

"So what happened?"

"Alec was so proud when he passed the course and got his license. He'd been saving his pay for some time, and it was his instructor who went with us to get the bike."

"Alec and Patrick have vacationed on Patrick's bike all up and down the coast. Alec thought his dad would be surprised. Pat came home a little over a week later, and he was surprised all right—"

She held her head in her hands and began sobbing as she uttered the words. "When he saw the bike in the driveway . . . he flipped. They fought and Alec took off. I wasn't there to intervene. Oh, Steven, what have I *done?*"

"You couldn't have known that Alec was going to get hurt. It does sound like your family could work on their communication skills. Jill has some wonderful counselors that work with both the patients and their families. Might be a great way for Alec and his dad to break the ice."

"I don't know. They're both pretty stubborn."

Steven tugged on Kristle's hand, and she stood. "Come on, it's getting late. You made progress by coming here. Say goodnight to your boy before you go. He's had a rough night."

Alec was snoring lightly, and all was quiet. "I'm not going to wake him, Steven."

Kristle rummaged in her purse and pulled out a phone. "Here, would you give him this tomorrow? His friends have been asking about him. Could you tell him I love him and ask him to call me?"

"Yeah, sure." Steven grabbed Sydney's notebook, writing on a page and tearing it out. "Call me sometime, and we'll talk more. We'll find a way to reunite your family."

"You're a good man, Steven Chandler. I'm glad Alec's got you."

Steven looked over at the kid who had tested every last one of his nerves since he'd arrived and turned his peaceful rehab experience on end. "I'll try to look out for him. Please be careful driving home."

"I will, thanks."

Kristle leaned down and kissed Alec's face, whispering, "I love you, son."

Alec mumbled a reply in his sleep.

"Goodnight, Steven."

"Goodnight."

Someone had re-made Steven's bed and folded the blankets back, the cord for the call bell was stretched across the bed and clipped to the sheet within his reach. He hit the button and waited. It was after 1 a.m. Stifling a yawn, he laid both his and Alec's phones on the table, and he set his charger next to them.

Randall, one of the orderlies, came in. "You ready to get back in bed, doc?"

Steven groaned. "My secret's out, huh?"

"You betcha. Everyone's talking about what you did tonight. Not many would have done that."

"I never had any choice. I'd never turn my back on someone else."

"I gotta ask what you did to get on Jill's good side. She's strutting around here like some proud mother."

Steven could picture the same expression she wore when one of her patients made some profound accomplishment. "Yeah, we, um, we go way back."

"You . . . and *Jill?*" he asked, disbelief lacing his tone.

"Oh God, not like *that*. She was my therapist almost twenty years ago when I first became disabled."

Randall laughed nervously and rubbed his face with his hands. "Gotcha. I've never pictured her with anyone. She's married to her job." He laughed. "Okay, doc. I can get a lift, we can use the board, or I can get another set of hands. Take your pick."

"I'm tired. Can you get someone to throw me into bed? I've had a long day."

"You got it!"

Steven considered calling Abby, but it was late. If he texted her, and she was sleeping, the chirp wouldn't wake her.

Hey, you awake?

*Yeah, what time is it?*

Late.

*Aren't you tired?*

I was sleeping, but Alec had an emergency.

*Oh no! Is he okay?*

Yeah, I got out of bed to help him. He'll be fine.

*You got out of bed? Are you okay?*

Yeah, it's all good.

*So, you were playing superhero.*

I GUESS YOU COULD SAY THAT. -ROLLS EYES-

*YOU CAN BE MY SUPERHERO, DOC.*

YEAH?

*YEAH. GET SOME SLEEP, STEVEN. IT'LL BE TOMORROW BEFORE YOU KNOW IT.*

GOODNIGHT, MY LITTLE DAMSEL. WINK, WINK.

*GOODNIGHT, STEVEN.*

He tucked his phone under his pillow and snuggled under the covers.

*Superhero . . . Yeah, Abby, I'll be your superhero!*

# Chapter Thirty-two

Randall came in and shook Steven. "Hey, time to get up."

Steven rubbed his eyes and looked around. "What time is it?"

"Six thirty. Someone called in sick, so I'm helping get people up before I go."

"Of all mornings to have to get up early."

"Sorry, man. Once you get in your chair, you can always recline for a while."

He'd spent hours reclining in the on-call room in his last electric. *Yes, I can go back to sleep.*

Randall pulled on Steven's pants and put non-skid socks over his toes. "Now, you're transferring into the chair this morning, yes?"

"I am."

"What else do you need me to do?"

"Spot me. I can do the rest."

"Good deal, man. You ready?" Steven nodded and Randall swapped the manual chair for the electric. Steven reached for his board and traversed the small space.

"All right, Steven, I'll see you later. I've got a few more to get moving before I go. Have a good day."

"You too, Randall. See you later."

"Bye."

Steven pulled on a shirt and threw on some deodorant. He brushed his teeth, combed his hair, and used the facilities. It was Alec's bowel training day. Steven had taken care of that the day before. He didn't want to tie up the facility when someone else needed it.

For fifteen years, Steven was able to manage bowel and bladder care completely free of dependence on others. People had no idea of the simple things they took for granted.

Steven left the bathroom and looked over to the other bed.

"Hey, man." Alec smiled hesitantly.

"Hey, how do you feel? Are you all right this morning?"

"Yeah. I'm okay."

"Good. I'm sure it was frightening."

"Yeah." He shuddered. "It was. It happened so fast."

Steven retrieved Alec's phone from his table. "Here. Your mom left this. She said your friends have been calling . . . and she loves you. She asked you to call her."

"My ma. Yeah, she's great. I'll have to wait till tomorrow to call her. *He'll* be home today. It's Sunday."

"She's worried about you. Don't make her wait, even if all you do is text her."

"I guess. Stress makes her physically sick—migraines, high blood pressure, stomach problems. I know how difficult my dad can be to live with. Calling when he's home may cause a blow-up."

Steven stopped in the doorway. There was something that needed to be said. Alec would spend the rest of his life living in regret if he didn't make amends with his parents.

"She told me a little bit about that. Look, I know he's being a jerk right now, but I know he cares about you. Don't shut your old man out. Life is way too short to hold grudges. When he does make an effort, and he will, don't push him away."

❖  ❖  ❖

Steven left Alec to think about that while he went in search of breakfast. He found Debbie sitting at a table, slurping a smoothie from a Styrofoam cup. A Danish lay on a plate in front of her.

Steven grabbed breakfast and two rolls of utensils. "Is this seat taken?"

Debbie laughed. "That sounded like some cheesy pick-up line. How are you, Steven?"

"I'm great. You?"

"I'm pretty good. But it's early."

"Is that your Danish?" He gestured to the pastry in front of her, and she frowned.

"Yeah, the aide who feeds me brought it, but she hasn't come back. They felt I was too thin for my age and height, so I have a smoothie with each meal. But if it weren't for the smoothies, I'd probably starve."

Steven was appalled. "Do they *really* forget to feed you?"

She laughed. "Not all the time. It's not like I'm missing much nourishment if I skip a Danish."

Steven held up a packet of silverware. "Would you be offended if I fed you? I didn't see any utensils on your tray."

She cocked her head and the corner of her mouth lifted up into a smile. "You sure you don't mind?"

"Nope, not at all. When I first went to med school, our class watched a movie about an experiment entitled Caring. A room of people whose arms had been immobilized were served a dinner. The servers left the room, but not a single guest could feed themselves. For the longest time, they sat, salivating over the mouthwatering meal until one by one, the guests began feeding the person across the table from them. It was an exercise to foster caring about one another."

Steven was cutting the Danish into bite-sized pieces as he spoke. "Can I hold your drink for you? I feel like you'll get a stiff neck."

"No, I've got it, but thanks. I've sort of gotten used to drinking this way. It's been eight weeks."

"Will you be shedding your casts soon?"

"Actually, the doc sees me tomorrow. I have to keep the back brace longer, but it would be incredible to do something like scratch my nose, you know?"

"I understand all too well. I'm so excited for you."

"Yeah, but then the work begins."

"And the sooner you'll be able to go home."

She moved her right index finger around in a circle. "Ooh-ooh! There's nobody home right now. Mom's on vacation, and Daddy is away somewhere for work."

She looked at his legs. "So how long have you got left?"

"I'm hoping about a week. I can't wait to get out of these things. It's been forever since I've seen my feet. I want to look to make sure they are still there."

Debbie giggled. "Was there ever any question?"

"Oh yeah."

"Wow, can I ask what happened? Is that too personal?"

"I'll show you mine, if you show me yours."

She snorted. "Okay, who's first?"

"I'll go. I've used a wheelchair since I was eighteen. I got hit by a car last October."

"Wait! You got hit while you were in your chair?"

He nodded slowly. "Yep."

*Cue the gasp and the hand over the open mouth.*

"Wow, that's messed up."

"Yeah, it is. I felt like I had the world in the palm of my hand. And it was gone in the blink of an eye. I'm lucky to be alive."

"You're quite a guy, Steven. You've got a great attitude."

He shrugged his shoulders. "Thanks, but I'm no one special."

"Well, I disagree. I think you're pretty cool."

"Thanks. I've got a great support system. I think it helps me take things in stride. What about you?"

"My accident or my family?"

"Either. You pick."

"Hmm . . . accident is easier."

*Interesting, but not entirely surprising.* "Go ahead."

"Okay, well, it started with the scoliosis. A couple of years ago, they found a curvature in my spine when I had a school physical. It wasn't very bad, maybe fifteen degrees. But in a year it had changed considerably, like an additional eight degrees, so they decided I should start wearing the back brace. I've had it since I was thirteen."

"But scoliosis isn't an *accident*. What happened to bring you *here?*"

Her breath hitched. "My doctor wanted me to start doing physical therapy to improve my balance and coordination. I thought he was suggesting yoga, or Pilates or something, but instead, he suggested I take a gymnastics class. My mom was all for it, you know, a reason to get me out of the house several days a week so she could have her *boyfriend* over."

"Go on."

"I wasn't supposed to be doing anything hard core, things like walking on a balance beam, using the parallel bars—stuff like that. There were these girls there, you know, 'Barbie doll types,' who think they're all that and a box of chocolates.

"They taunted me—little digs here and there about the brace, and the scoliosis, that I'd never have a boyfriend because I looked like Quasimodo. They teased me about my lack of ability. I couldn't even get gymnastics right. So they were working on the uneven bars, and I heard one of them bet the others I couldn't do it. I know now they said it to get a rise out of me, but I was so mad. Everyone was changing in the locker room. I figured I'd try it when no one was there to make fun of me, you know, to see if I could do it."

"You didn't."

"Oh, I *did*. I figured I'd use the springboard to get a hold on the high bar, and I'd try a swing to see if I could do it. My upper body strength wasn't too bad. I was doing okay, swinging several times. I planned to sneak in from time to time in the future and try more. I had been watching the girls each session, so I thought I could sorta, you know, self-teach or whatever. I swung to dismount and somehow I got tangled up with the springboard, and all my weight came down on my arms—broken radius and ulna in both arms, extensive ligament damage. Four hours in an OR suite with Dr. Wesley, and here I am, eight weeks later. That's pretty much it."

"And the family?"

"My dad is awesome, but he doesn't live with us anymore. Mom has custody but only because Dad travels so much for his work. He's a manager for a big online marketing company. He's overseas a lot. Mom is . . . well, Mom. She has a boyfriend, and he's okay. I don't think he digs kids. Or maybe he has an aversion to teenagers. I dunno. He's sort of distant. I don't see us ever being close."

Steven had a fleeting thought about how similar she was to Abby's mom. "Where's home?"

"Springfield."

"So you're about an hour from home."

"Yeah, give or take a few minutes."

"Your mom doesn't see you a lot?"

"She was here the first weekend, but other than that, we just talk on the phone. She's coming next weekend, I believe."

"Oh, I'm glad."

Steven popped the last bite of Danish into Debbie's mouth, and she chewed thoughtfully. "Eh, it's okay, I guess. My dad is coming home about the time I'll get out of here. I'm going to go home with him for a few weeks. He planned his vacation so that I could spend over a month with him. *That* is something to get excited about."

He looked at the clock; it was getting late. "Hey, is there anything else I can get for you before I go? I've gotta meet Daisy in about fifteen minutes."

"No, I'm good. Thanks for helping me with my Danish. I met Daisy; she's going to be the OT working on my arms."

"You'll like her. She makes you work hard, but she's nice. I'll see you around. Would you like to eat lunch with Abby and me?"

"Maybe. We'll see."

❖   ❖   ❖

Steven's current goal was getting in and out of a jacket independently, so he made a quick detour to his room to grab one. Steven heard laughing when he turned the corner and entered their room. He was pleased to see Alec up and dressed, talking on his phone.

"Progress," he thought to himself, smiling as he went to meet Daisy.

Steven was pumped when he returned from therapy. It had been hard to concentrate when his mind was occupied with thoughts of Abby's impending visit. He could hardly wait to see her.

He was waiting in the courtyard when she climbed out of the car, grabbing her laptop and messenger bag.

"Well, hello to you too," Abby said, giggling.

"I spoke with one of the nurses. There's a conference room with a nice-sized table, a Xerox machine, and a coffee maker next to the office. It's free all day if you want to work there."

"Sounds perfect!"

"How would you like to do this? Will we both read the reports?"

"I thought we'd split the stack in half. You skim over them and decide if it's something that can feasibly and safely be done in a school full of children. It can't be something hugely messy, nothing involving electricity—unless it comes from a battery—nothing involving fire, and no caustic chemical reactions."

"Gotcha. Anything else I should watch for?"

"Nope. You're my scientific consultant. Science only. I'll read for grammar and content. Set the questionable ones aside, and we'll try to find an alternative or something."

Steven read through the projects, and everything was pretty much science fair typical. A battery made from citrus fruit, a camera made from a paper milk carton, volcanoes made with baking soda and vinegar . . . One involved the use of a Bunsen burner, and another required putting water and drain cleaner into a soda bottle and adding foil balls to cause a reaction. *Too dangerous.* Steven added a sticky note suggesting Mentos and cola to create a soda geyser. It would need to be done outside, but it was kid-safe.

Abby vetoed several of her reports, and halfway through, they swapped. She was pleased to see that Steven was able to offer a kid-safe alternative for every project that was potentially dangerous.

Abby beamed when she packed up her messenger bag a few hours later.

"You know, I would have made these kids completely change the focus of their projects. Thanks to you, they can still do what they chose with some modifications. I've never ever approved every student's project. Thank you, Steven."

"You're quite welcome, Miss Harris."

"Wait outside with me?"

❖   ❖   ❖

Abby flopped down on a bench in the shade, and Steven parked himself right next to her. He grasped her hand, and she sighed, leaning her head on the back of the bench and closing her eyes. It was impossible to describe the way it felt, knowing they were becoming so much more.

The rumble of Sydney's engine broke the silence. Abby gave Steven a kiss on the lips before hopping into Sydney's car. Sydney beeped and waved as she pulled away.

❖   ❖   ❖

Steven went to the lounge to see if anything was happening—a game of cards, a jigsaw puzzle, maybe a movie. Steven smiled at what he found.

Alec and Debbie were sitting across from one another at the very end of a table, laughing noisily. There were two ice cream sundaes in front of Alec. They had the works—syrup, fruit, nuts, and whipped cream. Each of them had a spoon. Alec would scoop out a bite and feed it to Debbie, and then he'd angle the other bowl so Debbie could scoop out a spoonful and feed it to him.

Steven had hoped to introduce them to one another, but it was better this way. Steven laughed to himself. They were both wearing hot fudge and melted ice cream on their shirts. Alec called her Dollface, and she blushed. Cute.

That kid might be okay after all.

# Chapter Thirty-three

It appeared that Alec's moment of reckoning acted as a catalyst to break down barriers regarding the teen's attitude.

Steven was returning from PT when Alec approached him.

"Um, I was wondering . . . You told me something right after I got here, and I was being an ass and not really listening. I was hoping you could help me . . . investigate some things."

"What was it I said, Alec?"

"You said that just because I couldn't physically build bridges, there were other options that would still allow me to pursue a career with my parents' company. I know you have a laptop. Can we get on the internet here?"

"Yeah, sure. Why don't you ask Jill if we can use the conference room? If you explain what we're doing, I'm sure she'll be fine with it if it's not occupied. I've got to use the restroom, and I'll get my computer and come find you."

"Hey, thanks. I appreciate it."

"No problem."

❖　❖　❖

Steven found Alec near Jill's office talking with her about his parents. Alec went into the conference room, but Jill pulled Steven aside.

"I'm pleased that he's more receptive to spending time with you. I'll let Melanie know that neither of you will be seeing her today."

"Hey, thanks, Jill."

"You're welcome. He needs someone like you in his life. I can't think of a more positive role model for a young person. Go make me proud, Chandler."

"I'll do my best."

"I know you will." Jill patted Steven on the back as she walked away.

❖    ❖    ❖

"What are you thinking about pursuing?"

"I'd like to look into a degree in civil engineering," Alec replied. "I don't want to be too far from home, but if I started the application process when I get out of here, could I be ready to attend college next year? Does that sound feasible?"

"Of course you could. Now, where were you thinking of applying to college?"

"I think my mom would prefer that I stay close to home."

"New Haven University and Edmonds College both have good programs."

"Could you help me apply?"

"It would be my pleasure. I'm sure if you asked, Jill could make arrangements to get you out to the campus as some sort of vocational rehab. You should check it out before you apply."

"I wish my dad could meet you. My mom thinks he feels my life ended the day I got in the wreck. I think seeing you and understanding that you've accomplished so much after your accident might help him think a little more open-mindedly.

"You said you were like me at eighteen, and you became a doctor from a wheelchair. Why did you decide to become a doctor? Is that what you always wanted to do?"

"Whoa. One thing at a time. First, maybe we can find a way for me to discuss this with your dad without him feeling like he's being ganged up on. I don't want to alienate him further. Your mom knows me, so perhaps we can enlist her help."

Steven propped his elbows on the table and steepled his fingers. "Now, about my career—it is challenging to do some of the hands-on things I need to do with patients from a manual wheelchair. My chair is a custom deal."

Steven flipped a switch and demonstrated the stand feature as Alec studied it. "I've always had a stander. I'm not much different than anyone else. With a few accommodations, I can get almost as close to things as I could if I was standing on my own two feet. I can even drive it standing although I only do that on even surfaces. I've always had a fear of tipping over.

"Logan and Sophie are the reason I'm a doctor. Even though my father was dead set against it, I had enlisted in the armed services right before I became paralyzed. After I lost my parents, I felt I almost owed it to them to pursue a career in medicine. The two years I took to recover gave me time to mull everything over. It was the right decision."

Steven saw the curiosity on Alec's face that most people entertained about his relationship with Logan and Sophie.

"Logan and Sophie are my aunt and uncle. Sophie was my mom's older sister." Usually, Steven shied away from bringing up his history, but he suspected it would benefit Alec, maybe make him see Steven as someone who had persevered past the odds to obtain a fulfilling life despite his circumstances.

"Coming home from my eighteenth birthday celebration, a logging truck went out of control. Mom was in the front seat, and my dad and I were arguing. I was leaving soon for basic training, and he felt that I wasn't living up to my potential.

"Dad was distracted, and there was no time to swerve, no place to go. It all happened so fast. They both died in front of me while I was pinned in the back of the car."

"Man, I'm so sorry. I feel like an ass for the way I treated you. I don't'twanna know what brought you here now, do I?"

"Uh, probably not." Steven rubbed his face. Since he had opened up to Abby and had begun seeing Melanie, it had gotten easier. As a peer mentor, he'd be sharing the story for the rest of his life. *Might as well get used to this.*

"I was coming home from work last fall. I was leaving the hospital campus when I was hit by a car."

The color drained out of Alec's face, and Steven immediately reconsidered his admission. "Do you need a trash can?"

"Nah. Just give me a minute."

He stared at Steven's legs, looked up at his face, then back down at his legs. "You were only in the chair? Like . . . not in a car or anything?"

"No, not in a car. I was walking home from the hospital."

"So you got hit like a pedestrian?"

"Yes. I was traveling on the berm of the road like a pedestrian would."

"Damn, man, you're lucky to be alive to talk about it."

"You have no idea."

"I don't think I can ever apologize enough for my actions. Why are you even wasting your time on me?"

"I'm a doctor. I help people every day. They don't always appreciate it." Steven thought back to the day he met Abby. Yeah, she was pretty pissed.

"You're a bigger man than I'll ever be."

"No, I'm someone who has adapted and adjusted to my situation because I had no other choice. You can't turn back time, but I think you're beginning to accept your situation, and with acceptance comes adjustment. I have a truly wonderful life, and you can, too, if that's what you want for yourself."

"I do."

Alec looked down at his watch. It looked expensive, but Steven noticed the crystal bore scrape marks that Steven was more than familiar with. *Road rash.*

"We need to get to PT," Alec grumbled.

Steven closed his laptop and put it in his bag. "Can you hang my computer bag on the back of my chair? I can't reach it, but if we worked together . . ."

"Sure, man, whatever you need."

Steven was having trouble wrapping his head around the transformation that had taken place in Alec. Steven refused to act smug, but he knew that had he not intervened the night Alec had his emergency, the kid would have made no personal progress at all.

"Race you to the gym!" Steven yelled as he pulled away.

"No fair!"

# Chapter Thirty-four

Abby felt as if she were entering a home furnishing warehouse when Sophie lifted the door to the storage unit, and they walked inside.

"Before we buy anything, I'd like you to see if there's anything here that you like." Sophie began taking large covers off each item. After revealing a few beautiful articles, she uncovered a huge, overstuffed leather chair and ottoman.

"Yes. This is what I was looking for—Abby, dear, come try this out while we look for a few things." Itdidn't sound like a request, but the chair looked heavenly, so Abby didn't argue—she sunk into the most comfortable seat she'd ever encountered. The matching ottoman magically appeared under her feet.

"Sydney, would you help me with these?" Sophie asked. The duo uncovered piece after beautiful piece, eventually disappearing out of sight.

Abby studied the furniture she could see—solid and sturdy, yet not imposing, in rich, warm colors, burgundies, browns and greens—each seeming to complement one another. Abby didn't know how many choices she could make, but so many of the things she saw seemed like they were made for Steven's new home.

After what seemed like forever, Sophie came back out of the labyrinth she had been maneuvering and took Abby's hand. "Come, Abby, let's see what you think."

Abby sighed when she left the cozy chair, one Abby could see herself spending endless hours in, reading or grading papers. *I almost hate to leave it.*

Sophie trailed her fingers over the arm of the chair. "That was always one of my favorites as well."

Abby studied it longingly. "The leather is so soft and inviting. It's beautiful, Sophie."

"I was thinking it would look great in that little alcove next to the fireplace. I can't imagine a better place to snuggle with a book when it's cold and rainy outside."

Abby's breath caught as she tried to speak. "I love it, but are you sure?"

Sophie wiped her damp cheeks and turned to Abby. "This was my sister's favorite chair. It sat next to the fireplace in her home. I couldn't find it in my heart to take it to our house after the accident. It would have been a painful reminder for Steven then, but he's ready now."

Abby felt guilty for taking so many things for granted. She still had two parents who loved her, even if her mother was unorthodox in the way she showed her affections. *I am blessed.*

Abby heard Sophie say something and shook herself out of her inner musings. "Excuse me?"

"I'd love to put this bed in Steven's room. He'd like an adjustable base, so I need to figure out whether this bedframe can be adapted to accommodate one."

Abby ran her hand over the smooth, cherry headboard. Yes, this would be perfect for Steven. "You said everything had been in the family. Is all this stuff . . ."

Sophie interrupted before Abby had the chance to finish her question.

"Yes, dear, these are the things from Steven's home. After the accident, nothing was more important than his well-being. There were so many things to manage, arrangements to make. We hired a company to come in and pack everything, and we moved it here when we came to the city."

"The whole house?"

"Yes, Abby. One day Steven will have to come here and make some decisions, but for now, he's tasked us with picking and choosing."

"I was uncomfortable with his paying to furnish all the common areas of the house. I like this idea much better."

"If there's anything you don't want, we won't take it, and we can come here any time afterward and go through more things."

The place was a real treasure trove. Abby couldn't wait till Steven could come home and enjoy his things. It would be like seeing old friends.

"So he knows we're using his parents' belongings? I don't want to offend him."

"He's the one who asked me to bring you here. He wanted to come along, but as you can see, it's currently inaccessible for him."

"Once we move whatever you'd like, there will be room for Steven to navigate," Sydney said, running her hands over a lovely oak sideboard.

"Steven told me you sold your home as well?"

"Logan and I tried to have children. After several pregnancies that ended in heartbreak, we learned I'd never carry a child to term. Steven is the closest either of us will come to having a child of our own. Neither our home nor Steven's parents' would have accommodated his needs when he was ready to come home from the hospital. As you can imagine, even after his discharge, Steven spent a lot of time at the hospital.

"We moved from a tiny rural town to New Haven before he was discharged. Logan found work at Yale, and we found a home suited to Steven's needs. We love him like our own, Abby."

Abby was moved to hear Sophie speak with such devotion for the man Abby was certain she was falling in love with.

Luke would have moved heaven and earth for his daughter, but moving back home was not an option that could have fully accommodated Abby's needs.

Abby's mother was a different story. It seemed so easy for her to distance herself when Abby needed her most. Their mother/daughter relationship was nearly non-existent, which was, possibly, for the best. *Too bad we can't all have mothers like Sophie Chandler!*

Abby looked around the storage area, letting her fingers trail over the smooth wood and upholstered pieces. Everything was wood or leather or rich brocades—things she could never dream of buying on her teaching salary. Out of the corner of her eye, she noticed a large, dark piece. *Perfect.*

It was just the thing Abby wanted for Steven. Sophie tagged the mahogany desk and several large barrister bookcases for the movers. The desk was ornately carved and extremely heavy. The leather chair that accompanied it had the same deep carvings.

Steven wanted to use one of the bedrooms for a study. This would most definitely complete the room.

Sydney and Sophie helped Abby choose a few lamps and other decorative pieces. Sophie pulled out several large boxes, but Abby decided not to open any of them, knowing they held more personal mementos.

"If Steven is ready to look through other things from the house, we can bring a few boxes at a time."

"That sounds like a plan."

Sophie began leaving a trail of stickers on the furniture they'd be moving to the house.

"We'll have the movers put everything I've marked in the garage," Sophie said.

"I appreciate all you're all doing to help. I could never accomplish everything on my own as quickly as we need to, but I definitely plan to help. I'm sure Steven will too."

"I thought maybe we could make it a weekend—clean up after the builder is done so we can start moving everything in. There are curtains to hang, and you'll probably want to get your kitchen in order right away."

❖   ❖   ❖

A quick lunch came after visiting the storage unit, and then, a home decor store supplied bins and baskets for Steven's bathroom and bedroom closets, a way to keep supplies and sundries within reach but tidy and out of the way.

A kitchenware shop boasted every modern convenience. Abby took a deep breath and grabbed a cart.

"Steven gave me strict orders to let you get whatever your heart desires for the kitchen."

"I can't tell you how much I appreciate the generosity, but *I'm* buying everything my heart desires, and if Steven has an issue with that, he'll have to take it up with me."

❖   ❖   ❖

They delivered everything to the house, both Sophie's and Sydney's cars filled to the brim with packages.

Pillows and towels and picture frames; laundry baskets and odds and ends went into closets. Fatigued beyond words, Abby dropped into a folding chair and pulled her feet up.

"Give me a few minutes, and I'll help bring everything in."

"We've been going all day. Take your time."

Abby was overcome with guilt, but not so overcome that it kept her awake. She awoke to Sophie shaking her shoulder.

"Abby dear, we're almost done. Steven called. He'd love to see you if you're up to it."

Was she? Usually, Abby loved walking. If the weather was nice, she tried to walk every day, but the busy day had taken a toll on Abby. She didn't think she could make it to the bus stop unassisted, let alone all the way to the rehab facility and back.

"I'd love to go tell him all about our day, but I don't expect you to run me back and forth."

"Steven told me to ask you how many spoons you have left."

Abby swooned. Steven had introduced her to the spoon theory a few weeks before. It had become their own private language. It provided a way for Steven to ask about her well-being without alerting everyone in the room and for Abby to reply in the same manner. A finger against his lips was the silent question, her subtle display of a few fingers, her response.

"The drawer is nearly empty."

"I can take you straight home, or we can stop along the way. Steven asked if I could grab some sandwiches from the Italian deli. Are you up to joining us for dinner? Or, at the very least, will you permit me to pick up something for you, as well?"

"Are you sure you don't mind? You've been running circles around me all day."

"Not at all. *Do* you have enough spoons?"

"I think I have enough." Abby yawned. "I try to plan wisely. I've been so tired lately."

"Let's not delay."

Sophie pulled up in front of a sandwich shop and came back to the car with a large paper bag.

They stopped by Abby's apartment so Sophie could retrieve Abby's cane. It had been a long time since Abby felt so exhausted, and she was relieved that she'd had the foresight to buy it.

They found Steven playing cards with a young girl whom Abby recognized as Debbie, based on Steven's description.

Abby was pleased that Steven could more freely interact with others in this environment. It sounded like he truly enjoyed Debbie's company, and since Alec had experienced some sort of medical crisis, Abby suspected Alec and Debbie were becoming friends as well. Abby knew that "Dr. Steven" would never snub someone that he might have an opportunity to mentor, no matter how abrasive their first interaction might have been.

Abby was filled with pride at Steven's concern for others, his interest in their wellbeing at the root of who he was as a person, a doctor, a mentor.

Sophie smiled as she approached the table. Steven gestured to his companion. "Abby, Sophie, I'd like you to meet my friend, Debbie."

"Hello, dear. It's a pleasure to meet you."

"Nice meeting you as well, but please excuse me. I've gotta go call my mom. Steven, thanks for the game! One day I'm gonna kick your butt!"

Steven laughed. "Bring on the Slapjack!"

The girl stood, her arms hanging stiffly at her sides. She could be heard laughing as she disappeared down the hall.

"Private joke?" Sophie asked.

"When we first started playing cards, she said she'd play anything but War or Slapjack because her arms were casted, but now it's sort of a goal between us. Someday soon, she will kick my butt."

"She seems like a nice girl."

"Yeah, she is."

Reaching out, Steven took Abby's free hand. Abby hadn't failed to notice that he had looked at her cane several times but hadn't commented. "I overdid it a little today. A lot of walking, and I'm tired," Abby said casually.

"Are you sure you're okay to pack and move your things? I can round up some muscle to help you."

"I want to do this with my dad, but if I find that Luke and I need help, I'll let you know."

"All you need to do is ask."

"I know, thanks. My dad isn't entirely happy that I'm moving in with a guy even if you are a doctor, but I think he'll be more accepting of my decision to share your home if he sees the house firsthand and sees that I have my own private space. Asking him to move me has provided the perfect opportunity to spend some time with him."

Debbie returned to the large room and situated herself in the corner where some '80s sitcom was playing on TV.

Steven frowned and spoke quietly. "Debbie needs positive role models. Her mother has promised to visit a number of times, yet something always comes up. Jill has a waiver on file, permitting Debbie to leave the premises. I was wondering if you ladies would like to get her out of here for a day of shopping or maybe a weekend of food and fun."

Abby bristled. *Mothers are supposed to be nurturing. They should smell like sugar cookies and be soft and warm. They should be . . . like Sophie.*

And fathers should be like the role models she and Steven had had growing up. "What about her dad? Is he in the picture?"

Steven frowned. "He's an executive for some big corporation. Spends a lot of time traveling, but it sounds like they're close. I hope he makes time for her. She's an awesome kid. The teen years are so tough—trying to figure out who you are, who you want to be. Peer pressure is overwhelming. That's how she ended up here. I worry that she doesn't have enough positive support."

"A girls' weekend sounds like a blast, and if she's still here after you leave, we can find ways to spend time with her, have her over for dinner or a movie. We won't let her fall through the cracks."

"Speaking of dinner! I stopped by that little Italian bistro." Sophie began pulling sandwich after sandwich from a huge brown paper bag, setting them on the table.

*Oh my.*

Abby stood and crossed the room. "Join us for dinner? The deli gave Sophie too much food."

Debbie looked up. "Um . . . sure, Abby, if you are certain you don't mind."

"Not at all. Come join us."

For several hours they talked, ate, and played cards. It was a fun evening, but Abby was exhausted. She stifled a yawn, not wanting to be the cause of the little party breaking up.

"Abby, go home and get some sleep. It's been a long day for you. You've got to finish packing your apartment while you're off work. I feel terrible that I can't get inside to help you."

Abby stood and leaned into Steven, kissing him, before he pulled her onto his lap. Steven hugged Abby tightly, rubbing her back and nuzzling his nose in her hair. He kissed her lightly on the mouth and helped her step off his lap, steadying her with his hands on her waist.

"Please walk her inside, Sophie." Abby growled at Steven. He smirked, and Debbie laughed.

*I can walk myself inside, thank you very much.*

Sophie gave him a quick hug. "I will, son."

Abby had finally gotten used to the way Steven threw around names. Sometimes he called them Mom and Dad; other times, Sophie and Logan. Sometimes he introduced them as his parents and other times as his aunt and uncle. They often introduced him as their nephew, yet both of them lovingly addressed him as "son." It took Abby quite a while to figure it all out, but once she had, she realized it didn't matter how they addressed one another. They were a family who loved each other deeply. That was all that mattered.

"There's something I need to talk to you about, Abby. Can I call you in a while, or are you too tired?"

"Give me a half hour, okay?"

"Sure. Goodnight, love."

*There he goes, making me feel all warm and fuzzy, again.*

"Night, Steven. It was nice meeting you, Debbie!"

"You, too."

# Chapter Thirty-five

Steven couldn't begin to verbalize how it felt when Jill acknowledged that his time in rehab was half over. Less than a year earlier, his calendar had been full but between days in the office and nights in the lab, he wasn't truly fulfilled. It took a near-death experience to show him that.

Steven's injuries and the time he spent recuperating caused him to take stock. Abby stumbling into his life made him realize what he had been missing. Little by little, he'd been venturing out into the world with newborn eyes, experiencing it as a participant rather than a spectator.

Some of those things he had taken for granted were family and friends. He spent his time peering into the eyepiece of a microscope instead of maintaining those relationships.

So when his closest friends saw that he had almost knocked on heaven's door, they vowed to encourage Steven to begin enjoying life instead of letting it pass him by.

As soon as Steven received his first furlough to go home, Sydney spilled the beans to Spencer, and it was only a matter of hours before his buddies concocted a plan to get Steven out on the town for a boys' night of fun.

Steven felt guilty spending the time away from rehab with someone other than Abby, but Debbie had been given permission to go with the girls for a spa weekend, and both events coincided perfectly.

Steven gave Sydney money with directions to treat the girls to anything they desired. He hated the fact that he wouldn't get to see Abby until Sunday afternoon. She had schoolwork to complete before picking Debbie up, and by the time the girls arrived, he had already left with his friends.

❖   ❖   ❖

Their first stop was Richter's. It was New Haven's first bar and was drenched in local history. Dale and Jonathan had agreed to join them. Not planning to drink, Steven volunteered to be the designated driver, but Spencer refused. "We're not going to risk it. Jon is on call eleven to seven, and he'll drive us. He can't drink."

While they awaited the arrival of Steven's former roommates, Mac ordered a first round of drinks. A little waitress who was wearing a tiny vest and even tinier denim shorts sat a tall cold bottle in front of each of them. Steven looked pointedly at Owen, who shrugged.

"Sometimes you need to live a little, Chandler."

While he occasionally met the guys from work for a beer at the bowling alley, he was not a regular customer.

"I'm medicated. I have to be careful."

"When did you take your medicine?"

"I'm wearing a patch. It's a constant supply."

"Oh. You should be okay if you don't *over* indulge. I promise I'll take care of you."

"I don't know . . ." Steven hesitated. "I don't think this is a good idea. What if I have some kind of reaction?"

Spencer leaned in. "Come on, cowboy. It's only one beer." Then he whispered, "You know we'd never let anything happen to you. Didn't Sydney tell me they'd weaned you down to the lowest dosage? What's the worst thing that could happen?"

Steven's conscience was tapping him on the shoulder and muttering something about "famous last words." The little demon on his other shoulder echoed Spencer's thoughts. *What is the worst thing that can happen?* While he was probably right, Steven could think of a handful of worst-case scenarios.

Steven had seen firsthand as he lay on that road near death last October that he could trust Spencer with his life. Steven didn't know whether he could have been that cool under fire if it were a complete stranger, let alone someone he cared about. Hell, both these guys were medical professionals. What *was* the worst that could happen?

Steven watched the condensation bead into droplets and trickle down the bottle every few minutes. Finally, unable to resist any longer, Steven picked up his beer and took a swig. As soon as it hit his tongue, Steven had trouble remembering why, exactly, he had fought this with such determination. It had been almost a year since he'd sat at a table surrounded by his friends relaxing and shooting the breeze.

Spencer reached inside Steven's shirt, pulling off his patch. "Know what, if it makes you feel better, we can take this off of you, buddy." Spencer rolled it up in a napkin and pushed it down inside his empty beer bottle. "Now you won't have to worry."

The first beer went down smoothly, and soon Spencer was waving his hand and yelling across the bar. "Darlin', another round over here."

Steven shook his head vigorously. He'd had one beer. He'd come out with the guys to loosen up and relax. Goal accomplished—no need to tempt fate. Steven was a little buzzed, but he didn't feel impaired.

"Darlin'" set another bottle in front of Steven, and he watched as she walked away. When he looked back at the table, it was still sitting there, taunting him. Mac was slouched in his chair, grilling Spencer about his sibling.

*Don't go there, Mac. She will eat you alive!*

Steven heard a siren and realized it was coming from Spencer's pocket. He noticed several people watching them. Spencer shrugged his shoulders before he answered his phone.

He hung up with a frown.

"Dale's girlfriend is sick, food poisoning or something. He's not gonna make it."

"What are we gonna do now?

"Jonathan is gonna meet us over at Doc's."

"I've heard that before," Steven replied, thinking back to the last time Jonathan made him a promise. *No thank you.* "I think if we stop drinking now, get a late dinner, and people-watch for a while, we'll be okay to drive in a few hours."

Spencer shook his head. "Doc's is only a few blocks away."

Steven stammered. "You're not—you're not driving my new car drunk, and we're not leaving it here."

Mac said, "Steve, look, this place has the best parking lot. We'll go out and move it to the far corner of the lot. Take up two spaces if you want. It'll be less conspicuous farther away. They aren't gonna care. Tomorrow is Sunday. It's not gonna get towed."

Spencer was grinning, that boyish look on his face. "He's right, buddy. It'll be fine here, and we'll walk down to Doc's and get a bite to eat, play some pool, shoot a few darts. By the time Jonathan gets there, we'll be good to go. We can walk back for the car. It's only a few blocks."

Steven looked at his watch, surprised to see it was already after eight. "Hey, Mac, can you hand me my backpack? I need to empty my bladder before we move on to Doc's. I don't want to forget in case I get drunk or sick because of that patch."

Mac laughed. "Dude, I'm not doing *that* for you—drunk *or* sober. We'll wait for you."

"I never asked you to."

Steven was pleasantly surprised to see an accessible restroom. He had no trouble taking care of what he had to.

When he returned, Mac said excitedly, "Come on! Someone told us there's a band tonight. It'll be great. When's the last time you saw a live band?"

"It's been a while."

Spencer stood up and moved toward the exit. "Let's go. It's only four blocks away. It's still early; we can get a good table. We'll look for something near the back so the crowd isn't right on top of us."

❖ ❖ ❖

Doc's was relatively deserted when they arrived. True to his word, Mac found them something close to the back exit where they had easy access to the pool table and dartboard, yet they could see the stage from where they sat. A waitress came over for their drink order, but Steven shook his head. "I'd like something to eat. An order of plain wings, please?"

"Yeah, me too, only I'm no sissy. Make mine hot. I'll take two orders, and we need a basket of those homemade sweet potato fries you all are famous for." Mac was appreciatively admiring their waitress as she took his order.

Spencer turned on the Southern charm and flirted when it was his turn to order. "Hey, sweetheart, I'd like an order of the hot wings." He laughed. "And I think we could use three shots of tequila."

Steven's head jerked up. "No, no, no, no . . . we're here for food and a little fun. I don't think this is a good idea at all."

Spencer nudged Steven with his elbow. "Lighten up, Stevie. We won't let anything happen to ya. If anything *does* happen, we have one of New Haven's best ER docs in our back pocket. Even your dad would want you to loosen up and have a little fun after what you've been through."

"I'm not drinking anything else. I can have fun without getting hammered. Getting trashed and hung over isn't exactly convenient for a dude in a chair."

Mac gave Steven an innocent look. "It's all good. I'll drink yours. Don't worry, we won't pressure ya, man."

Steven closed his eyes and thanked God for someone who understood the voice of reason. "Sweetheart" set a shot of tequila in front of each of them and left quietly.

Mac leaned forward in his seat and looked past Steven. "So, Spencer, tell me about the infamous Brooke Grady. Your sister's quite the bombshell. You get the short end of the stick?" He laughed.

"Very funny, McCrea. You should leave Brooke alone. She's had a rough year, and she can be a real bitch if you rub her the wrong way."

"Whoa! That's not a nice thing to say about your only sibling."

"Dude, it's true. She recently came off a bad relationship. The girl wants nothing to do with men."

Mac had a determined look on his face. "Feisty is good. I like a challenge."

Steven squirmed in his seat. He wanted to explain, knowing it would put an end to the conversation, but he respected Brooke too much to spill her private heartache in a dirty New Haven bar.

Steven grabbed Mac's wrist and gripped it a little harder than was polite. "Don't. You have *no idea* what you're talking about. Leave. Her. Be."

"Hey there, Steve, no reason to go getting all possessive there. You've got a girl. Miss Grady looks lonely. Didn't you notice that haunted look in her eyes the day she visited you at the hospital? She needs a good man in her life."

"Mac, with all due respect, if you mess with Brooke, I'll kick your ass. I have no trouble defending her honor if I need to."

"What do you mean 'defending her honor'? I just wanna have a little fun with her."

"There are beautiful women all over New Haven. Why waste your time with the one woman who has no interest?"

Mac slammed back his tequila and turned his attention to Spencer. "So, you and Sydney? How many times does this make?"

"Mmm, dunno. Five, mebbe six . . . over about ten years. We're in a better spot now. I want her to move into my place when her lease runs out."

Steven was startled. "Isn't she living with me for a while?"

Spencer put a reassuring hand on Steven's arm. "Hey, buddy, don't sweat it. She'll be at your place whenever you need her. I'm not trying to take her away from you."

Steven sunk down into his chair feeling relieved. For a minute, he had been scrambling to find a new solution at such a late stage in the game.

Spencer took his shot as their waitress was setting the food down. With a concerned expression on her face, she asked Steven, "Honey, what's the matter? Don't you like your drink?"

"I'm sure it's fine. I think I've had enough to drink already tonight."

"Well, if you change your mind, sugar, let me know. I can bring you something else." And then addressing all of them, she said, "You boys enjoy your meal. If you need anything I'll be back around in a little while."

"Thanks, darlin'," Spencer drawled.

Steven took a bite of his food and moaned. The wings were exquisite. Though a small band was setting up in the front, the entertainment had already begun in the back. Mac was plowing through his food like a man eating his last meal. His lips were ringed in orange sauce, and it made Steven's lips burn thinking about it.

Spencer was methodically dissecting his wings, slipping an entire section into his mouth and pulling the succulent meat off before extracting a perfectly clean bone.

As Mac began loudly singing some nonsensical tune, Steven's silent prayers were answered, and the band on the small makeshift stage broke into a loud cover of Nirvana's "Come as You Are." Steven's mind drifted to the band that meant so much to him during his youth.

Steven's belly was full, and he realized he was comfortably drowsy, but not truly tired. It was more like that warm fuzzy state where you want to snuggle into a comfy seat and pull up something warm to cover yourself while you watch everyone else in rapt fascination.

*Life is good.*

Mac was getting boisterous, and Spencer was still trying to woo their server. If Sydney knew, she'd have his ass. As Steven let the music wash over him, he found himself starting to loosen up and relax. Steven had been uptight when he arrived, anxious about the guys' expectations for their night on the town, but this was enjoyable. At some point, another round of drinks had appeared. The guys made theirs disappear quickly, but Steven's were beginning to accumulate.

Spencer pushed one of the shots in Steven's direction. "Come on, buddy, you'll like it. I swear it's the best. This isn't like the tequila of our youth. This stuff is *smoooth*. Hell, sip it if you want. No one will care."

Steven's hand shook as he lifted the glass. It would be worse to be branded a thirty-five-year-old momma's boy than it would be to have one shot. He took a small sip. It wasn't bad. In fact, it was kind of tasty.

"Has a good flavor, doesn't it?"

"Mm, yeah, it's okay."

Steven sipped his drink and watched "Sweetheart" set a plate of appetizers on their table. Steven looked at Spence as he reached for a plate. "You won't get too drunk if you eat some more."

Spencer filled the small platter with munchable items and set it within Steven's reach. "There, that should do ya."

Steven set his empty glass down and picked up an onion ring, hand cut and battered. He licked his lips.

*Mmm.*

Steven began sipping his second shot and realized it wasn't nearly as bad as he had thought it would be. Before long, it was gone too. He ate a few mozzarella sticks. And then he discovered the potato skins. They were to die for, and he had a bunch. A third round of drinks appeared, and Steven took "Sweetheart" by the arm.

"I've had enough. I can't possibly drink anymore."

"Honey, those girls over by the pool table bought a round for ya. These are expensive. You should show your gratitude by accepting it graciously even if you don't finish it." She winked at him.

Steven raised the shot glass toward the ladies and took one sip. *I can do this. The guys brought me here to celebrate life. My life. Who am I to be the wet blanket?*

Steven shuddered, thinking about the scare he must have given Spencer that autumn night. In all the times Spence had stopped by to visit, he'd never once mentioned the night of the accident. Calm, cool, collected. That was Spencer. *I owe him my life.*

Spencer got up and walked over to where the girls sat, and Steven watched as his friend talked with animated gestures. Soon Spence was motioning for me and Mac to join them. Steven threw a wad of bills on the table for "Sweetheart." She had earned it.

"Boys, I'd like to introduce Lisa, Jamie, and Kim. I came over to thank them for buying our round of drinks. They'd like to shoot some pool with us."

They all shook hands and exchanged pleasantries. Spencer, Lisa, Kim, and Mac began to set up the table. The room wasn't readily accessible, but the pool table and the dartboard were close enough to one another that they were all still hanging out together.

"You playin', Stevie?" Mac asked.

"There's not a lot of room. I think I'll throw some darts."

"Suit yourself."

Steven went over to the dartboard and raised his chair. He heard the intake of breath that usually occurred when he stood up for the first time in front of someone, and he smiled to himself. *Yeah, I can be like any other guy.* Steven pulled the darts off the board and turned around.

"So, what's a nice guy like you doing in a dive like this?" Jamie asked.

"I had a serious accident, and I've been out of commission for a while. My buddies decided to take me out to celebrate my recovery while our girls have a night of their own."

"You're seeing someone?"

Steven nodded. "She actually looks a little like you."

"Have you been together long?"

"We have," he said, his face breaking into a smile. "We've been seeing each other exclusively since January."

"Too bad. I'd love to get to know you better, Steven."

"I'm sorry, I'm very happy."

"She's a lucky girl."

Steven laughed at the irony. *It's the other way around.* "I'm the lucky one."

"Aww . . . that's sweet."

He handed the girl three darts. She looked down at her hand and then back to his face. Embarrassed, she said, "I, uh, I don't know how to play."

"You've *never* played darts?"

"Not unless you count throwing the dart at a balloon to win a prize at the carnival."

"Uh, no. You need a little more skill than that. Did you at least hit the balloon?"

"Not often. Those things are rigged, ya know." She giggled as Steven tried to determine her level of skill, which was, apparently, non-existent.

"You can't rig a balloon."

"I think they file off the point on the dart so it bounces off."

"*No* they *don't!*"

Steven took the darts and moved over behind the throw line. "Come here, Jamie. Stand in front of me." She stood in front of him, but she was on the wrong side of the line.

He backed up some. "You need to stand behind the oche."

"The who?"

"Not who. What. The oche." Then he pronounced it. "*Ah-kee.* It's the line on the floor."

"Speak English, then. Why didn't you simply tell me to get behind the line?"

Steven laughed; he supposed that *would* have been simpler.

He tried to explain how to play 501, but they both kept laughing.

Steven handed her the three darts and told her to throw one of hers first. She threw and her dart bounced off the board onto the floor.

"See! I told you, this game is rigged!"

"No, it's *not*. Here, watch. You want to throw straight from eye level. Hold it like this with your index finger and your thumb. And you let it go like this . . ."

Steven threw his first dart and landed it in the bull's-eye.

She looked at him in wonderment. "How did you *do* that?"

He aimed the next one and landed it next to the first one. "It's all about lining up your shot. It's kinda like giving an injection with a hypodermic. You aim and shoot."

"Huh?"

"I learned to play darts in medical school. When they teach you how to give an injection, they use the same analogy." Steven threw his final dart to demonstrate.

"So you're a doctor?"

"Yeah." He gestured to his legs. "But I'm outta commission right now."

Steven didn't want to dwell on that though, so he redirected the conversation to the game at hand. He went over and retrieved his darts. "Come on, try again."

Jamie threw a bunch of practice shots and finally got the hang of it.

Steven found it difficult to try to explain to her how the object of the game was to get down to zero from a starting score of 501, especially when each throw had a point value, and she laughed when Steven stumbled over his thoughts. Another shot and a pretty, mixed drink had appeared on the table next to where they stood. He refused to drink it, regardless of who bought it.

Mac and Lisa came over to watch, finding a spot to lean against the wall and converse. Every time Jamie got a point, Mac would let out a whoop, and soon a small crowd had gathered.

Spencer came over and said, "Hey, we're gonna walk over to the Irish pub. They have karaoke tonight."

"We can't leave here. Jon is meeting us soon. He'll never find us."

"Nah, man, he stood us up. We're on foot tonight. If you want, we'll call one of those wheelchair cabs or something."

"They don't run this late. I *knew* this was gonna happen." Steven had that sick feeling earlier, but after a few drinks, his worries had moved to the back of his mind. Now, they were front and center again.

"Go on, finish your game. We'll worry about this when the time comes."

Steven turned back to Jamie and his round of darts. "I'm sorry."

"It's okay. Weren't you trying to teach me how to add or subtract or something like that?"

"Whose turn is it?"

She giggled and put her fingers over her mouth, shrugged her shoulders, and said, "I dunno."

Then she whispered loudly, "I gotta pee!" turned around and walked away. Steven looked at the clock, surprised it was after eleven, and decided that perhaps it would be a good idea for him to hit the men's room.

Steven lowered his chair and decided he could get the bag off his chair by himself.

Once Steven got the pack off in the restroom, he was home free. He put a blue pad on his lap and cleaned himself off. Steven had a little trouble getting the tube lined up with the hole and was glad he used the disposable pad. *Then* he didn't get the tube into the urinal as quickly as he normally did, and there was pee all over the pad. At least it wouldn't look like he peed his pants. As he was pulling the catheter out, he heard a drunken voice behind him. "Well, well, well, I didn't know they let cripples in this bar."

Steven could feel his face getting red, but he was determined to ignore it. *I'm not going to let some jerk ruin my evening.* They were leaving soon anyway, so he dumped the urinal and threw away his trash before turning to wash his hands. He quickly and carelessly shoved everything into his backpack and left it on his lap.

Hurrying out of the restroom, Steven drove over to the little table they had their drinks sitting on, bumping into it and spilling Jamie's drink.

Grabbing a napkin, Steven began to clean up the mess when some-one roughly shoved his shoulder. "I was talkin' 'bout you, pretty boy. You come here to pick up chicks?" His backpack fell to the floor as Steven grabbed ahold of his armrests.

"No, I, um . . ."

"Look at you, sitting there drinking a foo-foo drink."

Steven looked down at Jamie's drink, then over at his shot. He picked up the shot and slammed it. He wiped his mouth and attempted to look smug.

"Ooh, aren't you a tough guy?"

Behind the guy, Jamie stood, her face turning crimson. The jerk followed Steven's gaze and sneered. Almost immediately, he was in her face. "Hey, baby, wanna come back to my place?"

"Eww, Ryan, you're drunk. Go home."

Wait . . . she *knows* him?

Ryan took Jamie's arm, pulling her towards the door. "Come on, Jamie, let's go have a little fun. You know you wanna."

"Leave. Me. Alone! Don't *touch* me!" Her frantic voice turned heads. Steven prayed Mac would hear.

*Any time now would be nice.*

Spencer came up behind Ryan and drawled, "Hey, cowboy, I believe the little lady said no. Where I come from, no means no. Why don't you get a move on before someone gets hurt."

The jerk walked away from them but did an about-face as soon as Spencer left, turning on his drunken anger in full force.

"What's the matter with you, baby? You so desperate all you can get is some *crip?*"

Steven saw red, and for the first time in his life, he was *looking* for a reason to brawl. Ryan grabbed Jamie's jaw and pulled her against his body, kissing her roughly on the mouth. As soon as he let go of her, a resounding *smack* filled the air when her hand made contact with the side of his face. "I *said* don't touch me!"

"He's not even a whole man. Bet he can't even get it up."

*And there it is!* It was one thing for a disappointed, inexperienced ex-girlfriend to say it. It was a completely different thing for this jerk to emasculate Steven in front of a crowd of people. Steven stood his chair and drove into the guy, pinning him in the corner. *I'm ten feet tall—and bullet proof.*

Steven didn't know the girl, but he had an inexplicable urge to protect her virtue. "Don't you *ever* touch her against her wishes again . . ." Before he finished, Steven's fist came out of nowhere and struck the guy's jaw. He had never punched anyone before.

*That hurt!*

Steven tried to shake it off, but Ryan grabbed his shirt by the collar and was in his face, screaming, droplets of spit spraying across Steven's face. "She doesn't know what she wants."

Jamie stood off to the side, holding her hand to her chest, her face stained with tears. From a distance, she made herself clear. "You're a creep, Ryan. Stay away from me."

Steven chuckled a little too close to Ryan's face. "Like I said . . ."

*Well,* that *pissed him off.*

Steven's head slammed back into the headrest on his chair before he felt the pain of his teeth splitting his lip. Steven pushed his joystick, forcing Ryan further into the corner. Steven tried to hit the guy again, but Ryan punched Steven—hard. Almost simultaneously, the fist connected with Steven's ribs while the other hit him in the eye, making his head spin. Ryan pushed hard on Steven's chest, and Steven was afraid his chair would tip over. Steven backed up a few feet, and before Ryan could lunge at him again, a bartender grabbed Ryan from behind, around the chest.

"Let's go, big guy. Don't be giving the little lady and her friend a bunch of trouble."

"Come on, dude, she's not worth it," one of Ryan's friends said. Ryan jerked his arm away from his buddy and stormed outside.

Steven turned to a crying Jamie, taking her hand in his and examining it. "Does it hurt?"

"No, I'm fine." She looked up at him and gasped. "Oh, Steven, you're *bleeding*. I'm so sorry."

Steven reached up and touched his mouth. "So I am."

Spencer and Mac stood behind the girls, and of course it was Mac who chose to make a spectacle out of Steven. "*Dude*, who kicked *your* ass?"

"His name is Ryan. He and his buddies give us a hard time whenever we come here. He's got some sick idea that she's interested in him," Lisa said, motioning to Jamie. "The guy's a first-class jerk. Steven got a few good punches in."

Kim spoke up. "Ryan gives me the creeps. By the time we realized what was happening, it was all over. Thanks for keeping him away from her, Steven."

Lisa bent down and picked up Steven's backpack. She hooked it over his push handles and patted him on the shoulder.

"Thank you."

Next, Steven's boys were congratulating him. For a change, Steven felt ordinary, like he was the same as everybody else.

*This feels . . . good.*

"Come on, is everyone ready to go over to the pub?" Mac bellowed. "I want corned beef and cabbage. It's been years since my ma made it for me."

Spencer tried to quiet him. "Mac, *shhh*! We ate a little while ago. You *can't* be hungry already."

Mac rubbed his stomach convincingly. "I'm powerful hungry, Spence. Let's go!"

"Thanks, but I think I'm ready to go home." Steven looked toward Mac, frowning.

"Good luck with that. Thank you for sticking up for Jamie. I'm sorry you got hurt."

"I'm glad *she* didn't get hurt by that jerk. Please have a safe trip home."

"You too."

They all shuffled out behind the bar. Mac had suddenly found everything anyone said hilarious. Spencer was quiet, introspective.

"Hey, Steven. Do you think our girls are gonna be upset with us? Maybe this wasn't such a good idea."

Steven patted his hand. "Aww, I think it's okay, Spence. We were out in the open. Nothing sneaky went on."

Steven heard someone growl, and out of nowhere, Ryan slammed into Mac like he was a linebacker.

*Bad move, buddy.*

Mac grunted upon impact, and the two of them hit the ground. They rolled around behind the bar, getting in a punch here and there. Mac pushed up off the asphalt with his hands. He stumbled before he righted himself. Soon Ryan was on the ground holding his stomach.

❖　　❖　　❖

It was nearly midnight, and Steven didn't feel very well. It was hard to concentrate, and driving his wheelchair was a challenge.

They made it out of the alley and onto First Avenue. Liffey's Pub wasn't that far. Karaoke would be fun, and Mac could have his corned beef and cabbage if he wanted. The thought of it made Steven's stomach roll.

Ryan's group followed them out onto the sidewalk and began spewing abuse.

"Good for nothing cripple!"

"Hey, speed racer. Can you pop a wheelie?"

"I hope you have a license for that thing!"

Once in a while, either Mac or Spence would spit out a retort. When they were a block from the pub, a police cruiser passed them and slowed down. Luckily, they kept going, and Steven was relieved to see that Ryan and his band of fools had disappeared.

A very loud Spencer warned them to keep moving so they didn't get stopped by New Haven's finest, and Steven was never so relieved to see the front of Mac's favorite haunt.

Liffey's was brightly lit, and Steven could see people sitting around bistro tables in the small outdoor dining area. When they got to the corner, Mac stepped out into the middle of the street and put up his hand. "Stop, stop, *STOP!*" Spencer and Steven stopped on the curb. The light turned red, and Mac began directing the traffic on Whitney Avenue, yelling loudly and belligerently when cars didn't stop. Some of the patrons who were sitting outside began to laugh at Mac's antics. Spencer leaned down and whispered. "When the light turns green, we're makin' a break for it. Okay, buddy?"

Suddenly Steven didn't feel so confident about getting across. What if Mac told the wrong person to go when they were in the crosswalk? Steven felt sick. The light changed, and they made a run for it. Steven tried to find the curb cut but ran into the curb itself. Out of nowhere, he heard the unmistakable wail of a siren, and it wasn't coming from Spencer's pocket.

*Busted.*

Steven sat alone in the street while two officers had his friends pinned to the ground. A second car pulled up, and two officers got out, heading in Steven's direction. He hung his head in shame.

*This can't be happening.*

When an officer came toward Steven, he frantically tried to work his joystick to get away. Steven panicked when the officer walked around his chair, asking him how to turn it off. When Steven realized his attempts at fleeing were futile, the officer tried to flip the switch.

"Keep your hands where I can see them, buddy."

Instead of flipping the switch as Steven told him, he pulled two cable connectors apart and the onboard lights flickered off.

Trapped.

It seemed like they were all talking at once. Mac was sitting on the curb, hands cuffed behind his back singing, "I'm Henry the Eighth I am . . ." as bystanders watched and laughed. The cop who was with Steven sounded like he was talking from the bottom of a jar. The words were loud and confusing, and Steven couldn't seem to figure them out.

Steven felt the cold pressure of the handcuffs on his wrist as his other arm was wrenched behind his back—he cried out in pain at the unexpected contortion of his still tender shoulders. A big hand pushed him back into his seat, further hurting him.

Spencer lay squirming and swearing face down on the pavement. One of the officers rifled through his pockets, turning them inside out.

Another officer introduced himself as Officer Smith. He resembled a thug off the streets. His blonde hair was stringy and dirty, his face covered in stubble. "Are you armed?"

"Huh?"

"Do you have any *weapons* in your *possession?*" He loudly annunciated the words.

Steven shook his head.

"Illegal drugs?"

"No, sir."

"Are you intoxicated?"

"Yes, sir."

"What's your name?"

"Steven."

"Steven what?"

"Steven Maxwell . . ."

*That doesn't sound right.*

"Nooo . . . wait . . . no . . . I'm *not* him anymore."

Steven wanted to scratch his head, trying to think. "I'm Steven Chandler. Yep. That's me."

He leaned his head back against the chair.

*I need to lie down.*

The officer shook Steven. "I'm awake," Steven said while peering out of one eye.

"Do you have identification, Mr. Chandler?"

"Yeeup!" Steven smiled up at the officer. *If I'm happy, maybe he'll see I'm happy, and he'll be happy too.*

"I need to see your ID."

"I can't reach it."

"Where is it?"

"It's in my backpack with the John."

"The John?"

"Yes, John. They are in the pack together."

"I'm looking in your backpack now. Is there anything sharp in there? You don't have any needles or anything, do you?"

"Nooooope!"

Steven heard him open his pack, but he dropped it on the sidewalk and jumped back.

"Oh my God! That's disgusting! Now I've got piss all over my hands! Get me a pair of gloves!"

"I got gloves in there too. That's my bag of tricks. You wanna see some of my tricks?"

"No, buddy. We'll leave that well enough alone. But, I need to run your ID."

"Mmkay."

Officer Smith put everything back in his bag and zipped it up. "Someone is gonna have fun with that tomorrow."

Steven closed his eyes again.

*I don't like the red and blue lights. Make me feel sick.*

Officer Smith shook Steven again. "Your ID checks out, Mr. Chandler. We're going to play a few games, and then we're going to go for a ride."

Steven looked at Mac and laughed when he tried to walk along the crack in the sidewalk.

Officer Smith shook Steven. "Hey, pay attention. Look up here." He was pointing at his own eyes with his first two fingers.

"Well, I guess you can't walk a straight line."

"Yes, I *can*, but you turned my chair off. Come on, *plug it in*. I'll show you what I can do."

Officer Smith snapped his fingers to get Steven's attention. "Pay attention. I'm going to uncuff you."

*Ahh, that's better!*

"Arms straight out to your sides. Okay. Now, one hand at a time, bring your index finger in and touch your nose." The closer Steven got to his eyes, the bigger his finger grew. He giggled as he tried to touch his nose. "Other hand." It seemed Steven's left hand was as uncoordinated as the right one had been. Steven snorted as he slapped himself in the face. *"Touched it!"*

Officer Smith yelled to his partner. "Hey! A hand here?"

The other cop came over. "What do you need?" He studied Steven.

*Haven't you ever seen a gimp before?*

Smith fumbled with Steven's belts. "How do we get him out of here?"

The other guy scratched his head. "I dunno. Why don't you ask *him?*"

Smith got close and yelled in Steven's ear. "Sir, how do I get you out of this chair?"

Steven giggled; his board was in the car. "Na-nana-na-nah! You need a bo-ard . . . and you don't *have one*," Steven said in his very best sing-song voice.

"Come on, buddy. We don't want to hurt you or your chair, but we have to take you in, and we can't take the chair in the car."

"Ohhhhhh . . ." Steven pushed the button on his seat belt and swung his bar out of the way.

"There."

Someone pulled a car right next to his wheelchair, and Steven felt sick. The running car was too, *too* close.

Smith and the other cop each took Steven under the arm and tried to stand him. Someone hit his tickle spot, and Steven began to squirm and giggle. *"That tickles!"*

"Whoa, buddy. We don't wanna drop you. We gotta take you back to the station and get you sobered up."

"Okay. Can Spence and Mac come too?"

"Yeah, sure buddy, whatever."

They picked Steven up and tried to drag him to the car, his casts bumping along the ground. "Oww! Owww! OOUUCH!"

They stopped walking. "What's wrong? Did we hurt you?" Officer Smith asked.

*I made a joke.* "Gotcha!"

"Okay, enough fun and games from you."

They put Steven in the car and laid him down. Someone pulled his casts up onto the seat.

When they started moving, Steven rocked back and forth, and then the retching began.

*Blaaargh!*

"Eww! Brian, he's puking back there!"

"Oh God! I'm not cleaning that up!"

"Geez, open some windows."

Steven could smell puke, and there were pieces in his mouth. It tasted bad. He let out another round on the back of their seats, and he watched as the pieces slid down the leather. The open windows made it better, but it made him cold, and he began to shiver.

He didn't feel well. *I want to go home. I get a phone call. Don't I get a phone call?*

"Can I call my mom?"

"Not right now, buddy. You can call your mom after you're booked."

"I like books."

Someone in the front was laughing. "Always entertaining, aren't they?"

"Until they get sick. That's gross."

Steven woke up when they took him from the car, and three or four of them carried him inside and set him on a wooden swivel chair.

They took Spencer and Mac away, and Steven was all alone. It was noisy and bright, and all he wanted to do was sleep.

An officer came over with some kind of electronic device and took Steven's fingerprints. He kept looking at his fingers.

*Where's the ink?*

They gave Steven a card with numbers and took his picture. Right there in that chair. One of them teased that he was *special*. Steven didn't like that much. He knew what they were implying.

"Hey, can I have my backpack, I need to pee."

"Sorry, buddy, I think you already used it for that."

"Come on, it's time to pee."

"Here, pee in a cup."

"I can't pee in a cup. I need my special bag."

"No special treatment, buddy. Pee in the cup."

Steven slumped back into his chair, too tired to argue.

Steven slept until a door slammed.

"Hey, can I call my mom?"

"You're a big boy. I think you can wait till you sober up."

"No. You said I could make a phone call. They get to make them on TV. I'm a criminal now too. I want my phone call."

"Everyone will be asleep. It's 3 a.m. You don't want to wake your mom at 3 a.m."

"*Noooo*, don't wake mom. Let's call Brooke."

"Brooke is sleeping too."

"I want to go home. I don't like this chair."

"Sit still. We'll call someone in the morning."

What was the magic word that they used on TV? *Lawyer!* "I want to call my lawyer."

"You're gonna *need* a lawyer."

"I'm not talking anymore until I get a lawyer." *That's what they always say.*

"Good. Go back to sleep."

"I'm telling my lawyer you wouldn't let me call her. She'll be pissed."

"Fine. You call and wake her. She won't be happy."

# Chapter Thirty-six

The voice down the corridor sounded like a melody—the lyric of Steven's own personal savior.

*She's here! Brooke will help.*

The *click, click, click* on the floor grew louder, and it hurt Steven's head. When it stopped, he saw black, glossy pumps.

Cool hands touched Steven's chin, lifting his face to meet Brooke's gaze. "Oh, Steven. *Are you okay?* Sweetie, what did they *do* to you?"

Steven puffed out his chest and made his best smile. "I was in a fight!"

"*You* fought?"

"Mm-hmm."

"We'll get this all taken care of so we can get you home. Logan is going to shit a brick."

Brooke started to walk away, shaking her head.

"Brooke! I hafta pee."

"You do?"

"Uh-huh. It's time." Steven pointed at his cop. "He won't let me pee. I asked for my special bag so I could pee. But he says someone already peed in it."

*"Good lord.* Hold on, okay?"

"Kay."

*Brooke will fix this.*

Steven yawned. *I need another nap.*

Steven leaned his head back against the desk and closed his eyes.

When he woke up, the fog had lifted. He could hear every noise and feel every vibration. It made his head hurt and his stomach roll.

Steven sat, his eyes squeezed shut, while Brooke spoke quietly with the cop. Apparently they were acquainted with one another; and like most men, he appeared to be captivated by her beauty.

"Brian, I'm requesting a reduction in charges for my client from the DUI to a Public Intoxication charge. While Dr. Chandler admits he was operating his wheelchair under the influence, a criminal DUI charge seems ludicrous. The gentlemen who were accompanying him were both charged with disturbing the peace and public intoxication."

Steven still hadn't seen either of the guys since they had been brought in although he had heard Mac's drunken singing and Spencer's hooting and hollering off and on for what seemed like hours.

"Miss Grady, you know I could have charged him with a DUI for riding a *donkey* in the streets of New Haven while intoxicated. It *is* in the books."

Steven opened his eyes.

If he was found guilty of a DUI, he would lose his operator's license. He could go to jail for up to a year, and if those things happened, he would lose his job, and his entire adult life would have been in vain as surely as if he'd died in that accident.

❖　　❖　　❖

Steven trusted Brooke, and somehow she knew Smith. Perhaps they had worked on a case together.

"I understand, Brian, but it *wasn't* a donkey or a vehicle. It was an electric wheelchair."

"He could have hurt someone."

"Who would he have hurt? It's not a lethal weapon. It's a mobility aid."

"It's self-propelled, and he was driving it in the street."

"Would you have given him a DUI if he were on one of those little scooters the kids ride? Some of those are gas powered."

"Well, *no*, of course not. That would fall under drunk and disorderly."

"Suppose he were riding a bicycle?"

"Now, Miss Grady, you and I both know that I can't charge him with a DUI for riding a bicycle."

"Would you give him a DUI if he were using a wheelchair he could propel with his hands?"

"No, that's the same as a bicycle. You know the charge would have been public intoxication—drunk and disorderly."

"So in other words, the only thing you can use to make the charge stick is the battery that makes his chair go."

"Well . . . yes."

"Officer Smith, while Dr. Chandler's companions both failed field sobriety tests, none of the gentlemen were given a portable breathalyzer test on site, nor were they given breathalyzer tests here at the precinct. Dr. Chandler requested a blood alcohol test when he was brought in, but one was never performed."

Officer Smith blanched, apparently realizing he was caught in his own web. "Give me a break, counselor. We've been jumping through hoops all evening. A number of the officers are out in the field. It's been a wild night here."

"How can you charge my client when it was never confirmed that his blood alcohol level was over the legal limit?"

"He was swerving, bumping the curb. His friends were directing traffic in a major intersection when we caught them."

"You are still required to do a breathalyzer test, at the very least."

"Do you realize how much work it was to get your *handicapped* client into a squad car and then into the precinct here? I had to arrange for a van to transport the wheelchair. That man put me through all sorts of extra work. I had to get two officers to help carry him."

"I want to know what he's doing, sitting handcuffed to a desk chair instead of in the wheelchair that was designed to care for his special-ized medical needs. Dr. Chandler's body is prone to developing skin breakdown and pressure sores." She looked over at Steven and smiled sadly.

*I'm sorry I disappointed you, Brooke.*

Brooke continued to berate the officer. "Where is the chair, Brian?"

"You know we have no way to safely transport a prisoner in a wheelchair, and it had all these little pouches attached to the arm rests. I had no idea if he had a concealed weapon or something that could be used as a weapon. As it is, I was contaminated by urine trying to find his identification. That's a health hazard, you know. Who knows what kind of diseases your client has."

"*Where. Is. The. Chair?*" Brooke growled.

Smith gave Brooke a smug look. "Don't get your panties in a twist, Miss Grady. It's over at impound." He crossed his arms across his chest. "You can get it back first thing Monday morning."

"Brian, we both know all you have to do is make a phone call. My client can't leave here without that wheelchair. It's an eleven thousand dollar piece of medical equipment."

He shrugged. "*He* could stay here till Monday morning too. As for the value of the chair, it's no different than any other *motor vehicle*. There is still the matter of the impound fee."

"You and I both know you're not equipped to keep my client here any longer than you already have. He shouldn't be here in the first place." Brooke's foot tapped, and she looked like a pressure cooker—pressure, tension, building and building—ready to explode.

And there it was.

"*How much?*" she screeched.

Smith stepped back from the counter. "Two hundred bucks, and I'll have it returned to the precinct."

"And the DUI charge?"

"Well, here's the thing. I'm up for a promotion, and I don't know that it would be in my best interest if the good people of New Haven were to learn that I turned a drunk driver back out onto the street in-stead of charging him."

"It would look good if you acted like you had a heart and considered the special circumstances surrounding my client. Dr. Chandler is an upstanding citizen. He puts in long hours over at the university hospital; he spends his free time in the stem cell lab. He's never been charged with so much as a fine for jaywalking.

"Brian, do you go out and toss a few back when you're at the end of a rough day? Hang out with the guys to wash your troubles away with a few beers and the camaraderie of your friends?"

The officer nodded.

"Do you realize that my client has been in a facility twenty-four seven for more than six months? This is the first time he's been able to leave the facility and was celebrating his life with his friends. He's been under a tremendous amount of stress. This was a recreational outing. Is it so difficult to declare this a misunderstanding? He's a promising doctor. His entire career is at stake. There may be a day when he saves someone you love. It would be a shame if that opportunity was taken away over something like this."

Suddenly it was as if she remembered Steven's earlier request, and Brooke turned to address him.

"Steven, you've been here more than a few hours. When is the last time they offered you the restroom?"

Steven shook his head. His distended bladder was the least of his concerns. He wasn't sure where it was leading, but he decided he should answer. Brooke knew what she was doing. "I haven't gone since I was in the bar."

"Do you remember what time that was?"

"No. Maybe eleven?"

Brooke leaned in real close to Officer Smith again, "You realize my client can suffer life-threatening complications if he doesn't have access to proper medical care, prescription medication, and the use of a urinal? Do you realize he requires specialized medical supplies to be able to relieve his bladder?"

"I had no idea he had special toileting needs! He told me a few times that he needed the bathroom, but he refused to go without his wheelchair. I offered him a new Styrofoam cup.That's a reasonable accommodation. I know my rights!"

"Apparently, you've overlooked his. Have you offered him medical treatment? He is currently receiving care at an inpatient rehabilitation center. Have you contacted them to verify his medical needs? Both his legs are broken and need to be supported; they can't just hang there like that. Do you have any idea what kind of risk you've subjected him to by not contacting someone about his condition?"

"How was I supposed to know?"

"It's not rocket science. Your prisoner was arrested in an electric wheelchair. It never occurred to you that he might have special circumstances that needed to be addressed? Proper protocol would have been to call an ambulance and have them transport him safely to a hospital where he could be assessed and released when he was sober."

"We don't release DUIs when they're sober; we only do that for drunk and disorderlies. Speaking of which, you realize your brother is here as well."

"My brother is one of the reasons this man is here in this state. What did you charge *him* with?"

"A drunk and disorderly, same as that other guy."

"I'll worry about the two of them later." She paused. "I think we could overlook some of your *errors in judgment* concerning your handling of my client if you'd be willing to acknowledge your error in charging Dr. Chandler with a DUI."

The officer appeared deep in contemplation. "I suppose we could work something out."

"And the wheelchair?"

"I'll call the impound lot now."

"Good. I would appreciate it if you'd prepare the citations for my clients. I'll be taking care of their fines along with the impound fees."

"All three gentlemen?"

"Yes, all three. And the cuffs?" she asked.

"Oh yeah, sure. It's not like he'll run off or anything."

If looks could kill, Brooke's would have struck Smith dead.

"The paperwork will be ready by the time the wheelchair is returned." Smith stood and walked to where Steven sat. A few clicks and the cuffs fell away.

"Thank you, Brian."

He dipped his head and walked away. "Brooke."

Brooke pulled a chair next to Steven. "Do you need to use the restroom, Steven?" She spoke softly, and it made his head feel better.

"What time is it? I keep falling asleep." Steven realized whispering back to her didn't hurt as much either.

She patted his knee. "I know you do. It's after four thirty."

"How long till we go?"

"I don't think very long now."

"I've gone longer than this working the ER. Should be okay, but thanks for sticking up for me with your *buddy*."

She looked around and leaned in close. "He is a jerk, isn't he?"

"I don't like him."

"I don't like him, either, but I am glad someone was here that I knew. Your condition was the best leverage I had to get the charges reduced. I'm going to do my best to get the charges dropped completely, but for now, I want to get you mobile so we can get you home.

"You're sporting a pretty good shiner there, Doc. I think you might need that split lip stitched too. Logan is going to have a fit. Shit! I forgot to call your parents back. I promised to call them as soon as I got here. They were beside themselves. I was so distracted when I saw you here like this." She waved her arm up and down the length of his body.

Brooke pulled her phone out. "I'm with him," she whispered. "No, he's safe. He needs some attention. Can you please meet me with the van? West Precinct. DUI. No, I got them reduced . . . Yes, the other two are here someplace. They're the least of my concern. We'll be out when we're done. Yes, I'll tell him. Thanks.

"Logan said to tell you he's glad you're okay, but he's gonna kick your ass when he gets you home."

"I'm sorry you got dragged into this mess. It was only supposed to be a night out with the guys. I never intended . . ."

"Steven, we all understand. But your parents were frantic. When you hadn't come home, they tried to call your phone although now I realize you were already in custody when they expected you a few hours ago. They've been up all night waiting."

Frustrated, tired, uncomfortable, *ashamed* . . . The nausea began to rise in Steven's throat, and without warning, he violently heaved all over his clothing and the chair. Steven slumped in the chair, covered in vomit and too tired to sit up.

Smith stuttered out a string of expletives as he barked into the phone for someone to bring a bucket of hot water and a mop. Steven could feel the vomit soaking through his shirt, and the smell alone brought on another round.

Brooke demanded a roll of paper towels and a trash bag and began cleaning him up. Steven heard a scuffling sound off to the side and looked to see Mac and Spence at the watch commander's window, receiving their personal effects.

When Brooke was finished, she opened her purse and pulled out a pack of tissues. "Here, let me get your face, Steven. These are soft."

With tenderness Steven didn't realize Brooke possessed, she wiped Steven's chin and lips. He flinched when she touched the corner of his mouth. "I'm sorry. I know it hurts. I wish we could get you a clean shirt before they have to move you."

She looked over to where Smith stood. "I'll be right back."

Brooke returned with an NHPD T-shirt. She knelt and pulled Steven's shirt over his head. Silently, she worked to change him into the dry one. Brooke handed a Ziploc bag to Steven. Clumsy fingers fumbled to retrieve his watch, ring, wallet, and cell phone.

A man wearing coveralls pushed the wheelchair into the room where Steven was being held.

Steven watched as Brooke silently wrote a check and tore it out of her checkbook. She handed it to the man from impound. He tipped his hat and left. "Brian, can you get a few guys to get Dr. Chandler back into his chair, please?"

Smith picked up the phone and grunted a few orders into it. Two men came out and rolled the desk chair with Steven in it, until it sat perpendicular to his wheelchair. They lifted him under his arms, pivoting him into his seat. Brooke fastened his seatbelt. When Steven tried to take control of his joystick, it hung off the side of the mount, which was bent and broken. He looked up at Brooke.

*We didn't do that. I was driving when they stopped us.*

Brooke furrowed her eyebrows and shook her head.

*My beautiful chair. I waited seven long months for this chair. How could this happen?*

Brooke escorted Steven out of the room. She walked next to him, holding the joystick and driving his chair.

"We'll get it taken care of. They are responsible for any valuables in their possession. Right now, I want to get you home."

They turned into a corridor where Mac and Spencer sat on a wooden bench with their heads in their hands. When they heard the squeak of Steven's tires on the linoleum, they both jerked to attention. Mac had a badly bruised nose and a set of raccoon eyes. Spencer had a fat lip and a bruise on his forehead. Steven remembered watching him flopping around on the street while they were cuffing him. *I can only imagine how I look.*

Steven glanced at the clock. As a door opened at the end of the corridor, Logan and Sophie walked through. Steven didn't ever remember his aunt looking more beautiful than she did at that moment.

When Sophie saw Steven, she let out a strangled cry. *"Oh, my God! Look at you."* She knelt in front of Steven, touching his hands, his face . . . Steven winced and she pulled back. Then her expression changed to one he had rarely ever seen. She grabbed Steven by both biceps and shook him. "If you *ever* scare me like that again, I'll . . . I'll . . . Oh, Steven! We were worried sick!"

Steven didn't ever remember feeling more embarrassed or ashamed.

Mac walked over to Sophie, pulling out the key to Steven's car from his pocket. "Don't be mad at him, Mama Chandler. It's our fault. We encouraged him to let loose. He seemed okay when we left the bar to go to karaoke. He only had a few drinks."

"I hold all three of you equally responsible, Mac. There's nothing wrong with Steven's sense of judgment. Every one of you should have known better. I'm disappointed in all three of you."

Mac hung his head. "Yes, ma'am. I understand."

Spencer stood. "I'm sorry too. We all know he never would have done something like this on his own."

Logan barely acknowledged him. He simply said, "Let's get you boys home."

Brooke helped Logan back Steven onto the lift and get parked in the van. While Sophie was tying Steven's chair down, he heard Logan say the broken piece was a universal part, and he'd call Jill to get it fixed Monday.

"I'm sorry, Mom. I love you."

"I love you too, Steven. It'll be okay."

"Does Abby know?"

"She does, as does Sydney."

Spencer groaned from someplace behind Steven. "The sprite's gonna have my ass in a sling."

Mac laughed. "At least I don't have a chick to answer to."

Brooke stuck her head through the opening in the door. She pointed to the back of the van. *"You! Hey!* What's your name, Hercules?"

He snorted at her, which, Steven thought, probably wasn't such a good idea. "Name's Owen McCrea, ma'am . . . at your service."

Steven could imagine his blue eyes twinkling as he tried to impress the girl of his dreams.

"Owen, I want to see you in my office first thing tomorrow morning. Understand?"

*She isn't impressed, buddy.*

"Yes, ma'am!"

"And *you,* little brother. You'd better have your ass there too. Got it?"

"Yes, Brooke."

"Good!"

❖    ❖    ❖

The van jerked when they pulled out, and Steven's stomach lurched.

"How do you feel?" Logan asked.

"Sick."

"Does anything hurt?"

"My head."

Logan chuckled. "Aside from the obvious."

"Side hurts."

"Steven, son, how much did you have to drink?"

"Only a beer and a few shots."

"Why would you do that to yourself? You're still taking pain medication."

"I know, but the dose is so low that I thought I'd be okay. I didn't intend for this to happen. It's been so long since we did anything together . . . I just wanted to have a normal night for a change."

"Brooke said you've vomited several times. We need to be careful you don't get dehydrated."

"I need to pee soon, too."

"We'll get that taken care of."

"We'll have to call Jill too. I think you should go back to rehab tomorrow."

Steven felt panic begin to set in. "No! Casts tomorrow at seven. I hafta go back tonight!"

"We'll see."

They pulled in to his parents' home, and as soon as they were parked, Sophie opened the door and lowered the lift.

Lifting the broken joystick, Logan slowly and carefully drove the chair onto the lift.

When the platform touched down on the pavement, Steven's heart sank. Sophie's eyes were red and puffy. Steven was consumed with guilt as snapshots of recent months flashed through his mind . . . the endless nights Sophie spent by his side in the uncomfortable recliner next to his bed, her quest to help him find the perfect home, and the great effort he knew she expended so it would be ready when he had recovered. There was nothing she would deny her adopted son.

*I did this to her.*

"Oh, Steven, what are we going to do with you?" She reached out and touched his face where

Ryan had split it open.

"Let's get him inside. I'm going to need help getting him situated."

"Sydney is on her way with the girls."

Girls. *Girls. I don't want them to see me like this.*

"Please, can we go to my room now?"

# Chapter Thirty-seven

Despite the generous path of travel leading into the kitchen, Logan found himself challenged as he attempted to steer Steven's wheelchair using the damaged joystick.

Logan felt immense respect for the officers who sacrificed everything to keep the streets of his adopted town safe, but that morning, he cursed the bad apples who were partially responsible for the situation he found himself dealing with. Of course, his nephew played his own part in the mess, but there were so many factors with Steven's situation that his condition unquestionably warranted medical attention. There was no excuse for being negligent.

The entire situation was ironic. Logan didn't know how Brooke convinced the officer to reduce the charges, but they were seriously indebted to her for what she had accomplished.

A blood alcohol test proving Steven had been under the influence of both alcohol and narcotics would have seriously jeopardized Steven's career, not to mention his standing with the stem cell center, even if the law defined an electric wheelchair as a motor vehicle, which was ludicrous. Due to the nature of their research, Steven could not continue working there with a blemish on his record.

*Why would he even consider throwing away everything he's worked so hard for?*

Sophie sobbed the minute Logan explained Brooke's phone call, and then she swore in a way he'd never heard before. When they walked into the precinct, she was nurturing and left no doubt that Steven was loved. Still, Logan was glad it wasn't he who would be on the receiving end of his wife's wrath when Steven sobered up. Sophie might look like a pushover, but Logan knew better than anyone that she was not.

Like his wife had been earlier, Logan was assaulted with so many emotions at the sight of their boy and the sad state he was in. Logan was angry—so very angry—with Steven for acting so irresponsibly when he knew better than anyone what the repercussions would be, with Mac and Spencer for indulging with him, and yet, when Brooke rushed to Logan and explained the situation she had found Steven in, Logan felt like he would explode.

All the way to the precinct, Logan fought to understand the situation, and being the sensible adult—since Steven had apparently taken leave of his senses—Logan planned to take their boy home, let him sleep it off, and then lecture him unless Sophie beat him to it. However, that all changed with Brooke's interpretation of what had occurred while Steven was in custody.

Officers of the law were appointed to serve and protect all citizens, including his son, whose health was jeopardized while in their custody.

*Damn!*

❖   ❖   ❖

Logan intended to hash out the legalities of the incident with Brooke later, but for the time being, his greatest concern was ensuring Steven's safety and keeping him medically stable.

*First order of business: hydration and elimination.*

Logan went to the refrigerator and dispensed a cup of crushed ice. Steven had been asking for a drink since they'd gotten him secured in the van, but erring on the side of caution, Logan decided to treat his nephew as he would any patient with a queasy stomach. Logan understood—he'd had his fair share of cotton mouth during his youth—but he didn't want to instigate another round of Steven vomiting if it could be prevented.

Logan touched the spoon to Steven's lips. "Try this, son." Steven pulled the ice into his mouth and opened it again, immediately. "More." Logan frowned and offered Steven a few more slivers of ice.

"So thirsty, please."

"I don't want to give you too much, too quickly."

Steven snorted. "Come on, old man, you're doling them out with an eye dropper."

"Have you had anything to drink other than alcohol?"

"I had some cokes."

The clock over the sink read seven thirty. It had been almost eight hours since the boys had been picked up. "Did they offer you anything while you were in custody?"

"No."

"And you weren't given an opportunity to relieve yourself?"

"No."

"Let's try a few more ice chips while I sort this all out."

"Okay."

Once again, Logan studied his nephew, and what he saw made him want to scream—identical bruises encircled Steve's wrists. *Such a miscarriage of justice—not only removed from the sanctuary of his wheelchair but handcuffed to a wooden chair that offered no protection for his backside whatsoever.*

Steven's face was a mess, his clothing torn, and through the thin material of his sweatpants, Logan noticed the unmistakable swell of Steven's lower belly. Logan imagined all the potential complications that couldn't be seen: pressure sores, kidney infections, dehydration, and inwardly, he seethed.

"How are you feeling?"

"I've been better. Seriously, I'd be fine with slamming some water, tilting my chair back, and having a nap."

"We need to get some fluids into you, but you've already vomited several times. I'm reluctant to fill your stomach with liquids and let you go to sleep."

"Yeah, that probably isn't the best idea."

"We'll take care of you, son."

"So what's the plan? I'm fading fast."

"I got some supplies at the hospital."

"Yeah, I figured. Was afraid you were going to try and have me admitted."

"It crossed my mind. I'm sure I could have justified putting you in for observation, but there's nothing you need that we can't handle at home. I figured I'd save us both the embarrassment."

"Thanks, I guess."

"That split lip needs to be sutured, but my main concern is getting you hydrated and relieving your bladder. I picked up infusion supplies and a cosmetic suture kit to repair the laceration. I figured you'd spend a good portion of your day sleeping. If you're hooked up to some saline, you'll get rehydrated, and we don't have to worry about your getting sick and aspirating."

"Sounds reasonable."

❖    ❖    ❖

Logan went to the utility room, loading disinfectant wipes, paper towels, and a small trash basket onto the bottom of a wheeled cart. As he was loading his medical bag and the box of supplies from the hospital, he heard Sophie speaking softly to their nephew. He couldn't understand what was being said, but he did understand the unmistakable sound of retching moments later.

When Logan burst into the room, Sophie's eyes were as big as saucers. "I'm sorry. He was so thirsty."

"Nothing else by mouth." The words had no sooner left Logan's lips than Steven vomited again.

"Let's get him cleaned up."

Logan thoroughly washed his hands and covered his work area with a drape. He laid out clean gauze pads, sterile saline, then pulled on a pair of gloves. "I'm going to clean your face up a little and get you numbed up. While we're waiting on the lidocaine to work, we'll get your bladder emptied and start getting you hydrated, okay?"

When Steven nodded, Sophie slowly tilted Steven's chair back, and Logan rolled up under his headrest in a desk chair. "This is a nasty split. You're going to have a souvenir when it heals. I'll do my best, but I'm no plastic surgeon."

"I trust you."

Sophie had begun busying herself in the kitchen when Logan heard the garage door open. "Love, instead of upsetting Steven's stomach with the smell of food, why don't you and Abby take Miss Debbie over to Blue State for some coffee and breakfast? Sydney and I can get Steven sorted out and into bed. When you get home, we'll grab a few hours sleep too."

"I'm sorry, I was trying to stay busy."

"I know you were, dear. I was simply thinking that Abby's guest is young and impressionable, and has, to an extent, been entrusted to our care. We wouldn't want to jeopardize her ability to interact recreationally with such an exceptional peer mentor if she were to share that she witnessed a situation her parents might perceive in a negative manner."

"I understand. Abby and I will be back shortly."

Logan tied a tourniquet on Steven's arm, gently palpating until he found a vein that pleased him. He cleaned the site and inserted the cannula. After the saline lock was attached and flushed, he studied Steven's face. "How's the lip? Sufficiently numb?"

Steven gave Logan a thumbs up.

"I was thinking, maybe we should use a Foley to make sure your bladder is being emptied in a timely manner."

Steven groaned and opened one eye. "Is that necessary, old man?"

"Can you take care of business independently?"

"Probably not."

"Did you expect Sydney to do it for you?"

"No, not when I put myself in this situation."

"Let's take care of your bladder needs first. I'll stitch up your lip, and once you're changed and in bed, I'll hang some saline."

"All right."

Logan assembled everything he needed and got the catheter inserted. Immediately, there was a rush of urine; 750 ml ran into the bag before the trickle stopped.

The fact that Steven waited so long and had been visibly distended concerned Logan greatly. The return he got was dark and cloudy, not healthy and clear as it should be.

After Logan cleaned up, he touched Steven's lip with a gloved finger. "Can you feel that?"

Steven took a deep breath and relaxed his body. "Nope, my face is numb."

"Good. I'm going to begin suturing now. Don't move. Did you hear me?"

Steven opened his eyes, squinting from the overhead light. "Yes, I heard you. I won't move or talk. Go ahead." He closed his eyes and clasped his hands together on his lap. Logan laid a sterile drape across Steven's chest and began to work; he heard Steven's respirations slow and watched his body relax in slumber.

❖   ❖   ❖

Logan worked carefully but quickly and dropped the needle holder onto the utility cart, breathing a sigh of relief that he'd had time to finish.

*Logan was not usually nervous, but this was his son's face. He couldn't afford to make a mistake.* Logan removed his gloves and turned to the figure waiting in the doorway, greeting Sydney softly.

❖   ❖   ❖

In companionable silence, the two worked to clean up Logan's mess and prepared Steven's room while he dozed. Logan was relieved to see that Carol, the pharmacy tech, had packed everything he'd requested.

Sophie and Abby arrived sooner than Logan expected, entering the large kitchen as Logan was raising Steven to a sitting position. "Back already? I thought you girls were getting some breakfast."

Abby shrugged. The corners of her mouth turned up, but the smile didn't quite reach her eyes. "I wasn't very hungry, and Debbie had left-over pizza."

Suddenly, Steven grabbed Logan's wrist. His hazel eyes were as big as saucers when he yelled, "Bucket!" Logan got it under his chin right on time.

Abby squared her shoulders and took a deep breath. "I'm so sorry we fell asleep. Sydney was waiting for a phone call, but we knew it would be a while. We put in a movie and didn't wake up until we got that phone call from Spencer's sister saying you were at the jail."

Abby started to say something else, but when she took in the items on the table and studied Steven's disheveled appearance and bruised and bloodied face, she crumpled.

*"Oh, Steven."*

Logan took a hold of her shoulders as she swayed. "Maybe you should sit down, sweetheart."

Abby pushed away from Logan and dropped to her knees next to Steven's chair. She pressed her face to his soiled shirt and fisted both sides of it with her hands causing Steven to scream out in pain.

"Let go! Let go! Please!"

Abby backed away, her eyes brimming with tears.

Logan studied Steven. "Son, what hurts?"

"Ribs. Oh God, make it go away."

"What happened to your ribs? Did it happen while you were in custody?"

Abby's hand went to her mouth. "Should we take him for X-rays? What if they're broken?"

Steven's hands reached out for her. "Abby, please." Gently, Abby held his hand. When she looked into his eyes, they were filled with sadness.

"No, *they* didn't hurt me. That Ryan guy got in a few good punches although I do suspect Spencer got hurt when we were taken into custody."

Logan reassured Abby. "I don't think an X-ray is warranted. There probably wouldn't have been enough trauma from a fist to cause a break, and even if they were broken, we wouldn't intervene medically unless there was reason to believe Steven had sustained a punctured lung."

Steven reached out and pulled Abby in toward his chest. Logan heard her whisper, "Please don't scare me like this ever again."

"I'm sorry."

Logan watched as his son ran his fingers through Abby's hair, and for the first time, Logan noticed the cuts on Steven's hands.

Abby backed away from Steven, and he opened his eyes. "Maaaan! You reek!"

Steven chuckled quietly, "Abby, sweetheart, Logan's going to help me get cleaned up and settled into bed. Would you mind hanging out with Sophie for a bit? I promise, once he's done, I'm all yours."

"After you get cleaned up, I'll think about it."

As Abby passed, Logan said, softly, "Thank you for not giving up on him."

"I'm happy that he's here and in capable hands. We have boundaries to establish, but that's not for today."

# Chapter Thirty-eight

After Sophie plied Abby with a huge mugful of cocoa and a scone, Abby dragged herself to Steven's room and curled up in his recliner with a soft, fluffy blanket. Steven was already snoring. The relief of knowing that Steven was safe, of seeing him in the flesh, comforted Abby as much as Sophie's fluffy afghan did, and in no time, she was dozing in the recliner a few feet from Steven's bed.

Around three that afternoon, Abby woke with a start. She was livid and found it impossible to tamp down her anger. During the drive home after returning Debbie to rehab, Sophie's account of the things that had occurred at the police precinct ramped up Abby's temper to the boiling point—until she'd laid eyes on Steven's injuries. But in slumber, Abby found herself advocating on behalf of Steven and other individuals with disabilities. Abby already knew some of the horror stories, and while most officers of the law were courteous and compassionate, every once in a while, there was an individual who was ignorant and had no clue how to deal with someone with a disability.

Abby's chest bubbled over with anger. She was mad at the police department for their ignorant handling of Steven and his property. She was angry with Steven for putting himself into that situation, and she was angry with his friends for allowing it to happen. Abby was angry with herself and with Sydney, too.

*If we hadn't fallen asleep, we might have known something was amiss sooner.*

❖   ❖   ❖

Abby realized in the moments when no one knew Steven's whereabouts that she and Steven belonged together.

Steven had inexplicably wound his way into her life. Seeing him so vulnerable, Abby wondered how she could ever live without him now that their lives had become so entwined, but the past twenty-four hours made her realize that she needed to take some time to think. She needed to distance herself from everything to get her bearings. Abby knew if she lay there watching him until he woke, she was afraid she'd let the opportunity pass without addressing the questions that were on her mind: How does he view our status as a couple? *What can I expect from him if we choose to be exclusive?*

Before Steven awoke, Abby sneaked out to the kitchen for a drink and found Sophie at the table with her hands wrapped around a large mug.

"Would you like a cocoa or something? I can brew another pot of coffee."

"No, but maybe some ice water if that's okay?"

Sophie began to rise, but Abby stopped her. "I'll get it. I actually slept half the night. You didn't."

Sophie gestured toward the refrigerator. "Help yourself, dear."

"Thanks."

Abby trudged to the icemaker with a mug of her own, thankful that it had a handle, and there was no chance of it slipping through her fingers. Clumsy hands worked the dispenser, and Abby slowly carried the drink to where Sophie sat, slipping into a seat on the opposite side of the table.

"I wish you'd allow us to help you more, Abby," Sophie said, her smile sad.

"I'm okay. I promised Steven I'd let you know if I'm in over my head. Sydney has been a huge help with everything, and my dad is coming in a few days. You guys have done so much already."

"We're family, dear. We'll do whatever we can to help."

"Thanks. I'm whooped, and I have so much I want to get packed up at my house. Do you think someone could give me a lift? I'd take the bus, but I'm not as sure-footed as I could be today."

"Are you feeling all right? I've noticed that you seem tired, but I didn't want to pry."

"I figure if I pace myself, I can accomplish what I need to get done."

"If you need someone to pack things for you . . ."

"No, thank you, Sophie. There isn't that much, a few personal things and my dishes. The girls and I took a load over last night."

Sophie rinsed her mug and placed it in the dishwasher; Abby did the same. "I'm not going to disturb Steven. He was asleep when I came out," Abby said.

As Abby was pulling her jacket on, a disheveled Logan appeared in the kitchen doorway, wearing sweatpants and a T-shirt. Abby had never seen him in anything so casual. She covered her mouth and giggled. Logan scratched his messy head and smiled. "I'm a little worse for the wear, I'm afraid."

Abby looked down at her own casual attire. "I think we all are."

"I heard you say you were leaving, dear. I'm sorry your visit this morning wasn't more pleasant. We don't usually have this much excitement around here."

Abby gave Logan a wan smile. "That's probably a good thing. I don't know how much more excitement I can handle. I am still kind of frustrated. I want to be mad at him, but seeing him sick and injured makes my heart hurt, and I don't have it in me to stay angry. I need to work some of this out in my head."

"I understand, Abby. I know it doesn't help how you're feeling, but I'm so sorry you had to go through all of this."

"But see, you shouldn't have to apologize. Even though much of it was simply a series of unfortunate events, *this* could have been prevented. You're an innocent bystander the same as I am, and I've seen the concern etched all over your face. This is upsetting you too."

"It is," Logan said, "and I'm sure it'll hit me later, once I've had time to digest all of this."

She gave Logan's arm a little squeeze. "We'll be okay. He will be too. We need some time—and sleep. We all need sleep."

"I'm concerned that you're not taking care of yourself."

"I know I'm overdoing it, and I can feel it catching up with me, but for now, I think I'm okay."

"You'll let us know if you're getting in over your head with all this?"

"I promise. Thanks for caring so much."

"You're part of this family, sweetheart."

She wrapped her arms around Logan's waist and pulled him close. "Now you sound like your wife." Logan rubbed her back a few times before pulling away.

"Please promise you're not giving up on him."

"We'll be all right, but that doesn't mean I'm letting him off easy. I plan to get to the bottom of the situation with the officers involved too. I need to have a sit-down with Brooke. The Center for Independent Living has an attorney that deals with civil rights violations that happen to people with disabilities. I need to discuss this with her. We've had other consumers with hidden disabilities who have had issues with that same precinct. This isn't the first time they've treated a disabled person inappropriately."

"Thank you for promising to follow up on it. Please let me know if there's anything I can do and what your attorney friend has to say."

"I will."

❖　❖　❖

Logan was in his study checking on a patient when Sophie returned from taking Abby home.

"Steven is awake and is asking about his wheelchair. I told him you were on the phone, but I'd let you know," Sophie said, her voice a low whisper. "I'm going to go get some rest. You should join me."

"The day has gotten away from me. I need to shower and dress shortly."

"Maybe you should see if someone could cover your shift."

"That wouldn't be fair, but I will come in and snuggle with you for a while before I go."

Logan walked in to Steven's room to find him looking around. When he spotted Logan, he crossed his arms.

"Was all this necessary? Don't you think you went a little over-board, Dad?"

"No, son, I don't. You were severely dehydrated. You put yourself at risk for all sorts of potential emergencies. I couldn't stop the vomiting. I was very concerned."

Steven began peeling the Tegaderm off his IV site. "Well, you need to get me undone so I can dress and get back to rehab. I have an appointment in the morning."

"No, you don't. Jill doesn't want you to come back until I assure her you're well enough."

Steven's face turned red, his hands clenched into fists. "What have you *done?*"

"When you were *incommunicado,* I called to see if you had gone back to rehab. It was only common courtesy for me to call Jill today and let her know you were okay but obviously not well enough to return as scheduled. She instructed me to care for you at home if I was comfortable with that or admit you to the hospital."

"I don't understand why you think you need to keep me here. I'm fine now. I'd like to get up."

"I think you're making a mistake. You should be resting. Your body is still recovering."

"Get me up, and you'll see. I am fine!"

Logan grabbed a pair of boxers and a T-shirt from the dresser. He pulled the blankets back and picked up the urine collection bag, feeding it through Steven's pant leg before putting the shorts on.

"What the *hell,* Logan? A Foley? Seriously? Overreact much?"

"No, I did what was necessary. You needed fluids pushed. I wasn't going to ask Sydney to cath you every few hours, and you yourself admitted that you were in no shape to care for your bladder."

"Yeah, whatever, *Dad.*"

Steven couldn't have cut Logan deeper if he'd used a knife. Logan closed his eyes and drew in a deep breath, attempting to temper his anger before he said something that couldn't be taken back.

"You have two choices, son. Either you can act your *age* and treat the people who love and care about you with respect, *or* I'll call a transport van, and you can go back to the hospital where they can manage your care until you're healthy enough to leave. You won't treat me with disrespect because of circumstances that occurred when you refused to use a little common sense. Do. You. Understand?"

Steven hung his head in shame, remorse evident in his tone. "Look, I'm sorry. I know I screwed up. I'm sore and I feel like shit, and I know I have no right to take this out on you."

"Apology accepted. We'll discuss this when you're in a better frame of mind."

"I understand."

"It appears you have a lot of apologizing to do."

"I know," Steven whispered, his eyes welling up.

❖   ❖   ❖

"I'm going to try to move you now." Logan swung Steven's legs gently over the side of the bed. He straddled Steven's casts and grasped both his hands, swiftly pulling him into a sitting position. As soon as he was upright, Steven swooned, and nearly slipped from Logan's grasp.

"*Whoa!* Lay me down! Lay me down!"

"I thought you wanted to get out of bed?"

"Changed my mind."

"Wise choice." Logan put his arm under Steven's legs and swung them back onto the mattress.

"When you're feeling better, and during his office hours, you are to call Wesley. He will make an appointment for you to come into the office to have the casts removed."

"All right." Steven sighed.

"Look, I know you're not feeling the greatest, and I promised I wouldn't, but son, I have to say I don't understand. I know you believe strongly in the whole independent living philosophy, but do you see where your misguided attempt to do something independent became a huge error in judgment instead?"

Steven let out a frustrated sigh and moved his hands up to his face, pulling down on his cheeks, distorting them. "I didn't think I'd get this sick. I never meant to inconvenience you. I didn't mean to ruin anyone's weekend, and I never meant to worry any of you. Never in a million years did I think a few drinks would get this out of control."

"What made tonight any different, other than the obvious?"

"The guys in the bar. I'd never seen them before. When we left the bar, they were outside waiting for us. One of them jumped Mac, and they fought. After we walked away, they followed us. I remember them screaming obscenities at us. Mac couldn't keep his mouth shut."

"And someone called the police."

"I think it was a matter of being in the wrong place at the wrong time. When the cruiser drove by the first time, the other guys took off. If we'd made it inside Liffey's, we'd have probably been fine."

"You'd have probably been more intoxicated."

"I had a beer at the first place, and we were there for a few hours. Then when we went to the second place. I had two shots, but I ate quite a bit, and we were there for several hours. I didn't drink the third shot, and I wasn't going to have any more. Someone, I think one of those girls, bought me another shot. It sat there for a while when I played darts, and I wasn't going to drink it, but when that guy kept taunting me, I snapped and I slammed the last shot."

"What kind of alcohol was it?"

"Tequila. I've never had tequila, but I wasn't slamming them all evening. I pretty much nursed the first two for hours. I think it was that last one that did me in."

"I think you need to explain some of this to Abby. I know she's trying to understand everything that happened. She's upset about several aspects of this whole situation. I know it'll ease her mind to talk to you."

"Could you hand me my phone? I'd like to call her."

"Um . . ."

Steven's eyes got as big as saucers. *"What?"*

"She, uh, said she'd call you tomorrow. She'd prefer you give her some time."

Steven's lip trembled, and he squeezed his eyes shut but the tears escaped anyway. "I've ruined everything, haven't I?"

"We need to remember that Abby is under extreme pressure. She's helping put *your* new house together so it's ready when you get out of rehab. She is packing up her home, *and* she's working. The stress from this situation could take a real toll on her. You don't want something like this to push her into an exacerbation."

"Can I please call her? I need to apologize, and I need to know *she's* all right. I can't wait until tomorrow even if it does make her angry."

"I'll have Sydney bring your phone in."

"Didn't she go home?"

"No, she's staying the night. I've got to leave for work soon."

❖　　❖　　❖

Abby had just finished eating a frozen meal when her phone began to ring. By the time she made her way across the living room, the ringing had stopped, and the voicemail notification chimed. Abby pulled up the menu and saw what she already knew . . . *Steven.*

Abby took the phone and made her way back to her bedroom.

*Might as well get comfortable before I call him back.*

Before she could settle in, the ringing began again, but this time Abby answered.

Immediately, Steven launched into an apology. Steven begged for her forgiveness and tried with broken words to tell Abby what she already knew in her head and in her heart.

❖　　❖　　❖

Abby let Steven ramble until he was spent, knowing it was futile to interrupt. When he had purged himself, and it became her turn, there were a few things she had to know.

"Steven, I accept your apology, and I think we'll all feel better once we move past this. I think I'm able to look at this a little more objectively than your family is. While this entire escapade had to do with independence and letting loose, I think you need to think about how your actions have affected the people who care about you the most.

If they didn't care so deeply about your well-being, this wouldn't have escalated into a big deal."

Steven cleared his throat and his voice cracked. "I know, Abby."

"I overheard your dad talking while he and Sydney were getting you situated. He was so worried about your kidneys and the ramifications of the alcohol, the dehydration, the fact that you hadn't emptied your bladder in so long . . ."

"I didn't think things would get out of control. I thought we had a backup plan. And in my own defense, it hadn't been that long since I'd taken care of my bladder. I don't know that I've ever asked either of my parents when they last used the toilet. I know they worry, but seriously, Abby, I'm not five."

"You're right, and I couldn't agree with you more, but I guess for my own peace of mind, I need to know, since we're growing closer, if this is something that will be a regular occurrence. How do I factor into your life? As your *roommate*, as long as your actions don't cause upheaval or a dangerous situation that will affect me—I guess what you do is none of my business, and I have no right to get upset."

The air hung pregnant with unspoken words. The only sound in the room was the ticking of a clock, and Abby wondered if she had ruined everything.

Finally, Steven spoke, his voice barely audible. "I, um, I *thought* we were becoming *much* more than roommates. I sort of thought you were my girl. I think I love you, Abby."

Abby forged ahead, not allowing herself to get sidetracked by the admission that meant everything to her. "You need to understand, then, that I can't handle upheaval like this on a regular basis. I need to know that our future isn't going to be filled with nights like last night. Stressors cause upheavals with my MS. I can't afford to have an exacerbation right now. We both have too much at stake."

"I'm so sorry, Abby. I never thought about how this would impact everyone. I feel terrible for the thoughtless way I've treated all of you. I promise you this will *never* happen again."

"Please promise me that you won't take chances that will endanger your health or get you in trouble with the law. Okay?"

"I promise. Forgive me, Abby?"

"I forgive you, but I think we need to discuss this further when we're both not so emotional."

"Thank you."

Abby's heart hurt when they said their goodbyes, but Abby prayed they'd be okay.

❖   ❖   ❖

Sydney and Debbie came by Abby's apartment that night to help pack. The girls sat Abby down, put her feet up, and let her supervise while they packed everything except one dish, one plate, one glass, and one set of silverware. Abby had a handful of frozen meals she had gotten for the time before the move, so the pots and pans got packed, and by the time the pair left, Abby's kitchen was completely loaded into boxes.

They offered to come back the following night to help pack Abby's clothing and other non-essentials. She was going to decline, but in the end, she realized they were trying to help, and one of Abby's personal goals was learning to graciously accept offers of assistance, so by the time Debbie was ready to go back to the facility, the girls had made a date for the following night.

"Would you like to ride along? Steven seems to be feeling much better today."

"I'd like that."

Abby found Steven in conversation with Alec. The men sat by the window, their backs to the doorway as they looked out over the skyline. It was the first time she'd seen him since the incident. Her heart tugged at the sight. *Oh, my pretty, pretty man . . .*

Abby didn't intend to eavesdrop, but before she put her arms around Steven, Alec called Steven's weekend *cool*.

Steven bristled. "Alec, what we did wasn't cool. It was impulsive and irresponsible. I hurt my family, and I can't begin to tell you the remorse I feel for upsetting Abby. She's the best thing that has ever happened to me. I don't know what I'd do if I lost her."

Abby could feel her face heating up, wanting to announce her presence but needing to hear Steven's admission.

"Debbie said you were pretty sick. How much did you drink?"

"It doesn't matter. I was still taking medication, and I, of all people, should have known better. I thought I knew what my body could safely handle because I'm a doctor. By all rights, I should have been taken to the hospital. I became dehydrated and set myself up for all kinds of potential problems. I owe the people I care about everything, and I was horrible to them. I'm not sure how I'll ever make amends. It *so* wasn't worth it."

"So you and your girl—are you okay, then? You said she was upset."

"Yeah. She was. The stress of everything is bad for her health."

"Why? Is something wrong with her?"

"Wrong? *No*, not wrong, but she does have some medical concerns. That's not something I'm comfortable disclosing about her. No offense, but that's her business."

"It's all good, man. I understand. You're still together, though, right? There's no opportunity for me to step in and take your place?" Alec was laughing, and Abby had to cover her mouth to keep from laughing herself when Steven smacked him in the back of the head.

"No, not a chance, pal! She's the first *real* girlfriend I've ever had, and I'm gonna do everything in my power to make sure she's the last."

"Dude! How old *are* you?"

"I'm thirty-five, or rather I will be in a few weeks. Why?"

"What have you been doing all these years? Living in a cave? How is it possible that she's your first girlfriend? Don't tell me I'm going to have to wait that long for a girl."

"I *knew* this situation was hopeless."

"I went to college for four years. Then I went to medical school and did my internship. I wrapped up my residency, took a job as a neurologist, and worked a few days a week as a fellow in the stem cell lab to work off some of my student loan debt. I led a busy life!"

"So— what? No time for a girl until you had an accident, and you were forced to sit still?"

"Something like that."

"And she's the first girlfriend you've *ever* had? Dude, you're one hell of a late bloomer."

Then Abby saw it in the slump of Steven's shoulders. She knew where his mind was going to go, and she refused to let him put himself through that sort of humiliation. Abby knocked loudly on the door, and Steven jumped. He turned toward the door, and Alex peered around from behind him.

Abby walked over to Steven and ever so gently placed a hand on each cheek, lifting his face so she could assess it. His eyelids fluttered shut. One was a rainbow of color, from vibrant purple mixed with bright red to brown and greenish yellow around the edges. The other was black as night. He opened them, not taking a breath as she looked over the rest of his face. When she lowered her eyes to his lips, Abby frowned. Right next to the corner of his mouth was the split Logan had closed.

"May I?"

"Mm-hmm."

Even more gently than she had held his face, Abby slipped her thumb inside the front of his lip, pulling it down carefully so that she could see the rest. Steven's teeth had left some nasty marks on the inside. Abby lowered her face until they were eye to eye. She placed butterfly kisses across Steven's mouth, not wanting to hurt him. He moaned, and Abby heard Alec pretending to gag. She pulled away, and they both began to laugh. One of Steven's hands went to his ribs, and the other pressed against the corner of his mouth.

"To what do I owe this surprise, Miss Harris? I thought you'd be packing your little heart out all week."

"Oh, I've *been* packing."

"And is the house becoming a home?"

"The house is incredible, Steven. The curtains are up, there's artwork on the walls, and the cupboards will soon be outfitted with all of my kitchen things."

"What kinds of 'things,' Abby? *Food?*"

"Oh no, Steven. *You're* taking me to the store to buy food. I'll cook it, but you're picking out your own stuff."

"I can hardly wait."

Abby reached down and took Steven's hand. "Walk with me. Hey, you got it fixed!"

"Yes. Jill had the guys take care of it when I got back. It was a bracket that held my controller. It must have gotten bumped when it was lifted into the van. Who knows? It's fixed and it's been paid for. I'm fortunate it was nothing serious. Had it been something like a joystick module, it would have been a long time until it was repaired."

Abby looked down and saw the blue fiberglass sticking out of the bottom of his jogging pants, his bare toes pointed in different directions. "So . . . you've still got them?"

"Till tomorrow afternoon. I have to go over to the orthopedic department at the hospital."

"Good luck. Do you think he'll put them back on?"

"No. He wants to get me into the whirlpool. I haven't gotten any more flexion. I've got less than two weeks to get bending."

"And then you'll be home."

"Yes, and then I'll be home . . . and you're still planning to be there too? I haven't scared you away with my lack of judgment?"

"Yes, I'll be there. We'll talk about your judgment soon, okay?"

Abby gave him another kiss when they reached Sydney's car.

"Good night, Steven."

"Good night."

# Chapter Thirty-nine

Wesley removed the casts on Tuesday. He was extremely pleased with the range of motion Steven had gained and added whirlpool therapy in addition to the ultrasound he'd been receiving. Wesley also prescribed an anti-inflammatory gel to be used with the ultrasound to help ease any discomfort or inflammation Steven might have as a result of the adhesions.

Steven looked down at his legs in awe. They were ugly, scaly, red, scarred, and emaciated—but they were still there. Every other time the casts had been removed, he was lying on his back. Steven had been able to push himself up with his elbows, but this was the first time he was able to sit and look at them. He couldn't help himself.

Steven called Sydney during the ride back to rehab. "I need a shower. Can you get me a loofah or one of those puffy, foo-foo things you girls use?"

She laughed. "Yes. *Why?*"

"The skin on the front of my legs is crawling. Lotion. I need lotion too."

"You have cocoa butter in your cupboard there, Steven. I'll be over soon."

❖   ❖   ❖

Steven grew concerned the moment Sydney entered his room.

He watched as she quietly gathered his things and trudged to the bathroom, her shoulders hunched, no spring in her step.

Steven followed her into the room, reaching for her wrist when she turned on the shower.

"Syd? What's wrong?"

Steven's breath hitched when she met his gaze.

"Is it Spence?"

Sydney shook her head, her eyes awash with sadness.

"Is Abby all right?" *Sure she is. Isn't she? She was fine last night!* Steven's heart pounded against his ribs.

"Do you know something, Sydney? Is she leaving me? She promised we'd work this out. Oh God, I told her I loved her." Steven began tugging at his hair.

Sydney pulled on Steven's hands. "Steven, stop! She seems . . . under the weather. I called her school this morning because her phone went to voicemail, but they said she took a sick day. I'm sort of worried about her."

*If I did this to her, I'll never forgive myself.*

❖ ❖ ❖

"She's been working hard. She may have taken a lazy day. She's probably sleeping."

Sydney went home, promising to let Steven know if she heard from Abby. Steven tried to call throughout the afternoon, and finally, Sydney called after eleven to say she had spoken with Abby, who thought she was coming down with something and had gone to bed early, promising to call Steven in the morning.

Early Wednesday morning, Abby did call. When Steven looked down and saw her name on the display, he was relieved beyond words. It didn't matter where she'd been or what she was doing as long as she was safe.

*Is this how I made her feel when I was out with the guys, and she couldn't contact me? Lord, forgive me.*

"Abby," Steven said, her name barely a whisper.

"Hi, Steven."

"You okay? You sound exhausted."

"I *am* exhausted."

"Didn't you sleep?"

His girl let out a stuttering sigh. "I slept, but I don't feel rested. I'm not—the past few days have been rough. I think today will be a better day."

"Sydney said you took yesterday off. I tried to call you. I was worried sick."

"I'm so sorry. I didn't mean to worry anyone. I was so tired when I got up that I called work and went back to bed. My phone was dead. I would've called when it was done charging, but I fell asleep after Sydney and I hung up."

"It's okay. I'm afraid you're taking on too much. I'd die if anything happened to you."

She chuckled quietly into the phone. "You wouldn't *die* without me. Don't be melodramatic, Steven." And then, barely above a whisper, she said, "I'll be fine."

"Well, I should let you get ready for work. Will I see you at lunch-time?" *I miss you.*

Steven's question was met with a long silence. "I'm not sure. I took today off too. I wanted to take a little time to rest up before the big move, you know?"

Steven did know, and he was glad she was taking some time for herself, but he still worried.

"Good for you. Stretch out and read a book. Do something for yourself, okay?"

"Yeah, I'll try. I'm sorry I worried you."

"I'm glad you're all right."

"I'll talk to you later, Steven."

"Okay. Take care, love."

"I will." And the line went dead.

❖    ❖    ❖

On Thursday, Steven requested that Abby come for dinner. With some prodding, she agreed. Steven had had a good day, and he hoped that his mood might rub off on Abby and raise her spirits.

Steven was reading a medical journal that Jeff had dropped off. He was looking forward to getting back to work, his recent progress encouragement that anything was possible.

His heart stopped when Abby walked into his room. She glanced up from the floor with sad eyes, and it was then that Steven noticed Sydney's arm linked through hers, not in a friendly gesture but one of support. With her other hand, Abby gripped her cane.

"Baby, what's wrong?" Abby's hoodie was swimming on her, easily several sizes too large. It hung to her knees, and even though she had the sleeves bunched up, her hands were barely visible. When she got closer, Steven noticed the Woodstock FD insignia on the upper left side.

Steven hurried over to his girl and motioned for her to sit on the bed. Sydney carefully guided her across his side of the room and helped her sit down.

Abby motioned toward a bag on the foot of the bed. "I brought dinner, and I'm as hungry as a horse. Can we please eat?"

"Sure, may I give you a ride?"

"Yes, please," she said, again with the small, sad smile. Steven couldn't wait until they were alone. On the inside, he was freaking out, but he refused to create a scene if it was something Abby wanted to remain private.

Sydney smiled at the two of them and quietly left the room.

Steven parked perpendicular to the edge of the bed and raised the wheelchair armrest closest to the bed. "Can you scoot across onto my lap?"

"I think so."

"Use the remote to raise the bed a little." When the mattress was even with the tops of Steven's legs he said, "That's it."

"I don't want to hurt you."

"Just watch the toes. Do you remember transferring into your wheelchair?"

The corners of Abby's mouth turned down. "I'd rather not."

"Humor me. Scoot to the edge of the bed." Steven patted the other armrest. "Can you get ahold of this one?"

Abby slowly reached across Steven's lap, and he put an arm behind her, lifting as she began to transfer onto his lap, helping her turn as she made the transition.

Once Steven was certain Abby was secure on his lap, he grabbed the bag of food and gave it to her. He didn't know if he could wait the five minutes it would take to get her safely tucked away somewhere, like the conference room. He didn't know how he'd ever eat with his insides all twisted up.

"Baby, you have to tell me what's wrong."

"As soon as we're someplace private, okay?"

*Definitely gonna lose my mind.*

"Sure. Hang on."

Steven reached across her lap, his arm holding onto both of her legs while she wrapped her arm around his shoulders.

Steven drove as quickly as he could safely go. Thankfully, the conference room was unlocked. He swung the door open and reached inside to turn on the light.

Steven drove to a loveseat that sat in a far corner and deposited the bag of food. He released his hold on Abby. When she turned, Steven took hold of her waist to steady her while she stood.

When Abby lost her balance, Steven reached for her wrist, making her hiss in pain. He felt something under Abby's sleeve, and as soon as he tried to pull it up, Abby backed away, covering her hand.

"Baby? What's wrong? Are you hurt?"

"It's all right. I can explain. I was going to tell you when we were alone."

Abby sat and pulled her leg up underneath her. Steven transferred onto the loveseat, and turning to face Abby, reached for her hand again, but Abby pulled it away and blurted out, "I went to see Dr. Jeffries this morning. I'm not trying to hide anything from you. This has been the day from hell."

"What's wrong, baby? Are you having an exacerbation?"

Abby began to cry. She wiped her face with her sleeve, her eyes wide. "Dr. J called it a . . . *pseudo flare?*"

Steven's heart sank. *This is the last thing she needs.*

"So, not actually a full-fledged exacerbation. Tell me about your appointment. What's going on?"

"Um, I woke up yesterday, and it felt like my feet were asleep. Only . . . they didn't wake up. I've been so tired . . . dead tired. I was in bed almost the whole day."

Steven clenched his hands, his breaths coming in gasps. He wiped the beads of sweat from his forehead with the back of his hand.

"Why didn't you call me?"

One of Abby's hands went to her hip. The other pointed at him with an accusing index finger. "I *know* how you get. You'd get into this self-deprecating mood, and I'd have trouble pulling you out. I can't afford that right now. I wanted to talk to Dr. Jeffries today and find out what we were dealing with. I had *every intention* of telling you as soon as I got home, but I had to pee. Then my phone was ringing off the hook. It was Sydney."

Steven thought back over the little things he had pushed aside hoping he was wrong: the balance issues, the fatigue, her shaking hands, the way she rubbed her eyes when she tried to read something, the cane she bought on Good Friday . . . little things that nagged at him here and there but not all at once . . .

*If I had been on my A-game, they'd have been glaring like a neon light!*

Steven looked at Abby's face, *really* looked at her. Her cheeks were bright red, but the rest of her was so pale. The pupils of her eyes were dilated.

*She's on some kind of therapy.*

She picked up the bag that sat between them. "Can we please eat while we talk? I'm starving."

"Can I see your arm first? I need to make sure I didn't hurt you."

She held her arm out to him, and he gently rolled the huge sleeve to reveal an IV catheter. Steven looked over the infusion site, and there was no blood. He hadn't dislodged the catheter or blown the vein when he grabbed her arm.

*Thank God.*

"What are you taking, love?"

"A three-day steroid. I, um, I had the first one in the office. I'm doing the other two at home."

"How do you feel?"

She crumbled and the tears started running again. "Mis-mis-miserable."

"Come here, baby." Steven tugged on her hand, and she melted into the side of him. "Crawl right up on my lap. You won't hurt me."

Abby carefully crawled into Steven's embrace.

"That's better, isn't it?" Abby nodded but seemed to be deep in thought. "Abby, sweetheart, can you be more specific?"

"All of it?"

"Yes, please, all of it. I need to know how you're tolerating everything."

"I'm exhausted, and I'm hungry . . . no, starving, but when I eat, I'm nauseous. I have terrible heartburn, and my mouth tastes funny."

"Like metal?"

"Yeah, and I'm peeing like crazy too."

"Do you go into the office, or does a nurse come tomorrow and hook up the infusion for you?"

"No, I'm on my own. I don't get a bag tomorrow. I get one of the little balls."

"Like an I-Flow?"

"Yeah, that's the name of it. I have two of them at home in my fridge."

"I hate for you to be alone while you're taking it. Would you like Sydney to stay with you for a few days? I'm sure she wouldn't mind."

"She's been working so hard helping me with the house, running errands . . ."

"Abby, she might be family, but she's getting *paid* to do those things, so don't feel like you're inconveniencing her. I can ask her if you like."

"No, I think I'll be okay, but I felt like my heart was going to burst out of my chest when I was getting the bag. Maybe she could come over tomorrow morning while it's hooked up, in case I have any problems."

"She wouldn't mind at all. I'll ask her to make sure she doesn't have any plans. Have you ever had this medication?"

"No, I had another treatment before, but I don't have time to do a seven to ten day hospital stint. I didn't plan on taking time off this week. I'm off all next week."

"I'd plan on taking the rest of the week off, Abby. I doubt you'll sleep much tonight, and even though you're exhausted, you'll probably feel like running a marathon tomorrow. The day after you come off can be pretty bad. You'll crash hard if you don't taper off. Did Jeff prescribe any oral steroids?"

"Yes, along with something for my stomach and a sleep aid. I was only going to get the oral steroid. I never have trouble sleeping, and I don't usually get heartburn, but it's started today." She dropped her head in her hands and moaned. "I'm not myself."

"Please, love, get the sleep aid and the antacid. You'll feel much better if you have both. Get some kind of hard candy too; it'll help with the bad taste. Something minty. I've heard root beer barrels are good too. Buy something that has a strong flavor."

"You do have insurance to cover it, yes?" They'd never discussed anything financial other than how he was going to pay for the house. If her insurance wouldn't pay for treatments, he wanted to make sure Abby was taken care of. Her access to proper healthcare was paramount.

"Yeah, it's all covered except for a small deductible."

"Good. Then get everything filled, even if you don't need them. You'll be glad to have it in the middle of the night when nothing is open."

"Do you think Sydney would mind stopping at the drug store?"

"Not at all. Are you sure you don't want her to stay over?"

"No. I'm a big girl. I can handle this."

"Are you still hungry?"

"I'm famished, and I ate right before I came here."

"Uh, yeah." Steven laughed. "This stuff can make you ravenous." Abby reached into the bag and pulled out a Mountain Dew. "Um, you might not want to drink that right now."

Abby growled at Steven. "And why shouldn't I drink this? I thought you were all about drinking caffeine even when you know it's bad for you. Please don't tell me what to do."

"You're already amped up on all kinds of steroids. You'll never get any sleep." Abby gave Steven the evil eye, and he decided it was time to shut his mouth. Steven held his hands up in surrender.

*Moving on to dinner . . .*

Steven opened the bag and laid out a burrito on the couch. It wasn't an ideal place to put food, but at least he had a wrapper between the couch and the food. Using one hand, he unwrapped the paper and then peeled the burrito open.

"Abby, can you hand me the condiments one at a time?"

"Mm-hmm." Despite being under the weather, there was a glint in her eye, and Steven remembered that day, his favorite meal ever shared with Abby. He ran a strip of each condiment on the burrito and carefully flipped the flour tortilla closed.

Steven lifted it to Abby's mouth, and she took a healthy bite. He'd never fed someone he was in love with before, and watching her tongue sweep over her lips to pick up the tiny morsels was so damn hot. If she weren't so miserable, his mind would have gone straight to the gutter. Steven had never felt this kind of overwhelming devotion to anyone before.

*This is amazing.*

Abby finished her burrito in a few bites.

Steven began preparing one for himself, but when Abby licked her lips and turned those sad eyes on Steven, he fed it to her instead.

"Oh my God, you're not going to want me if I keep eating like this. I'm going to be as big as a whale before the weekend is over!" Her breath hitched, and Steven feared the waterworks were right around the corner, but she recovered herself.

"Abby, sweetheart, you're *not* going to be as big as a whale. There's *nothing* in this world that could make me *not* want you." He reached out and put his hand to her cheek, softly pulling her in for a kiss. "I love you, Abby."

And then it started. She got quiet and closed her eyes, and Steven felt the trembling before the sobbing began. Her breath hitched between sobs, but she uttered those words right back to him. "I"—sniff—"I love"—sniff—"I love you too."

That's how Sydney found them almost a half hour later. Hugging and kissing and sobbing and sniffling—a big, blubbering, ecstatic mess.

"Sydney, could you run Abby past the pharmacy on your way home? She can tell you which one."

"Sure, no trouble at all."

"They close soon. You should get moving."

And then, because Steven really wanted to hear her reply *to be sure he hadn't imagined it,* he whispered, "I love you, Abby."

With watery eyes, Abby met his gaze. "I love you too, Steven. Thanks for taking care of me tonight."

Steven wrapped her in a crushing hug. He didn't want her to leave. He didn't want her to be alone, to go through this with no one there. He knew this was only the beginning of the rollercoaster ride, and before the meds would make her feel better, they would most likely make her feel worse. "You're welcome, love. Please, promise you'll call me if you need *anything.* I'm here for you. I don't care what time it is. I can't come to you, but Logan can and will. You know you only need ask."

She nodded and answered quietly. "I understand. Thank you."

"Take the burritos."

"But you haven't eaten."

"There's plenty of food here."

"Thank you."

"Sydney," Steven asked, "could you ask someone at the desk to come help me off this couch? It's a little too soft, but you have got to go. She needs those scripts filled."

"Will do. Why don't you call me once you're in bed? We didn't discuss your schedule for tomorrow. I'll be up."

"Thanks, I will. Goodnight, ladies."

In unison they chimed, "Goodnight, Steven."

❖   ❖   ❖

Steven was asleep before ten, but his phone was vibrating by midnight. Abby was too hot, sweating profusely, had soaked several T-shirts, and threatened to strip and *sleep naked*.

*Good lord.*

He talked her down off the ledge after more than an hour of trying to reassure her that it wouldn't go on forever.

At two she called and said she had tossed and turned and had counted sheep, then all but stood on her head.

By three the itching began. He told her to take an antihistamine, hoping it would help with the insomnia, too, since she refused to take the sleep aid. *Stubborn woman.*

She called back around four and said she was exhausted, but she couldn't shut her body or her mind down. Her thoughts were all over the place, and she couldn't stop fidgeting. "Oh God, Steven, *please do something!*"

*She never took the antihistamine.*

Finally, she took the sleep aid. He hoped that it kept her asleep all day. Thank goodness she had given Sydney a key. *Smart girl.*

Sydney called at eight thirty to tell him Abby was dead to the world. "Should I hook up the IV without waking her?"

"No, let her sleep a while. The heart palpitations will wake her. They were horrible yesterday, and she needs to rest."

❖   ❖   ❖

At some point, Steven realized that *Dr. Chandler on fentanyl* would not have been functioning as sharply as he was now. Suddenly, the effects of drugs on his mind came into sharp focus.

Another call came at ten when Steven was in the gym. Jill answered his phone and handed it to him. Abby was awake, and they were hooking up the ball that would provide her medication.

*Good. Get it over with as soon as you can.*

At noon it was the hiccups that had started over an hour earlier. Sydney tried to scare her, made her hold her breath, and gave her countless spoonfuls of sugar.

*Oh God, not sugar! Her blood sugar will go through the roof!*

"Keep an eye on her, Syd. She might need insulin if her blood glucose gets too high."

The ball finally emptied and was disconnected.

At two o'clock, she'd had a rush of energy, and Sydney couldn't rein her in. The apartment was spic and span. Boxes were all packed.

"Would it be okay for Abby to sleep in your bed at the new house until her dad moves her furniture?"

*Move her in, Sydney.*

By four, she'd eaten several meals that would put a lumberjack to shame.

"Let her do her thing, Sydney. She's bound to wind down soon."

At six, they packed a bag for Abby, then stopped to get a bag from Sydney's place.

*They are both sleeping in my new bed.*

Abby was snoring by nine, and Sydney was exhausted.

"It's been a long, tiring day." And with that, Sydney hung up.

Steven was nearly as tired as Sydney sounded. He hadn't been on the phone so much in one day since, well, since he had patients he was keeping tabs on. Not since I was Dr. Chandler.

*I miss being that guy.*

Steven put his phone under his pillow. He was out before ten, but he knew the phone would buzz at some point. He hoped he wouldn't be too tired to hear it.

Abby didn't disappoint. Around three she called, sweat-soaked and starving. She threatened to strip and cook naked if Sydney wouldn't wake up. Steven asked her to shake Sydney and give her the phone.

"Sorry, Sydney, it's gonna be another long night."

Abby was back out before five, and Steven got to sleep through until Leslie came and helped spot him as he got into the shower. The shower was so rejuvenating, he almost forgot how tired he was. *Almost.*

Steven fell asleep in the whirlpool. He didn't hear from the women again until lunchtime. The final dose was finished, and the catheter was out of Abby's arm. The nightmare was coming to a close. But—the women had been bickering all morning.

Abby swore Sydney was the anti-Christ, and Sydney was waiting for Abby to do her best Linda Blair impression.

Steven called that night at seven. He hadn't had a call in hours. Abby was ecstatic. She said she was walking so much better and could feel every little thing she stepped on. However, she was exhausted, and her stomach was upset. If it wasn't the heartburn, it was the hiccups.

The hiccups got so bad, Abby had to put Sydney on the phone because she couldn't talk anymore. Steven made a few suggestions— nothing that was proven, mind you, but when Abby sucked on a big spoonful of peanut butter and held her breath as she worked it around her mouth with her tongue, they finally went away.

*"You are the man!"* she said and Steven fist pumped.

*Yes! I* am *the man!*

Sydney called at nine and said Abby had worn herself out, asked for the sleep aid, and was sleeping soundly.

*The crash is coming. I can feel it.*

Steven called at eight o'clock on Saturday morning. Abby was still sound asleep. She staggered to the bathroom with Sydney in tow two or three times but was currently down for the count. Sydney would have loved to sleep on the couch, but she wouldn't leave Abby alone.

*Apparently, Abby snores like a freight train.*

Jill promised to have Steven's routine completed before lunch because Sophie was coming to get him with the old van. He was going to his house for the day.

❖   ❖   ❖

On the way, Steven bought Gatorade, fruit sorbet pops, and bananas to restore some potassium Abby had depleted. She was still sleeping when he arrived, but when she finally woke up, she was sensitive to light and had a headache. Steven gave her some Tylenol, and Sydney slipped a sleep mask over her eyes. Steven transferred into his bed and curled up next to Abby, spooning with his girl for the very first time.

A very surprised Abby woke up to find Steven's arms around her. Despite her pleasure at this discovery, Steven was now in full doctor mode. He made her push fluids and threatened to wake her at regular intervals so she wouldn't get dehydrated. It was surreal that Abby's physical needs mirrored Steven's needs from the weekend before, and it hurt his heart because he knew he'd been responsible for some part of her downward spiral, too.

When it was time to leave, Steven was torn. Abby needed help, and he hated to go, but she was in capable hands with Sydney, and Steven had a job to do.

❖   ❖   ❖

On Wednesday, Abby walked into Steven's room at rehab. He didn't know that he'd ever seen her look stronger or stand taller. Her gait was perfect.

Since they hadn't seen each other in three days, Abby lunged at Steven when she saw him. His chair was in the standing position, and for a split second, Steven feared they were going to topple over.

Abby took Steven's face in her hands and stared at him as if she were parched, and he was an oasis. Her hands and lips were everywhere.

"Oh my god, Steven! I'm so sorry. I feel terrible. I was horrible to everyone."

"Abby, it's okay. It wasn't you. It was the meds."

"Oh no, it was *all* me. I knew what I was saying, but I had no control. How could you possibly love a harpy like me?"

"Oh, Abby. How could I not love you?" Steven replied, and then he kissed her.

# Chapter Forty

Balancing the highs and lows of MS was something that continued to challenge Abby.

Spring whipped Abby's life 'round like a whirlwind—beautiful weather, parent teacher conferences, long, healthy walks, the science fair, preparations for an unexpected move, Steven's lost weekend—gathering momentum until it peaked with Abby's flare.

The flare, she had almost anticipated—the Chandlers' reaction, not so much. Abby had never been nurtured Chandler-style. Not in the way Steven wielded his expertise to help her navigate the episode nor in the way Sydney stayed by her side around the clock. She never expected Logan's appearance in the middle of the night simply because Sydney called him. His gentle hands, soft and cool, touched Abby's face, palpated her pulse. "How do you feel, Abby? What hurts? Are you thirsty?"

Attentive, quiet, compassionate—even though Abby wasn't herself.

Abby awoke to Sophie wiping her face with a cool cloth, holding her hand while she lay nauseous, her eyes squeezed shut.

Every member of Steven's family enveloped Abby in a love that was genuine and unconditional, ensuring that she was comfortable and safe while her body did battle with an invisible assailant. And this, Abby realized, was why Steven chose to ignore the overreach—because their actions were borne of love.

❖   ❖   ❖

*That which doesn't kill you makes you stronger.*

Abby realized the mantra she repeated in her head while she was under the weather could be applied to relationships, too.

She and Steven had navigated a challenging week, but instead of growing apart, they'd grown closer.

Despite their recent declarations, they had so much to learn about each other, which was how Abby found herself sitting behind Oliver Maxwell's mahogany desk as Sydney worked to clean Steven's bedroom and bathroom.

Abby ran her fingers over the dark wood, which had been waxed and buffed until it gleamed. The buttery leather chair cradled Abby in comfort, and she giggled when she spun in circles, imagining a youthful Steven doing the same.

"What's so funny, Miss Harris?"

Abby gasped, her palm slapping her chest. "Steven! How did you get here?"

"I drove."

"Seriously?"

"For real, babe."

"Has this been happening much? This driving thing?"

"Only for the past week or so."

"Did you come alone?"

"Jill and I were out for a drive. I saw Syd's car, so we stopped. Sydney is giving Jill a quick tour. She said I'd find you in here.

"You look like you belong behind my father's desk, my dear, but I don't know if we can both work in this study at the same time. You're very distracting."

"Then we'll have to take turns because I like this study."

"You look so professional with your hair up and your glasses on. I bet the little boys in your class all have crushes on you."

Abby hung her head and blushed. "They're too young to think like that."

"Au contraire, Miss Harris. I remember having a crush on a particular teacher when I was about their age."

Abby gasped. "Seriously? I don't even want to think about that."

Steven chuckled and pulled as close to Abby as he could. Turning his father's big leather chair by the arms, he guided it until his footrest fit perfectly between the wheels. Steven put his hand behind Abby's head, pulling her to him, and he murmured oh-so-quietly as he kissed her, "Oh, the things you do to me, Miss Harris."

Abby's chest grew warm, and she felt the blush creeping up her neck to her face. Abby fanned herself, and Steven chuckled low and sexy, making Abby's blush deepen.

"You seem to forget, Dr. Chandler, that we have some important things to discuss. Let's not put the cart before the horse."

Steven frowned. "Yes, you're right. We do. Would you like to go out for dinner this evening? I know this little place."

"How will we get there?"

"I'm not comfortable driving independently yet, but I'm sure I could impose on a family member to provide transport tonight."

"Okay."

Steven grasped both her hands in his and pulled Abby close. "We'll be okay, baby. I'll do anything to make you happy. Anything." He leaned into her hair, nuzzling her neck. "I'm never letting you go," he whispered.

Abby wrapped her arms around Steven and squeezed with a strength she didn't know she possessed. "I don't know that I could bear to live a life without you in it, and that scares me to death—to be so dependent on another person."

"I've never experienced feelings so intense either, but I have experienced losing someone, and I know I can't live without you." Steven backed up. "Come on, let's go talk to Syd about that ride."

They wandered through the house, and Steven stopped in the living room, turning to face Abby. "I was thinking. Your father is coming soon."

"I pushed it back a day. I was feeling so terrible. I, um, I didn't want him to know how bad things had gotten. I wanted to give my body some time to get back on track."

"You should be honest with him, Abby. From what you've told me, I imagine he'd be hurt if you kept it from him."

"He would be, and I promise I'll talk to him about it. I don't want him to coddle me. I want to have a peaceful weekend without his worrying that I'm overdoing it. I didn't realize how run down I was until yesterday when I began feeling so good. I apologize. I think I derailed your train of thought."

"I was thinking that if you weren't too terribly upset with my friends, perhaps you'd let them move your things before your father arrives."

"Oh, no, that's not happening. Can't go there, Chandler."

"Why?" Steven asked. "You know they feel terrible about what happened."

"It's not that. My dad is coming here specifically to move me. What's he going to think if my stuff is already here?"

"That he's got a nice, quiet weekend to spend with his daughter? Let me arrange this for you. Mac and Spence could move the heavy stuff, set up your bed, carry in your dresser and whatever boxes you have."

"I don't know. I suppose it wouldn't hurt. When?"

"Tomorrow morning? I already took the liberty of asking both of them if they were free."

"Of course you did. You're incorrigible, Chandler."

A wide grin split Steven's face. "I know."

"Thank you."

"You're welcome."

"So, tomorrow? I can't believe it's here already."

"I know." Steven sighed. "I wish it was moving day for me too."

"Eight days," Abby whispered.

Steven's head jerked up. "You're counting?"

"Every day since we decided to do this."

"Wow. Here I thought I was the only one."

"Have I told you how proud I am of you?"

"I think you just did."

Abby snaked her arms around Steven's neck, closing her eyes and kissing him, softly at first, and then he pulled her onto his lap and intensified the kiss.

Somewhere in the distance, a throat cleared. "Time to get back to work, Chandler."

Steven groaned, pressing their foreheads together. "I tell you, she's a sadist."

Jill laughed. "Let's go, Loverboy. You'll have plenty of time for that next week!"

Steven caressed Abby's cheeks with his thumbs. "Tonight, Abby. Wear something comfortable."

She leaned in and pecked his lips a few times. "Okay."

He patted Abby on the backside. "Up you go, then." Holding onto her hand, Steven steadied Abby as she climbed off of his lap.

"I'll see you later."

"Why don't you call your dad and ask him to be here sometime Friday afternoon? He's leaving Sunday, yes?"

"Yeah."

"Good. That'll give you the entire weekend to take it easy. I'd love to do this for you."

"Thanks, I'll call him. We don't spend enough time together."

"I'll see you tonight."

❖   ❖   ❖

Sydney popped her head into the study right after Abby hung up with her dad. "So, Mac and Spencer are moving your stuff?"

"Yeah, they seem like okay guys. I can't blame them for what happened. Steven's a grown man, and I'm so ready to move forward."

"And Steven? Do you blame him?"

Abby closed her eyes and flopped her head back. "I'm upset with him for getting into a situation that endangered his well-being, but I can appreciate the need to do something that lets you forget about your troubles, if only for a little while. So, no, I have no right to blame him for trying to cope with everything he's gone through."

"I'm glad. You're good for each other."

"We're going out tonight. I guess he asked you for a ride?"

Sydney nodded.

"We need to talk. Anything he may have done has been forgiven from the beginning, but I need to know what I can expect if we're going to move forward in this relationship. I won't be one of those girls who sit by the phone while her guy is out carousing with his friends half the night. I can't do that. My dad is a first responder. When I lived at home, I slept with the phone nearby while he worked all night. I know Steven is used to working long hours and covers call after hours; I don't expect Steven to report his every move to me, but it's common courtesy when you're in a relationship to let your significant other know you're safe."

"I understand, Abby. I do."

Abby wondered if Sydney and Spencer would ever make amends.

"Are you going to be okay with the guys moving my things, Sydney?"

"I'm a big girl, Abby. I'll be fine." But the way Sydney's lip trembled and her eyes welled up told Abby she wasn't.

"Oh Sydney." Abby held her friend as she sobbed.

As suddenly as Sydney had started crying, she stopped and pushed away from Abby. "That's enough of that. I'm not going to mourn a romance that wasn't meant to be. He's always been a flirt, and I've ignored it all these years, but I feel like he was on a date with another girl at a time when we were planning our future. I'm ready to settle down but not with a man who isn't one hundred percent invested too."

"Maybe you should go somewhere else tomorrow."

"What, and give him the impression that I'm all brokenhearted? No way, Abby. I'm a strong woman. I'm not letting any man affect me like that."

"You are a strong woman, Sydney. I don't think I could do it."

Sydney chuckled sardonically. "The man has given me ten years of experience. This isn't the first time something like this has happened. I think it's time for me to see what else is out there. I'm not stringing him along; he knows we're separated. I haven't given him any reason to hang on to false hope. There's this dreamy, single doctor I know . . ."

Abby's stomach was in knots on the ride to pick up Steven. Sydney had offered to do her hair and makeup, but this wasn't a date where she was trying to impress him.

The late spring weather was warm, and Abby didn't want to get too hot, so she dressed in a button-down shirt and a pair of cotton slacks. She also pulled her hair up into a ponytail and wore her favorite pair of chucks.

*He said to dress comfortably!*

When the girls pulled in, Steven was waiting outside, wearing his trademark smile. Abby had been seeing more and more of it as Steven got closer to his release date.

Abby remembered thinking way back when they first met that he was such an incredible man—inside and out—and how she had longed for someone like that.

*He was so far out of my league! He still is! I'm so lucky!*

It amazed Abby how fate brought Steven into her life, for in as much as she loathed the frustration that sometimes came with her disability, Abby would never have crossed Steven's path.

Abby stepped out of the car so Steven could get in, and Sydney lowered the ramp. "Do you want to drive? I can move the seat."

"No way, Sydney, not with you and Abby in the car. I'm not ready yet. Jill can control the car if I have a problem."

"So, when will you start driving this?"

"We're going to move it here this weekend, and I'll drive it the rest of my stay. I have a license, but I still get anxious about being out in traffic."

"I can sort of relate to that. I haven't driven in two years."

"We have to work on getting your license re-instated, Abby. You're capable."

"When they put a stop on it, it was because my reaction time was slow. Dr. Gilmer reported it to the DMV."

"At the time, it was an appropriate action, and by law, if a doctor doesn't feel a patient can drive safely, it's his responsibility to report it.

They give the patient every opportunity to appeal and test expedient-ly."

"I wasn't ready to drive then. I couldn't even walk." Abby's voice was barely a whisper.

"I know, baby, but it's not like that now. You're strong and healthy."

"I wasn't that strong or healthy last week."

"I suggest that during a period when you're well, you get your license. You could go years without another setback. If the day comes where you feel that you're not able to drive, exercise caution, and let other people transport you."

"I don't think I could go out on the road if the examiner was some-one like that guy who arrested you, someone who would be waiting for me to make a mistake. I'd be under so much scrutiny, I'd fail." Abby shuddered thinking about it.

"It doesn't exactly work that way, love. You'll have a medical review first, and after you've been approved, you may attend the driver train-ing program operated by the DMV. Once you demonstrate that you can safely operate a vehicle, you're eligible to get your license."

"You make it sound so easy."

"It'll be like riding a bicycle, Abby."

The vehicle slowed, and Abby looked out the window. She hadn't been paying attention to her whereabouts, and they appeared to be in a park or something.

It was as if Steven could read her mind. "This is East Rock Park. You've never been here?"

Abby shook her head.

Pulling into a parking space, Sydney opened up the vehicle so they could get out. Abby stepped out first so Steven's path was unobstructed. Sydney pulled out a picnic basket and a jacket for each of them.

They strolled up a secluded path and stepped into an open area with a little gazebo. The gazebo was ramped and had a small round table with three small benches and an opening for a wheelchair.

Steven looked at Abby hesitantly. "I hope this is okay. You asked for something private, and mom put together a nice picnic for us. I haven't been here for a few years, but it's peaceful."

"It's fine, Steven. What a beautiful spot!"

Sydney covered the table with a paper tablecloth and set out two divided plastic dishes, plastic utensils, napkins, and bottles of water. She laid the jackets over the railing and picked up the basket.

"Sophie said to tell you everything is disposable. I'm taking the basket with me. Call me when you want to be picked up, okay?"

Steven seemed to be mulling something over. "Let's plan on seven thirty back here at the gazebo in case I don't have service or whatever." He looked at Abby. "Better safe than sorry?"

"Seven thirty is fine with me. See you in a bit."

After Sydney left, Steven asked, "You want to eat first or talk?"

"I think the eating part will come easier after we talk. I sort of have butterflies right now." They were fluttering so frantically that Abby feared one would come out each time she opened her mouth. Her hand was on her stomach, and suddenly, this didn't seem like such a brave idea.

Steven held his hand out. "Come on, sit on my lap. We'll go for a little stroll along the river. We can talk while we're on the move."

Hesitantly, Abby climbed up onto Steven's lap. He guided her so he could reach the joystick.

Abby felt a jerk, and the chair tipped back. She let out a squeal and grabbed hold of Steven's arm.

"It's okay, Abby. I won't drop you. I wanted to tilt you to be secure if we hit a bump."

"I'm not afraid."

"Good."

They traveled down the path a short distance in silence. Finally, Steven said, "So, you wanted to talk. I presume about us?"

Abby tried to get it out, but she couldn't form the words. She didn't want him to think she didn't trust him; there were areas like her health, where she would trust him with her life.

Steven stopped driving and looked at her, patience written all over his face.

"You know," Abby began. "A week ago when you had your illustrious weekend with the boys, I was prepared to make you grovel for my affections." Nervously, she tugged on the button of his shirt.

"I was so frustrated, and when I left you sleeping in that bed, all I wanted to do was make you feel as desperate as I did watching you while you were so sick. My gut instinct told me to leave you stewing, let you wonder if the whole situation was the straw that would break the camel's back." She looked up into his worried hazel eyes. "But I'd spent my afternoon in that recliner thinking, trying to understand why I was mad. And even though I wanted to dish out some punishment to make you think about how I felt, in the end, I realized that my anger stemmed from the frustration of the entire situation, and I couldn't truly be mad at you for everything that happened."

Steven tentatively stroked Abby's knuckles. "When I woke up, and you were gone, Logan told me to give you some space. My heart was shattered because I was sure I had lost you forever."

Abby's heart twisted at Steven's tortured expression.

"I don't know that I can live without you, Abby."

Steven tipped them back again, then strolled further down the trail, going slowly enough that they could continue talking but still moving along the scenic route.

"I'm beginning to feel the same way, and it scares me. I want to believe what happened last weekend was the result of a series of unfortunate events, but I guess I need to know if it's a common occurrence."

Steven opened his mouth, and Abby shook her head, putting her fingers over his lips. "Please, Steven, let me have my say, and then I promise to give you my undivided attention."

Suddenly, Steven's calm facade cracked, and the chair came to a complete stop. Taking his hand off the joystick, Steven reached down and flipped the power switch off.

"And you have mine."

Abby turned in Steven's lap. She covered his hand with her own and squeezed. Abby stared into Steven's big, brown eyes. Without breaking contact with his gaze, she began to speak.

"There are some things I need to share with you. I hope this will help explain why the entire incident was so stressful for me. I'm humbled that you felt safe sharing what happened with Courtney. I've never shared my history with anyone else."

When Steven silently nodded, Abby drew in a calming breath and let it out slowly. Her insides twisted at the thought of sharing, but this was Steven, and she knew in her heart that she could trust him with anything.

"My life has changed so much in the year and a half since I met you. I see life differently now, and I can't—I won't—take things for granted."

Abby worried the hem of her own shirt. "A couple of years ago, I dated someone who drank and was unpredictable. Being with Trent was like being with a ticking time bomb, and he roughed me up a few times. I know that the circumstances surrounding what happened last weekend were extenuating and magnified because of your medications, but I can't go through something like that again, Steven."

As Abby spoke, Steven's free hand curled into a fist held so tight, his knuckles had turned white. His expression had grown stormy.

"What do you mean he 'roughed you up'?"

"He took hold of me a few times and left handprints on my arms. I got pushed around a few times too."

"I'd like to leave a handprint on him." Steven grumbled under his breath. "Abby, you gotta know I'd never hurt you, baby."

"I know you'd never mean to hurt me, but now that I'm living with MS"—Abby took a haggard breath—"I need to know that I can count on you to take care of yourself.

"Steven, I know you'd never intentionally do anything negligent, and this probably sounds so far-fetched, but last weekend shook my resolve. You have to know that ideally, I want to be able to trust you, as my partner. I want to rely on you to take care of me if I need you, if I'm no longer able to take care of myself." A tremor rippled through Abby, causing her to rub her hands up and down her arms.

"Even if you're only able to monitor me, or make a phone call if I get into trouble." Abby swallowed a lump. Giving voice to her feelings was harder than she thought it would be.

"A week from now, an exacerbation could hit, and I might be blind or unable to talk or swallow or walk. As long as your condition remains static, and you don't have some secondary condition that flares up, you could remain as healthy as you are now for a very long time."

Searching his eyes, she continued. "I'm scared, Steven. I don't know what my future holds, and it's terrifying to put all my trust in another person even if he is a promising neurologist and a whiz-kid scientist. But you're still human, and as we experienced last weekend, you make human mistakes."

"I, uh . . ." He began to interrupt, but she had to drive her point home before her train of thought got derailed.

"Please, hon, let me say my piece. I need to do this." Steven nodded silently.

"I have a friend from Buddies. Let's call her Mary. Two years ago, Mary was a 911 dispatcher. The stress of her job caused her to become so debilitated, she had to crawl out of the basement of the courthouse she worked in, practically on her hands and knees. Finally, after being rushed to the hospital, she was diagnosed with multiple sclerosis. Today, she uses a wheelchair full-time. She can't even do something as simple as hold a drinking glass. She got hit hard with it—chronic progressive MS. Her husband John provides nearly all her personal care. She has remained homebound and has recently begun to tap into the resources of her local Center for Independent Living. Her mother brings her to the Buddies meetings, and the agency that sponsors them provides an aide so she can participate. She is on a waiting list for attendant services and has to rely solely on family members to provide interim care." Abby trembled. *That could be me.*

"Her mother sits with her during the day, but her parents are elderly and most of the responsibility falls on the husband. John drinks to cope. The scary part is that he holds his liquor so well that she has no idea how intoxicated he is. She shared at the last meeting that she wishes she could give him an ultimatum, but she has no one else to care for her and fears she'll end up in a nursing home.

"A few months ago"—Abby could feel the tears welling up in her eyes—"he took her into the bathroom and sat her on the toilet. He had already begun his after-work indulgence, but by the time she had finished in the bathroom, he was passed out in bed. Mary didn't have the phone with her and sat on the toilet for over eight hours before he woke up and found her. Another time, he took her to the local grocery store, and when he pivoted her out of the car, he got confused about what he was doing, pulled up her skirt, and dropped her panties, thinking she needed to sit on the toilet." Abby's tears flowed, imagining the humiliation her friend had endured.

Steven wiped Abby's cheeks with his thumbs. "He shouldn't even be caring for her, let alone operating a car she's a passenger in." Steven softly spoke, easing the ache in her heart.

"No, he shouldn't, but right now, he is the only person she has to rely on. I'm terrified of having to rely on someone else for my basic needs. This sounds terribly selfish, but if I'm making a commitment with you, I need to know that you'll be there for me with your wits about you if I get in a bind."

"Abby, I'd never jeopardize your health under any circumstances. Hearing stories like that makes my blood boil. You can't honestly think I'd ever leave you in that kind of situation!"

"No, I don't think you would. But you said yourself that alcohol took away your inhibitions and allowed you to do things you would never do sober. I didn't think my own mother would abandon me like she has or like she did when I was a small child."

"She abandoned you? You honestly don't think *I'd* leave you."

"No, I don't think you'd intentionally leave me, but do you know that in the state of Connecticut, a DUI carries a twelve-month sentence for a first offender?"

"I didn't before the incident."

"I've come to rely on you, Steven, to depend on you in my life. I'd be lost without you for a year, and where would I go if you were locked away?"

# Chapter Forty-one

"That charge was ludicrous, and you know it!"

"And Smith was also completely within the law to charge you. As long as the DMV defines your wheelchair as a vehicle, the law is entirely enforceable."

Steven was looking off somewhere in the distance when he said, "We both know they don't have the facilities to . . ." before Abby interrupted him.

"You're right. The state of Connecticut doesn't have facilities that are properly equipped to care for a paraplegic. However, there are over three hundred inmates currently incarcerated in Connecticut state penitentiaries who are either paraplegics or quadriplegics. I can't imagine the care is any better than substandard."

"You would still live in the house. No one could take that away from me."

"I could never afford to live there alone."

He looked down at Abby. "You honestly think I'd allow you to be put out on the street?"

"No, I don't, but you're not above the law. Your special circumstances and your hard-as-nails attorney saved your ass."

"I don't ever plan on something like that happening again, Abby. Honest to God. I won't ever go out drinking again if that's what you want. I'll stay home. I promise."

"That's not what I want, and it's not fair to you or your friends. I'm not going to tell you that you aren't allowed to socialize, but I do expect to know what your plans are so I'm not at home worrying, and I expect you to have a back-up plan if you need a ride. No more public drunkenness."

"I understand."

"I trust you, Steven." Abby touched his arm.

"I know that seeing is believing." Steven entwined his fingers with Abby's. "And so far, I've shown you that I can be irresponsible, but Abby, that wasn't really me. I want you to know that I can be trusted to be there for you."

"I believe you, and I understand there are gonna be nights when you're working late. I guess I need to know that you're safe. I lived with my mom for a while, and when I moved back in with my dad, there were so many nights when I had no idea if he was okay. He'd get called to a fire, and I'd sit up all night by the phone. I just—I don't handle stress well anymore."

"I promise, baby, I'll be considerate."

"That's all I ask."

Steven hung his head and asked, "So, I'm still permitted to see my friends?"

"You're a grown man, Steven. I wouldn't dream of driving a wedge between you and your friends."

"Is there anything else on your mind?"

"Actually, yeah. Tell me about this girl Jamie. I heard that you got all busted up defending her honor. Your face looks great, by the way." Abby had been in her own little world as it was healing. Now, the sutures were gone, and the bruising had faded. There was a fine pink line that ran down about half an inch from the corner of his mouth. It almost pulled his lips down into a frown when he wasn't smiling. Abby knew in time it would fade and become a silvery line, and she'd be the only one who even realized it was there.

Steven scratched his head. "Hmm . . . Jamie. That's not the entire story. The guys missed half of it. When we were in the bar, I had run into the restroom, and as I was cathing, this jerk came in and started making derogatory remarks about them letting people like me into the bar."

"Oh, Steven!" As Abby realized where the story was leading, she saw red.

"I crammed everything back into my backpack. I didn't stop to rinse the urinal or anything. He was drunk, and I was intimidated. The things he was saying were truly hateful."

"That's why everything had urine all over it."

"Yes. Anyway, the jerk came after me. Apparently, he and his band of idiots have harassed the girl and her friends in the past. When he got rough with her, I lost it and hit him. Abby, I swear, when I looked at her scared face, all I could think of was you. We only played one round of darts. We might have been talking a total of fifteen or twenty minutes—tops. She knew I was committed to someone. Nothing happened. You have to believe me."

"No, I don't *have* to do anything of the sort, but I *do* believe you. You've been up-front about that from the very beginning. I don't believe you'd be unfaithful."

"Thank you for giving me the benefit of the doubt. I know I don't deserve it. I'm so sorry about everything, Abby."

Steven looked so sad . . . so humble. "We'll be okay, Steven. I know we will. We're a team. We just have to remember that."

"Abby? Why didn't you tell me how bad you were feeling? In a way, it's along the lines of what you just told me. We need to be honest with each other. Why didn't you tell me you were in trouble?"

Steven had her there, and Abby knew she owed him an explanation too. "I, um, where do I start? I didn't realize until the day you were sick in bed at Logan's that I was having some kind of episode. Both your dad and Sydney commented that I didn't look well. I was off-balance, and I was so tired. But I really thought I had just overdone it."

"But, you weren't okay."

"No, I wasn't. I wanted to come to you, but I remembered something Logan said once, that I'd have to decide whether I wanted you to be my doctor or my boyfriend. Because if anyone where you worked realized you were caring for me as a patient, and then we ended up in a relationship, you would end up in front of the ethics board, and you could lose your license."

Steven dropped his head. "You're right. I probably would."

"Right now, there's no official record of you ever treating me as a patient. You ordered tests, and you came to talk with me, unofficially, but that's it. You are my boyfriend. I don't want you to be my doctor. I promise I'll come to you for advice, but I couldn't do it last week. Once I got in that office, everything happened so fast. I blinked, and the next thing I knew, I was sitting in a recliner with a needle in my arm. I was so gobsmacked that I didn't fully realize what I'd agreed to until it was already in motion."

"I understand. It just hurts that you didn't tell me you were in trouble."

"I didn't really know that I was. I know better now what to look for. I promise not to let things get out of hand. Just don't smother me, okay?"

"I'll do my best to curb my doctor tendencies."

"Thanks." Abby reached up and pulled Steven's face down for a kiss. As their lips connected, Abby's stomach growled, and Steven threw his head back laughing.

"Come on, Abby, let's get you fed."

Steven stopped a few feet from the table and lowered the front of the chair. Always the gentleman, he helped Abby off his lap and held onto her until she was on her feet. Abby uncovered the dishes.

Awaiting them was an antipasto with fresh veggies along with ham, cheeses, and salami. There was also a salad with raw broccoli, cauliflower, bacon, and cheese.

Abby found two fluffy, homemade croissants and a fresh cup of fruit for each of them too.

"So how does your dad feel about us moving in together?" Steven asked.

"Um, he doesn't know the whole story." *How am I ever going to con-*

*vince Luke that this is a good idea?*

"What does he know?"

"That I'm moving in with a disabled guy I met in the hospital. I explained that I was renting a room and that your house was accessible, and I couldn't beat the price. I reminded him how hard it was for me to get in and out of my house. And I might have mentioned that it was a community where a lot of people with disabilities lived, and our arrangement wasn't all that uncommon."

"So, in other words . . ."

Abby hung her head. "I lied to him."

"Are you ashamed of me, Abby?" Abby's head jerked up, and she met Steven's sad eyes.

"What? No! Of course not!"

"But he doesn't know we're a couple?"

"Uh, not yet. He doesn't know you're the doctor who diagnosed me either. I mean, he knows who that doctor is, but he doesn't know you're that doctor. Are you following me?"

"So how do you plan to explain things to him?"

"I don't know. He's just so gung-ho for me to move back home to Woodstock. I don't want to move back in with my dad. If he knows I was having trouble last week, it'll just validate his argument. Everything I love is in New Haven. You, your family, my volunteer work at the CIL, my job, the kids I counsel . . . He doesn't understand. He thinks I should drop everything and come home and get a job at my old elementary school. My dreams are bigger than that. I love Luke—so very much—but I can't live in that house. If something were to happen, the bedrooms and toilet are on the second floor. I couldn't do it when I first got sick, and I can't do it now."

"Have you explained that to him?"

"I've tried."

"Abby, you need to be honest with him."

"I promise I'll explain this weekend. We've got plenty of time together, thanks to the generosity of your friends. I really do appreciate that, by the way."

Abby heard the crunch of tires on gravel, and Steven looked at his watch.

"Sydney. I suppose it's time to go back."

Abby sighed. "I guess so."

"Promise you'll have a talk with your dad. It's important to be honest with him, Abby. You're not close to your mother, so you don't want to alienate him. Life's short."

"I promise."

❖   ❖   ❖

Sydney drove Abby to the old apartment on Friday morning. They walked through to make sure she hadn't forgotten anything.

Someone pounded loudly on the door, and Abby hurried to open it. When she grabbed the doorknob and yanked it open, she looked up, expecting to see Mac's huge form hovering over her. Instead, Abby was graced with Steven's smiling face.

Abby felt her mouth drop open.

"Earth to Abby."

"You're here?"

"I hope it's okay."

"It's better than okay! Did you come to keep me occupied so I'd stay out of trouble?" Abby asked with her hands on her hips. This was a diversionary tactic; she was certain.

"Actually, I realized we won't see each other again until Monday."

"Oh." Abby's spirits fell.

"I'm really going to miss you, Abby."

Abby lowered her hands and moved from her spot in the doorway. "Come inside. There's not really any place for us to go. We can hang out in the kitchen, but it's really cramped. I'm sorry." She looked behind Steven, but the hallway was unoccupied. "Where are the guys?"

"Mac was bringing me up the steps when the Goodwill truck pulled up. Spence went to talk with them."

"Perfect timing. After they take the living room furniture out of here, we'll have so much more room to navigate the other things. As you can see, I don't have a lot of stuff."

Abby's kitchen was a galley, and there was very little room. "You'd better back in as far as you can . . ."

He poked his head into the kitchen. "When it's empty, and we're not in anyone's way, you've got to show me around. I can't imagine how you navigated this with a wheelchair and an aide. How did you both manage without tripping over one another?"

"Oh, it was the most fun the few days both my dad and the aide were here."

Steven turned around, and looking over his shoulder, backed carefully into the kitchen. "Did you seriously wheel all the way in here to get to the fridge and then back out? This is testing my abilities, and I've got a few years of experience under my belt."

Abby was embarrassed and hung her head as she answered. "Uh, no. When I was in the chair, my friend Corey loaned me one of those dorm refrigerators and a pint-sized microwave. I kept them both on the table. My aide cooked meals for me and left portioned servings in little microwave dishes. There was enough room in the fridge for a day of meals and snacks and enough space on the door for a day's worth of bottled water. I kept a cup on the bathroom sink too. She forgot the bottles of water a few times."

Abby heard Steven's sharp intake of breath at that. "She left you without a drink?"

"No, she left me without a cold drink. I was fine, Steven."

"But . . ."

"But nothing. I had food. I had drink. And I had a way to serve myself. It was okay. I managed."

"But drinking out of the bathroom faucet—"

"I do it every day when I brush my teeth. Sadly, the bathroom is no more accessible than the kitchen is."

"I'll have to see that."

Abby heard Mac clomping down the hallway before she saw him, and she smiled to herself. Mac grabbed Abby in a suffocating hug and picked her up off the ground.

"Hey, Abby!"

"Hey, yourself! Put me down, you big oaf. Please."

Abby snickered at his embarrassed expression. Mac gently lowered her feet to the floor. "Sorry, you've always just been a patient. I've never known you as Stevie's girl. I've never known *anyone* as Stevie's girl. You've completely changed his outlook on life."

Abby put her hands on her hips again. "'Just a patient'?"

Mac shrugged sheepishly.

"Yeah, well, I'm still mad at you, so behave yourself, okay? I don't want to be in a foul mood when my dad gets here in a few hours."

Abby heard Steven's voice behind her as he responded with an exasperated quip. "And quit calling me Stevie."

"You're entirely too stuffy, *Steven*."

Spencer stood in the doorway, accompanied by two men wearing uniforms. "Hey, Abby, these gentlemen are here for your furniture?"

Abby looked past him to the guys in the hallway.

"Hello. Come on in. Everything is in the living room." Abby walked a few steps and pointed out the things that were going. Spencer smiled and looked around.

"It's much emptier than last time I was here." It took Abby a minute to follow—-she'd forgotten that Spencer was there during her first ill-fated Christmas in the place.

Hopefully, Abby's next home wouldn't be so unlucky, or perhaps it was just her, and then she realized the past two Christmases had been the same for Steven as well. Making new memories would be welcome.

"I had a houseful of people too. You remember coming here?"

"Oh yeah, I remember. Your dad was barking out orders like a drill sergeant. I remember thinking the only reason he needed us was for our ambulance."

"Yeah, that would be my dad. I try not to think about that day too much."

"Makes sense."

Abby realized that poor Steven was still marooned in her tiny kitchen. And Sydney, Abby couldn't be sure where she was, but she wasn't in sight.

"The bed needs to come apart, and you'll probably want to take the drawers out of my dresser. It was my gran's. It's, uh, it's made out of real wood, so it's kinda heavy."

Mac snorted. "Not a problem, little lady. Lead the way."

When Abby passed the closet, she heard noises coming from inside. *Guess I found Sydney.*

Abby showed the guys to her room, and once she knew they were occupied, tapped on the closet door. Sydney reached out and grabbed Abby, yanking her inside the confined space.

"Oh, Abby, this is harder than I thought. Just seeing him makes me all befuddled. I want to stand my ground, but it would be so much easier to pretend nothing ever happened. I thought I could be strong."

Abby wanted to empathize, but she couldn't. She still had Steven, and she truly believed they could go in no direction but forward.

"What are you doing now—here in my closet?"

"Oh." Sydney smiled. "I was just sorting out the things you won't need. What do you want to keep?"

"Definitely the wheelchair, um, probably the walker, maybe the bed rail thing? I won't need anything for the bathroom. It's all been sanitized."

Sydney nodded. "Okay, so while the guys are in the bedroom working, I'll get things out of here. Maybe I can just stay out of their way. Busywork is a good distraction."

"I'm proud of you, Sydney. If it gets to be too much, just go for a walk or something. I'll sit here until you get back."

"Thanks, but you need my help today. I'll be all right."

Abby leaned over and gave Sydney a big hug. "Thanks for everything, Sydney. I can only imagine how hard this is for you."

"You're welcome, hon. It is, but come on. Let's get busy."

Abby stepped out of the closet and looked around. The Goodwill guys had a chair and some accent tables to take. Abby peered into her bedroom. The bed was gone, and her drawers were stacked in a corner.

*I feel like I'm forgetting something.*

Abby walked around, looking behind doors and in corners. She stepped past the small bar that divided her kitchen and living area and looked down. Abby's heart dropped.

*Steven.*

Abby covered her face with her hands, peeking out from between her fingers. "Oh, Steven. Why didn't you say something? I completely forgot you were even here. I got so caught up in the moment. I'm a terrible girlfriend."

He reached for her hand with a smile. "Hey, don't be so hard on yourself. I knew you'd be busy when I chose to come along. I just wanted to be a part of this in some small way. I'm just hanging out until they get the big stuff outa here."

"I need to catch the Goodwill fellows when they come back in. I have some medical equipment I'd like to donate."

"Is that what Sydney's doing?"

"Yeah. She's having a hard time being here with Spencer. I found her in my closet."

"She'll be okay. This isn't the first time this has happened. I just don't know how many times they can bounce back. He was going to ask her to move in with him when her lease is up at the end of the month."

"She told me. She's going to stay with us for a little while instead."

"Yes, that was the original plan. Not forever, just until I'm self-sufficient. Is that going to be a problem? I should have discussed it with you first."

"It's fine. I've known for some time that she was going to stay on as a live-in for a few months. She said she was thinking about putting down some roots. We stopped by a realtor's office one afternoon when we were picking things up for the house."

"I'm so happy for her! She's always lived a Bohemian lifestyle. Having a place of her own will be good for her."

Abby saw one of the guys from Goodwill walk past with her shower chair.

When Abby looked into the living room, her TV sat on the floor with a few other electronics, and her wheelchair and other durable medical equipment were up against the wall next to them. The rest of the room was bare, save for the dust bunnies that were still residing in the corners.

"Come on, I believe it's safe now. All the big stuff is out."

"I'm fine in the cubby hole here."

"I need to make some food for Brutus, and you're in my way."

They both laughed as Steven moved. He narrowly missed getting smacked with a set of toilet safety rails.

Abby watched as Steven turned into the living room, backing himself into a corner to stay out of the flow of traffic. Soon there would be nothing left to remove.

Abby threw the pizzas in the oven and began setting bottles of water on the bar. One of the men taking the furniture handed her a slip of paper. "This is a list of the items you've donated. You can enter an amount you feel is an appropriate value to be used for tax purposes. Thank you for your donation."

"Oh, thank you for coming and taking it. I hope someone can get some use out of it."

"I'm sure they will, Miss Harris. Best wishes in your new home."

*In my new home.* It was the first time someone outside Abby's circle of friends had said it, and she felt all warm and fuzzy inside.

"Thanks."

The door was barely closed, and Mac's booming voice could be heard throughout the tiny apartment. With hardwood floors and nothing to absorb the sound, Abby feared the neighbors would be pounding on the walls to quiet them down.

"Abby! Where's the food? We had a deal!"

Abby laughed and smacked his bicep; her hand stung. *Geez, the guy is solid.*

She pushed a basket across the counter. "The food will be done when the timer goes off. Have some chips if you can't wait."

Abby approached Steven and batted her eyes. "It appears all my furniture is missing, Dr. Chandler. Would you care to help a girl out? I need someplace to sit."

Steven held out his hands. "It would be my pleasure, Miss Harris."

Thankful that his toes were safely protected by new sneakers, Steven sat Abby down sideways. She swung an arm up around his shoulder. They hadn't had any physical contact since the evening before, and she was feeling a little needy.

Abby took Steven's face in her hands, pulling him in for a deep kiss. He opened his mouth, and soon they were exploring and teasing each other with their tongues. It seemed like it had been forever since they'd kissed like that. Abby felt Steven's arm snake around behind her before he put his hand on her thigh and pulled her bottom in closer to him. Abby had just reached around his neck, fisting her hands in his short curls, when someone cleared their throat from behind.

*Busted!*

"Abigail?"

Abby pressed her forehead against Steven's and groaned. *I guess we'll be having that conversation sooner rather than later.*

"Dad."

# Chapter Forty-two

Placing her lips next to Steven's ear, Abby muttered, "Just give us a few minutes, okay?"

*I'm so not ready to have this conversation.*

"I'll have Syd check on the pizzas. Are you up to taking a walk with your dad?"

"I haven't felt this good in a long time. I'm okay."

"Once the guys eat, we'll go. We'll talk later, love. Is that all right?"

"Yes, thank you. Love you."

"Love you too."

Ever cautious, Steven held onto Abby until he was certain she was sure-footed.

Luke stood in the doorway, a scowl on his face. Before things got out of hand, and he said something Abby knew he would regret, she wanted to give him the explanation he deserved.

There was no reason to hide what she shared with Steven. Luke would have reservations, and that was understandable, but Abby knew her father would treat Steven with respect and acceptance.

She put her arms around Luke's waist. "Hi, Dad."

"Hey, kid. You're looking good." He waved his arms around the interior of her apartment and then asked a little more quietly, "What is all this? Who are these people, and where's your stuff? I thought I came here to move you!"

"Come on, let's go for a walk. I know a nice place where we can sit and visit for a while."

"Will your place be all right?"

"Of course. The guys are leaving shortly, but my friend Sydney is here. She'll lock up if she leaves. It's all good."

They walked to Abby's school and found their way to the quiet, shaded playground. Luke always seemed to be calmer when he was outside, so Abby chose to sit on the swings.

*Calm is good.*

"I thought you and I would be spending some time together. It doesn't look like you need me here."

Abby let out an exasperated sigh. "Dad, I'll always need you. My friends thought it would be nice if they pitched in and helped move my stuff so you and I could spend a nice, relaxing weekend together. I haven't seen you since Easter!"

"But what's with all the guys? Don't you have any female friends?"

"Of course I have female friends. I'm moving heavy furniture. You met Spencer. He was one of the paramedics who came and took me to the hospital that Christmas."

"Now that you mention it, he did look sort of familiar."

"The big guy is Mac. He's a physical therapist. He works with me every time I'm in the hospital."

"I don't remember this Mac."

"He's a nice guy, trust me."

Luke crossed his arms and huffed. Abby forged ahead.

"The girl is Sydney. I know you'll like her. She's really helped me out a lot."

"I suppose it's good to have so many professional people around, you know, with your condition."

"Daddy, I don't have them around because I've got a disability. They are my friends, and they're here to help me move."

"So you brought me here under false pretenses?"

Abby clenched her fists in frustration. "This conversation isn't going the way I intended at all. I think we need to start over."

"Okay. Let's start with the fellow in the wheelchair who had his hands all over you. Who is *he*?"

*Fair enough.*

"That's Steven."

"This is the guy who had a serious accident, the one you 'picked up' at the hospital'?" Luke asked, using air quotes.

*Why, oh why, do you have to remember that tiny conversation from Easter weekend?*

"I didn't 'pick him up' at the hospital. We've known each other for a while. We tend to run in the same circles."

"What do you mean?" Luke asked, cocking his head as he studied his daughter.

"He's involved in a lot of disability issues, the organizations we volunteer for, some of the places we receive services. We're both involved in a lot of the same things."

"And *you* are really *involved* with this Steven?"

"He's a great guy. I know you'll love him if you get to know him."

Luke snorted. "I don't know about that."

"I'm asking you to give him a chance, Dad."

Luke stared off at the New Haven skyline. "Abby." He sighed. "You forget I know a little something about people in wheelchairs."

Luke's closest friend, Miles Tucker, was also a person with a disability, but he acted bitter, and Abby suspected he found comfort in the attention he received from the people in his life since his son moved to a place in the city.

"And I'm asking you not to have preconceived notions about Steven when you haven't had a chance to get to know him. He's a hard-working, independent guy."

"Then maybe you should tell me about him so I can try to understand. I want you to be happy, and ever since you were so sick, I've wished you had someone to take care of you. I don't want you to be alone, but there are so many things going through my mind right now.

"How's he ever going to be able to take care of you? He looks like he needs a lot of help. I remember a time when you couldn't walk across the room or use the toilet by yourself."

"Okay, first of all, Steven is incredibly independent. He refuses to let me help him because he has his own attendant. That girl, Sydney, is his private nurse. And Steven is more than capable of caring for me. You need to give him a little credit."

"Abby, I've seen you at your worst. There is going to be a time when you have another episode. Then what?"

Abby forced herself not to laugh. *Steven has seen me at my worst. He and his family rode that roller coaster with me!*

"I should have probably called you, but I've been busy getting ready for the move, and it really wasn't an issue. I had a flare-up recently. Steven took care of me when I was having trouble, but when he couldn't be there for me, either Sydney or one of his parents were. I'll be okay with him, with them. I'm in good hands here in New Haven."

Luke looked troubled. "Was it another exacerbation?"

"No, not exactly. I think it was a little bit of everything—stress, being overworked—plus it's getting warm outside. Dr. J put me on steroids for a week, and it resolved quickly."

"Don't tell me you were in the hospital and kept it from me."

"No, I wouldn't do that."

"So you're not having a bad spell now?"

"No, it's over, whatever it was. I haven't felt this good in a long time. My doctor says I may have to take steroids more often. I'll do what I need to do."

"I worry about you, kid. You're so far away, and you don't really have anyone to rely on if you get into trouble. Are you sure I can't convince you to come home?"

"Sorry, Dad, no can do. My job is here, the kids I counsel are here, and I like living here. Woodstock can't offer me all the things I have in New Haven that allow me to live independently."

"You can't blame me for trying. I'd even remodel the house if you'd come home—make things easier for you. I'm so afraid this thing will get worse, and you won't be able to live on your own."

"Thank you for your concern, but I need you to trust me to know what I need and how to access those resources."

"But if you need me, you'll let me know?"

"I promise. I love you, Dad, but I need you to believe in me."

"I do. This Steven is going to be around a while, isn't he?"

"Oh, I hope so."

Luke silently stared off across the schoolyard for some time. Abby pushed herself gently with her feet.

Luke smiled over at Abby. "So, I thought we'd be busy all weekend. What will we do now?

"Well, the guys were going to load up the van and go to the house. They've offered to set up my bedroom furniture. I still have a ton of stuff to unpack."

"So do you even need your old man, or should I go back home?"

Abby pushed off with her feet and swung into Luke, checking him hard with her shoulder.

"Of course I need you. Come on, let's go grab some lunch."

When they got back, the apartment was vacant.

Using the bathroom for the last time, Abby quickly went through the closet and vanity. Sydney had left no stone unturned. Everything was pristine.

There was nothing left behind except for some pizza and a handful of napkins. Two bottles of water sat on the top shelf of the fridge.

Abby looked around the place, thinking about life since she'd first moved in. *My life has changed in so many ways.*

"I guess this is it. I just need to take the garbage to the dumpster and drop off the keys."

❖   ❖   ❖

Abby had been trudging down the sidewalk behind Luke and looked up when he stopped at a cute little hybrid. "What's this?"

"I figured since I plan on retiring, I'd get something that's a little easier on the pocketbook."

"Cute!"

Abby directed her dad through town until they got to her new neighborhood. Luke whistled under his breath when he pulled into the entrance. The gatekeeper waved to Abby and opened the gate.

Luke drove around asking questions about the development as they went. Finally, Abby pointed to Steven's house. "It's that one with the stone front."

When they pulled into the drive, Abby unbuckled her seatbelt. "Let me see what's in the garage. I don't know where they put everything."

"Sure, sure, Abby. I'll be right here."

The garage was empty except for a stack of boxes that Abby recognized from the storage unit. There was plenty of room for Luke to park and still leave room for Steven's car. Abby hit a button and the door began to rise.

Luke pulled in carefully and parked.

"Come on, I'll show you around."

They walked through the foyer and into the living room. Abby was surprised to find the bookshelves partially filled. On the coffee table, she spied a small envelope lying on top of a well-loved book of sonnets. Abby slipped her finger under the flap and pulled out the enclosed card.

*Abby,*

*I asked Sophie to dig out some of my mom's books. I know she'd be delighted to know I fell for someone who loves the classics as much as she did. I hope you find enjoyment in these and that they help you pass the time until I get home.*

*Love,*

*Steven*

Abby wiped her eyes on her sleeve and walked over to the bookshelves, fingering the spines of Grace Maxwell's treasures.

Abby looked forward to whiling away the hours in Grace's chair, and she could hardly wait for the weather to cool off enough so she could enjoy the fireplace.

Abby looked up to see Luke watching her warily. "I'm sorry, it's the books. They weren't here this morning. Steven left them for me."

Luke's eyes darted around the room, trying to take everything in. "Wow, Abby, this place is really over the top. Are you sure he can afford this?" Luke whispered the last part, sounding suspicious.

"We're alone, Dad. You don't have to whisper, and yes, he can afford it."

"I worry about you, kiddo. I know we didn't have a lot, but we were always happy, weren't we? I can see why you wouldn't want to come home. This place is gorgeous."

Abby had never thought about it like that. Her happiness had nothing to do with things and places but rather the people who were part of her life. She could live under a rock and be happy if her loved ones were with her.

She walked over and wrapped her arms around him. "I had everything I ever needed when I lived with you. I have never thought I missed out on anything."

"My best friend is disabled, and he can barely make ends meet. Abby, please don't be offended, but how is it possible that this guy can build a house like this? Did he get a big settlement from that accident he was in?"

Abby stepped back from Luke and looked up at him. She'd hoped that their conversation at the playground had put the inquisition to rest.

"I'm not offended, but I will only tell you a few things. I won't share Steven's personal business. I hope you understand. He didn't get anything from his accident. He uses an electric wheelchair and crossed in the middle of the street. They were installing curb cuts, and he couldn't access the corner, but he was found completely at fault."

Luke blanched. "Are you, are you serious?"

"Yeah," Abby whispered.

"Does he work? He's not involved in anything illegal?"

She snorted. "Steven? You've got to be kidding me."

"I'm sorry, Abby, but look around you. Don't you feel like this is too good to be true?"

Before she answered him, Abby thought about the past six months of her life. The ups and downs, the insecurity, and finally, the way Steven grounded her and made her feel wanted, loved.

*Yes, it is too good to be true. He's too good to be true.*

"The circumstances that made it possible for Steven to build and furnish this home in the manner that he has came with a great amount of sacrifice. I know without a shadow of a doubt that he would give it all up in a heartbeat to change the things that made all this possible. You have to trust my judgment on this, Dad. He's everything I've ever wanted, and he's all I will ever need."

Luke inhaled deeply before he nodded. "I guess this means you're a permanent fixture in New Haven, then. In the back of my mind, I secretly hoped one day you'd come home."

"New Haven is my home. I'm happy here. Now come on, let me give you the tour."

Before walking through the house, Luke stopped at the massive bookcases surrounding the fireplace, picking up little things he recognized. Luke smiled as he studied pictures of him and Abby at Walker Pond during a camping trip to Wells State Park with Corey and Miles.

Luke picked up different pieces of sea glass that sat interspersed with pebbles in a heavy glass bowl, little trinkets they'd picked up over the years on various outings together.

Luke drew in a breath when he picked up a picture of his parents, Grandpa and Grandma Harris.

*I know. It seems like they've been gone so long, doesn't it?*

Luke smiled when he picked up the ugly ashtray Abby made for him in first grade.

"Hey, you gave this to me for Father's Day!"

"You quit smoking! Do you want it back?"

Luke shook his head.

"Are you sure? It was a Father's Day gift."

"No, it's okay."

"I thought, perhaps, we could have a barbeque before you went home. Celebrate Father's Day a week early. I'd love for you to meet Steven's family."

Luke set the ashtray down and smiled in a way that told Abby he had accepted her choices.

"I'd like that, Abby. If you're going to be spending time with these people, I want to get to know them too."

Luke's smile became sad when he came to the picture of himself with Abby's mom from Christmas Eve—the night before Abby had been rushed to the hospital. It was the only picture Abby had of herself with both of her parents. They were all laughing and looked happy.

*Sometimes appearances are deceiving.*

Abby and Penny talked on the phone from time to time, but their relationship was always rocky. Abby found that it was easier with distance. Their relationship fluctuated over the years. Either Penny was Abby's best friend or her greatest source of contention. Luke always made up for what was missing in Abby's life though—calm and quiet, yet imposing and stable if Abby needed that.

Out of the corner of her eye, Abby saw Luke move to the fireplace. He picked up the photo of Steven and his parents, studying it before he replaced it on the mantle.

She didn't want to dwell on it or have to field questions that weren't hers to answer. "Come see my kitchen, Dad. It's to die for."

Abby took Luke's hand and practically dragged him down the hallway. He laughed at her enthusiasm, and she felt like a ten-year-old girl again.

Abby's kitchen was quite the conversation piece, and she laughed to herself when she realized how possessive she'd suddenly become.

*My kitchen.*

Luke whistled appreciatively. "This is beautiful, Abby. I know you've always wanted a fancy kitchen. You've never needed that though. You're an incredible cook even when you only have the bare minimum to work with."

Abby thought back to Easter and smiled. Yes, she could make anything with practically nothing. She couldn't wait to shine in this kitchen though.

"We'll have to test your theory tonight. I might have a fancy kitchen, but I'm still working with the bare minimum. I don't want to buy too many groceries until Steven is home and can be a part of it."

Luke cocked his head off to the side. "What do you mean, 'home'?"

Abby motioned toward the small dinette set. "Why don't you sit down, and I'll make us some coffee."

Abby pulled two saucers out of the cupboard and placed them on the island with silverware and a stack of napkins for the napkin holder. She lifted a box from a shelf behind her and plated two pieces of chocolate cake. While she was returning the box to the shelf, Luke took everything to the table.

Abby hit a button on the coffee maker. She had set it up earlier so she wouldn't have to fuss while they were visiting.

While the coffeemaker hissed and gurgled, Abby got two mugs out and put a healthy dose of sugar and creamer into hers. Luke took his black.

Abby pulled out the carafe and filled their mugs. As she carried them to the table, she thought back to the week before. She could barely walk, let alone carry something hot. Abby felt fortunate to be feeling so good. Luke reached out, taking the mugs when Abby got to the table.

"Thanks, Dad."

"Mmm, you're welcome. I saw the box, so I know you didn't make this, but it's still delicious."

"There's a bakery close by. Steven's mom stops there from time to time. She knows this is one of my favorites, so she bought a cake for us to make the weekend easier. She knew we were moving things."

"So you didn't tell her either that you were having your things moved before I got here?"

*Smart aleck is looking a little smug, isn't he?*

"It was a snap decision. I was afraid if I told you I'd already moved, you might change your mind. I liked the idea of just having you to myself. It seems we don't get much of a chance to talk."

"No, you're right. We don't. I guess I should ask you to give my thanks to your friends. It was a kind gesture."

"Steven's always thoughtful like that. He wanted us to have quality time together."

"Tell me about him. We started to talk, but then we moved the conversation out here. What does he do, since you assure me he's not a criminal?"

Abby wasn't sure why she had braced herself for this conversation. She guessed mostly because the two of them rarely discussed things that were personal in nature. Now that her dad was in front of her, Abby wasn't suffering from the nerves she had anticipated when Steven was trying to convince her to be open with her dad.

"He's a doctor."

Luke's wide eyes were priceless. "Like a *doctor*, doctor? Or do you mean he's a teacher? You know, like a doctor of education? Do you work together?"

Abby laughed. "Yes, he's a *doctor* doctor. He'll be going back to work soon, I suspect."

"I can't shake the feeling that I know him somehow, and I just can't figure it out."

# Chapter Forty-three

"Steven is the neurologist who diagnosed my MS."

"That's why you said he's capable of caring for you! He already does. Oh, Abby, is that even ethical? Won't he get in trouble?"

"No, he has never treated me. He doesn't treat me now. His uncle was the doctor who saw me initially in the ER. Because of the holiday, they couldn't get anyone from neurology to order the tests I needed. Steven was a patient then, too, and as a favor to his uncle, he called in the orders from his hospital bed so they could begin running tests the day after Christmas."

"I thought you said you met in the gym or something."

"Well, after he diagnosed me and helped arrange a bunch of services for me, we didn't see each other again. When I was admitted for treatment over Christmas, I ran into him at the gym and recognized him. We didn't really become friends until then."

"It looked to me like you're a little more than friends." Abby could feel herself blushing.

"This move didn't start out under false pretenses, but our friendship has evolved. I've fallen for him, Dad. He's the piece of my soul that I didn't realize was missing. I've never felt like this about anyone."

Luke reached out and squeezed her hand. "That's all I've ever wanted for you. Will I get to know him a little better this weekend? Where will he be? You said you didn't want to really shop until he was home. You never did answer my question."

"I'm sorry, I got sidetracked. It seems like there's so much to talk about."

"How about starting at the beginning?"

"Well, Steven's had a disability for a long time, since he was a teenager, but this latest accident occurred when he was returning home from work one night in his wheelchair. He was struck by a car. Like I was saying, they were doing a curb cut project near the hospital, and he was attempting to cross the street. He had no way to get far enough off the road. The driver said she never saw him." Abby shook her head, still in disbelief.

"I don't understand how she didn't get charged with something, reckless endangerment, something."

"Steven's parents wanted him to fight it, but he made the decision to drop the suit. He has the means to support himself, and anything related to his disability is being paid for. The lawsuit wasn't about the money. It was more about bringing awareness to the public about what happened. Given the circumstances . . ."

"I still think someone should be held responsible in some way, if not the driver, then maybe the municipality. How badly was he hurt? When we discussed him over Easter, you said he'd been hurt seriously, but he'd be released soon. That was a couple of months ago."

"It was, and he was released from the hospital. He's been going through rehab at a local facility. He's coming home in a few days," Abby said enthusiastically. "He's working so hard. He's a very independent man."

"I can't imagine what would happen if Miles got hit by a car. That would be devastating. Steven's lucky to be alive."

Abby shivered, and goose bumps stood up on her arms. She rubbed her hands over them. "He is. He's a medical miracle," she whispered, thanking God that Steven was still alive.

*I nearly lost him—before he was ever even mine.*

"I suppose someone who has been through something like that

would appreciate life and those around him a lot more than someone who hasn't come so close to losing it all."

*You have no idea, Dad.*

"I don't think he takes anything for granted. He's truly blessed. We both are."

Luke scooted his chair over and gave Abby a hug. She wasn't used to such affections from him, and it warmed her physically and emotionally. "I'm happy for you, Abby. I look forward to getting to know him."

"I look forward to that, too, but come on. I want to show you the rest of the house, and I'm not sure what we have to do to get bedrooms ready for the weekend."

Luke followed Abby down the hallway. She opened the door to the study and noticed several new boxes on the floor that were labeled "Medical."

"This furniture is beautiful."

"Logan and Sophie have had it in storage since before Steven was in college." Abby knew these pieces meant far more to Steven than he let on, and she wondered how he'd cope having them in his space all the time. If personal possessions were all Abby had left of Luke, she wasn't sure if she'd feel comforted being surrounded by them or if the pain would be too much to bear.

Luke stopped to study another Maxwell family portrait.

Abby knew Luke would have questions when he met the Chandlers and realized they weren't the same people from the photographs, but that wasn't her story to tell. *I guess we'll cross that bridge when we get to it.*

"Come on, I want to show you my room." Abby pulled Luke into the room, and her breath caught when she saw Grandma Harris's bed all set up and made with the new linens. Her dresser and nightstands were in their proper places.

"Mom's furniture looks great in here. I'm glad you kept it, Abby."

"Yeah, me too. It does look pretty, doesn't it?"

Luke nodded before looking out the window. He smiled when he took in the view.

"Oh, this is nice. I love this room. I've never been an avid reader, but this little spot couldn't be more perfect for you. I really like the window seat."

Luke followed Abby into the bathroom, and she tried to picture everything through his eyes. The bathroom was bigger than her old room at his house. Abby still couldn't believe that this was her home now, and she wanted to pinch herself every time she thought about Steven living here with her.

As Luke stepped out of the bathroom, he shook his head. "Wow, Abby, it looks like they've taken everything into consideration."

"All the houses in the development are visitable. They aren't all as accessible as Steven's though. There are multi-level homes that have an accessible bathroom and bedroom. The main living area is accessible, and there's at least one no-step entrance even if the second floor isn't accessible. The developer specializes in accessible housing. There isn't much that Steven can't access in his chair."

"I can understand now why you wouldn't want to live in my two-story house. I'm sorry, Abby. I didn't mean to be so pushy. I still miss you when you're not around."

Luke looked around. "Is there a guest room in this place?"

"The study was the guest room in the house plans. There's a bedroom in the basement, but there's not a bed or anything yet. That will be Sydney's room until Steven is able to take care of his overnight needs. You can sleep in either my room or Steven's. They're both made up with fresh bedding."

"Do you mind if I sleep in your room? I feel a little odd sleeping in Steven's room. He doesn't know me."

"You can sleep wherever you like. He won't be home until next week."

"Please thank him for his hospitality. I appreciate having the time to enjoy your company. Once or twice a year really isn't enough, kid."

"No, it's not. We'll both have to make an effort to remedy that. I just get so busy. My life is really full, Dad."

"I'm glad to hear that."

"You'll love the backyard—they built a big fire pit with benches. It's going to be awesome this fall when it begins to cool off."

Luke followed Abby through the kitchen and out the back door. Taking her dad's hand, she led him to the benches that circled the pit. Abby realized that maybe he didn't know everything she was involved in. "Have I told you about my kids I have after school?"

"You said you counsel some of them. I didn't understand, but it didn't seem appropriate to pry."

"I'm a peer counselor because I also have a disability. I spend time with them a few times a week, trying to help my kids cope with the aspects of their disabilities. It might be helping a child discover a creative way to remain on task. Or perhaps one of my kids would benefit from a piece of technology to get the most out of their education . . . maybe funding for a laptop or accessing services that would provide an extended school year or an aide to help them get through their school day. Sometimes, it's just sitting and listening while they vent their frustrations about another student who treats them differently because they are disabled."

"Well, it certainly seems like you have your plate full. Sounds like those kids are lucky to have you."

"Some of them don't have parents who are willing to devote the time they should. Some parents simply have no idea how to get the things their kids need. Because I volunteer at the CIL, I'm able to tap into resources that I wouldn't normally have access to as just a teacher."

"That's a good thing, right?"

"Yes, it's a very good thing."

"The other kids honestly pick on the ones who have, um, problems? When I was growing up, you always looked out for the underdog."

"Do you remember when I was a kid, and my teachers thought I was lazy and uncoordinated? I had two left feet. All the kids picked on me relentlessly. Dr. Chandler thinks that I may have actually been exhibiting signs of my MS even then. It's become alarmingly prevalent in children."

Luke laughed before he asked, "It's *Dr.* Chandler, now?"

"Oh no. I didn't mean Steven. I was talking about Logan, Steven's dad." Abby thought Luke already realized there were two of them.

"Logan Chandler? That name sounds so familiar."

"He was the doctor who admitted me to the emergency room—tall, attractive, older gentleman? You'll see him this weekend."

"Oh, okay. It's scary to think there are children getting MS. You never heard of things like that happening twenty years ago."

"I don't think it's so much that it didn't happen but more that people didn't realize it was happening in children. There were signs, but they were attributed to other things—clumsiness, the need for glasses—no one understood. It was actually in the 1950s that childhood MS was acknowledged. It's not common, but it happens. Steven says two to five percent of all people with MS exhibited symptoms before they were sixteen. He was working on a project to link Epstein-Barr virus and MS. It seems there is some connection. Kids who show MS symptoms often test positive for that virus as well."

"And Steven volunteers at this place too? This CIL place?"

"No, not at the CIL. Steven started the support group I attended when I was first diagnosed. During his pre-med studies, Steven realized there was no local support group for people who had recently become disabled. He wanted them to have some place to go to find the things they needed, to have peers to lean on. For me it was a stepping stone to my volunteer job at the CIL. They both offer similar services, but the CIL was a better fit for me."

"How does Steven find the time? Doctoring isn't a nine to five profession."

"He works in a private practice with another neurologist. I don't think he works a forty-hour week, but he is on call for emergencies, plus he's reducing his student loan debt by working at a research center which is affiliated with the hospital. His research is focused on finding answers to MS and other neurological diseases."

*He found the time because he never had anyone to go home to.*

"It sounds like you won't even see each other a lot."

"There may be times we don't, but we're both secure in each other's independence. We'll be all right."

"This is really nice, not just the house, but the fact that you seem so happy. I am happy for you, kiddo. It doesn't sound like this is something you just jumped into."

"No, it's not, but we've still got a lot to learn about each other. I've never really known Steven as anyone other than as a patient in a hospital. I've seen him sick, hurt, and recovering, but it wasn't until just the past few weeks that I've really been reacquainted with the go-getter I met nearly two years ago. We're not rushing into anything. We've got separate rooms. We're sharing expenses."

Abby loved Steven and trusted him, and for now, that was all that mattered. She knew he felt the same way. The rest they'd discover together in their own way in their own time.

"I'm happy for you, Abby. Really I am. I hope you find everything you're looking for with this guy."

"I already have."

"That's good. I hope he treats you right."

Suddenly Luke's stomach growled. Abby looked at her watch and was shocked to see it was almost six. They had talked all afternoon.

"Sydney and I grabbed a few steaks. I could throw one on the grill."

"That sounds great, kid."

The table was set by the time dinner was done. Abby couldn't have timed it better. The potatoes that had been pre-heated in the microwave, then finished on the grill, were tender. The corn, roasted in the husks, was golden brown, and the steaks—just a little pink but still juicy.

"This looks wonderful. I don't know how you ever learned to cook like this. Neither your mother nor I were very good cooks."

"And you wonder how I learned, silly man."

After they were done, Luke helped Abby carry everything to the kitchen. "Abby, would you mind terribly if I went over to the precinct? I need to follow up on a lead for an arson case I'm working."

"The police precinct? Why wouldn't you go to the fire department?"

Abby shuddered at the thought that one of Luke's acquaintances might have been involved in Steven's arrest.

"Abby, what is it?"

"Hmm? What's what?"

"Wait. When you asked me what the guys at home do regarding suspects who are in wheelchairs, you were talking about your boyfriend? He was the one they mistreated? You had me sold on this guy. What aren't you telling me, kid? I thought he sounded too good to be true."

Abby felt like shrinking under her dad's scrutiny, but what happened with Steven was a miscarriage of justice, and Abby was committed to defending his honor. Steven Chandler was an honorable man.

Abby gave Luke a condensed but honest version of the story— enough to ruffle his feathers.

"They never should have treated him like that, but there are always a few bad apples in every basket," she said.

"Yes."

"Well, The Center is going to provide sensitivity trainings for the city. I'm a little hesitant about getting involved. I don't think I could keep my mouth shut if I had to deal with the guys who busted Steven."

"Well, just be happy that his lawyer got the charge reduced to a D&D. It really could have been worse."

"I know. Brooke is a strong adversary, and I wouldn't want to be on her bad side."

"Well, I'm glad you have someone you can count on. If you ever need an attorney, that's what you're looking for."

"Yeah, it is."

"Well, I better get going. I'll be back in a few hours. Will you be awake?"

"Yeah, I have things to unpack. It'll take me some time to get it all organized."

"If you need help lifting things, wait for me. Please don't be stubborn."

"Thanks, but I'll be okay." *As long as you don't play avenging angel at the police station.* "It's mostly small stuff."

# Chapter Forty-four

As soon as Luke was gone, Abby grabbed a shower and changed into something comfortable and cool so she could work. She opened the windows and put on some music. In no time, her books were all shelved. *The Complete Sherlock Holmes* and *David Copperfield* graced the shelves along with *War and Peace*, *The Time Machine*, and C. S. Lewis's *The Screwtape Letters*. Abby pulled open another box, and they were joined by *Oliver Twist* and *Madame Bovary*.

Abby decorated the shelves in the living room with other curious items as well. She set out a Mason jar with a wire bale and a glass lid, filled with marbles collected while playing with the neighborhood kids. Abby smiled, thinking of her childhood in Woodstock.

Added to the novelties were vintage pull toys and an old tin spinning top that once belonged to Grandma Harris, and even a tin bank shaped like a globe of the world with maps so old, some of the places could only be found in history books.

Abby stood back and studied her work with satisfaction. *I like it.*

Some of the antiques had remained in boxes since Abby had left home, and it was exciting to pull them out and be able to enjoy them again.

Abby came across a framed portrait of herself with Luke, so she placed it on the mantle next to the Maxwells.

❖   ❖   ❖

With a book, Abby climbed into Grace's chair, but she found her mind drifting to the conversation she'd had with her father.

She chuckled to herself, remembering the day she parked illegally in an accessible space at the supermarket. She'd had so many preconceived notions about people with disabilities until she'd become disabled herself. Now she understood that disabled folks lived full, satisfying, stimulating lives. She hoped by being honest with Luke, he'd embrace Steven as the person Abby had chosen to build a life with.

Abby snuggled down into the chair and hugged the book of sonnets to her chest.

*I'm home.*

❖   ❖   ❖

Abby awoke to Luke gently shaking her shoulder. "Abby, honey, I'm back. It's time to go to bed."

Abby groaned and struggled to get out of the chair. Luke grabbed her hands and pulled. "Off you go." He gave her a gentle nudge toward Steven's room.

"I'll see you in the morning, Dad. Sweet dreams."

"Same to you, kiddo. Good night now."

Abby clambered up into Steven's bed, pulling his pillow down in front of her. She snuggled into it, but it didn't smell like him anymore. She was lonely, so she pulled out her phone.

YOU AWAKE?

NOPE. ARE YOU?

Abby stifled a laugh. Always the jokester.

YES, BUT BARELY. I MISS YOU.

MISS YOU TOO. ARE YOU IN BED ALREADY?

ALREADY? IT'S AFTER MIDNIGHT.

SO IT IS.

ANYTHING NEW AND EXCITING HAPPENING?

Yes! You'll never guess.

*What?*

Never in a million years.

*WHAT?*

Debbie is going home on Wednesday.

*Wednesday, like four days from now Wednesday?*

That would be the one.

*I wanted to do something with her before she went. :- (*

Let's have them over Sunday. Mom just loves Debbie. Would Luke mind if we included them?

*Not at all. Sounds like a plan.*

I'll take care of the arrangements on my end. Sophie offered to help with food.

*Please thank her for me. Sydney did too.* Abby yawned. *I'm sorry. I'm tired, but I'm glad we talked. I needed this.*

Me too. Get to sleep, silly girl. I have work to do tomorrow.

*Okay. Good night.*

Goodnight, love, I'll talk to you soon.

*Love you.*

Love you too.

*Love you more . . .*

Impossible. Go to sleep!

*Allright.*

NOW!

*Don't yell. I'm going.*

Love ya, babe.

*You too.*

❖   ❖   ❖

Abby awoke and looked at her clock. It was early, but it was a sunny Saturday, and her guess was that Luke was already bright-eyed and bushy-tailed. On a usual Saturday, he'd have been at the station house or out on the water.

Abby hopped into the shower and dressed for a carefree day with her dad. She looked around Steven's space, spying some of the supplies Sydney had delivered.

Abby loaded towels and washcloths into baskets on shelves within Steven's easy reach. She put out paper products and set up the closet in a manner that was nearly identical to the one at Steven's parents' home.

Abby looked around, satisfied that the room was ready for Steven. When he arrived, everything he might need would be ready and waiting for him. It was spacious enough for two people in wheelchairs to be able to pass one another without great difficulty. Abby knew Steven well enough by now to know that nothing was left to chance.

❖　❖　❖

Abby found Luke in Grace's chair, wearing a pair of sweats and a T-shirt. She couldn't remember when he'd looked so comfortable. His sock-covered feet rested on the ottoman.

"Mornin', Dad."

"Hey, Abby. Did you sleep well?"

"Like a baby. You?"

"Yeah. It's a nice spot. I slept with the window open, and it was surprisingly quiet."

"Are you hungry?"

"You don't have to go to any trouble. I picked up a dozen donuts last night while I was out. If you don't mind brewing some coffee, we'll be set."

"I don't know if I can get through the day on donuts. How about some French toast or something? I have some sausage I got from one of the butchers at the market."

"That sounds better than yesterday's donuts."

"All right, let me make some coffee, and I'll get started on food."

"I think I'll grab a quick shower if that's okay with you."

"It's fine. I've laid clean towels out in the bathroom. Use whatever you need."

"Thanks, Abby."

She looked up to answer him, but he was already gone.

❖    ❖    ❖

Abby was cracking eggs when Sydney called, and Abby happily invited her to breakfast. Sydney was a master at juggling a dozen different things, always helping everyone.

*Who is helping Sydney? She's barely keeping it together. Was her decision to break things off with Spencer a knee-jerk reaction she's already beginning to regret?*

Since Drunkgate, Sydney had described a long history of miscommunication and frequent separations over the past decade, but Abby's heart hurt at the longing she heard in her friend's voice when she mentioned letting go of the man she thought was the one.

Still, no one would've guessed Sydney was nursing a broken heart when she bounced into the kitchen and hopped up onto the island, snatching a pancake off the plate as she passed Abby.

Luke walked to the coffeemaker, filled a cup, and went to sit at the table, warily keeping an eye on Abby's friend. As easily as Sydney had gotten up onto the island, she hopped down, got herself a cup, and settled at the table as well.

"Hi, Luke. I'm Sydney. Abby has told me so much about you." She extended her hand, and he took it with an amused expression.

"Er, nice to meet you, Sydney."

Abby smiled to herself as she finished cooking. By the time they finished eating, Luke had volunteered to help move whatever was left in Sydney's car, stating he was determined to move something that weekend.

❖    ❖    ❖

Abby began an inventory of the groceries she needed to properly set up her kitchen. She texted Steven to remind him that he needed to make a list of his own.

Abby laughed out loud when she read his reply.

REAL MEN DON'T MAKE GROCERY LISTS. THEY AD LIB.

Abby heard Sydney's engine rev just as Luke was coming through the back door.

"I like Sydney. She's a nice girl."

"Steven's entire family is nice."

"I look forward to meeting them. I'm glad I came down."

"Me too."

"So, kid, when were you going to tell your old man there was a widescreen TV and a game room in the basement?"

"I did say it was a finished basement, and I'm sorry if I omitted the details. The satellite guy has to come back to hook us up. We do have a TV up here if you want to watch it."

Luke sat down and watched Abby finish putting things into the cupboard. She considered hanging around the house for the day, but it was gorgeous outside.

"You want to go do something? It's not supposed to get too hot today."

"I'd like that. Do you have something in particular in mind?"

"Have you ever been to Old Mystic?"

"You mean the seaport?"

"Yeah. There are some great places where we could grab a bite to eat. I've always wanted to check out the aquarium too."

Luke's smile grew significantly. "That sounds great. I've always wanted to see the whaling ship."

"Yes, there's that too." Abby couldn't help but laugh.

"Can we spare the time to drive down? Do you have more stuff to unpack?"

"It's only about an hour away. Do you mind driving?"

"Not at all. Let's do this!"

❖   ❖   ❖

*He's like a kid in a candy shop!*

Abby watched her dad gather brochures and rummage through the T-shirts like a tourist. They wandered the old seaport, walking through all the old buildings that had been staged with furnishings and period decor. They bought a boxed lunch and people-watched from a bench in the shade near Chubb's Wharf. Children ran and played, and couples walked hand in hand. It was a beautiful Saturday afternoon, and it felt like all of Connecticut had turned out to enjoy it.

"So, what's new in Woodstock? Any gossip I should know about?"

Luke's face grew a little red as he tugged at the collar of his shirt. He coughed a few times and mumbled, "I may or may not have asked Sherry if she wants to get hitched."

"Really? Oh Dad, I'm so happy for you—although I hope you were a little more romantic than that."

"You know I don't mince words. That's exactly how I asked her."

"What did she say?"

"I thought you were never going to ask!"

"And just like that, you're engaged."

"I guess we are."

Abby wrapped her dad in a strong hug. She hoped her death grip let her old man know how happy she was. "Congratulations!"

No one who knew the couple doubted their relationship, but they deserved the happiness and security that would come from making it official.

Theirs was one of those slow-burn romances. Sherry's husband, one of Luke's classmates, had been killed in an accident the summer before Abby started sixth grade. Luke had been one of the firemen on the scene that day, and he was different when Abby came home from her mother's at the end of the summer. He'd never divulged the horrors of the accident that had claimed the life of his friend, and Abby had never asked.

Colby Michaels, Sr., left behind a widow and two small children, and over time, Luke became their self-appointed protector. In the beginning, it was stopping to mow the lawn or shovel the sidewalks. When little Colby Michaels asked Luke to help him build a soap box racer for the annual derby, Luke began volunteering for his Scout pack.

That winter, when the Michaels' old wood stove caused a flue fire nearly destroying the cedar plank house where they resided, Luke rallied his buddies, and they installed a high efficiency furnace that would not only keep them warm but keep costs low for the single income family.

When Mrs. Michaels began working the following spring, it was Abby she called upon for assistance. Abby was almost twelve when Sherry offered her the after-school job watching Jojo. Colby spent his days with an older woman who only watched pre-K kids, and Sherry simply couldn't afford the local after-school program. The seven-year-old was precocious and well behaved, often sitting quietly with a book while Abby tackled her homework.

Evenings often brought barbeques in one back yard or the other, followed by a ride to the local custard stand for a shake or a sundae for dessert.

Sherry worked long hours to keep a roof over their heads and their bellies full, and because she flatly refused Luke's assistance, he took it upon himself to do random acts to make her life easier—the covert ops at Christmas and Easter when Luke brought home bags of goodies that Abby wrapped for Jojo and Colby. Luke would wait until late at night to sneak the large box of gifts and food onto the porch and ring the doorbell.

Abby watched from the front seat as her father ran like hell before slipping back into the car. The pair watched from the shadows as a sleepy Sherry would open the door in her robe, searching the darkness for her secret benefactor. Once the heavy boxes were dragged inside and the porch light turned off, Luke would start his car and hurry away.

As time wore on, the two families became inseparable. Sherry's kids felt like siblings to Abby, and Sherry had always been motherly toward Abby when she came back home to Woodstock. When Abby called home from Miami, it was often Sherry who calmed her mood after Penny had pulled some hair-brained stunt.

This was good news, happy news.

Abby had missed seeing them the last time she was home because Sherry and Jojo were in Hartford, visiting family for Easter.

❖   ❖   ❖

Luke pointed out an exhibit that wasn't present during Abby's last visit a few years before.

"You see her? Isn't she majestic?"

"She is rather pretty for an older gal. What's her story?"

"She's an endangered species, that one—the last American steam yacht in the country. There are only three like her in the entire world."

Luke leaned back with his hands behind his head and sighed deeply. "Ahh, that must be the life. To be able to travel anywhere you want on the water like that."

"You should have gone into the service—Navy, Marines. You could have seen the world on the government's tab. Do you ever regret our quiet, little life?"

"Never, kiddo. Nothing could make me happier than the memories we share."

Luke glanced down at his watch before looking up and studying the horizon. "Come on, it's getting late. Let's make sure you've got everything ready for tomorrow."

They took their time walking back to the car. Once in a while, Abby would catch Luke watching her. She could tell he was trying to be discreet, but Abby knew he was trying to gauge her condition. Finally she had to acknowledge it.

"Dad, I'm fine, really. I'm better than I've been in months."

"Sorry, I can't help it."

"I can't sit around waiting for the other shoe to drop. Life's short. Ask Steven."

That was exactly why Abby decided she wasn't going to waste any more time trying to figure out what she felt for Steven, the reason she'd so willingly agreed to his proposal to move in.

"I'm sorry. I understand. I'm glad you have such a positive attitude."

"I'd miss out on so many things if I sat around waiting to have a relapse."

The ride back to New Haven was quiet but enjoyable. They took scenic Highway One, which was preferential to the rapid-paced traffic on I-95.

They pulled in to Edd's Place, an old-time diner not far from Grove Beach. Abby had never been, but her dad seemed to know the place.

When they went inside, the cook raised his spatula in welcome.

"Hey, Luke!"

"How are you, Henry?"

"Doing great. How 'bout yourself?"

"Couldn't be better!"

"Good! Who's the beauty on your arm? Is this the future Mrs. Harris? You're old enough to be her father!" Henry grinned and winked at Abby.

Abby laughed and yelled over the hum of the fan. "He is my father!"

"I know, honey! He and Sherry tell us all the time about their beautiful daughter, Abby."

Abby blinked and wiped her eyes with her sleeve before looking up at her dad. "She really tells people that?"

Luke rolled his eyes. "Silly girl. She's always been more of a mother to you than . . . well, she thinks the world of you. Don't act so surprised."

A girl about Abby's age in a retro restaurant uniform came over to the table and took their order for burgers and sweet potato fries. She was gone a few minutes and came back with two tall and frosty strawberry shakes. Abby had to hand it to Luke. He knew his all-American diners.

Abby was so full she could barely move. When they finished talking and laughing over coffee, they crawled back into the car and headed home.

Abby was exhausted when they got inside the house, and she was suddenly relieved beyond words to know she didn't have to cook a huge meal for everyone.

Just as she was drifting off, her phone began to ring. Steven.

"I just wanted to let you know Debbie and Alec are both coming. Sydney is going to pick them up with the van."

"Oh, good."

"Hey, I was wondering. Would you mind if I offered to sell my lift van to Alec? He's going to need something when he leaves here. We don't really need it, and well, he wants to go into construction. It is in fairly good mechanical shape."

"Doesn't it belong to Logan and Sophie? Shouldn't you be asking them instead of me?"

"I already asked them, and they said it was mine to do with as I pleased. Once we're all moved, I don't see any reason to keep it now that we have something I can actually drive. You don't want to drive it, do you?"

"Who, me?" Abby squeaked. "Drive that big thing? Hell no!"

"I didn't think so. I just wanted to clear it with you before I offered."

"Well, it's got nothing to do with me, so no, I don't mind."

"Thanks, Abby. I wanted to be considerate and include you in the decision. I've got to go do a whirlpool session. See you in a few hours."

"All right, see you then."

Abby had barely cleaned up the breakfast mess when Sophie and Logan arrived. Luke studied them warily and then gave Abby a look that clearly said they'd talk later. Abby made a quick introduction. "Logan, Sophie, this is my father, Luke Harris. Luke, this is Logan and Sophie Chandler, Steven's parents."

Choruses of "Pleased to meet you" and "How do you dos" echoed around the room, but suddenly over the cacophony, Abby heard it . . .

Abby made a beeline to the front door and looked toward the driveway. There sat Steven in all his independent glory.

She practically ran to greet him.

"You drove here."

He puffed out his chest. "I did."

"How did it feel?"

"Oh, Abby, it was liberating."

"First time?"

"On my own? Yeah."

Abby stole a quick kiss. She'd been deprived since Luke arrived early on Friday. Steven framed her face with his hands and kissed her back.

"I'm so excited for you." Steven let go of Abby's face and patted her behind.

"We should go inside."

Abby sucked in a deep breath. "Yeah, I left our parents in the kitchen."

When they entered the living room, everyone was visiting quietly. Steven took Abby's hand. "This looks really nice. I'm proud of you. I was afraid you'd ignore me and put your things out only in your own room. I like this."

"Me too. I was hoping you might have treasures of your own to contribute."

"I may. We'll have to look. I'm not sure if I'm ready for that yet."

"It's okay. We'll talk about that later. We're supposed to be having fun today."

Everyone looked up from their conversations. Luke's gaze went immediately to Abby and Steven's joined hands. He stood and took a few steps in their direction before his face broke into a smile.

When Steven fumbled with the switch on his chair, Abby grinned at his nervousness. With a quiet whir and a few pops, the actuator began to turn, and soon Steven was towering over Luke. She'd never seen him stand so straight or look so proud. He might not have been ten feet tall or bulletproof, but he was her Superman, and Abby had never been happier or more sure of their relationship than she was at that moment.

She swooned as Steven confidently thrust his hand toward her father.

"Welcome to our home, Mr. Harris. I'm Steven Chandler. I intend to marry your daughter one day, sir."

# Acknowledgements

Fourteen years ago, I entered the opening chapter of this series in a "Write What You Know Contest," thinking it would be a fun exercise. I never imagined that exercise would evolve into the community of friends I've amassed. I am grateful for each and every one of the readers who have accompanied me on this incredible adventure.

None of this would have been possible without my family. Your love, support, encouragement, and patience through the journey of bringing this story to my readers continues to be a priceless gift. I love you so much! Thank you for understanding that I need to see this through.

I would be remiss for not thanking the following for their contributions to this project:

To Mom and Alec for being such powerful forces behind this story. Representation is everything, and I promise to keep your memories alive by telling stories that matter. Mom, you taught me to follow my dreams; Alec helped put them within my grasp. Thank you both.

Cindy—I would have never written a story so powerful, had it not been for your journey. I have the upmost respect and admiration for you and your contributions to the disability population. Thank you for the gift of your friendship. (And for having the courage to share your very personal photo to add authenticity to my book cover.)

To the many friends from the disability population who showed me the importance of inclusion, accessibility, disability etiquette, and representation. It is my goal every time I pick up a pen to share these fundamental things with a world that might not understand in hopes of changing perceptions.

Amy Argent for helping me sort the wheat from the chaff. Thanks for taking me under your wing, for your words of wisdom, and friendship.

Susan Atlas of Atlas Edits—your attention to detail astonishes me. I feel like this relationship was a learning experience for us both. I can't wait to work on another project with you. I hope we get to have that cup of coffee someday.

My PR team, Patti and Jae, your tireless, daily pimping of my work is appreciated more than words could ever express. You girls are rock stars!

My team, The Roll Models—betas, pre-readers, brainstormers. The gift of your time is precious to me; the success of this series belongs to you too.

My fic wives—Debbie, Sherry, Angie—your friendship and support are priceless. Thank you for believing in me and this story.

Tiffany—webdesigner, technical guru and fixer of glitches I can't begin to comprehend—I can never thank you enough making my internet presence amazing. You are incredible!

Gel of Tempting Illustrations, I love the graphics you create for my teasers. It's always a pleasure working with you.

Thank you to all the new reader/reviewers who jumped on my runaway train to read ARCs and review right through release day! I can never thank you enough.

My beloved MTK—your love and support for other authors has encouraged so many of us to follow our dreams. I can never thank you enough for making me a priority any time I needed you. Huge, squishy hugs to you.

Thank you to Dr. Robert Baer, author of Is Fred Dead? A Manual for Men with Spinal Cord Injuries, for providing wonderful reference material.

My new family at Lights! Cameras! Access! for helping me see the value of my work and for helping me explore new avenues to get my stories into the hands of more readers.

To Jd Michaels and Stories About Us for your continued guidance and support in making this project a reality. Jd, your brilliance astounds me. You are the master of kick-ass covers! Your friendship means the world to me. I couldn't have accomplished this without you. A million thanks could never be enough.

Hello,

I am a lifelong disability rights advocate. I am the director of a firm called Autistic Reality, and I am also the author of books of essays on disability, pop culture, fandom, and much more. I am also a professional pop culture critic, and write reviews for a number of sites. I also speak on disability representation at a number of conferences and conventions. In addition, I have at least fifteen disabilities myself.

I have had the immense pleasure of knowing DA Charles for several years now. I can attest that her devotion to the disability cause is absolutely pure, and comes from a very good perspective. That perspective is absolutely authentic, as Charles has disabilities herself, as do a number of her friends and loved ones. Not only that, but Charles has spent decades dedicated to improving the quality of life of the disabled population.

DA Charles has labored on this book and other creative works for years with much love and dedication. The quality of Charles's work is absolutely sterling, and her writing will move you and help you become a better person. For quite some time, she did not believe she would ever see this work published, and with the help of the Stories About Us initiative, of which I am editor, Charles has proven her doubts absolutely wrong. The lesson is this: never let anyone or anything keep you from your dreams. Charles's dreams have become reality, and so can yours.

Alex Frazier

For more than thirty years, **D. A. Charles** has been involved in disability rights advocacy. With the aim of furthering disability awareness, she writes about individuals with disabilities with respect and realism, portraying dynamic and realistic characters complete with flaws and vulnerabilities, each navigating to fulfill their dreams and desires.

Ms. Charles maintains an information and referral website with links to agencies and organizations that provide goods and services for the Disability Community.

D. A. Charles can be found at **https://linktr.ee/dacharlesauthor**

Readers are encouraged to join *The Roll Models Street Team:*
**https://www.facebook.com/groups/impactstreetteam**

**D. A. Charles**
**P.O. Box 63**
**Linden, PA 17744**